JUST BENNY

Alex Banwell

BROAD PLACE
publishing
broadplacepublishing.co.uk

First published in Great Britain in 2022
Second edition published in Great Britian in 2025

Broad Place Publishing
Broadplacepublishing.co.uk

Cover image
https://pixabay.com/photos/child-freckles-happy-joy-portrait-2844209/
Cover model courtesy of giselaatje at Pixabay

British Library Cataloguing-in-Publication Data.
A catalogue record for this book is available from the British Library.

Print Book: ISBN 978-1-915034-60-1

Books can be purchased from broadplacepublishing.co.uk

In loving memory of my father, Jeffrey Lyn Durbin, (1948-2017)

who always encouraged me to 'Do to others whatever you would like

them to do to you.'

I miss you, Dad, but I know that because of our shared belief in

Jesus, we will meet again in Glory.

Author's note

During my early teens, I attended a boarding school for the blind, where my roommate Sarah Tummey and I discovered a shared passion for creative writing. We enjoyed inventing characters and writing plays about them. I think we are both glad none of our crazy jottings will ever see the light of day, but they were a wonderful way to pass the time.

Shortly before I left the school, we began a new project about a group of teenagers growing up in a quiet, unnamed rural village. I carried on working on it for many years, and looking back, I'm amazed by how my simplistic and naïve writing style matured as I did. Some of my ideas were wild and unrealistic, but I was young, so I still had a lot to learn.

I gave up writing about fifteen years ago, thinking that part of my history was over. It was time to turn my attention to more serious things such as my marriage and my home, but I still found myself occasionally re-visiting those old documents, if only to laugh at my younger self.

Following another re-read early in 2021, I felt the urge to write again. The characters remained alive in my mind. I could still anticipate what they would say and how they might react to certain situations. So I wrote a few more scenes, and it all came flooding back. Then I remembered the play's humble beginnings. I don't have the first part anymore, because I lost the braille volumes during one of my many house moves. I wondered if I could start again, writing about those same people, but from an adult perspective, and once I got going, I couldn't stop. Writing was just as addictive as ever.

The play has become a source of light relief, a bit of nonsense I only share with my closest friends. It is my favourite way to unwind. However, I felt compelled to take it a step further because one of my fictitious teenagers intrigued me more than the rest. Being the baby of the group and the most overlooked, Benny Wellander had always been the least developed of my characters. He was just Benny. He had issues, but I never explored what they were. Re-writing the play gave me the chance to breathe new life into his story, and Benny surprised me by emerging as one of my main protagonists.

As my writing progressed, I wondered if I could turn parts of my play into a book. I had toyed with the idea of writing a novel, but I never thought it would be about Benny. I began to feel there might be a deeper purpose in telling his story. I have met a lot of youngsters like Benny; children born with disabilities or problems that either alienate their parents or cause them to become overly protective. Having a disability myself meant I could empathise with some of his struggles. Is there some of me in Benny? Undoubtedly. There was a time when I failed to relate to my peers and became overly introverted, although not to the extremes he does.

You may wonder why I chose to write about epilepsy rather than blindness, which is something I understand all too well. My honest answer is that I don't know. I needed a reason for Benny's damaged brain, and unmanaged epileptic seizures were the first thing that came to mind. Those who understand epilepsy better than I do might argue that Benny's constant sickness is unrealistic. It is rare for epileptics to vomit so violently after seizures. However, while doing some research, I discovered a rather scary sounding rare vomiting disease about which little seems to be known. I therefore imagine epilepsy is only one of his problems, possibly coupled with a mild form of autism, and that the full extent of his limitations is yet to be explored. I have seen this for myself in the blind world. Once a diagnosis of blindness is given, people hardly ever look for other underlying conditions unless they are forced to do so.

I hope you enjoy this novel, and that you will grow to love my characters as much as I do. What happens next? Well, I already know the rest of their story beyond the close of this book, and since I have plans for a sequel, maybe one day you will too.

Prologue

July 1999

The muffled whispers of excited voices ebbed away as Benny Wellander lay still and silent, his blond head poking out from the top of his sleeping bag. Now all he could hear was the rustling of the tent in the night breeze. Benny breathed a sigh of relief. He had made it through the first day of camp, and the others were too excited about their big adventure to think about taunting him like they usually did. He would be the last one chosen for team games. No one wanted Benny on their side. He didn't really care because he hated games. He was only joining in because his older sister said that was the right thing to do.

Benny tried not to think about how this was his first night away from home, or of how much he missed his mum tucking him in and lying beside him holding his hand. If he could sleep, it would soon be morning. There would be loads to do, even if he was unlikely to enjoy any of it. He just had to get through one more day. Then it would be Sunday. His mum and dad would pick him up, and he could go home pleased at having completed the camp with his classmates.

Maybe Emma was right, and the other kids would stop bullying him before they started secondary school in September. For now, he was doing okay. He even felt a bit proud of himself.

Time passed, and Benny woke up with a jolt. At first, he couldn't figure out where he was. Then he remembered. Dizziness and confusion overwhelmed him, and there was a sharp pain in his head. Knowing the signals all too well, Benny's heart began to race as he anticipated what was about to happen. He possibly had a few minutes left before his world started spinning and his body took on a life of its own. Emma had warned him he would likely have a seizure while he was away, because stress or change often brought them on. Barely a week went by without him having at least one, although they varied in severity. Perhaps tonight it wouldn't be so bad, and he'd be able to use some of the coping strategies his sister had taught him.

One thing was certain. Benny couldn't stay in the tent. He rose shakily, edging his way towards the entrance while hoping none of his three companions would wake. The boys in this tent had drawn the short straw, but someone had to share with him, despite their loud moans.

'He throws up all the time! And he's a cry-baby! And...' The list went on and on, and Benny had tried to close his ears to it. He had to sleep somewhere, and he was grateful he wasn't in the same tent as Henry Keith.

The night air hit Benny as he slipped outside and released the breath he hadn't realised he was holding. Now he could lie on the grass and wait. If the seizure didn't come, he'd be able to go back to bed. Maybe the fresh air would make him feel better. Was he just stressed because he'd woken up in a strange place? If the worst happened and he threw up, at least no one would know about it.

After a lifetime of epilepsy and some coaching from his elder sister, Benny knew enough to keep himself relatively safe. However, he had never faced a seizure alone. Normally he woke his mum. She looked after him, cradling his head, muttering soothing words, and attempting to contain the vomit. He couldn't have a fit without being sick to his stomach.

'Mum?' had he whimpered the call aloud, or was it only in his mind? It was coming. Tears fell as he lay on the grass and surrendered to the inevitable. His last coherent thought was that Dale Moss was right. He was Weedy Wellander. He was stupid, rubbish at everything, and he missed his mum. She was the only one who loved him for being just Benny.

1

'I'm sorry, Mr Wellander. You're going to have to fetch him.'

It was 2 a.m., and the voice on the phone sounded tired as Ola Wellander sat up in bed and shrugged off the urge to slam the receiver down, turn over, and go back to sleep. He had known this was a bad idea from the start. The boy wouldn't cope with one night away from home, let alone three. Ola was surprised Janet had even allowed him to go. It had been Emma's doing. His seventeen-year-old daughter had persuaded her younger brother that he needed to be a part of this final school trip before graduating from the juniors to the local secondary school.

'If you want to make friends, Benny, you've got to do what everyone else is doing. They'll think you're weird if you don't go.'

'They think I'm weird anyway.'

Ola had overheard his children's conversation several weeks earlier while cleaning his car. Emma and Benny were sitting together on a garden wall drinking hot chocolate. No doubt Emma had made it to butter him up and bring him round to her way of thinking. She always thought she knew what was best for Benny. So did Janet, but mother and daughter rarely agreed. This left Benny torn between the love and coddling of his over-protective mum and the advice of his sister, whom he desperately wanted to please. Emma was everything Benny desired to be, and despite their frequent squabbles and Emma's constant lectures, Ola knew Benny idolised her.

'So show them you're not,' Emma had said.

Ola couldn't see their faces, but he could picture the fear in Benny's eyes. The boy had always been timid. He was scared of his own shadow and clung to his mum like a life raft. Janet blamed it on his health. Emma said he was just spoiled. Ola chose not to have an opinion, because that would mean becoming emotionally entangled with a child he could barely tolerate.

'What is it, Ola? Is it Benny?' Janet leaned over to switch on the bedside lamp.

Ola blinked and scowled. It was always the same. When Benny was at home, he woke her because he couldn't sleep, because he'd had a nightmare, or because of one of his seizures. The boy only had to hint he felt sick for Janet to go running with a towel and a bowl. If she had her way, he'd still be sleeping next to their bed, as he had for the first four years of his life, until Ola put his foot down.

'If the seizure's over, surely he can sleep it off?' Ola said into the phone, ignoring Janet. 'He'll be fine if he rests.' He was determined not to give in to Benny this time. There had been enough of that. Besides, his family had made plans. They were going on a boat trip in the morning, and Emma was looking forward to it. They could never take Benny on boats because he got seasick, and car sick, and sick with fear… Ola thought his son might as well live with his head in a bucket, then chided himself for his cruelty. Why had his heart become hardened to a boy who needed him so badly? Yet the more time passed, and the more apparent Benny's problems became, the less Ola had to give.

'He's crying for his mother,' the teacher explained. Clearly, Benny's teacher wasn't willing to persevere with him. Ola didn't blame him. There was no reasoning with his son once panic got a hold. The only person who could pacify him was Janet, and she did it with cuddles and babying; not the sort of mothering Ola felt was suitable for a twelve-year-old boy.

'We have to get him!' Janet was already out of bed and pulling on her clothes.

Ola realised there would be no more rest for him tonight. Why hadn't he insisted his wife learn to drive so she could go by herself?

Pulling her hair into a ponytail, Janet continued, 'I should never have let him go.'

For once, they agreed on something, but for very different reasons. While Janet was reticent to let Benny out of her sight,

10

Ola had known it would be a disaster from the beginning. Well, he had been right again!

'Okay,' Ola consented. 'We'll be there as soon as we can.'

He moved to put the phone down, but Janet wrestled it from him. 'Let me speak to his teacher.'

She peppered their caller with questions about the length and severity of Benny's seizure as Ola groaned and stretched his long legs.

Satisfied that on this occasion her son would not need to be hospitalised, Janet put the receiver down and continued getting dressed as Ola headed into the bathroom, coming back out five minutes later where he met Emma on the landing.

'What's going on, Dad? I heard Mum talking. It sounded like she was in a state.'

'Benny's teacher phoned.'

'At this time of night?' Emma yawned and stretched.

'He's had a seizure.'

'So?' She didn't seem shocked. 'He's always having them. I warned him before he left that he probably would. I said he should let it pass and get on with having fun.'

'Well, he obviously didn't take a blind bit of notice. Why doesn't that surprise me?' They exchanged a knowing glance. 'He's crying for your mum, and she's determined to go to him.'

'You're not going to bring him home?' Emma threw up her hands in frustration.

'What choice do I have, Em?'

'If you do that, things will get even worse for Benny. He keeps moaning that he doesn't have friends, that the other kids make fun of him because of his seizures and how slow he is at learning. They'll do it even more now. They'll call him a cry-baby because he couldn't even spend one night away from his mum and dad!'

'And they'll be right.' Ola struggled to contain the anger rising in his chest.

'You should refuse to go. Tell Mum to be sensible for once.'

He should reprimand Emma for disrespecting her mother, but he didn't have the heart because he wished he could comply with her suggestion. 'If I don't take her, she'll get there somehow. You know what your mum's like with Benny. If he wants her, she'll move heaven and earth to get to him.'

Janet chose that moment to walk out of the bedroom and join them on the landing. 'Has your dad told you what's happened, Em?'

Emma replied with a nod. His daughter likely knew she'd lose it if she opened her mouth. He might well do too.

'You'll come with us, won't you?' Janet begged.

'Why do you need me?' Emma put her hand on her hip. She wasn't going to pamper Benny. She'd probably keep out of his way tonight, but only because Benny couldn't handle it when she gave him what for. Ola wished he could correct his son to toughen him up a bit, but Janet refused to discipline him, and Ola had given up trying. It wasn't worth it.

Janet was still trying to convince Emma. 'I was hoping you'd help your dad navigate. I'll have to sit in the back with Benny in case he's ill.'

'He'll always be ill, Mum. Just give him a bucket or something.'

'Emma!' Janet wailed. 'Your poor brother's got himself into a state. He needs us.'

That was always the way. Benny needed them, and only Emma had the ability to phrase things right. His daughter might get Benny to see a glimmer of sense, where his parents always failed.

Less than half an hour later, the Wellanders were in the car, heading for the campsite where Benny and his schoolmates had gone on their excursion. Ola and Emma waited while Janet quietly retrieved her tearful son, and they were on their way home before the sun rose.

Exhausted by the physical and emotional rigours of his seizure, Benny fell asleep on the back seat with his head resting on his mother's shoulder. He said little, but cried and clung to Janet until her endearments settled him.

'I wish I didn't have to wake him,' Janet said, as Ola pulled into their driveway.

'He's too old for me to carry him now.' Ola got out of the car, slammed the door, and marched towards the house. He'd well and truly had enough and intended to make the most of what little rest he could get.

Still, something compelled him to glance back. The slammed door had woken Benny. His twelve-year-old son sat up and surveyed his surroundings with bleary eyes, his vacant expression worsened by the confusion of having been roused with a jolt.

'Let's get you inside and into bed.' Janet helped Benny out of the car, guiding him into the house as Emma followed. 'Want some warm milk?'

Sighing at the way Janet was treating Benny like a toddler, Ola closed the door behind them and locked it. Benny nodded and sat down opposite his sister.

'Anything for you, Em?' Janet asked. She was already preparing Benny's drink.

'No thanks.'

As Ola headed towards the stairs, Emma's eyes followed, pleading for him to stay. He knew she was still angry at Benny, for she hadn't even acknowledged him during the journey home. However, unlike his own, Emma's bouts of anger were soon replaced by love and pity.

Emma reached out a hand to cover one of her brother's. 'Wanna tell me what happened?' She spoke in hushed tones. If Janet heard, she'd tell her not to question Benny when he was tired.

'I didn't wanna be stupid, Emmie.' As Benny fought tears, Emma squeezed his hand, letting him know it was okay. He seemed to take courage from her nearness and continued speaking with more assurance.

Why doesn't he ever respond to me that way? Ola thought.

'I knew it was gonna happen, so I went outside and lay on the grass.'

'You didn't wake anyone?' Emma asked.

'I thought I'd try and be brave and handle it by myself.' He shrugged. 'I know I've gotta learn.'

Emma nodded her affirmation.

'It wasn't really bad, and I knew I wouldn't be sick over no one's stuff if I was outside.'

'That was brave, Pestie.'

Ola had overheard his children having several long talks before Benny left, where Emma helped her brother come up with some coping strategies, convinced they would work if he remembered to put them into practice.

'So what went wrong?' Emma asked. It was obvious something had.

'Henry Keith must've followed me.'

'He's the class bully, isn't he?'

Benny nodded. 'He's the one who tells the others to make fun of me. He likes to watch me having a seizure. He tells everyone how stupid I look and how sick I am. He reckons I do it on purpose.'

Emma gave a disgusted grunt. 'There may be some things you do to get attention, but it's not that.'

Benny drew his hand back at her criticism, and Ola internally scoffed. His son did loads of things to get attention, and his offense at Emma's little comment showed his over-sensitivity.

'So what did this Henry Keith do?' Emma asked, refusing to be put off.

'He told me I should be in the special unit with the disabled kids. He said I'm mental and I shouldn't have gone on camp with them cos I was gonna spoil it for everyone.'

'And you believed him?'

'I woke up Mr Fletcher and told him I'd had a seizure and I wanted to go home.'

'So you might have stuck it out if it hadn't been for Henry Keith?' Emma was trying to be positive, but Ola didn't share his daughter's optimism.

'I dunno,' Benny admitted. 'I didn't like it much. I hate sport and stuff. No one ever picks me for a team. I'm always last, and the others moan cos I'm too slow or I run the wrong way.'

'You only do that when they wind you up and you panic. You know what to do.' Emma seemed desperate to turn the tide of negativity that ruled her brother's young life.

'I'm rubbish at everything.' Those were Benny's favourite words, and he seemed to be set on making them a reality. 'And Dad's really angry with me again.'

His son's observations might have bit into Ola's chest years ago, but right now, they were just true. Of course he was angry. Once again, Benny had ruined everyone's plans.

At that moment, Janet pushed back into the siblings' conversation. 'Let's get you upstairs and into bed.' She draped a protective arm around Benny's narrow shoulders. 'I'll carry your drink.'

Ola retreated into the shadows as Benny rose and followed Janet out of the room. Emma remained sitting at the table, tapping her fingernails over its varnished surface. Ola joined her once Benny and Janet were safely upstairs.

'You heard all of that, huh?' Emma asked, and Ola nodded. 'How can I help him? He'll never cope with secondary school the way things are. Will he ever claim his independence, or will Mum always insist on keeping him as her baby?'

Ola shook his head. He had no answer. Emma's unspoken words hung between them – the ones about his own relationship with Benny, or lack of one. He'd left Benny floundering without guidance from a strong male role model. Yet it wasn't all his fault. Nor had it always been this way. There was a time when the Wellanders had been a normal, happy family.

2

Why did it have to rain the day they finally moved into their own home? Ola Wellander stared out of the hired removal van in despair as he attempted a cautious manoeuvre to reverse it onto his new driveway. He supposed he shouldn't be surprised. Moving in January was always going to be chancing it.

Looking back at the three-bedroom red brick house in the middle of a quiet cul-de-sac, he couldn't believe he and Janet had come this far. Not only was he the owner of this beautiful home, albeit with a hefty mortgage to repay, but he had also landed his dream job at a local garage. Far removed from the young man who'd left Denmark with little more than the shirt on his back and a rudimentary education, Ola had learned his lessons by living rather than in a classroom. His mechanics training had come in stages as he wandered from place to place, gradually learning his trade.

Climbing out of the van, he reached out to steady five-year-old Emma as she came dancing towards him, her pigtails swinging in the breeze. His heavily pregnant wife stood in the doorway, less eager to get pummelled by the rain.

'I love our new house, Daddy!'

Ola swung Emma up into his arms and kissed her cheek. 'That's good, Em, because I hope we'll be living here for a long time.' His accent contained only traces of his Danish heritage, as he'd made it his business to perfect his English. Ola had always wanted to blend in. He despised being questioned, and a foreign accent and broken English aroused curiosity.

'I've got the kettle on.' Janet smiled as he approached, still carrying their daughter. 'I expect you'd like a coffee before you start unloading.'

'You know me well.'

Ola couldn't fault Janet as a wife and mother. She greeted him after a long day's work with strong black coffee accompanied by a slice of home-made cake, and an eager ear ready to take in whatever he wished to share. He knew she listened because she asked intelligent questions. Ola and Janet were an insular pair. They had few friends, having seldom stayed in one place long enough to make them. Now, as Ola glanced around the street that was to be their new home, noticing the gentle rise of the hill and the mixture of older houses and 1960s properties like their own, he hoped all that would change.

Although Ola was a stoic and private man, he wanted more for his wife and daughter. Emma brought laughter and light wherever she went. She made friends easily, always willing to make the best of what she had. Her curiosity and enthusiasm for life could not be contained, even when financial difficulties had forced them to live huddled together in a two-room flat with a shared kitchen. Ola felt guilty about that, but his little girl had smiled and laughed him through it. She had even taught him a little about the value of laughter, although he preferred watching her antics from a comfortable distance.

Meeting Janet had provided purpose to his previously nomadic lifestyle. They met when he worked afternoons at a small-town petrol station in the days before his mechanics training began. He had noticed the short, dumpy brunette, who always arrived alone, treated herself to a chocolate bar, and slipped silently away with barely more than a greeting. She was shy at first, but she responded to him with a smile, and the normally tight-lipped Ola felt a strange compulsion to get to know her. They chatted awkwardly until several months and tentative conversations later, he plucked up the courage to invite her on a date. He was pleased to discover she was more than ready for a serious relationship.

Janet was twenty-one when they married, two years Ola's junior. She didn't have any strong career aspirations and was overjoyed at the birth of their daughter, Emma Jane. Although the pregnancy wasn't planned, the baby fitted easily into their lives, with Janet choosing to stay at home with her while Ola worked.

Their search for home took them up and down the country until they found themselves here in a medium-sized Gloucestershire village. It was conveniently located a short bus ride into town, with a local shop for essentials and a park for Emma to play in yet was far enough away from the bustle to offer his family the quiet life they craved.

With Janet now pregnant with their second child, Ola knew it was time to settle down. The garage where he'd found work seemed to have a line of steady business, and he was now a trained mechanic with a regular income. He indulged in a satisfied smile as he thought of his father in Denmark and wondered what he would say if he could see his only son now.

Ola had never related to his father. He supposed he had inherited his disposition, but where Ola was quiet and withdrawn, his father could be violent and unpredictable. That hadn't been helped by his love of alcohol. Ola had witnessed his steady decline until he gradually drove everyone away. Ola's mother had left when her son was sixteen, refusing to take him with her and declaring that he was old enough to stand on his own two feet. Looking back, he supposed she was right. He had always been independent. From the time his mum left, Ola began making plans. He had his goals, and he soon figured out how to achieve them.

'One of the neighbours dropped by earlier and offered to help.' Janet ushered her family into their new home, closing the front door to shut out the rain. 'He said he works with you at the garage.'

'That'll be Peter Moss.' Ola put Emma down in the kitchen and reached for his coffee. 'He seems like a decent guy.'

'He's got a little girl, Daddy. And she's five, like me!' Emma's eyes danced with excitement.

'A little friend for you, maybe?' Ola suggested.

'His wife looked nice too…'

Ola noted Janet's hesitancy, and he knew this was in deference to him. Janet had always been cautious about making friends, all too aware of how he hated others knowing about their private business. Although Ola realised it was the years of living with his father that had made him closed and suspicious, he struggled to know how to break the habit of a lifetime. An alcoholic father was something to be ashamed of, a secret best kept behind closed doors. The fewer people knew, the less they talked. Yet he and Janet had nothing to hide, so why was he still holding back?

'You should invite her round for a cup of tea. Em and her little girl can get to know one another.' He could tell his suggestion pleased Janet, and it satisfied him to know he'd made her happy.

'Can I help you take everything out of the van, Daddy?' Emma was always eager to help, and sometimes didn't appreciate her own limitations.

'No.' Ola regretted his stern retort as he registered the hurt on his little girl's face. He never could find the correct line between love and discipline and tended to err more on the side of the latter. Yet Emma never held it against him. She always forgave and came back for more. 'Sorry, Emma. It's just slippery out there with the rain. You stay safe inside. There's a good girl.' He was determined that his children would never be scared of him. They would never know the fear of an unpredictable and hostile alcoholic father. He would always be approachable; always be their daddy.

Ola hoped this second child was a boy. Then their family of four would be complete. He liked the idea of having a son to work alongside him and was committed to giving him all the teaching and direction he had never received. No, Ola Wellander would never turn into his father.

'What are you hoping for? Boy or girl?' Karen Moss sat opposite Janet at the kitchen table, her two-year-old son fast asleep on her lap. The cheerful voices of their two daughters playing in the lounge brought a smile to her face as Karen accepted a cup of tea.

'I'd be happy with either, but I know Ola wants a boy.' Janet rested her hands on her enlarged stomach as the baby kicked.

'That's how I felt when I was having Dale. I already had two girls.' Karen's elder daughter Judy was in her early teens, while Erin was five, like Emma.

'How long have you and Peter lived here?' Janet rose to replenish the teapot.

'We moved in just before Erin was born. We lived in some pretty rough places before that. Then Peter got a break, and we could afford our own home.'

'Sounds similar to what's happened to us.' Should Janet have admitted that much? Would Ola be cross? He had encouraged her to make friends, and surely friendship involved a certain amount of openness.

'I reckon he and Peter have both landed on their feet at that garage. Lewis Hobbs is a good employer.' Karen reached for a chocolate biscuit as Emma and Erin bounced into the room.

'Can we have biscuits too, Mummy? Please?' Emma's eyes lit up with excitement.

'Just one or two.' Janet held out the plate and the girls each took one, as Dale stirred on his mother's lap.

Emma crammed her treat into her mouth then reached for another, while Erin nibbled daintily, settling for only one.

Janet had marked during their brief acquaintance that Erin seemed to be a serious child, and she questioned whether this would make her a satisfactory companion for her playful daughter. She often wondered where Emma's insatiable zest for life had come from. She certainly wasn't like either of her parents. Although Janet longed for a close friend, she had always held herself apart from her social peers. She was the girl the others included when there was no one else around. She'd followed them from place to place, hoping to find a best friend in one of them, but it had never happened. Would it happen now with Karen Moss? She seemed like a sensible woman, a homemaker like her.

'Does Dale want a biscuit too?' Emma smiled at Karen. Taking the plate, she moved around the table and offered it to the toddler.

'Oh no you don't.' Karen pulled Dale back as he made a grab for the contents of the plate, and his squeals of protest made Emma giggle. 'You can have one, but only if I give it to you.'

'Dale likes biscuits.' Erin's tone was matter of fact as she turned to her new friend.

'Everyone likes biscuits! Especially when they're chocolate.' Emma took Erin's hand and dragged her out of the room, calling over her shoulder that they were going to play some more.

'What will you do about her when you go into labour?' Karen attempted to stop her squirming son from taking another biscuit.

'I don't know.' Janet sighed. 'I guess we haven't thought that far ahead.'

'Just call me. I'll come round and take her back to my house.'

'Thank you.' Janet's relief was palpable. It had been years since there was someone she could call upon during a time of need. Her parents lived miles away, and although her mother had briefly mentioned visiting after the baby's birth, Janet knew she didn't really want to.

Besides, she wasn't sure how Ola would react if Carol came. He had never got along with her family because Ola gave nothing away. He seemed to become even more sullen when others were around, and her parents failed to understand what Janet saw in him. They hadn't visited since her marriage, and Janet knew Ola wouldn't stand to have relative strangers staying at their house. It was better this way. If Karen cared for Emma, Janet would soon be home with her new baby and able to provide for her family's needs.

As she stood with Emma on their doorstep, waving at Karen's retreating back, Janet sighed with contentment. Life was good. The sunshine over the hill hinted at the springtime to come. Her family of three was about to increase to four. Ola would be a devoted father, she an adoring mother, and Emma a happy older sister. There would be no more moving. They were settling into their new home, and Janet was even making friends. Could life get any better than this?

3

'Ola!' Janet's cries roused Ola from slumber.

'What's wrong?' He rolled over, peering up at his wife in bewilderment. She sat bolt upright in bed, clutching her stomach then reached to turn on a bedside lamp.

'It's time. I'm in labour.'

'Are you sure?' She was only 38 weeks, and she'd had lots of stomach tightenings this pregnancy.

Janet swung her legs round, got up and leant over the bed. 'Of course I am!'

She almost never snapped. The pains must be coming with rapid intensity.

Ola climbed out of bed, moved to her side, and wrapped a reassuring arm around her shoulders. 'Do you want me to call the Mosses?'

Janet nodded, biting on her lower lip so as not to cry out with the pain. This baby was in a rush. If they weren't careful, they wouldn't make it to the hospital in time.

Half an hour later, Emma was safely deposited with Karen Moss, and Ola drove at a frantic pace, while Janet held onto the passenger door, groaning with every pain.

'Hang on in there, Jan,' he urged, grateful there wasn't much traffic on the road at this late hour. Why was their baby in such a hurry? Was something wrong?

'I need to push!' She screamed piercingly with yet another contraction.

'You can't!' He didn't mean to shout, but there was no way Ola was going to deliver a baby at the roadside. He was a mechanic, not a midwife.

Ola released a sigh as the lights of the hospital came into view. He parked the car in the first available space and rushed off to find help. Soon, Janet was being wheeled into the delivery room. It was all happening at once. A doctor telling her to push. Janet screaming as she bore down, and their son shot into the world with a hearty wail. Tears of relief welled up in Ola's eyes. They had made it. Janet had delivered their baby surrounded by the safety of the doctors and nurses.

Janet cried with joy as she held their son, covering his tiny body with kisses. It was over. The pain of a sudden labour had been worth this moment of sheer joy. Their family was complete. Ola had his boy.

The midwife shuffled over to tell him the baby weighed six pounds. A little small considering Emma had been a hefty eight-pounder, but the little boy had instantly latched on to feed. He'd soon catch up.

Suddenly the baby's body stiffened. What was happening? Janet's eyes widened as their son's tiny face turned blue. She looked up and screamed for Ola. He stepped forward as the infant was wrenched from her arms and whisked away by the midwife. He held his wife's shoulders, trying in vain to console her while stone cold fear froze him in place.

When twenty minutes had passed, Ola began to pace the hospital room. Janet lay on her bed, sobbing. He had long since run out of comforting words. Time dragged by, and although a nurse came to check on Janet, there was no news of the baby. Ola questioned and even demanded, but the answer was always the same. Their son was undergoing tests. They were trying to stabilise him. He had suffered a seizure, the cause of which was a major point of concern.

Janet attempted to rise, but she was in no fit state to wander the hallways, and Ola had to pin her back down. Exhaustion from the labour claimed her, and she fell into a brief, fretful sleep until a doctor entered the room and gave them the news that rocked their world. They needed to run more tests to be certain. However, their baby was likely epileptic.

Ola hardly comprehended what he heard. Their tiny, perfect son was saddled with something that might affect him forever? The doctor muttered reassurances. Epilepsy was treatable with the right levels of medication; their boy would most likely live a normal life. But his words just seemed like unintelligible noise. Then Janet's panic set in. She demanded to see her child, repeating over and over, 'Why has this happened to us? Why our baby?'

When Ola's wife and child were finally reunited, Janet held their boy possessively, vowing she would never let him go. She fed him again, but this time, he only took a little of her milk. He fretted and fussed, and she sang and cooed while Ola stood by helplessly. He hadn't even held their son yet. Had Janet even realised? When she reluctantly released the baby into Ola's arms, he let out such a loud cry that Ola quickly handed him back, presuming he must still be hungry.

The baby had another seizure that afternoon, and an even worse one just hours later. Janet would not return home as quickly as she had hoped. Ola rang the Mosses, and Karen assured him she and Peter would be happy to care for Emma as long as needed. Yet he felt so frustrated over his inability to help Janet or their son that he returned home later that night, taking Emma with him. He bathed her and read her a story, then snuggled her up with her favourite teddy before returning to his empty bed, where he slept fitfully.

Every time he woke, he wondered what was happening at the hospital. Although he wanted to be with Janet and his son, this situation was beyond him, and Ola didn't like things he couldn't control.

The following day, he took Emma to see her baby brother. Janet was on edge after a sleepless night, and she didn't seem to want to let either of them near the baby. She hovered over the boy like a mother hen, her eagle eye watching his every move for the slightest sign of another seizure. Ola didn't ask to hold him again, and Emma shrank back in fear.

Janet came home five days after their son's birth, and Ola hoped their lives would slot back into a regular routine. However, it soon became apparent that normality would be a thing of the past for the Wellanders. Ola had set the cot up beside their bed, but after several sleepless nights, Janet announced she and the baby would sleep in the nursery. She excused her behaviour by reasoning that her husband was going back to work and needed uninterrupted rest. At first, he was happy to have it. Yet as the days turned into weeks, he missed his wife's presence at night and the intimacy they'd shared.

Janet's every waking moment revolved around the baby, whom she and Ola had named Benjamin. She carried him around the house in a sling, feeding him almost constantly because he often fell asleep at her breast. She was ever watchful for his seizures. Janet's despair deepened as the weeks turned into months and the doctors tried various treatments, and Ola's only hope was that the baby would outgrow his epilepsy.

One unusually mild afternoon in January, Emma bounded out of school with Erin at her side. Janet waited in the playground beside Karen with baby Benny strapped to her chest in his sling. She had shortened his name to Benny because it sounded sweet, though Ola favoured Ben. Ola had little to do with his son, who could only ever be pacified by Janet and cried whenever his dad went near him. So Benny had stuck.

'Did you have fun at school today, sweetheart?' Janet held out a hand to her beaming daughter.

'Yes! Can Erin come home for tea?'

'I don't know.' Janet saw Emma's instant look of disappointment and was loath to be the cause of it. 'Benny's had a bad day with his seizures. Daddy and I might have to take him to the hospital later if he doesn't start feeling better.'

'Why don't you let her have tea at our house?' Karen took a firmer grip of Dale's hand as the toddler attempted to escape into the crowd of excited children.

Janet smiled down at the little boy who was always on the move. Dale never walked anywhere - he ran. He was boisterous and extremely outgoing; everything Ola had wished for in a son. She sometimes caught her husband watching Dale playing in the street with Emma and Erin and was convinced she could read his thoughts: Benny would do none of those things.

They'd always have to keep him close because they never knew when a seizure would convulse his little body. He was a sickly child; especially after an episode, and she worried over his inability to keep anything down. Yet Benny was growing. Not as steadily as Emma had, but the doctors put that down to his poor health and reassured her it was enough.

'Can I, Mummy?' Emma bounced up and down as Janet looked down at her grizzling baby. He was likely hungry again, or wet, or was this the precursor to another seizure?

'Yes, I suppose so.' Emma deserved a treat. Janet had little time to play these days, and Ola was at home less than ever. He worked long hours at the garage and had taken up golf in his spare time. Janet supposed she should be glad he'd made friends with Karen's husband, Peter, but surely she deserved his support too?

When Ola arrived home that evening, he found his house quiet and seemingly empty. After dropping his keys on a kitchen worktop, he heard noises from upstairs, and followed the sounds to find Janet, Emma and Benny in their daughter's room. Emma sat on her bed with Benny on her lap, while Janet stood over them wearing a beaming smile of pride. Emma was tickling her baby brother, and Benny laughed up at her. Ola mused that he had never seen him laugh before. As far as he knew, Benny only cried.

Unaware of her husband's presence, Janet gazed lovingly at her two children. Ola was surprised she'd finally let Emma hold Benny, who could only sit up with support. He was much slower in his development than his sister had been, and every seizure seemed to knock him back. Just when his eyes brightened, and he became more aware of his surroundings, several days of illness would leave him lacklustre and listless. Now Benny sat smiling up at Emma and pulling on a strand of her hair, like any normal child.

'Stop it you bully!' Emma was firm but gentle as she disentangled herself from his grasp. 'Erin's baby brother pulls hair too. He hurts more than you!'

Benny babbled up at her, causing his sister to laugh louder. 'What's he saying, mummy?'

'I don't know.' Janet deftly pulled Emma's hair away from her face and out of Benny's reach. 'I suppose he's enjoying playing with you.'

'I love you, Little Pest.' There was a tenderness in Emma's tone as she rocked him, imitating the movements she had seen her mum make hundreds of times during the last ten months.

Benny nestled into her and quietened, as Ola watched in wonder, feeling a sudden surge of love for both his children.

Janet glanced at the clock on the bedside table. 'Time for bed, Em.'

Ola wished his wife wouldn't break the peaceful moment. Benny was responding to his sister when he usually wanted no one but Janet. Even Karen's experienced arms couldn't satisfy him – he cried until Janet was forced to take him back.

I'm his own father, Ola thought, *And I've held him only a handful of times.* On each occasion Benny had become inconsolable. Janet never allowed him to persevere. She always took his son right back.

Janet reached down to extract Benny, then turned towards the door. Her eyes widened when she saw Ola. 'How long have you been home?'

'I only just got back.' He moved further into the room and bent to kiss his daughter's cheek. 'Night, Em. Have you had fun today?'

'Lots! I played with Erin after school, and I think Benny likes me now.' Emma grinned up at him showing the gap where her front tooth had recently fallen out.

'Of course he does. You're his big sister.'

After tucking Emma in, Ola followed Janet downstairs.

'Your meal is keeping warm in the oven. I wasn't sure how late you'd be,' she said.

He nodded, unwilling to admit he could have been home at least an hour earlier.

'Could you hold Benny while I get it ready?'

Ola reached out to take his now sleeping son. The only time Benny consented to be held by him was when he was asleep, and he rarely stayed that way for long. He should be grateful she'd asked. Instead, he bit back a retort about how it would do the boy good to be put down for a few minutes.

Janet smiled warmly as Benny settled in his arms. Her smile fortified him for what he wanted to say next. 'Jan?' Ola prepared to broach a subject that had been hanging in the air between them ever-since Benny's birth. 'I think it's time for you to come back into our bedroom.'

'You know I can't.' Her tone was plaintive, and Ola saw the fear in her eyes. She thought he was trying to tear her away from her baby, and she wasn't about to let him.

'You're my wife, and I need you.' His voice was quiet but firm.

'But Benny…'

'He'll have to learn to sleep by himself.'

'We can't leave him alone,' she argued. 'What if he has one of his seizures?'

'Then we'll have the cot in with us until he's older. We can't carry on the way we are. We need to get back to how we were.' Ola wanted to reach out, to pull her into his arms and tell her he still loved and needed her, but as ever, the baby was between them.

'He'll keep you awake. He still cries a lot at night.'

'Then he needs to learn not to, and perhaps you shouldn't pick him up the minute he starts.' His resolution not to let his irritation show crumbled with every objection she made.

Benny seemed to sense the tension. He stirred and let out a cry, his eyes darting in search of his mother. Ola tried to hold him more securely, but his attempts proved futile.

'It's all right, my love,' Janet soothed as she took him back. 'Mummy's got you. It's all right.'

'I'll deal with my food.' Ola's shoulders slumped. Another battle had been lost. There was a new man in Janet's life – a sickly and demanding baby. Did he have the right to be jealous of his own son? Ola knew he ought to be ashamed of his emotions, but although he didn't want to admit it, he was growing to resent Benny.

4

'I love Christmas!' Nine-year-old Emma's eyes darted back and forth as she bounded through the busy shopping centre, colourfully decorated for the festive season. There was so much to see and experience. Emma didn't want to miss a thing. By contrast, Ola loathed shopping and only consented to join them to help shoulder the bags.

'I didn't think it would be as special for you this year, Em.' Ola attempted a smile. His little girl was growing up. Following her birthday in September, she had proudly announced that she was too old to believe in Father Christmas. This meant some of the wonder of the season had faded for Ola. It didn't matter that his son still believed, because so much went over Benny's head.

Even though the boy had reached the age of three, his vocabulary and skills were impaired by his regular and prolonged seizures. Janet feared they were damaging his little brain, but Ola thought his son was lazy. Why should Benny learn to communicate when Janet, and sometimes even Emma, catered for his every whim? His slightest squeak had his mum running to his side. Benny and Janet had a language all of their own, a private world they let no one else enter.

'Can we have a hot chocolate, Dad?' Emma asked.

Her joy was infectious, and Ola found his mouth twitching. 'I suppose we can.'

Benny had been trotting along happily, holding his mother's hand. Suddenly, he came to an abrupt halt, forcing Janet to skid to a stop alongside him. He whimpered, released her hand, and held up his arms imploringly.

'Can you carry him, Ola?' Janet begged.

Ola was tempted to give in, to pick his son up and place him on his shoulders, but that wouldn't satisfy Benny. Only his mum would do for him. 'He's old enough to walk,' he chided.

Janet's helpless glance moved from his face to her son's. Her hands twitched, revealing her yearning to pick Benny up and cuddle him.

Benny hated crowds. On the rare occasions when strangers visited their home, he crouched in a corner or hid behind the sofa. He was used to Karen and would sometimes play with Emma and Erin, but Dale's boisterousness scared him.

Emma's attitude to her brother varied according to her mood. Sometimes loving and playful, she soon tired of him if he became difficult. Emma favoured Ola in many ways, including displaying a number of his character traits as she matured. However, she was the spitting image of her mother with brown hair and eyes. Benny had inherited Ola's pale skin and blonde hair, which made him look even more pallid when he was ill.

'Don't be a baby, Pestie.' Emma held out her hand with a dazzling smile, calling Benny by her favourite pet name. 'You're going to be four soon. Mum and Dad can't keep carrying you everywhere. Come on. Dad's gonna let us have hot chocolate! And we'll see more Christmas lights.'

Benny couldn't resist Emma's enthusiasm. He took her outstretched hand, and the two walked ahead of their parents. Disaster averted, Janet led her family into yet another shop. The crowds seemed to multiply with everyone searching for the best Christmas bargains. Emma asked when they were going to have their hot chocolate, and Janet said they only needed to go into one more shop. Benny protested more as the crowds grew thicker until Ola's patience and Emma's enthusiasm wore thin.

They were moving amongst several racks of clothes when Ola lost sight of his children amongst the shoppers. As Janet was further back, he wasn't overly worried. Benny couldn't move fast and would only be about three or four steps behind her. Then he spotted Emma darting from under a rack. She tugged on his sleeve and spoke quietly, her eyes wide with fear.

'Dad! Benny's gone.'

'What do you mean?' Janet's head shot up, and her gaze swept over their surroundings.

Emma's attempts at subtlety had failed. Her brother's name, however quietly whispered, was enough to alert their mum.

'I'm sorry, Mum.' Tears sprang into Emma's eyes. 'I didn't mean to lose him.'

As Janet panicked, Ola thought practically. 'When did he let go of your hand?' He was more irritated than worried. The boy needed discipline. He'd be having words with him later, no matter what Janet said.

'I don't know!' Emma wailed.

After that everything happened at once. Janet marched to the nearest shop assistant and threw her hands in the air, announcing loudly to anyone and everyone that she had lost her baby.

'He's not a baby, Jan. He's three.' Ola's temper flared. He was angry with Janet for over-reacting, with Benny for disappearing, and with Emma for letting him go. This was why he abhorred Christmas shopping.

'He's going to be so scared!' Janet pined. 'He'll be crying for me.'

Soon everyone was joining in the search for the missing boy, turning the whole place upside-down. Of course Ola wanted to find Benny, but this sort of attention was exactly what he hated. As Janet voiced her anxious fears – *What if someone had taken Benny? What if he was hurt, or he had a seizure when she wasn't there to look after him?* – Ola felt humiliation burning within.

'It's all my fault! I should never have let go of his hand,' Janet cried.

Emma, no doubt blaming herself too, looked to her father for reassurance, but Ola had none to give.

After a thorough search, a security guard found Benny hiding behind a large cardboard box. He had been missing for less than thirty minutes, but it had felt like hours. Benny cried and shook pitifully as he was returned to his mum's arms. Convinced he was likely to have a seizure, Janet left Ola and Emma to struggle with the bags while she comforted Benny.

Ola drove his family home in stony silence. As soon as they were safely inside, he marched out of the house, spending what remained of the evening drinking at the Frog and Parrot. As he downed his sixth pint, he wondered if he would turn into his father. Was this how it happened? Had frustration driven his dad to drink? He vowed yet again that he couldn't follow in his footsteps, no matter how strong the temptation. Emma needed him. With her mother's attention consumed by Benny, Emma often got neglected. He wouldn't neglect her. She deserved more.

❧

The following summer, Emma begged her parents for a holiday by the sea. All her friends went away, but the Wellanders hadn't left home since Benny's birth. His frequent hospital visits ruled their lives.

Ola was working increasingly long hours at the garage in the hope of one day buying the business from its ageing owner. Although Peter Moss had worked there longer, he was less ambitious and would be just as happy to take orders from his friend.

When Emma mentioned her desire for a holiday, she already had the whole thing planned out. 'Erin says we can hire two caravans together. We'll all enjoy the seaside, and Mum will have Karen to help with Benny,' she said.

At first Janet seemed uncertain, but the thought of having Karen close by comforted her.

'It's a good idea,' Ola confirmed. 'If we have to take Benny to the hospital, Emma can stay with the Mosses.'

Ola hoped it might even be a chance for them to recapture some of their former closeness. Although Janet had abided by his wishes and moved back into their bedroom, Benny still slept beside her. The only alone time they shared was when Emma let their son stay in her bed.

Ola had already been dropping less than subtle hints about Benny sleeping in his own room. However, Benny hated being by himself. He followed Janet constantly, whether she was in the house or working in the garden. Her silent little shadow. Janet claimed he was placid when they were alone and only displayed fits of temper when Ola or Emma threatened to rob him of her attention.

And why shouldn't we? We're your family too. As Ola compared Benny to his sister at the same age, he recalled how Emma had chattered and played, creating her own imaginary worlds. Benny seemed to lack imagination. Few toys or games interested him unless someone was on hand to show him what to do. He could sit staring into space for hours.

'I wonder what he's thinking?' Janet mused one Saturday afternoon while preparing Ola's coffee.

'Likely nothing at all,' Ola was hot and irritable, having just mowed the grass.

'That can't be true.' Janet handed over the mug. 'I'm sure his thoughts are more advanced than his speech. He just finds it easier to express himself in other ways.'

'Like in tears and temper tantrums.' In Ola's opinion, his son was spoiled and unmanageable.

Benny's seizures came in waves, and prolonged bouts of illness caused him to regress further, sleeping for hours cuddled up on the sofa with his favourite blanket. During his better spells, Janet insisted she saw glimpses of the boy he might become, when he took more interest in his environment.

Ola didn't share her optimism. But as the time for their holiday drew closer, even he looked forward to their week away with the Mosses.

❦

When the day of their departure finally dawned, Emma chattered away nineteen to the dozen as they loaded the car and set off. She sat in the front seat beside Ola, while Janet monitored Benny in the back. Predictably he was car sick, but Janet had become adept at reading his signals and acting accordingly.

'I can see the sea!' Emma bounced up and down in her seat. Ola revelled in his daughter's happiness, determining to let nothing spoil her holiday.

When they arrived at their destination, Emma, Erin and Dale ran in and out of both caravans while the cars were unloaded.

The more reserved Judy sat on her parents' veranda with a book, but the younger children were eager to explore every nook and cranny of their new surroundings. Although Karen and Janet griped when they got under their feet, Ola suspected they were secretly delighted in the children's unbridled joy.

'Come and play with us, Pestie!' Emma squealed.

Ola watched from his seat on the veranda as he and Peter shared a couple of beers. Emma charged about wildly and when she grabbed Benny's hand, her brother followed her willingly. Ola had rarely seen Benny run and play with other children. Watching him now, it was difficult to believe the boy was so sickly.

A chase ensued, with Benny last in line. In his efforts to keep up with others, Benny outran himself, falling face down on the grass. His cries of frustration soon brought Emma to his side, and Ola watched as she helped him up, speaking in firm but loving tones.

'You're all right. You didn't hurt yourself.'

Benny stopped crying, but Ola still expected him to run inside to his mum.

'Come on. Hold my hand, then we can go faster!' Emma said.

Benny smiled, and brother and sister dashed off in pursuit of Dale and Erin as Ola looked on in amazement.

❧

That afternoon, the two families had their first look at the sea. The Moss children knew what to expect, and Emma passed on her wild excitement to Benny. Soon they were both asking if Benny could go paddling too.

Ola was about to say 'Of course' when Janet overruled, hesitant to let her youngest near the waves. 'He won't like it, Em. He'll fall. He'll end up swallowing sea water and making himself sick.'

So, Janet held Benny on her lap, forcing him to watch the others from afar. Ola expected Benny to kick up a fuss, but fortunately, he laughed and smiled as Peter chased Dale, Emma and Erin in and out of the water and jumped them over the waves.

'Come and play with us, Daddy!' Emma pulled on Ola's arm, and despite his usual reticence, he found himself being drawn into her games. They had a few rounds of bat and ball before Emma jumped back in the water and Ola sat down, eager to swig the coffee in his thermos.

Benny was growing restless now.

'Someone wishes he was in the sea with his sister.' Karen reached over to Benny on Janet's lap. 'Want Auntie Karen to take you?'

'Yeah!' Benny disentangled himself and placed his hand trustingly in Karen's.

'You don't mind do you, Jan?' Karen asked.

Ola watched for Janet's reaction. He expected her to make excuses, but Karen was a responsible mother to her own children. If Janet refused, Benny would cry, and Ola would get really cross. *It's been a peaceful day so far, Jan. Don't ruin it.*

'Alright,' Janet said. 'But don't let go of Auntie Karen's hand.' Janet's eyes remained glued to their retreating backs as Karen led Benny towards the sea. He turned back to smile and wave, copying his sister. Ola saw Janet fighting tears as she waved back and blew him a kiss.

Karen paddled with Benny, gradually acclimatising him to the icy water. The first time a wave came towards him, he retreated with a cry, but he soon looked as happy as any of the others. When Ola was dragged closer by Emma again, he caught some of the conversation between Karen and Dale.

'Will you play with me now, Mummy?' Dale tugged at Karen's arm.

'Not now, Dale. I'm holding Benny.'

Dale stuck his tongue out. Patience was not one of the six-year-old's virtues. He approached life fearlessly, as a boy should.

'Now, don't be like that,' Karen said. 'Benny is younger than you.'

'He doesn't need holding. Mum. He's four. I did lots of scary things when I was four. I can remember! I didn't cry all the time, and I could talk good.'

'Perhaps you can play with Benny?' Ola saw the glimmer of hope in Karen's eyes.

'No! I want to splash and go under water. Benny's scared of all that stuff.'

Karen glanced their way, clearly caught between her promise to Janet and her desire to play with her own son. She waved Ola over. 'Can you take him while I play with Dale?'

Reluctantly, Ola agreed. At least if he went, Janet couldn't stop Benny having fun.

Karen placed Benny's little hand in his much larger one, then turned back to her son. 'Come on, Daley! Let's see if you can drown Mummy!' Dale's idea of playing definitely wasn't suitable for Benny.

Dale pelted into Karen's outstretched arms, chattering non-stop about how much fun he was having and how much he loved the sea.

Ola looked down at Benny standing rigidly at his side. He'd stiffened the moment their hands touched. Was he scared of his own father? Ola searched for something to say, then shook his head. The boy wouldn't understand. Just as he'd resolved to take him back to Janet, Emma appeared, grasping Benny's other hand and urging Ola to help her jump him over the waves.

'He won't like it, Em,' Ola argued. 'He'll cry.'

'No he won't!' Emma leaned closer to Benny and hissed, 'Don't cry. It'll be fun.'

As another wave crashed towards the shore, Ola and Emma lifted Benny and all three of them sprang into the air. Emma laughed uproariously, and after the second and third attempt, her brother joined in.

Ola lost himself in the joy of playing with them until Benny's hand slipped out of his grasp, and he lost his footing in the water. He grabbed his son just in time, and suddenly Benny was up in his arms, too surprised to cry. Emma waved up at him, and any trace of fear was replaced by a smile. No words were exchanged, but Ola enjoyed the momentary closeness with his youngest child.

However, Janet's eagle eye had witnessed the mishap. She was upon them before they knew it, reaching for Benny, and offering comfort he didn't even need. 'Come to Mummy,' she said, pulling him from Ola's arms and carrying him back up the beach, where he sat with her and Judy watching the rest of them paddling until it was time to pack up and return to their caravans.

Ola didn't have the energy to override his wife. Sooner or later, Benny would have cried. It was better this way. He'd had his moment of fun, and he was happiest with his mother.

Later that night, the Wellanders sat on their veranda eating popcorn. When Janet tried to cajole Benny to sleep, he said an emphatic no, even though it was well past his bedtime. Emma reasoned they were on holiday. It wouldn't hurt him to stay up later. Ola had been relieved to hear her promise Benny he could share her bed. At least now he didn't have to wonder if Janet would force him out onto the sofa.

'Tell us about when you were a little boy, Daddy.'

Ola hated it when Emma asked those kinds of questions, usually deferring them to Janet.

'You never talk about when you were little.' Emma spoke with her mouth full of popcorn. 'Did you have holidays in caravans too?'

He shook his head, hoping to put an end to the conversation.

'Your father grew up in another country, Em. I'm sure things were different there.' Janet fiddled restlessly with the blanket on her lap. Her arms looked empty without Benny, who sat on the floor beside his sister tucking into the popcorn bowl. Soon, Janet picked up a magazine from the table next to them.

'I bet Dad had holidays too,' Emma persisted.

'I can only remember one.' Ola didn't know what made him talk. Perhaps it was the intimacy of the moment with his family, or the fact that he felt more relaxed after sharing a couple of drinks with Peter.

'Where did you go?' Emma asked.

'To England with my mum. That was when I decided I wanted to live here when I grew up.' He didn't feel the need to explain that they had taken the holiday to temporarily escape his drunken father, or that the vacation had been a gift from his maternal grandmother the year before she died. She'd known of their predicament and had begged her daughter to leave and make a new start. But Ola's mother was convinced she could cope – until she couldn't. By then it was too late. She was so hardened that she didn't even want her son.

'Did you go to the sea too?' Emma was full of questions tonight.

As Ola looked down at his children, he even saw Benny gazing up at him expectantly. He sometimes wondered whether the boy could understand more than he could say. 'Yes, but I liked the fair best.'

'What's vat, Daddy?'

Was this the first time Benny had braved asking him a question? Ola was so startled that it took him a few moments to plan a suitable reply. 'I expect we'll see one before we go home. There are all sorts of exciting things at a fair, like rides that swing you round and round and up and down, and toy horses to ride. All kinds of things.' Ola used his hands to demonstrate as he spoke, recalling how he had communicated such concepts to Emma when she was Benny's age.

'You won't be able to go on any of them.' Emma snatched the popcorn bowl from Benny, who glowered at her with disappointment in his eyes. 'And you can't eat any more of that.'

'Why?' he challenged.

'Cos you'll be sick.'

'I no be icky! Ew mean, Emmie!'

Ola was fascinated by the exchange between his son and daughter, and fortunately, Janet was too distracted by the magazine to notice their brewing row. Normally she would have jumped to Benny's defence.

'Tell him, Dad!' Emma seemed sure her father would be on her side. 'He will be sick, won't he?'

'He might if he eats too much popcorn.' There was amusement rather than sternness in Ola's voice, and Benny laughed up at him. 'But the same applies to you, Emma, so you'd better let me eat the rest.'

Benny poked his tongue out at Emma, grabbed the half-empty bowl and tossed it up to his father, who caught it with alacrity. Father and son exchanged the first conspiratorial smile they had ever enjoyed, and Ola realised he had underestimated Benny's understanding.

'Well, you still can't go on the rides at the fair.' Stubborn Emma was determined to have the last word.

'The only place the two of you will be going right now is to bed.' Ola rose and held out a hand to his daughter but was surprised when Benny took it. His little hand felt trusting in Ola's much larger one, and a momentary surge of love swept over him.

'I'll see to him.' Janet rose and pulled Benny away, carrying him into the caravan. Ola glanced at his empty hand then shrugged it off, turning his attention back to his daughter.

'You're not gonna let him go on the fair are you, Dad?' Emma clarified.

'I doubt if he'll want to when he sees how fast everything moves.'

Ola was right. Benny was less eager to go on the fairground rides when he saw the crowds and the flashing lights. However, he surprised his father by pointing up at Dale sitting on Peter's shoulders and falteringly asking if he could do that too. So Ola spent the whole evening with Benny happily watching proceedings from an elevated position, while Janet looked bereft and Emma, Erin and Karen went on all the rides. Peter took Dale on a few too, but Judy, Ola, Janet, and Benny had no desire to join them.

Eventually Janet relaxed, slipping her arm through Ola's as they strode through the fairground. Ola wondered if this would be a turning point for their family. Would Benny outgrow his seizures and his clinginess? Would Janet learn to let go?

However, later that night, Emma woke her parents by rushing into their room declaring that Benny was really ill. One seizure followed another until Ola and Janet found themselves in an unfamiliar hospital before dawn. When the seizures subsided and they were told they could take their son back to the caravan, he was listless and emotional, only letting Janet near him. He lay on her lap all morning until she declared they needed to take him home. Ola dreaded having to tell Emma, and he didn't blame her for her dramatic outburst when she saw Janet packing everything away.

'We've only been here two days,' she wailed. 'It's not fair! Benny will get better. He always does.'

'He's scared, love,' Janet explained. 'He needs to be at home where he feels safe.' She had Benny tied to her chest in a sling. As he was small for his age, she could still carry him that way when he refused to let her put him down.

'He's silly!' Emma marched out of the caravan, slamming the door behind her.

Ola found Emma lying on the veranda sobbing her little heart out, and the love he'd felt for his son the previous night turned to anger as he once again witnessed the effects of Benny's illness on his sister.

'I'm sorry, Emma.' It was all he could say. He remained silent during the journey home and said little for the next few days.

Sensing his anger, Benny withdrew even further, and the void between them only became wider.

5

As Benny's first day of school drew near, Janet's anxieties hit an all-time high. Although he was starting a year late, Janet was convinced he was still too young. Ola had wanted Benny to begin his education at the accepted age of four, but fortunately the school had been on Janet's side, agreeing their son wasn't ready. They had insisted on him having speech therapy at home, hoping this would help him overcome some of his verbal delays.

At five and a half, Benny would now be the oldest child in his class. In theory he would be closer in ability to his peers, but during the extra year at home, Benny had made minimal progress, prompting Janet to beg Ola to consider delaying things further. Surely Benny's health and under-developed learning gave them the perfect excuse?

Her husband remained resolute. 'He should go to school like every other child,' he insisted. 'He's only epileptic.'

'They still can't find any medication that works,' she'd argued. 'He has too many seizures, and he's always in and out of hospital.' Janet's endless pleas made no impact on her husband who had one strong argument on his side.

'If we wait another year, Emma will be going to secondary school. It's far better if she's there with Benny in the beginning.'

Janet couldn't deny this, so she reluctantly devoted the summer to preparing Benny for the world of education. Her fears remained close to the surface as she told him about all the fun things he would do. 'You'll learn to read and write and do sums. Your teacher will tell you exciting stories, and there will be loads of other children to play with.' Janet didn't know why she added the last part, because poor Benny struggled to relate to other children.

'Don't wanna go, Mummy.'

His speech was still limited for his age, and when anything upset him, he reverted to baby talk. This was another worry, because she knew how cruel children could be.

'Wanna stay with you.' Benny entwined his spindly arms around her neck.

Janet held her child close, enjoying his need of her comforting presence. She kissed the top of his head as she rocked him back and forth on her lap. He was still so small and thin. It was easy to presume he was younger than his five years. However, there would be no hiding his age when he started school. 'It'll be fun.' Tears threatened as she tried to offer encouragement she didn't feel.

'*We* have fun, Mummy.'

Janet was all her little boy needed, and although she was ashamed to admit it, she liked being at the centre of his world. 'We still will, sweetheart. You'll only be at school for a few hours. When you come home, we'll have hot chocolate and biscuits, and you can tell me all about your day.'

'No. Not gonna go.' It was an emphatic statement from a child who was often accused by his elder sister of not knowing what he wanted.

Janet would have to get Emma on-side if they were going to cajole Benny into cooperating, so she urged her two children to play schools as often as possible. Emma took the role of teacher gladly, and under her tuition, Benny was a compliant student. She even got him copying his name on paper.

However, the concept of numbers was foreign to him. Benny's idea of counting to five started with one, skipped two three and four, and went straight to five. When a frustrated Emma asked him what had happened to the missing numbers, he emphatically declared: 'Don't want them, Emmie.'

He seemed to have a logic all of his own and was a literal thinker. Emma once asked him to put the rest of her lunch in the bin, and Benny tossed it in, plate and all. Later, when she asked where the plate was, he simply told her he'd done what she'd said.

It was a warm early September morning when Janet and Emma walked Benny into his classroom on his first day. He clutched both their hands and seemed to be in denial until they prepared to leave him. When they headed for the door, he automatically made to follow, reaching for his mum's hand.

'You've got to stay here, love.' Janet wanted to escape as quickly as possible so neither of her children would see her cry. 'Mummy will pick you up later.'

'No. I been school now, Mummy. Wanna go home.'

Janet kissed Emma goodbye as Benny clung to her legs, unwilling to let go. She bit down on her lip, trying desperately not to give in, as the teacher attempted to pry Benny, shaking and screaming, from her embrace. Mrs Lowell reassured Janet that she was used to handling distraught little ones, but she couldn't possibly understand. Benny wasn't like other little ones. He was vulnerable and helpless. Guilt at betraying her son pierced Janet's heart, and she battled whether to obey Benny's pleading eyes or the teacher's.

Janet almost capitulated and took her baby back home. 'You don't understand. He's going to end up having a seizure!' How could anyone look after him as vigilantly as her?

It wasn't until the teaching assistant stepped in and practically marched Janet out of the door that she allowed her reluctant legs to move. She emerged into the sunshine, where Karen waited, eager to offer her invaluable support.

Things had gone much more smoothly for the Moss children, with Dale flat out refusing to let Karen accompany him into his new classroom. He was seven. He was going into the juniors, and that meant he was a big boy. He didn't need his mum to show him where to go.

'If Benny has problems, they'll handle it.' Karen draped her arm around Janet's shoulders. 'They know about his seizures, and I'm sure he's not the first epileptic child they've had to deal with.'

'But even his doctors say his case is more complicated because they can't seem to bring it under control. You don't realise, Karen. The seizures leave him tired and listless for days. How's he going to cope with that at school?'

Karen chewed on her lip, obviously wanting to say more but choosing to refrain. 'How about you come to my house for a cuppa?'

'I can't.' Janet shook her head emphatically. 'I want to be near the phone in case Benny can't cope and I have to fetch him.'

'Fine. We'll have tea at your house.'

Janet had barely brewed their tea when the call came. Benny had made himself sick with crying. Could she collect him? By the time Janet returned to the school, Benny had also wet and soiled his clothes. She was used to carrying spare clothing around as he still had occasional accidents. She hadn't even attempted to toilet train him through the nights. He slept fitfully, often waking up grizzling and complaining about bad dreams. Janet feared they were caused by the medication he took for his epilepsy, but the doctors' hands were tied. Without the tablets, Benny's seizures would be even worse.

Back at home, Benny refused to get off Janet's lap. He begged her not to make him go to school, and Janet was at her wit's end. He cried hysterically when it was time to pick Emma up. Sensing he was afraid of returning to the source of his fears, Janet phoned Karen and asked if she would walk Emma home.

Emma was sympathetic when she found out what had happened. She cuddled her brother while Janet prepared their tea, then rushed him upstairs to play when it was time for their father to return home. Janet was sure Emma expected Ola's reaction, which was even worse than she had feared.

'You brought him home?' Ola bellowed. 'For goodness sakes, Jan. Can't you see that was what he wanted? The more you give in, the worse he's going to get!'

'I couldn't leave him there,' Janet sobbed. 'Please try to understand.'

'The boy's got to go to school.' Ola refused to discuss it further, and he ignored Benny for the rest of the night.

Thankfully Benny seemed not to notice. He rarely shared more than a few words with his father. Occasionally Ola included him if he was doing something with Emma and Benny showed an interest, but mostly he pretended his son didn't exist.

'What're you gonna do, Mum?' Emma asked when Janet was sitting on the edge of her daughter's bed. Benny lay sleeping next to his sister, reassured by having been told he could spend the night with her if he was good. He slept much better when he was with someone else, and Ola was so angry, she didn't dare suggest he slept with them that night. Though Benny's bed remained in their room, Janet often snuck him in beside her once Ola started snoring. When Ola spied him in the morning, he would sigh and glare at her before getting up to start his day.

'About Benny?' she asked.

Emma nodded as Janet smoothed the blankets over her treasured youngest child.

'I don't know. I wish he didn't have to go to school. I'm sure he can't cope.'

'He can cope with more than he thinks.' Emma's tone was grown-up and assertive, but Janet disagreed.

After further unsuccessful attempts at encouraging Benny to stay in his classroom, his teacher realised they needed to hatch a plan. By then he was having regular and intense seizures and regressing in other ways. His classmates were already singling him out as the weird boy who had accidents, cried all the time, and had to go home an hour after he arrived. Janet wanted Ola to accompany her to meet with the headmistress, but he would have no part in it. So it was Karen who went.

Several options were discussed until the teachers agreed. Benny would begin with half days, with Janet staying with him in the classroom, leaving him alone for longer periods each day until he could manage a morning, then an afternoon, then all day without her. Amazingly, it worked, although it took until the following January for Benny to consent to being left all morning. Janet enticed him by making detailed plans of what they would do when he came home, devoting the afternoon to him until Emma and Ola returned.

Ola's attitude to his son during this period became even frostier. He started insisting upon Benny sleeping in his own bedroom. Benny cried himself sick, and Janet spent most of the night going in and out to see to him until Emma suggested they move Benny in with her. Although Ola wasn't happy, Emma persuaded him it was the best way of transitioning her brother into sleeping by himself.

~❧~

Spring turned to summer, and Benny's first school year was ending. During the final half term, he stayed all day, and although he still said he didn't like it, Janet couldn't deny that his confidence was growing. Mrs Lowell had taken a liking to him despite their rocky start. Sensing his struggles with basic learning, she gave him practical tasks that made him feel important. He took responsibility for putting the crayons away or tidying the toys after playtimes. These things he did willingly because they didn't tax him, and he begrudgingly admitted he liked Mrs Lowell.

Janet wondered whether they would end up back at square one when Benny changed classes in September, but Mrs Lowell was one step ahead of her. During the last two weeks of the school term, she introduced Benny to his new teacher, who liked mothering him even more than she did. They carefully explained what would happen, and he told Janet about it on the last day of school. He would have six weeks to play at home, then he had to go into Mrs King's class. That was fine for now, but Janet feared he would forget about it by September. There was also the added strain of Emma no longer accompanying them on the daily walk. She would travel to her new secondary school by bus.

Janet slept fitfully the night before Benny's return to school, expecting him to come running into her bedroom at any minute saying he wouldn't go without Emmie. He still slept in his sister's room on weeknights, although they had struck a deal whereby he stayed in his own room on Fridays and Saturdays. If he cooperated, Emma took him to the local park on Sunday afternoons to play. Those were Benny's special times with his sister, and no one else dared to intrude.

At first, Janet felt left out, but she soon appreciated the growing bond between her children. Emma was as good as her word. When Benny declined to keep up his end of the deal, she refused to back down, and there were no Sunday afternoon outings, however loudly he cried. When he realised this, Benny did his best, except on the nights he was ill. Emma allowed for that most of the time.

❧

'Why's Emmie got different clothes on?' Benny was becoming more observant, and Janet couldn't deny his progress. Yet she dreaded giving him an answer.

'She's going to the big school today, remember?' Janet steeled herself for tears.

'Oh yeah.' Benny nodded his understanding. 'And I've gotta go in Mrs King's class.' He climbed down from his chair, leaving behind a half-eaten piece of toast. Persuading him to eat regular meals was proving to be yet another challenge. He didn't seem to need food the same way most children did. Janet supplemented his limited diet with endless cups of hot chocolate or warm milk. He ate half a meal if she fed him or made a game out of it, but he soon tired of the task and told her he was full.

The only food Benny never refused was ice cream, and he loved dipping biscuits in warm milk or in her tea. He was painfully thin and prone to catch any cold or sickness bug that was going around. He still had long periods of illness which meant that despite his progress, Janet had to keep him home from school more than was helpful.

Janet and Benny waved Emma off on the bus then walked to the infants' school. She could tell he was nervous when she left him in his classroom. Mrs King took hold of his hand and said he would be fine with her, and Janet almost believed her.

Although Benny was tearful when she left, he didn't try to follow, nor make a sound as he joined the other children in a circle for story time.

Two weeks later, Mrs King called Janet aside to tell her she was proud of Benny. He had managed to stay at school after one of his milder seizures. He trusted her enough to sit on her lap for the rest of the day while she directed the class. Her only regret was that he still hadn't made friends. The other children's attitudes had grown worse over time as he continued to struggle with his academic limitations, and his teacher found his seizures impossible to hide.

Janet was thrilled to have something positive to report to Ola. She hoped he would encourage Benny, but he simply grunted a reluctant, 'Well done, Son,' before returning to his newspaper. Father and son still barely communicated, even though Benny's speech was clearer, and his little personality was developing.

Emma settled well into secondary school and enjoyed making new friends, although there was still a special bond between her and Erin. The Mosses and the Wellanders mingled regularly, but although Dale was only two years older than Benny, he refused to consider him as a playmate, calling Benny a silly baby. Nothing anyone said could persuade him to change his mind.

6

'Your sister's got a boyfriend!'

Eleven-year-old Dale never talked to Benny unless it was to taunt or tease him. Dale's friend Brian Brooks spoke to him occasionally, but Dale said he couldn't understand why.

Benny liked Brian, and he sometimes wished he was his friend instead of Dale's. It was strange to watch Dale and Brian playing together, because they didn't like the same things. Dale loved noisy games and sport, but Brian was quiet and good at his schoolwork. Even Auntie Karen had told his mum it was an odd friendship. Benny heard them talking about it one day while they sat in Auntie Karen's kitchen. He usually ignored them when they talked, unless they were talking about something interesting, and hearing about Dale and Brian was interesting.

Benny longed for a best friend. When he was younger, he had thought his sister was his best friend. Emmie was growing up now, and the lots-of-years between them meant she no longer had the time or patience to play with him. She was wearing makeup to school, and she spent loads of money on clothes, CDs and other boring things.

If Benny had money, he would spend it on ice cream, or chocolate. Or maybe on a bike. Yet, he mused sorrowfully, even if he had a bike, who would teach him to ride it? Uncle Peter had taught Dale, and now Dale rode around everywhere. Uncle Peter also played football with Dale and Brian in the street, whereas his dad watched TV, read his newspaper, or occasionally did something with Emma.

Benny wondered how he would feel if he had a daddy like Peter. Although he loved his mum, it wasn't the same. He saw other boys with their dads. Sometimes they picked them up from school and took them out on adventures. The boys boasted to one another about how strong their daddies were, and how they were teaching them cool things. Benny did none of those things, because his dad had no interest in doing them with him. He helped his mum in the garden instead and sometimes played with Emma, though she didn't want to play much anymore.

Dale had been given a shiny new bike for his birthday, and Benny wondered what he'd done with his old one. If he was braver, he might have asked, but he was scared of Dale, so he did his best to avoid him.

Now Dale had sought him out, but it was only to show off because he thought he knew something Benny didn't.

'No she hasn't,' Benny replied. 'Emmie hasn't got a boyfriend.'

Dale was causing trouble again. Benny's mum said trouble was Dale's middle name. He thought she was wrong about that though, because he'd heard Auntie Karen calling him 'Dale Peter Moss' when he was naughty. Benny wondered why he didn't have a middle name like Dale. Or maybe he did, and he just didn't know it. He would ask his mum if he remembered.

'She has. I saw her kissing him!' Dale's eyes gleamed with cruelty, and Benny longed for the courage to stand up to him. 'I see lots of things now I'm at big school with your sister. Not like you! You're still a baby.'

'You're a mean, nasty boy, Dale Moss.' Tears sprang to Benny's eyes. He wished anger didn't make him cry. It just happened. It wasn't even better now he was nine.

Dale laughed at his tears. 'You're a silly little cry-baby, Weedy Wellander.'

Benny struggled to handle his emotions at the best of times and didn't stand a chance when Dale backed him into a corner. He escaped into the house where he knew his mum's arms waited.

'What's the matter, my love?' Janet opened them wide.

Benny jumped into the security of her cuddles, even though he knew he shouldn't indulge in them. Dale was right. He was a cry-baby. He was stupid and rubbish at everything he did. Knowing that made him cry even harder. 'Dale was nasty to me,'

Janet pulled him onto her lap, and Benny wept into her chest. Was his mum the only person who loved him? Emmie used to, but she got stroppy these days. The way he behaved probably didn't help. He tried to get back at her by telling tales to their mum, like he was doing now with Dale. Only with Emmie it always backfired, because she had Daddy on her side.

Now Benny was growing up, his dad was less restrained with his discipline. If there was one thing Ola couldn't stand, it was taletelling. While Janet loved and fussed, he shouted and threatened; and all Benny could do was cry.

'Don't worry about Dale Moss.' His mum dried his eyes with a tissue and planted a tender kiss on his cheek. 'You wouldn't want to be friends with a naughty boy like him.'

Benny wondered what Auntie Karen would think if she heard his mum calling Dale a naughty boy. He supposed Karen loved Dale as much as Mum loved him, but she didn't show it the same way. People were confusing.

Once he was feeling better, Benny went back outside to see what was happening in the street. If Dale was still there, he could hide at the side of his father's shed and the older boy would never know. Benny watched most of the happenings from his spot beside the shed. It was his favourite spying place. Had he a better imagination, he might have invented some spying games, like the teachers read about in stories at school, but he was rubbish at thinking up games; and anyway, there was no one to play them with. So he just spent his time watching and listening.

The cul-de-sac was quiet, and Benny soon became bored. He returned to the kitchen to ask his mum if he could meet Emma off the bus. She'd stayed late with her friends for an after-school activity.

Janet's eyebrows lifted at his request. She still didn't like letting him go anywhere by himself, even if it was just round the corner to meet the bus.

'Please. There aren't any busy roads to cross, and I know the way.' He used to go with his mum before Emma decided she was too big to be fetched from the bus stop.

'Why don't you wait for her here?'

Benny recognised the reluctance in his mum's face. She couldn't refuse, could she? Not when he asked for so little. Benny never knew what he wanted for his birthday or Christmas, and he hardly ever asked to go anywhere. He just wandered around the house or garden unless she gave him a task to do. 'I like seeing Emmie get off the bus.' He gave her his best puppy-dog eyes.

That did the trick. 'Come straight home. If she's going anywhere with her friends, you tell her I said she's to see you home first. Okay?'

Benny nodded and ran out the front door with his mum chasing after him.

'Benny! Don't run. You'll fall.'

Ignoring her warnings, Benny pelted down the road. Houses and cars sped by as he ran even faster, free and alive, like the birds he loved to watch whizzing through the sky. He didn't know how long it was till Emma's bus arrived because time had never meant much to him. Whenever it came, he would be waiting. Perhaps he'd persuade her to take him to the shop for ice cream if he was really good and grown-up and didn't get on her nerves.

Loads of people were waiting at the bus stop, so Benny hid round the corner. He would still see the bus coming from there. Benny hated being surrounded by strangers. He only wanted to see Emma.

The vehicle pulled in and crowds of noisy teenagers jumped off. Benny saw Erin Moss and Brian's sister, Kerry. Where was Emmie? He craned his neck to look for her. Had she got into trouble at school? Would she have to stay even later? He knew that happened sometimes because his sister told him about some of the antics of the naughty boys in her class. Benny shuddered at the thought.

Then he saw her. Emma walked off the bus holding hands with a tall boy whose long hair was done up in a ponytail. Boys weren't supposed to do that! Ponytails and plaits and things were for girls. Boys had short hair, didn't they? Perhaps it wasn't a boy, but a girl who looked like a boy. Then Benny heard them talking, and he knew it was a boy.

Emma laughed as her companion whispered into her ear. Then she reached up and kissed him right in front of the other kids from the bus.

Benny couldn't believe it. His sister was kissing a silly boy! He was angry and jealous. She wouldn't play with him anymore because he was 'childish', but she seemed happy with that other boy. It wasn't fair. He was gonna tell on her. She'd get in loads of trouble. Dad would ground her, and she wouldn't be allowed to go out again for ages. The boy would find someone else to play with, and Emma would want to be with him again.

Benny had changed his mind about letting his sister know he was there, and he ran home another way. His mum would be angry if she found out because she said it wasn't safe, but even if there were nasty people lurking in the quiet alleys, he was running too fast for them to catch him.

Back on his own road, he caught sight of Dale Moss's shiny new bike. Dale had left it outside on his parents' front lawn. It would serve him right if someone stole it. You were supposed to look after new things, especially expensive presents like bikes you got for your birthday. Benny didn't know exactly how much a bike would cost, but it was much more than he would ever have. His money box was empty, because he didn't get pocket money like Emma.

Benny looked around gingerly. Satisfied there was no one watching, he moved closer. The bike drew him like a magnet. He had watched Dale loads of times, and he was sure he knew what to do. Dale wouldn't know if he just took it for a little ride. His mum and dad said stealing was wrong. Would it be stealing if he took the bike? Wouldn't it only be having a lend? Dale and Brian always shared their toys. It wasn't his fault no one wanted to lend him nothing. If he had a bike, he'd share it. Not with Dale, because Dale would wreck it just to be mean, but he'd share it with Brian.

Glancing over his shoulder, Benny wheeled the bike out onto the street, gazing down at it in awe. He just wanted a little go. His mum and dad would never let him have one. This would be his only chance. He would put it back after one quick ride. No one would know.

Benny gritted his teeth and climbed onto the bike. It wobbled at first, but he thought if he went really fast, he might keep his balance, whereas if he went slow, he'd have time to get scared and fall off. He started peddling and shut his eyes. That was a bad idea. He couldn't see where he was going. 'Stupid!' he muttered. He opened them again to focus on the road ahead.

Ola Wellander chose that moment to drive around the corner on his way home from work. Attuned to the children playing in the street, he was already going fairly slowly, yet the last thing he expected to see was his son tearing towards him on Dale Moss's bike. Ola slammed on his brakes as bike and car seemed set to collide. He yelled, 'Benny. No!' knowing his son couldn't hear him.

Ola's heart pounded as he sprang from his car. There'd been no impact, but Benny lay sprawled on the tarmac breathing heavily, with the bike tangled between his feet. Ola's initial impulse to yell stalled as Benny stared up at him with tear-filled eyes and whispered, 'I'm sorry, Daddy.'

Noticing a graze on Benny's knee through a hole in his jeans, Ola reached down and helped him up. His reaction seemed to surprise them both, as they stared into each other's eyes. Benny was obviously expecting an angry tongue lashing, and Ola had been ready to give one, until love and pity took over. Love was a word he rarely thought about in relation to his son, but sometimes it swept over him at the most unexpected moments – like this one.

'What were you doing on Dale's bike?' His question came out more gently than he'd expected, and he noticed that Benny's flow of tears had quickly dried up. By now, he'd usually have been carrying his son yelling and screaming to his mother.

'I only wanted to have a go, Daddy. It looks like fun when Dale and Brian ride their bikes.'

'Haven't we taught you not to steal other children's toys?' Ola's gaze remained locked with Benny's.

'I was only borrowing it.'

'Did you ask Dale?'

Benny shook his head, having the good sense to look contrite. 'Dale's mean to me, Daddy. He never lets me share none of his toys.'

Ola felt a surge of compassion... and something else. Was it pride? What a strange time to be considering such an emotion. Yet when he had seen Benny hurtling towards him, he'd smiled before the panic set in, and he realised he was about to hit him. Benny had looked so normal, riding along with a cheeky grin, reminding Ola of his own childhood, in the days before he felt the impact of the world's cruelty.

'You'll have to say sorry to Dale for taking his bike without asking.'

'Okay, Daddy.'

Again, Ola had expected protests and tears. He turned to inspect the bike. Nothing was broken. They could return it without the Mosses knowing, but Benny would fail to learn a valuable lesson about taking responsibility for his mistakes. Ola took hold of the bike with one hand and reached for his son with the other. 'Come on. The sooner you get it over with, the better.'

Benny's eyes widened, seemingly surprised his father was offering to go with him. Then he stuck out his chin and stood on his own two feet, clinging firmly to Ola's hand. Facing Dale with his daddy by his side must be making him feel a lot braver.

The deed humbly done, Ola sent Benny home to Janet while he stood chatting to the Moss's in their front garden. Dale had been predictably angry, but Karen had said it was brave of Benny to come and say sorry, and she and Peter hadn't felt the need to punish him. After Benny and Dale left, Karen also confessed admiration for Benny's determination - getting on a bike and riding it by himself. She had always been sure Benny was more observant than he let on, and today had proved it. He had clearly been watching Brian and Dale, studying what they did and how they did it.

Ola took her words to heart and was surprised to find himself agreeing with her assessment of his son.

'So are you going to get him his own bike?' Peter grinned once the two men were alone.

'I doubt it. His mother will say it's bad for his health.'

'What do you say?' Peter stared at Ola intently. 'He's a little boy like my Dale. Little boys love riding bikes, and they like it when their dads teach them.'

'I can't teach Benny anything,' Ola confessed. 'I haven't got the patience.'

'You taught him to come round here and say sorry. We both know Jan wouldn't have done that. She would either have done it for him or tried to cover it up.'

'No doubt he's having cuddles and sympathy right now.' Ola scowled.

'Well, he looked very grown-up when he came into our house holding your hand.'

'It never lasts with Benny. He's got major limitations and trying to work with him on anything is too frustrating. Perhaps it's wrong of me to admit this, but patience has never been one of my strong points. Sooner or later, Benny will remind me of how much of a spoiled and pampered baby he still is.'

Benny proved his father right much sooner than even Ola could have predicted. When he got home, a full-scale argument was in progress between his two children.

'I saw you,' Benny said.

'So what?' Emma tossed her hair.

'You were kissing a boy. And I'm... I'm telling Dad.'

Seeing him enter, Benny ran towards him. 'Emmie has been kissing a boy!' He pointed at his sister, screwing up his nose. Had their moment of camaraderie led him to think Ola would take his side?

Anger flared up again. 'Haven't you already caused enough trouble for one night?' Ola waved him away dismissively. 'You know it's wrong to tell tales.'

'But... but Daddy!' Benny persisted.

'Enough!'

Benny shrivelled. His eyes momentarily opened wide at Emma, before he turned back for one last plead. Ola blocked him out. Whatever was going on with Emma, he wanted to hear it from her, not a little snitch.

Benny got the message and did exactly what Ola expected. He ran to Janet, crying and telling her Daddy and Emmie were mean. Ola groaned and after Emma stomped up to her room, he grabbed his coat and disappeared to the Frog and Parrot.

❧

Little changed for the Wellander's in the following two years, until, just after his eleventh birthday, Benny was hospitalised with the worst series of seizures he had ever experienced. He was in and out of consciousness for several days as the doctors tried to stabilise him. Through it all Janet sat at his bedside or held him on her lap when he whimpered in distress. By the time it was over, his speech and basic skills were dramatically affected.

When his parents brought him home, he struggled to walk and talk and had very little control over his bodily functions. As the weeks wore on, he made slow but steady progress, and when he returned for his final year of primary school six months later, he was physically back to where he'd been before.

However, a thicker fog seemed to have descended over his brain. Whether it was because he had missed so much school, or because he had sustained further brain damage, Benny found his schoolwork harder than ever. He soon lost interest, realising he was only there out of necessity. He did as little as he could to get by and continued to daydream about having a bike, a best friend, or someone to love him other than his mum.

He knew Emmie loved him again at least. They had talked about the boyfriend and how you loved different people in different ways, but they still weren't as close as Benny wished they could be. Emma let him sleep in her bed sometimes if he had a nightmare, or he was feeling sick, but it happened less often as she grew older. Mostly she told him to wake their mum. When he did, Ola became cross; especially when Benny couldn't make it to the bathroom in time.

His bouts of sickness grew worse as his stress levels increased. Simply being around his father made him anxious, so whenever they went on family outings, he was car sick. Sometimes Emma prevented it by sitting in the back and distracting him with silly games, but that only happened when she was in a really good mood. Mostly she travelled in the front with their dad, and Janet sat alongside Benny ready with cuddles and a bowl.

Benny hated being sick all the time. He was ashamed of his seizures and of being rubbish at school, but what could he do about it? Dale Moss was right. He was a pathetic, silly little boy, and it wasn't surprising no one wanted to be his friend.

As Year Six progressed uneventfully, and secondary school loomed, Benny became increasingly insecure.

'I'll never have a friend,' he said to Emma as he curled up on her bed one night.

'You mustn't think that way.' Emma patted his shoulder. 'You can't let boys like Dale Moss win.'

'Yes, I can.' Benny chewed his fingernails.

Emma shook her head. 'No. If you want to be like other boys, you have to prove you can be. And I'm going to help you. How about we start with the end of school camping trip?'

7

They had started with that camping trip, and Benny had almost made it, Emma considered as she sat at the breakfast table the morning after they'd picked Benny up. Why did that kid have to be so mean? Benny had managed to cope with the seizure all by himself. He could be there right now, making friends and growing up ready for secondary school – if Henry Keith hadn't been an idiot.

'You'll have to go on the boat without me.' Janet was saying.

Emma glanced up from her eggs on toast. Her mum had dark circles around her eyes.

'It was supposed to be a family day out,' Ola grunted.

'Emma understands, don't you love?'

Before Emma could answer, Ola beat her to it. 'Why should she have to?'

'Benny can't help being ill.'

Emma rolled her eyes and picked at her food. Why did they have to argue all the time? They weren't like this before Benny came along. Not that she'd swap her brother for a peaceful house. She loved him, despite the challenges he'd brought.

'You'll still have a good time without me.' Janet scraped the remainder of her cereal into the bin.

Her mum was right, but that wasn't the point, and Dad knew it.

'What do you think, Em?' Ola asked. His eyes begged her to side with him.

'We could never take Benny on a boat.' Emma shrugged. She didn't want to choose sides. What would that achieve? Their family was already divided.

'You and I could go shopping together instead, love. Maybe next Saturday?' Janet suggested.

'We'll see.' Emma wasn't willing to commit to something that would change at a moment's notice if her brother became ill, and their mum felt he couldn't do without her. Benny would always be Janet's priority. It was something Emma had learned to accept.

Benny trundled into the room, stretching his arms.

After fussing over him a bit, Janet went outside to hang clothes on the washing line, and Ola retreated into the lounge to watch the morning news, leaving Emma alone with her brother in the kitchen.

'Are you and Dad going somewhere?' Benny asked.

'Help me wash up.' Emma had filled the sink with water and begun her task. She pointed at the items already waiting on the draining board. 'Grab a tea towel, dry the dishes, and put them away when you're done.' Experience had taught her that Benny needed step-by-step instructions. If she just told him to wipe the dishes, he would stack them on the worktop until the piles toppled, and they'd find themselves surrounded by broken glass and china. Then their mum would come running, afraid he'd cut himself on the fragments. 'You know where it all goes, don't you?'

'I think so.' Benny looked around aimlessly. He took little notice of where the cups and plates were kept. If he needed anything, he asked, and their mum always obliged. But he clearly didn't want to admit his ignorance, and today was a good opportunity for him to learn.

Benny nodded and his nose twitched. 'It can't be that hard.'

'It's not hard, Pestie. I trust you.'

Benny's eyes lit up. He grabbed the towel and the first mug.

'Dad's arranged to take me and Mum out on a boat,' Emma explained.

'Can't we all go? A boat trip sounds like fun.'

'No. You'd be sick.'

'I'd try not to. Please, Emmie?'

She couldn't stand the wheedling tone he sometimes used. It made him sound a lot younger than his twelve years. 'If you're ill,

Dad will get cross, and the day will be ruined. It's better if he and I go, and you stay here with Mum.'

Benny looked at the cup in his hand. Emma noticed his fingers trembling and his nostrils flaring. She wondered if he might throw it in temper and braced herself for the repercussions. Their dad would hear from the living room and shout.

'Babies throw things. I'm not a baby no more,' Benny muttered before searching for the right cupboard and putting the cup back in its place.

Emma breathed out and a proud smile spread across her face.

'You don't need to do that, sweetheart. I'll help your sister.' Janet had returned to the kitchen with her empty washing basket.

'I like helping Emmie.' Benny's words earned him an extra smile of approval.

'But there are sharp knives!' Janet fretted.

'Mum!' Emma sighed and swished the dish water a little too ferociously, causing bubbles to slosh out over the sides.

Benny saw the funny side and was soon rubbing some of the frothy water on her nose. She responded by aiming her wet washing up sponge for his chest.

'Emma. Be careful!' Janet warned.

Emma knew it might end in tears. Benny could only cope with so much teasing. But today he was doing well, and she was enjoying the playfulness.

'He started it!' Emma imitated Benny's customary whine, and Benny threw the damp dish towel over her head.

'For goodness sakes! You two.' Janet clicked her tongue before exiting the room in search of more washing, and Emma returned the towel to Benny.

'You're not going to get out of it that easily, Pestie.'

'I know.' He re-focused on his task as Ola joined them from the lounge.

'Ready to go, Em?' he asked.

'I'm nearly finished here. I've just got to clean my teeth.'

'The glasses don't go that way up,' Ola barked. 'Can't you see how the others are stacked?'.

Benny shuddered at their father's harsh criticism, and Emma worried the glass would slip from his hand. She moved to stand at his side, took it from him, and placed it in its rightful position, before methodically rectifying his mistakes. Then sensing his need for a hug, she reached out and pulled him close. 'Thanks for helping, Pestie.'

His task unfinished, Benny left the kitchen without a backward glance.

'That's typical of your brother. He never finishes what he starts.' Ola retrieved the towel and deftly dried the remaining crockery.

'He was doing okay before you came in and made him nervous.'

'What are you trying to say?' His eyes flashed.

'Nothing, Dad.' Emma sighed. It was no good starting their day out together with an argument. If Ola left the house in a bad mood, he would carry it through the morning. Emma had been looking forward to their outing, and she was determined not to spoil it now. It was bad enough her mum couldn't come.

Janet was in the bathroom rifling through more washing when Benny joined her. She greeted him with a loving smile as she knelt on the floor organising the clothes into piles.

'What are you and me going to do today?'. He'd had a rotten night, and she wanted to make it up to him.

'Dunno.' There was rarely anything Benny wanted to do except go to the park or eat ice cream.

'Louise Brooks invited me to a coffee morning at her church yesterday. I said I couldn't go because I had plans with your dad and Emma, but I'd much rather go to the church with you.'

'I don't like coffee.'

Janet laughed lightly, ever reminded of her son's literal brain. 'There won't just be coffee, sweetheart. There'll be tea too, and lots of cake and biscuits. Probably home-made.'

'Will they have hot chocolate?' he asked.

'I expect so.'

'There'll be lots of people.' Benny sat on the edge of the bath. Janet was glad Ola wasn't around to warn him about breaking it.

'Not too many, and they'll be quiet because it's in a church.'

Benny looked up and sighed. 'Okay.'

'Put a clean t-shirt on while I put this lot in the machine. And brush your hair. It's sticking up.' Janet missed dressing and washing him. She had been forced to let go a little during the last few years and it jarred against her protective instincts.

Benny ambled out of the room to do her bidding, and Janet completed her task with the laundry.

Half an hour later, they set out for the church, walking hand-in-hand because Janet still didn't like him crossing roads by himself. Benny dawdled as they passed a shop with skateboards in the window, and she caught the look of longing in his eyes.

'Dale's got one of those,' he announced. 'He had it for his birthday.'

'Yes, I know, but Dale's older than you are.'

'Only two years,' he grumbled.

'Come on, or we'll miss out on the best cakes.'

'You and Dad won't even let me have a bike.'

Janet frantically searched for an explanation. How could she help her precious boy understand her constant fears for his safety? 'You'd hurt yourself if you had a seizure on a bike or a skateboard, sweetheart.'

Benny looked so dejected as he studied the pavement that Janet almost felt guilty. It was for his own good though, wasn't it? It was much better if they just went for ice cream, like he always enjoyed.

❧

The church was busier than his mum had promised. As soon as they entered, the noise hit Benny's ears, and he stuck like glue to her side. She found a space at a corner table, and he sat so close he was almost on her lap. He followed her when she fetched their drinks and buried his head in her shoulder whenever someone came to talk. She made excuses about how tired he was.

'No Emma today, Jan?' Louise Brooks bustled over to their table with a cloth in her hand. She was Brian's mum. Benny didn't think she knew his mum very well.

'She's gone on a boat trip with her father.' His mum smiled back but the smile looked nervous, and it seemed to make the black circles under her eyes even bigger. Were they his fault?

'So you get to spend the day with your wee lad here.'

Benny loved Brian's mum's Scottish accent. Mrs Brooks was gentle, and she never forced him to talk. He lifted his head from Janet's shoulder and smiled, earning him one of her beaming grins in response.

'Are you getting yourself ready to start secondary school in a few weeks, young Benny?'

'I don't wanna go.' He liked Mrs Brooks enough to tell the truth. She wouldn't make fun of him. Benny wondered if Brian's family were nice because they went to church. He didn't know a lot about church, but they had Bible stories at school, and it seemed like God and Jesus expected you to be kind. Were God and Jesus real? And if they were, what would they think of him?

They would probably think he was stupid, like everyone else. You had to be good for God to love you, and Benny wasn't. Not always. He could be if he wanted to, but too often his temper got the better of him and he started crying because he was angry, and fed up, and bored, and rubbish. He wished he could be like Brian Brooks. Brian did well at school, and everyone said he was a nice boy. No one liked Benny except for his mum and Emma.

They stayed at the coffee morning until Janet said it was time to go. She wanted to get some chores done while Ola and Emma were enjoying their trip. As soon as they got home, she set to work with her mop and duster, while Benny went into the front garden to see what was happening up and down the street. Thankfully, Dale was nowhere in sight, so Benny didn't have to worry.

He wasn't sure how long he sat on his parents' front wall. He saw Mr Brooks going out in his car, and another neighbour taking her dog for a walk. Benny wondered what it would be like to have a dog. He wished he could find out, because maybe a dog would love him despite his stupidity and his seizures. However, he knew deep down that his dad would never want a dog in the house. Even his mum would complain about the mess. He thought about how he would train a dog. It wouldn't be that hard. You only had to be firm and fair. Benny didn't know how he knew that. It just seemed to make sense.

'Hi, Benny,' Brian stood in his parents' front garden and waved. He wouldn't be doing that if Dale was around. 'Mum told me you were at the coffee morning earlier.'

'Yeah.' Benny wished he could think of something useful to say. Brian was Dale's friend, so there was no point talking to him.

'She wanted me to help out, but I got out of it. I had homework.' He paused, then added, 'Mum said you're pretty nervous about starting secondary school in September.'

Benny nodded.

'It's not too bad,' Brian encouraged. 'Some of it isn't that different from junior school.'

'Emmie says you have lots of tests and stuff.' Benny finally found his tongue.

'Well yeah, but no one expects you to get everything right. If you ever want help... Well, you could always ask.'

Benny couldn't believe Brian was offering to help him. He guessed Dale didn't know. 'Dale wouldn't like it if you helped me with my homework.'

'It's not up to Dale.' There was firmness in Brian's tone. 'You can't help being younger than us, and you can't help being ill.'

The older boy turned around and strolled back into his house, leaving Benny to stare after him open-mouthed. It was nice of Brian to offer. Would he ever have the courage to ask?

8

'Benny, can I come in?' Emma stood outside her brother's closed bedroom door waiting for a response. In the past she had strolled in and out as she pleased, but he was a teenager now, and he deserved some privacy.

'Yeah.' His voice sounded muffled.

Emma guessed he was lying with his head buried in a pillow. He was supposed to be studying, but that never lasted long with Benny. Even at thirteen and a half, his attention span was terrible.

'I thought you were catching up on schoolwork.' Emma entered the room to find him just as she had expected, sprawled out on his bed looking half asleep.

'My head's hurting.'

That was his favourite excuse. Although it worked with Janet, it didn't wash with Emma. 'You're going to have to get caught up, or you'll struggle even more.'

Benny had missed three weeks of school in the first term of Year Eight, spending over half that time in hospital while the doctors tried to find yet another medication to lessen his seizures. As a result, he'd been given loads of work to do over the half term holiday.

'I'll never catch up.' He scowled.

Emma sighed, aware it was true. Benny's first year at secondary school had been a nightmare of poor results and failed tests. The teachers didn't show him the sympathy he'd enjoyed at junior school. They viewed him as a stubborn boy who refused to try. So, Benny had withdrawn even more, becoming quiet and sulky, and only speaking when absolutely necessary.

When Emma asked him what teachers he had, hoping to give him tips to keep them happy, he didn't even know half the time. She suspected he sat at the back, staring into space, when he should have been paying attention. When she tried to help him with his homework, it was obvious that even though he was in the year below, his standard was still well behind his peers.

There had been rumblings about him being placed in the special needs group for Year Eight, and Benny had been so alarmed that their mum had begged for him to be given a second chance. They'd given him one, until he'd gotten in such a state about going back at the start of the year that he'd made himself sick again.

'You can do more than you realise,' Emma encouraged. 'You've just got to try harder.'

'What's the point?' He blinked back tears.

'If you don't, you'll be moved in with the special needs kids. This is your last chance, Pestie. They're serious this time.' She had to make him understand.

'I don't wanna be with them. Some of them are scary.'

He looked so young and vulnerable that it melted Emma's heart, and she reached for his hand. 'How about if I help you more tonight?' She could usually get the best out of him if she exercised patience. 'I'm going round to Erin's now. I'll be back after tea.'

'Okay. Thanks.'

Emma had discovered Benny could express his thoughts verbally, but he lacked the ability to write them down. She didn't know how this information could help him, since his teachers seemed unwilling to adapt. In their eyes, all the blame lay at Benny's door. They insisted that if he only worked harder, he would surely achieve more.

'Why don't you get some fresh air? It will clear your head.' He spent far too much time hiding away in his room.

Benny looked out of the window. 'There's nothing to do outside.'

Although he still longed for a bike, their mum refused to consider it. Emma resolved to broach the subject again with their dad. Benny needed something to motivate him into going out, and a bike would be just the thing. It would stop him spending the whole of the holidays in his room.

'At least you've stopped having so many seizures.' She tried to sound upbeat. During his time in the hospital, he'd had at least one a day. It was yet another stressful season as they all worried about the damage they inflicted on his brain.

'I wonder if Chloe's gone home yet,' Benny mused.

Emma smiled at her brother's uncanny way of switching subjects without warning. Chloe was one of the girls he'd met at the hospital. 'I guess she might have.' She saw his shoulders droop and squeezed his hand. 'Had a soft spot for her, didn't you?'

'It's not fair to be so ill when you're only six. She was really happy and bouncy, Em. She wanted to do loads of stuff, but she couldn't.'

Chloe had been on the Children's ward because she had cancer. Her bed was next to Benny's, so he had devoted hours to drawing with her or doing jigsaw puzzles. When her treatment made her ill and she cried, Benny held the little girl's hand and rubbed her back. Emma had never seen him interact that way with another child, and even Janet was amazed. Normally his hospital stays were met with tears and tantrums. This last time had been different. He had instantly taken to Chloe, who asked a million questions and chatted all day about her brothers and sisters, her friends at school, and the things she planned on doing when she got better.

However, Benny had overheard the nurses talking, and he knew the awful truth. Chloe wouldn't get better. She was going to die. They were just trying to help her stay strong for as long as possible. The night he discovered this, their mum found him crying into his pillow. When she asked him what was wrong, he said he felt sick. So she lay down on his bed and cuddled him all night like she had when he was little. The following morning, Benny told Emma the truth, confessing his guilt over being such a baby when Chloe was so brave. He'd decided to do everything he could to make her happy.

After that, Benny's days in hospital were filled with 'I spy' games and walks in the garden. When exhaustion kept Chloe in bed, he made up silly stories to take her mind off her troubles.

Emma heard him telling one once. It made her smile. He'd sounded like her when she was a child playing with her dolls. She hadn't known he could be inventive.

Chloe hadn't been afraid of his seizures. She'd even held his head over the bowl when he was sick, and when he became upset about going for more scans, she'd told him bluntly he needed to be brave. Emma hadn't seen that, but Benny had told her all about it.

Chloe had clung to Benny when he left the hospital, and he hadn't wanted to leave her.

'I'll come and see you,' he'd promised.

That had been a fortnight ago, but every time he mentioned it to their mum, Janet made excuses. This made Emma cross. Benny should be allowed to go. Unless it was too late?

'It's hard to understand why kids like Chloe get cancer, isn't it?' Emma sighed as she leaned down to hug her brother. 'You were really there for her, and it meant a lot to her parents.'

'I like little kids.' Benny smiled. 'They're funny. Chloe was funny, and she liked me too. Not many people like me.'

Emma turned and walked towards the door. 'Try not to get wound up about going to school, okay? It won't help.'

'I wish I didn't have to. What's the point if I'm so stupid?'

'I bet if you could ask Chloe right now, she'd give anything to be well enough to go to school.' Emma hoped her words would give him a fresh perspective.

'She told me I've gotta work harder too.' He laughed. 'I said I'd try.'

'So, honour your word, Pestie.'

Emma left his room and meandered into her own to put her makeup on. Although she and Erin had nothing special planned, she wouldn't think of going out without looking her best. You never knew who you might meet.

'See you later,' she called, checking her appearance one more time in the hallway mirror.

'Have fun.' Janet responded from the kitchen.

'Don't go spending all your money,' Ola called from the lounge.

'I won't, Dad.' Emma grinned.

'I had hoped earning your own money would give you a sense of value,' he grunted.

'Are you going to give me the lecture about saving again?'

'Well, if you want a car…'

'You work in a garage, surely you can find me a decent old banger that won't cost a fortune.' She winked at him.

'The older the car, the more it'll cost to keep it running.' Ola's expression remained stern.

'I've got you for that!'

Her father actually laughed, as Emma heard Benny clattering down the stairs, and she turned with a smile. 'Who's after you?'

'The ice-cream van's outside,' he enthused.

She should have known. Benny only ever moved that fast over one thing.

'Your mother will have tea on the table in an hour,' Ola reprimanded. 'She won't appreciate it if you spoil it by eating ice cream.'

'Benny hardly eats anything else, no matter what's on the table.' Emma tousled her brother's hair and reached into her purse to hand him some change. 'Have a treat on me.'

'You're as bad as she is.' Ola returned his attention to his newspaper as Emma and Benny headed for the front door.

'Don't let it lock behind you,' Emma warned. Benny heeded her advice, putting the latch up.

'See you later.' Benny waved at his sister as she headed towards Erin's house, and he joined the queue at the ice-cream van. A toddler in front of him grew impatient over the seemingly endless wait, so Benny distracted him by making funny faces. Cries of distress soon turned into delighted giggles, earning Benny a smile from the boy's mum.

'Thank you.' The woman handed her toddler his ice cream, and Benny put in his order as she led her son away.

Having received his cone, Benny stepped back onto the pavement, almost colliding with a tall, willowy girl with long red hair, wearing the skimpiest top he had ever seen. His dad wouldn't let Emma go out dressed like that. She looked like one of those Spice Girls on telly.

'Oops. Sorry!' She held up a hand to prevent the collision.

It was too late. Benny had already jumped and dropped his ice cream. He stared down at it in despair, fighting the urge to cry – and to scoop it up with his fingers.

'I'm sorry. I bet you were looking forward to that.' She had a soothing voice and a slightly posh accent. She wasn't from the village.

Benny wondered where she'd come from. Then he realised. She must be part of that new family who'd moved into the house that had been up for rent for ages, sitting empty until two weeks before. He'd heard his dad moaning about the new neighbours because they were city folk, and they dressed and talked differently from the locals.

Seeing and hearing this girl, he knew what Ola meant. Still, Benny thought it was unfair of him to talk about them that way. Especially considering he still had traces of a Danish accent. His parents were the newbies in the village once. What had the old people thought of them?

'It was my fault.' The girl smiled with a toss of her hair. 'I should buy you another one.'

Benny stared after the retreating ice cream van, as its *Teddy bear's picnic* jingle faded away. 'The van's gone now, so you can't.'

Benny's father wouldn't want him talking to strangers. He was forever laying the law down about people who were a 'bad influence.' The only time Ola spoke to him was to tell him something he shouldn't do.

'We could walk to the corner shop, and I could get you one from there?' She checked her watch. 'There's just about time before it closes.'

Benny knew he shouldn't, but something about her intrigued him. Besides, he wanted his ice cream. It wouldn't hurt to walk to the shop. It was only round the corner. Even his mum let him go there now, sending him on errands to buy milk or bread, or giving him money for chocolate or sweets.

73

'Okay. Thanks.' His confused gaze fell to his dropped ice cream melting in the gutter as he wondered aloud, 'What should I do with that?'

'I guess you'll have to leave it there to melt. It'll make a horrible sloppy mess if you put it in the bin. If the cone's still there when we get back you could throw it, but I bet someone's dog will have eaten it.'

He nodded and fell into step beside her, amazed he'd had the courage to speak. He never spoke to strangers. Why was this girl so fascinating?

'You're Emma's brother, aren't you?'

How come she knew Emmie? 'Yeah.'

'I'm Shanette Thompson, but most people call me Nettie.' Her bright smile was rewarded with a tentative one from him. She paused expectantly, then prompted, 'I can't remember your name.'

'Benny.' It sounded pathetic on his lips. Why hadn't his parents called him something more sensible, like Ben? Benny was a little boy's name. He'd always hated it.

'Oh yes. I remember Emma telling me now. Weren't you in hospital for a while?'

'I'm epileptic.' He chose not to explain further because admitting his weaknesses made him shy, and he didn't want to be shy with Nettie Thompson. 'Do you like living here?' He needed to change the subject, yet as soon as the question was out, he wished he could take it back. He never asked questions!

'It's quiet compared to where we used to live.' Nettie smiled as if she had been waiting for him to ask. 'I've always had a lot of friends. It's sad. People around here seem to be wary of strangers.'

'Lots of them have lived here for years.' She was obviously older than him, and he wanted to come across as mature. This was a new way of thinking, and Benny fleetingly wondered what was going on.

'I get the feeling they're suspicious of me and my parents. It's a shame.' She sighed. 'We're just like the rest of you. We can't help it if we talk and dress differently.'

'Yeah.'

They walked on in silence, and soon reached the shop, where Nettie kept her promise and bought him an ice cream. She had one too, and she was slower eating it than him because she talked a lot. Benny liked listening to her, as she shared observations about the various houses in the village and the people who passed them on their walk home. As they approached her front gate, he was sorry to see her go.

'Thanks for the ice cream.' His mum had drummed it into him to be polite. No matter how scared he felt, he must always say please and thank you.

'You're welcome, Benny. It was nice chatting to you.' Nettie waved as she walked up her parents' driveway and disappeared into the house.

Benny stood still, watching her go. Maybe today would be the only time she'd speak to him. She'd soon realise no one cared about stupid Benny Wellander. Or would she? He'd talked more than usual, so perhaps he'd made a friend. She was a lot older than him; at least sixteen or eighteen like Emma. It was difficult to tell because of the way she dressed and acted.

As soon as Benny walked through his parents' front door, he found he was in trouble from both of them. His mum was in a state because he had gone out without telling her. She'd presumed he was only going to the ice-cream van. Dad was cross because he had left the front door unlocked. He practically hit the roof when Benny explained his mistake by letting it slip that he'd been chatting to Nettie Thompson.

'We don't talk to people like that. You hear me?'

'Why?' Benny rarely answered his father back, and Janet visibly shuddered, anticipating what was to come.

'Because I say so.' Ola's voice seemed to thunder through the house, and it was enough to silence Benny.

He felt the tears stinging as the back of his throat constricted, and he rushed upstairs, unwilling to let himself cry in front of his dad.

❧

Later that evening, with Ola at the Frog and Parrot, Benny thought it was safe to question his mum. 'Why doesn't Dad like the Thompsons?'

'It doesn't matter. Just do as he says and keep your distance, there's a good boy.'

'Dad's scared of anything different,' Emma stated. She had returned from Erin's, and Benny hadn't realised she was listening.

'Nettie seems nice.' Perhaps Emma would talk to him more if he took the positive approach.

'She is.' His sister nodded. 'I've talked to her a few times.'

'I wish you wouldn't, love,' Janet fretted.

'I'm an adult, Mum. It's not up to Dad who my friends are.'

'He would say that, as long as you're living under his roof, it is.'

'So what will you do? Cross the street every time one of them comes near you?'

'If I have to.' His mum wiped the worktop for the third time and Benny wondered why they couldn't be kind to everyone.

Emma let out a frustrated sigh. 'You give Dad way too much power over you.'

'He's my husband.' Janet turned her attention to Benny. 'It's time for you to get ready for bed.'

He wanted to argue. It was still early. But if he stayed up, Emma might make him do schoolwork again. So he escaped to his room. He was glad he had his own space now, because his mum had finally given in and let him have a portable TV on his thirteenth birthday. There wasn't anything he particularly enjoyed watching. It was just something to do that didn't cause arguments.

9

'I thought you'd like to know.' The caller's voice was sombre, and Janet gripped the telephone receiver more tightly, wondering how she was going to break this devastating news to Benny.

'Thank you.' Her response was subdued. 'I'm so sorry. Chloe was... such a special little girl.' She fought the sting of tears. She couldn't cry with Chloe's father on the phone sounding so brave.

'She was the joy of our lives.' His guard dropped enough for Janet to hear the emotion bubbling under the surface. 'She talked about your Benny right up until the end.'

'I'm sorry I never brought him back to see her.' Janet fumbled over her words as she attempted to explain. 'Benny's an emotional little boy. I thought he might upset her.' Janet had been convinced that watching Chloe fight for her life would be more than her son could handle. He might have asked questions to which she had no answers.

'We understand.'

Chloe's father hung up, and Janet leaned against a kitchen worktop, resting her head in her hands.

'Mum? What's the matter?' Benny had snuck into the room without her being aware of his presence, and Janet swallowed down her tears. Benny's arms were instantly around her, causing her to cry even harder.

'Oh Benny!' She held him close, not wanting to taint his innocence with the news she had to share. 'That was Chloe's dad on the phone, sweetheart.' She paused, inhaling deeply. 'Chloe... She died, Benny.'

Her darling boy sniffed and squeezed her a little more tightly. 'I knew she was gonna.'

'How did you know?' Janet couldn't hide her surprise.

'I heard the nurses talking. That night when I told you I felt sick and you stayed on my bed, I wasn't telling the truth, Mum. I was sad cos Chloe was gonna die.'

'Why didn't you tell me?' It wasn't like Benny to keep things from her.

'I didn't think I was supposed to know,' he admitted. 'I don't think they told Chloe. I only said something to Emmie one time, when Chloe was in the shower so she couldn't hear.'

The maturity of his reasoning startled Janet. This was new for her son.

'Mum?' Benny pulled away and looked up into her doleful eyes. 'She'll have a funeral, won't she?'

'Yes. There's always a funeral after someone dies.' Since this was Benny's first encounter with death, Janet didn't want to presume he knew more than he actually did. She still preferred to shelter him from life's hardest lessons.

'I wanna go,' he stated. Janet's eyes widened. Benny must have noticed her look of horror for he added, 'I can, can't I?'

'Funerals are very distressing, Benny. And this one will be worse than most because of Chloe's age. You'll get upset. It's better for you to remember her as she was.'

'She was my friend. You and Dad sometimes go to funerals.'

Janet shuddered at his words. There had only been a couple because they didn't have many friends. One of Ola's colleagues at the garage had died the previous year and Janet had coped fine with that, but when they had travelled a fair distance to attend the memorial service for a distant cousin, she'd found it extremely difficult, even though she hadn't seen her cousin for years. Benny probably remembered it because he had stayed with Karen after school.

'Funerals aren't suitable for children, Benny.' *Nor should they be about children.*

Janet's hopes that he would drop the subject were dashed later that evening when she heard Benny discussing Chloe's funeral with his sister.

'I'll take you if you want to go,' Emma promised.

'Emma. I told him no!' Janet burst into the kitchen where her two children had been chatting. She hated refusing Benny anything, but this was for his own good.

'He's got the right, Mum.' Emma stood facing her, hands on hips. 'Like he said, Chloe was his friend.'

'He won't be able to handle it.' Janet was determined. 'He'll get himself worked up, and he might have a seizure.' That wouldn't just be bad for Benny. It would distress everyone involved, on likely the most painful day of their lives.

Yet her daughter wouldn't give in. 'I'll look after him,' she said.

Emma kept her promise. She took Benny to the service, and he did cry. He clung to his sister's hand as they sat in the back pew, and everyone talked about what a special little girl Chloe had been.

Benny agreed. She was special, and he liked the way they talked about her. Chloe's family were Christians, like Brian Brooks. So although they were sad, they spoke about how Chloe was with Jesus in heaven. Benny hoped they were right. If Jesus was real, surely he'd look after a good little girl like Chloe.

When Emma asked if he wanted to go to the graveside, Benny said no. He hadn't known what went on at funerals until his sister had patiently explained it all the night before. Thinking about Chloe's little body being lowered into a hole in the ground felt too scary, and he was afraid to watch. Being with so many strangers was harder than he would admit, but he drew strength from Emma's closeness. She didn't have a go at him for crying. She passed him a tissue, hugged him as he wept, and whispered words of encouragement.

'You're being really brave, Pestie.'

'No I'm not,' he sobbed.

'Everyone cries at funerals. It's normal. You're not making a scene.'

Emma sang loud and clear during the hymns, but Benny remained silent. He didn't know them, and he hated singing.

That night his mum hovered over him expecting a seizure that never came. Benny lay on his bed thinking about Chloe, wishing he had seen her one more time before she died. He hoped she was in heaven. It sounded like a nice place.

10

After October half term, there was a new boy in Benny's year. In his own way, he was as different as Nettie Thompson. Benny had only seen Nettie a few times since the day of the ice cream, but every time he did, she waved at him and smiled. He knew Emma and Erin were getting to know her. Emma had told him Nettie was sixteen, and she wasn't at school anymore. She had a job on the checkouts at a local pharmacy.

Damian Maubry also looked and talked differently. His was a harsh-sounding cockney accent, and he was black. There had never been a black boy in Benny's class, so the other kids didn't know what to make of Damian. He seemed friendly and outgoing, but since their class had already completed one year of secondary school, friendship groups had automatically formed, and it was difficult for a newcomer to find his place amongst them.

Benny was startled when Damian sought him out one blustery November morning at break time. Benny sat in his usual spot on a low wall, always alone amid the crowd of noisy teenagers.

'All right?' Damian said.

Benny often struggled to understand when Damian spoke in class. He definitely didn't want to get drawn into a conversation with him now. He wouldn't know what to say.

'Yeah.' He replied without lifting his head, presuming Damian would immediately walk away. However, when he looked up, Damian hadn't moved. 'What d'you want?'

The other kids only spoke to Benny to make fun of him. Most likely Damian had heard about his fits and the way he threw up in class, although he hadn't seen it yet. Benny had gone two weeks without a seizure. That was a record. He was marking the days off on a calendar on his bedroom wall because he wanted to know how long it would last.

'You're Benny, aren't you?'

Everyone knew his name because he was the thick kid who failed his tests and brought in notes from his mum, excusing him from reading aloud in class.

'Yeah.' He hoped Damian would go away. He had nothing interesting to say.

'It sucks being at a new school.' Damian's eyes clouded and Benny felt sorry for him.

'School sucks anyway. Doesn't matter if it's new or not.' The two boys exchanged a smile which bolstered Benny's confidence. 'At least you do better at it than me.'

'It's not fair, the way they all make fun of you for being at the bottom of the class.'

'I don't care.'

'Bet you do,' Damian insisted.

Benny wasn't willing to admit how much.

'I've heard the other boys talking about how you get ill all the time.'

'I have seizures,' Benny confessed.

'I haven't seen you have any.'

'That's cos I haven't for a few weeks.'

The bell rang and the two lads returned to their classes.

The following day, Benny found himself standing behind Damian in the dinner queue.

'It looks disgusting.' Damian pointed at the unappetising food on offer.

'It is.' Benny laughed. 'I don't like food much, even if it's nice.'

'You don't?' Damian whistled. ' I love food, especially my gran's home cooking.'

'I only like ice cream and chocolate.' Benny grinned impishly.

'We all like those, Stupid.'

It didn't sound so bad when Damian used the insult, because he accompanied it with a smile.

'Bet you'd like food if my gran cooked it.'

'What about your mum?' Benny surprised himself with his boldness.

'I don't live with her.' Damian's expression sobered. 'She's always working so she sent me to live with my gran.'

'Where's your dad?' Benny was waiting for Damian to tell him not to be so nosy, but the more they talked, the friendlier the other boy seemed to become.

'I don't know much about him,' he answered.

'I dunno much about mine either.' Benny sighed.

'How come? Doesn't he live with you?'

Benny nodded. 'He doesn't talk to me unless he has to.'

'Why not?' Damian probed.

'He doesn't like me.' Benny shrugged. 'He only likes my big sister Emmie.'

'I'd love to have a brother or sister,' Damian admitted. 'I hate being all on my own.'

A week later, Benny wondered if this was how it felt to have a friend. Damian sat next to him in class, and they spent their lunch breaks together. Some of the other boys had gradually started warming towards Damian. When they taunted him for associating with Benny, Damian stopped them in their tracks. Benny was his mate, and nothing they said could make a difference.

⁓

When Emma caught wind of her brother's new friendship, she asked when Benny was going to invite Damian home for tea.

'I've never done nothing like that before,' Benny mused. 'It'd probably be a bad idea.'

'Why?' Emma asked.

'Mum will make too much fuss, I don't know where Damo lives, and Dad doesn't like the Thompsons, so he won't like Damian either.'

Emma accused him of being daft. When he still showed no signs of telling their parents about Damian's existence, she decided to take matters into her own hands. Then she saw Damian alighting from the school bus on the other side of their village, which sealed it. Benny had no excuse not to have him round if he lived in their village. She broke the good news to their parents one evening while Benny was in his room.

'Benny's made a friend. He lives close by, so I think we should encourage him.'

'How do you know?' Ola didn't even glance up from his newspaper.

'He hasn't said anything to me.' Janet looked hurt.

'I suspect he's wondering how you'll both react because... Well, Damian's black.'

She waited anxiously for Ola's reaction. Fortunately, he hardly flinched.

'How old is he?'

'He can't be much younger than Benny.' Emma smiled at her dad. 'They're in the same year group.'

'Might do him good to have a friend I suppose.'

Ola's calmness amazed Emma when she compared it to his aversion to Nettie Thompson. 'Benny was worried about how you'd take it, Dad. You were pretty mad when you found out he'd been talking to Nettie.'

'That's different. The Thompson girl is sixteen, and she's obviously a bit on the loose side.'

'She's not like that.'

Ola dismissed Emma's defence of Nettie with a wave of his hand.

'Should I ask Benny to invite him home for tea?' Janet always deferred to her husband on such matters.

'If he wants to.' It seemed Ola didn't care either way. Emma supposed she shouldn't be surprised. He didn't care about much where Benny was concerned, but she'd hoped he'd show a bit more interest. Particularly as having another boy around might help Benny grow up and stop him clinging to their mum.

Damian's first visit to the Wellander home occurred a week later. Emma was pleased with how it went. Damian was the total antithesis to her shy and withdrawn brother, and she had never seen Benny laugh so much. Her mum was amused by Damian's cheeky smile and his cockney accent. Even Ola noted the boy was polite, and that Benny's behaviour improved when Damian was in the house.

At Damian's instigation, Benny dared to ask again for a bike, and Ola surprised them all by stepping in and overriding Janet's fears. Benny's eyes lit up when their dad presented him with his early Christmas present.

'He'll fall!' Janet fretted. 'He doesn't know what he's doing.'

'Doesn't look like that from where I'm standing.' A rare look of pride had crossed her dad's face as Benny cycled off down the street with his friend. He'd told Emma the story of nine-year-old Benny cavorting on Dale's bike. He clearly had no doubts his son could ride. Besides, anything Benny didn't know Damian would teach him.

Benny wobbled a bit going round the corner and, without thinking, Emma ran after him. He'd kept his balance that time but as he laughed about it with Damian, the inevitable happened. Emma watched him hopelessly topple and land at the roadside with his bike beside him. Benny's cheeks coloured but he didn't cry, so Emma held back. What if he didn't want her help in front of his friend?

Sure enough, Damian swung round and came back. 'You okay, mate?'

Benny nodded, not meeting his gaze.

'I fell off loads in the beginning. It gets easier.' Damian held out a hand.

'Bet you were really little when you had your first bike though,' Benny mumbled.

'Well yeah. My mum never fussed over me the way yours does.' Damian pulled Benny to his feet. 'Want to go to the shop for ice cream?' He obviously knew how to cheer Benny up already.

'I ain't got no money.'

'I don't mind buying if you do next time.'

The two boys were soon back on their bikes heading for the village shop, and this time Benny stayed on. A grinned crept onto Emma's face. He was alright. He was going to be alright.

'You're what?'

Benny could hear his mum's voice from where he stood in the garden, washing his bike next to Damo. Dale's mum was round and she must have just said something important.

'It came as a shock to me and Peter too.' Karen laughed. 'At first, I convinced myself I was on the change. That's why I was so late finding out. We've had time to get used to the idea now, and we're happy.'

'Isn't having another baby at your age dangerous?' Benny's mum continued. Wait, Karen was pregnant? Benny peeked through the window.

'There are risks, but the baby will be worth it.' Karen was leaning back in her chair, a contented smile settling on her face. 'Have you ever wanted more children, Jan?'

'I used to think I'd have more when I was younger.' His mum sighed. 'Ola hoped for one of each, and that's what we got. We agreed that would be enough for us. Even if I had wanted more, there's no way I could've done it with Benny needing me so much.'

'He seems to be a little less needy these days,' Karen stated. It was hard to hear her because Damian's portable CD player was blaring out some of his awful chart music. Benny turned back to his bike, not caring that the temperature was approaching freezing as he dipped his cloth in the bucket. 'I think it's wonderful that he's made a friend,' Karen continued.

'So do we. Every child needs a friend. I just hope... I hope Damian will understand his limitations.'

'I'm sure he's already seeing them, but he's sticking around. I'm only sorry my Dale is the way he is with Benny.'

'I suppose we can't dictate who our children make friends with.' Benny wondered if his mum was thinking about Emma's budding friendship with the Thompson girl, which he didn't think his dad had figured out yet.

Suddenly, his fingers felt like they might fall off, and Benny knew the solution. 'Can we have hot chocolate?' he asked, clattering into the kitchen with Damian close behind.

His mum smiled benevolently. 'Yes of course.'

When she reached out to hug him, Benny realised he'd forgotten to say please but conscious of Damo, he pulled away, trying not to notice when his mum looked hurt. Was this the first time he'd refused her hug? It wasn't that he didn't love her - he still liked her to lay on his bed at night holding his hand until he went to sleep. He was just growing up, that was all.

After drinking their hot chocolates, Benny and Damian headed to the park on their bikes. Benny was disappointed to discover that Dale was there. Thankfully, Brian was with him, and Dale usually ignored him when Brian was around. It was only when they were alone that Dale taunted him.

'Race you!' Damian already had a head start.

Benny put all his effort into catching up, until a familiar warning signal took over. He jumped off his bike, letting it clatter to the floor, and just got to the soft grass before the seizure hit. Now everything was happening around him. Although he could hear it, he felt like he was being dragged down a dark tunnel, totally out of control as his body convulsed.

He mustn't panic. He couldn't! It would soon pass. If he gave in to fear, it would get worse. Benny's thoughts spiralled as his world came in and out of focus. If his mum found out, she would take away his bike. Now Damo had seen him having a seizure, he wouldn't want to be his friend. He was stupid, and he was gonna be sick.

'We've gotta get some help!' he heard Damian yell. 'I don't know what to do.'

'He's fine.' Dale's voice. 'He has them all the time. It's his way of getting attention.'

'No it's not.' Brian argued. 'Sometimes he has one after another. We should get help.'

'Your mum's with his.' Damo again. 'Go and get her.'

'Why me?' Of course, Dale wouldn't want to help.

'Why not you?' Benny sensed Brian approach, move the bike away and kneel beside him.

'I'm sorry, Benny. I don't know much about seizures. I heard once that people can choke, so I'm just going to…' Brian tugged on his left arm, then manoeuvred Benny's head onto it. 'Hopefully that's the right position?' he muttered.

Benny was helpless to respond. His body kept shaking, making his stomach turn, as he heard Brian speak again.

'Please, Lord? Please help Benny. Please show us what to do. Please stop this seizure and help him get over it quickly so he doesn't have to go back into hospital and miss more school.'

Suddenly, Benny's eyes flew open. The seizure stopped, his stomach convulsed, and he vomited into the grass. Tears pricked then poured as he retched in front of Brian, who put a comforting hand on his back. Though his body had stopped jolting from the seizure, Benny now shook with tears of shame and embarrassment. He buried his head in his hands, hoping he'd not been sick over his clothes. He had tried not to, but sometimes everything was so out of his control after a seizure.

'Hey, come on.' Brian's voice was soothing. 'Calm down, or you'll be sick again.'

Benny looked straight at Brian, seeing compassion in the older boy's gaze. 'I'… I'm sorry.' His words came out falteringly through his gulping sobs.

'You can't help it, can you?' Brian rested his hand on Benny's shoulder. 'Is there anything I can do?'

'I'll get up in a minute. It's just…' Benny cleared his throat and attempted to re-compose himself. 'Everything feels weird.'

'I bet.' Brian let go of him and sat back.

As Benny looked down, he saw with relief that his t-shirt and jeans were unstained, but he still felt ashamed for throwing up in the park. Emma would say he'd been sick everywhere, so what did it matter? But it mattered to him.

'Want me to help you up?' Brian held out a hand and Benny took it.

Rising shakily, he could feel everything coming back into focus. It hadn't been a bad seizure.

Damian shuffled sheepishly towards him. 'Dale's gone to get your mum.'

'Okay.' Spotting a bench in the distance, Benny headed for it with Damian and Brian in tow. He had to sit down. He put his head between his knees, momentarily afraid he was going to be sick again, and forcefully reminding himself he had it under control. There wasn't much left for him to throw up.

'Who were you talking to when I was lying on the grass?' he asked as Brian put his jacket around his shoulders to stop him shivering. Benny had heard words he couldn't understand. His brain played funny tricks on him during a seizure.

'To God.' Brian didn't flinch at the question.

'Why?' Benny had never heard anyone talking to God like that.

'You were ill, and I believe God's the only person who can help.'

'He won't wanna help me.'

'Of course he does. Why wouldn't he?'

Everything about Brian was mature. His voice had broken, and he used big words. Benny felt like a child next to him. 'Cos he knows I'm stupid, and I do silly stuff. I'm not nice to people, and I'm a baby.'

Brian's eyebrows drew together, and his voice softened. 'He still loves you. I'm sure of that.'

That didn't make sense. 'How can you be?'

Brian smiled. 'Do you know anything about Jesus?'

'Only bits from school.' Benny shrugged. 'I don't remember a lot.'

Before Brian could continue, Benny heard his mum shouting. 'Where is he? Where's my baby?'

Benny's face got warm as Janet swooped in and pulled him up. She'd probably have carried him out of the park if he wasn't too big.

'What about my bike?' Benny pointed backwards.

'I'll wheel it home for you,' Brian said.

11

Benny feared the day of his seizure in the park might mark the end of his friendship with Damian. However, Damo proved him wrong by turning up the following morning like nothing had happened.

'You coming out on your bike, mate?' Damian offered one of his cheeky grins, and Benny felt pleased and proud to have him as his friend.

Then his mum embarrassed him by fussing again. 'I don't know if he should. Not after yesterday.'

'The fresh air will be good for him, Jan.' Once again, Ola startled Benny by taking his side.

Benny took full advantage of his dad's support and left with Damian. When he saw Nettie Thompson coming out of her parents' house, he lifted a hand to wave and was pleased when he didn't lose his balance and fall off his bike. When they passed the bus stop where Emma used to get off, Benny stared at it longingly.

'Watch where you're going!' Damian shouted, screeching to a halt as Benny's front wheel hit his back one.

Benny applied his brakes and shoved his feet down, stopping without falling off.

'What's up with you?' Damian said.

'Sorry. I was just wishing I could take the bus.'

'Why don't you?'

'Mum won't let me.' Since Benny had started secondary school, his mum had taken public transport to the school and met him at the gate. He'd never been concerned about that before, but lately it had annoyed him. All the other kids went home by themselves once they started big school. Even Emma had. Why were the rules different for him?

'Mum says it's because I shouldn't be by myself in case I have a seizure, but I'll have to be alone sometimes when I grow up. Why shouldn't I get used to it now?' Benny knew he sounded moany, and he hoped Damo wouldn't get annoyed.

Instead, his friend chewed his lip before saying, 'Well, how about I stay on 'til your stop? Then you won't be on your own.'

'Really? You'd do that? You'll have to walk further to get home.'

'That's alright, mate. I don't mind. Tell your mum she doesn't need to worry about you anymore. We can get the bus together.'

Benny returned home just before dark feeling excited and weirdly hungry. This was a novelty. He usually claimed food was seriously overrated. His stomach growled as he put his bike away in the shed, and he wondered if his mum might cook him sausages and chips. Tempting though it was, he knew better than to ask for ice cream for tea.

As he turned to enter the house, Benny spotted something black and white skulking near Janet's prized rose bushes. Upon further inspection, he realised it was the Thompson's cat. The stupid animal had got into their garden again.

'Dad's gonna throw a bucket of water at you if you don't clear off.' Benny expected the cat to listen and obey, but it just sat and stared at him. 'Go home.' He waved and pointed toward the Thompson house. The intruder didn't move. 'You're a stupid cat.' Benny bent to stroke it, enjoying the soft fur under his fingers. 'Maybe cats don't listen like dogs.'

He lifted it warily into his arms. Although his mum had always warned him to keep away from animals, fearing they would bite or scratch, this one seemed friendly. 'I'll take you home before Mum and Dad get cross. Come on.'

Benny carried the cat around the house and onto the main road, where he gingerly approached the Thompson's driveway and knocked on the door. Should he leave the animal on their doorstep and walk away? He never went visiting except with his mum. What had got into his head to make him consider doing this? He was thinking of running home when the door opened, and Nettie stood in front of him. There was no going back now.

'Hello.' She smiled warmly, her fiery hair shining as it fell in waves over her shoulders.

'Your cat got into our garden again.' He held out the animal and Nettie took it.

'Been causing trouble again, have you?' She spoke tenderly. She must love the cat.

Benny was ready to leave, but before he could turn away, Nettie spoke again.

'Hey, do you want to come in for a drink?'

He should say no. His father's warnings rang in his ears, yet he was intrigued by this girl's friendliness, so he said *yes* and followed her into the house.

'Do you like hot chocolate?'

He nodded, and Nettie led him into the kitchen where she introduced him to her mother. 'This is Benny Wellander from down the road.' Then turning to Benny, she added, 'This is my mum, Mary.'

'Nice to meet you, Benny.' Mary seemed edgy.

Sensing her unease, Benny's shyness took over and his feet itched to escape.

'Will you make the drinks while I take Benny into the other room, please?' Nettie asked her mum.

Wait. Nettie wanted him to stay? Benny could hardly run home now, even if her mum was scary.

'I suppose so.' Mary muttered with no enthusiasm.

Nettie led Benny into a lounge similar to theirs. 'Are you feeling any better?' She pointed him to a chair while she sat on the sofa.

'Yeah. I haven't been back in hospital.'

'That's good.' She asked him a few more questions, and when he only managed one-word answers, she broke into peals of laughter. 'Don't say a lot, do you?'

'Sorry.' He shuffled nervously in his seat. 'My mum says I'm shy.'

'I bet you're only shy when you're nervous.'

How did she know? Nettie was drawing him in again. How did she do that?

'I think you'd have a lot to say if you were confident enough to say it.'

'Dunno.' He looked away, then back at her. 'Lots of what I do say don't make no sense.' He'd just proved his point by sounding like a seven-year-old.

Nettie seemed unphased as she bent to stroke the cat that had followed them into the room.

'What's your cat called?' It was the first question he could think of.

'Jess.' She laughed. 'Wasn't an inspired choice, was it? If she hadn't been black and white like Postman Pat's cat, I might've come up with something else. I was only three when my dad brought her home. I guess I went with what I knew.'

'She's a really friendly cat. She didn't try and scratch me or nothing.'

'We've got her pretty well trained.' As Nettie spoke, the doorbell sounded, and she rose to answer it.

Benny's anxiety increased as he wondered who was at the door. He was relieved to hear his sister's voice.

'Did I see my brother coming over here, Nettie?'

'Yes.' Nettie answered Emma in her usual friendly way. 'He brought the cat back because she was wandering in your parents' garden. I invited him in for hot chocolate. Do you want one too?'

'Mum sent me looking for him. She's got tea on the table.' Emma sounded awkward as Benny joined them in the hallway. 'Dad will be home any time now. He'll be cross if he finds out Benny's gone wandering.'

'I guess we'll have to drink that hot chocolate another time.' Nettie either hadn't picked up on Emma's awkwardness or she didn't care. Her reassuring smile filled Benny's insides with warmth. 'Thanks for bringing Jess home, Benny.'

'It's okay.' He followed Emma out of the Thompson house and headed for home.

His sister turned to face him once she was sure they were alone. 'I need to talk to you.'

'What's the matter, Emmie?' Why did she seem angry? He'd only returned Nettie's cat.

'I'm not going to tell Dad about what just happened.' Her brown eyes bore into his. Why would their dad care? He never paid attention to anything Benny did unless he was doing something wrong. 'Listen to me, Benny.'

That meant she wanted him to look at her. She made him do that when she needed to be sure he was understanding her instructions. So much that was said around him went over his head.

'Why're you cross, Emmie? I didn't do nothing wrong.'

'You know Dad doesn't want us talking to the Thompsons.' They stood under the light of a streetlamp.

'You talk to Nettie. I've seen her with you and Erin.'

'That's different. I'm nineteen and Dad trusts me. He has different rules for you. He gets frustrated enough as it is. Don't push him by doing things you know he won't like. Stay away from her, Benny. You hear me?' She wagged a finger for emphasis.

'I haven't always gotta do what you say just cos you're my sister.' It was rare for him to fight back, but he didn't like her bossiness.

'You will if you know what's good for you.' Emma's tone turned tender as she pulled him into a hug. His defences crumbling, Benny relaxed in her arms.

'Nettie's older than you, Pestie. She's sixteen.'

'She's nice. She asks me about stuff.' He wasn't sure how to express the things he appreciated about Nettie.

'She was being polite. She'll make friends her own age. Anyway, you've got Damo. Don't rock the boat now Mum and Dad are letting you have more freedom.'

As Emma lay in bed that night, she hoped she had said enough to put Benny off any further contact with Nettie Thompson. She struggled with guilt because she genuinely liked Nettie. However, her dad's opinions hadn't changed. Nettie's low-cut skimpy outfits had sealed her fate, convincing Ola 'she and her sort' would lower the tone of their quiet little neighbourhood. Why would a family accustomed to city life move to such a rural area? None of it made sense.

Emma mulled over the gossip flying around the street. Peter Moss reckoned it was because of John Thompson's job, but her dad argued the man still got up at the crack of dawn to catch a train to work. He must work far away. Why up sticks and move?

Emma knew her dad could smell a rat a mile off. Once his suspicions were aroused, his guard went up. Though he usually took little interest in Benny, if he caught wind of the fact that Benny had visited 'the Thompson girl', there would definitely be trouble.

12

Despite Emma's warning, Benny kept bumping into Nettie. The following Saturday he was out alone on his bike when he got a puncture. He was heading back home, half-pushing, half-carrying his bike, when he spotted her.

'Hey, Benny,' Nettie called. 'Are you by yourself?'

'Yeah,' Benny muttered. 'Damo had to go. Don't tell my mum.'

'Is Damo the guy I saw you with the other day?'

'Yeah. He's my mate.' Saying that felt like a novelty.

'I bet you've got loads of friends because you've lived here all your life.' A shadow crossed Nettie's face. 'Emma told me your parents bought their house before you were born.'

Benny nodded. The sadness in Nettie's eyes made him want to say more. She was new to the area, and the locals still treated her family with suspicion. She probably missed her city friends. Benny was sure she had loads. Who wouldn't want to be friends with a girl like her?

'I didn't have no mates till Damo.' He hoped his confession would bring her comfort. 'He just moved here, like you.'

'You're good at welcoming newcomers.' Her sadness transformed into a smile.

'I dunno.' Benny was glad an elderly lady chose that moment to pass them on her mobility scooter. It gave him an excuse to focus on moving his bike.

'Thanks, love,' the woman acknowledged with a wave.

Benny considered saying goodbye to Nettie and continuing his journey home, but she still stood watching him. Did she want someone to talk to?

'I thought Damo would stop hanging round with me after I had a seizure in the park.' Why was he blurting stuff out? Nettie didn't need to know. Well, he'd started, so she might as well find out how stupid he was. Maybe then she'd avoid him, like everyone else. That would make his dad happy.

'I'm glad he didn't.' She sounded sincere.

'I bug him sometimes.' Her eyebrows shot up, so Benny explained. 'I act like a baby.' He cleared his throat, looked away and fumbled on. 'Damo's more grown-up cos he lives with his gran. His mum doesn't worry about him, and he does okay at school. He plays football. I hate football. I was jealous when he joined the school team and started hanging out with the other kids.' Benny watched Nettie carefully, waiting for her expression to change.

When it didn't and she still seemed interested, he dared to go on. 'I got in a grumpy strop, and Damo walked away and left me in the park. Then he acted like nothing had happened the next day, and I was pretty confused. So he told me I bug him sometimes, and when I do, he needs space. I'm learning now. Damo always comes back, and he sticks up for me. When the other kids are mean, he tells them to leave me alone cos I'm his mate.'

'Good.' Nettie adjusted her sparkly hair clip, tucking in a few loose strands. 'I hate the way some kids pick on others just because they're different.'

'Me and Damo are really different.' Benny grinned. 'My mum would wanna wash his mouth out with soap if she heard him swearing, so I don't tell her about that.'

Nettie laughed. 'Hey, remember that hot chocolate we never got round to sharing? Fancy one now? We could go to the inn next to the cricket green. My treat.'

Benny chewed on his lip. The inn did the best hot chocolates, with cream, marshmallows, and sprinkles. His mum wasn't expecting him for a while, but what about his bike?

'You can leave it in this alley. We'll grab it on the way back and I can help you with it then?' Nettie said, reading his mind.

That convinced him, and once he had a mug of warm cocoa in his hands, his shyness disappeared. He even talked to Nettie about his struggles at school and his fears over being moved into the special needs class.

'Isn't there anyone who could help you?' She sipped her hot chocolate appreciatively.

'Brian Brooks said he would ages ago.' Benny lowered his head.

'Great. Why don't you take him up on it?' The charm on Nettie's bracelet jangled as she absent-mindedly stirred her drink.

'Dunno.' Benny stared into his half-empty mug. 'Emmie tries to help me, but she gets cross when she has to explain stuff loads of times cos I'm so thick.'

'Don't put yourself down.' Nettie reached out to cover his hand. 'You can't help it if your seizures have damaged your brain.'

He had never talked about his epilepsy until he met Nettie. Even Damo wasn't interested. Yet Nettie was full of questions about his seizures, how they felt, and what effect they had on his life. A whole hour had passed before Benny realised he had to get home, or his mum would be fretting.

❧

The second time Benny bumped into Nettie was when he and Damo jumped off the school bus on Wednesday.

'Alright, Benny?' Nettie called as he slung his backpack over his shoulder.

As she came over and started chatting, Benny was glad his mum had started allowing him to travel with his friend. Nettie jabbered for a while. Benny wasn't totally sure what she was on about, but he was happy to listen and smile until Nettie waved and headed in the other direction.

'Who was *she*?' Damian said. His eyes had been popping out of his head the whole time they talked, and Benny knew he'd been itching to ask.

'Only Nettie Thompson. She lives in our street. Her family just moved here.'

'How come she talks to you? She's way older than us. And she's gorgeous!'

'I dunno.' Benny had wondered the same thing. 'Maybe she feels sorry for me cos I've only got one friend. She hasn't got no brothers or sisters. Maybe she wishes she did.'

'Nah. That can't be it. Who'd want a brother like you? There must be something else.'

Benny didn't take offense. 'She hasn't made many friends yet.' His shoulders shrugged and he suddenly felt bad for revealing that much about Nettie.

Unphased, Damo wiggled his eyebrows. 'I'll be her friend!'

'Oi.' Benny gave him a shove as Damo laughed and turned for home.

'Benny, Wait!'

Benny was bounding down the street trying to avoid the puddles when he heard Nettie's call. The icy December rain had caught him off-guard on his way back from the shop. His mum would moan at him for not wearing a coat, but he hated coats. It didn't matter whether it was summer or winter. They were heavy and annoying.

'I've got an umbrella if you want to share it,' Nettie offered.

He should tell her he was fine. He didn't care about getting wet, and Emma's warning still rang in his ears. But Nettie's friendliness was so appealing. Why shouldn't they be friends? Hang on. Why did he want them to be?

Benny shook his head. There were so many unanswered questions, and he wasn't accustomed to caring about such things. He'd never even had a friend before Damo. Nettie was nearly three years older than him, and she was the one instigating their conversations.

Nettie didn't wait for his answer. She held her umbrella up over them both as they dodged the puddles and dripped their way across the road.

'I hate rain,' she complained.

'I don't.' He laughed as they ducked under some low-hanging branches and droplets of water ran down Nettie's neck. 'It's fun.'

'You reckon?' She rolled her eyes and shivered. 'I guess I still thought everything was fun when I was your age.'

'Why does stuff have to stop being fun when you grow up?' he asked.

'You start seeing the harsher side of life.' Although Nettie's expression was unreadable, Benny sensed something was making her sad.

'Are you okay, Nettie?'

'Yeah. It's just... Never mind.'

Benny saw her fingers twitch around the umbrella. Then a great splosh of rain fell off it and splashed up their legs.

'Ewww,' Nettie complained.

'I could give you a hug if you like.' Hugs usually made his mum feel better when she'd had a fight with his dad or Emmie.

Nettie's lip twitched. 'That would be nice. It's been ages since anyone gave me a hug. But it's probably not appropriate. You're a bit... young.'

Benny shrank back, feeling like a small child again until Nettie swiftly changed the subject.

'Have you thought more about getting help with your schoolwork?'

'You mean like asking Brian?'

Nettie nodded.

'I can't.'

'Why?'

'Brian is Dale's best friend, and Dale hates me,'

'I can't imagine anyone hating you, Benny.' Her tone was gentle.

'Lots of people do. The kids at school do cos they make fun of me, and Dale does cos he calls me Weedy Wellander, and my dad does cos...' Benny paused for thought. Why did his dad hate him? 'I dunno why. He just does.'

'Parents can be weird sometimes. They get disappointed if we don't do things the way they want. I don't think they ever really hate us.'

'My dad does,' Benny insisted. 'He loves Emmie, and he hates me.'

They had reached their street, and Nettie raised a hand to wave at Karen and Erin who were fighting their way out of Karen's car with armfuls of shopping. Judy had already made a dash for the front door, leaving her mother and sister to grapple with the heavy bags.

'Karen's having another baby,' Benny blurted.

'How did you know that?'

'She told my mum.' He grinned up at her. 'I don't think Dale will like having a baby in the house cos it'll cry more than I do.'

'Babies are hard work,' Nettie stated.

'Yeah, but they're cute and funny.' Benny glanced at his house and realised his mum would probably be worrying over him getting caught in the rain. 'I've gotta go. Thanks for keeping me dry.'

'I don't know if I did very well at that.' Nettie laughed. Despite the umbrella, they were both drenched.

'It don't matter.' He darted away before she could say more, stopping to wave once he reached his parents' driveway. 'Bye, Nettie!'

Later, Benny pondered Nettie's words about his schoolwork. He'd been mulling it over more than he wanted to admit. His problems weren't going away, despite his best efforts to push them to the back of his mind. Damo had warned him he was within weeks of being moved into the special needs class. His avoidance tactics were no longer cutting it. Something had to be done, but he didn't have the courage to tackle it. His best option was to get his mum on-side.

That night as she lay beside him, he tried to persuade her to do what he couldn't. 'Mum?'

'Yes, sweetheart?' Her face brightened as he cuddled into her and held her hand.

'I'm really messing up at school.'

'No you're not.' She pressed her lips to his cheek and held him even tighter. 'You can't help it. You've missed a lot of school.'

'They're gonna make me go down, and the only place left is the special needs class cos I'm already a year behind.' There was a lump in his throat as he spoke. No doubt Emma would say he was turning on the tears, but this time he was genuinely worried.

Janet shook her head. 'They told us they wouldn't do that.'

'Damo says…'

'You worry too much about what Damo says.' She stroked his cheek and tucked the blanket in tighter to ward off the winter chill. 'Damo doesn't know everything.'

'He knows a lot more stuff than I do.' His mum didn't respond, so he went on. 'He thinks I should ask for help after school.'

'From whom?'

'Brian Brooks. He's pretty brainy, and he's already done Year Eight.'

'I don't know, love. That sounds like a big ask…'

'You and Dad could pay him.'

Janet's eyebrows raised and she paused before answering. 'Alright. We can ask if it'd make you feel better.'

Janet hated seeing Benny looking so worried. Stress brought on seizures, and seizures meant prolonged spells in hospital. With Christmas fast approaching, she didn't want him having to face that all over again. She wasn't particularly concerned over his schoolwork, and Ola said little about it except to grumble when he read his annual report, or when the truth came to light at the obligatory parent teacher evenings.

But when Benny nodded, leaned over to kiss her, then buried his face in the pillow and drifted off to sleep, she gazed tenderly down at the child who had consumed her heart and life for nearly fourteen years, resolving to do whatever she could to help him succeed at school.

She found Ola in the kitchen making coffee and cautiously broached the subject of their son having private tuition from Brian Brooks. 'It's not like him to ask for something like this, Ola. He's genuinely worried.'

'So he should be.' Ola didn't even turn to face her as he reached up into a cupboard and took hold of the biscuit tin. 'You should talk to Brian's parents. If the boy will do it, tell them we'll be happy to give him some extra pocket money.'

'He's a responsible lad. I think it's his Christian upbringing.'
'Maybe.'

Janet knew Ola had no faith, but he had to agree that the Brooks clan were a nice family, unlike others they could mention.

Following some discussion between Janet and Louise Brooks, arrangements were made for Brian to begin tutoring Benny in the new year. He would come to the Wellander house every Tuesday after tea. They all hoped this would be enough to get Benny's teachers off his back. Now they could concentrate on looking forward to Christmas.

13

It was another wet and dreary day as Ola locked up the garage, preparing to head home for the Christmas break. He had a lot on his mind. His boss was retiring, and he had offered Ola the chance to buy the business. This was more than he could have dreamed of when he left Denmark practically penniless.

'Should I start calling you gaffer?' Peter grinned at his friend.

'Not yet.' Ola shrugged. 'I've still got some thinking to do.'

'Come on, Ola. You know this is what you've been hoping for.'

'Are you disappointed he didn't offer it to you?' Ola didn't want bad feelings ruining a good friendship.

'I've never wanted to run my own business,' Peter confessed. 'I'm a follower, not a leader like you. You've had boss written all over you ever-since you walked into this place almost fourteen years ago.'

'Has it really been that long?' Ola had lost track of time as he focused on giving his all to his work.

'Jan was ready to drop your Benny when you moved here, remember?' Peter laughed.

Ola sighed. 'A lot has happened since then; and now you're the one who's about to become a father again.'

'Bit of a surprise that.' Peter smiled with pride. 'Typical of my Karen. She's always loved throwing me curve balls.'

'Well, you all have a good Christmas.'

'You too.' The two men shook hands and headed for their cars.

The garage would be closed until the New Year. No doubt Ola would see Peter at the Frog during the festive season, but it was unlikely the two families would get together. Janet and Karen often met up while their husbands worked. However, once Ola was home in the evenings Janet scarcely left the house, and they never invited their friends over for dinner.

As Ola drove the short distance home, he considered discussing the latest developments at the garage with his wife. If they were going to face the financial burden of buying a business, she deserved to have her say. Though she always deferred to him, he had to give her a chance. He hadn't been fair with Janet during the years since Benny's birth. He could blame her for obsessing over the boy, but it took two to make a marriage, and Ola had been emotionally distant. Was this their opportunity for a fresh start? Benny was less needy now. Perhaps he and Janet could re-discover the connection that had brought them together and made them strong during those early years of moving from place to place with little Emma.

Ola thought about buying his wife something special for Christmas. Tomorrow was Christmas Eve. He had left it a bit late, but perhaps Emma would give him some advice. If he talked to her nicely, she might go with him to the shops and help him choose. He would make it worth her while.

Ola smiled as he turned into their street, but his joy rapidly transformed into anger as he saw Benny standing on the Thompsons' driveway talking and laughing with their red-headed brazen hussy of a daughter. As Shanette gesticulated over something, his innocent son was all smiles. Ola understood enough of Benny's inhibitions to recognise this wasn't a recent acquaintance. Despite his warnings, Benny had been fraternising with the Thompson girl behind his back. His son had defied him, and Shanette was taking advantage of that! Ola's rage hit boiling point as he parked on his driveway, slamming his way out of the car.

'Benny!' His voice roared across the space between them. Benny turned, his face blanching. 'Inside. Now.'

Benny stared at his dad, hesitating. He didn't want to leave Nettie. She was his friend.

She tipped her head. 'You'd best go.'

'I'm sorry, Nettie.' He remained rooted to the spot for a few more moments before running after his father.

Ola had stormed into the house, leaving the door open. Benny crept in gingerly, hearing raised voices from the kitchen.

'Ola, please…' His mum was crying, and she sounded afraid.

'It's well overdue, Jan,' his dad raged. 'He thinks he can do what he wants and get away with it. Well not anymore!'

'What's he done?' she pleaded.

Benny entered the room to find his father pacing and his mum standing at the sink sobbing.

'He knows what he's done.' As his dad turned and glared, Benny darted a glance from one parent to the other, unsure of how to react.

'Benny?' Janet held out her arms. That settled it. He fell into the safety of her embrace.

'It's too much of that he's had.' There was disgust on Ola's face as he watched them. 'I had hoped you'd changed. Since your friendship with Damian, you've started to show more maturity. We trusted you, Benny. That's why we've been giving you more freedom. How do you think it feels to know you've thrown it back in our faces?'

'Ola, I don't understand.' His mum squeezed tighter, shielding him from his father's anger.

'He's been spending time with the Thompson girl when I specifically told him not to,' Ola spat.

'It can't be true.'

'I just saw them. We both know Benny doesn't make friends easily, but the way the two of them were… Well, it's obvious this wasn't the first time.' Ola resumed his pacing, his face contorting as he fought to control his mounting fury. 'I told you what kind of girl she was. She's sixteen, and the way she dresses… It's obvious she only has one thing on her mind.'

'She knows Benny's only a child!'

'That won't matter to a girl like her. Maybe she thinks a boy like him would be an easy target. I know her kind.'

'Don't be mean…' Benny's fear had turned to an anger that caught even him by surprise. He pulled away from his mum and faced his dad head-on, their blue eyes meeting in battle. 'Nettie's my friend. She's nice. And she cares about me – a lot more than you do!' Benny's body shook as his words tumbled out. Was he going to have a seizure right there in the kitchen?

'Benny, calm down.' Janet reached out an arm, but he shrugged her off as he continued to stare his dad down.

Ola soon recovered from his surprise. 'You won't see her anymore. Do you understand?'

'You can't tell me what to do!' Benny shouted.

'Yes, I can, because I'm your father.'

'Only when you wanna be!'

Ola looked away, as if Benny had hit him in the face.

It gave Benny the strength to continue. 'You don't wanna be my dad when I need you. Only when you're cross cos I've done something wrong.' He could barely speak through his tears. He rushed on anyway. 'You hate me. But that's okay, cos I... I hate you too!'

Benny stormed upstairs, leaving his parents staring after him in utter bewilderment. Throwing himself onto his bed, he sobbed into the pillow. Moments later he heard the familiar slam of the front door. No doubt his dad was off down the pub again.

Janet sat in the kitchen shaking with fear, anger, and every other negative emotion she could muster. She was still processing what had happened when she heard the retching. She climbed the stairs to find Benny lying on the bathroom floor, recovering from a seizure. It had all been too much, just as she'd anticipated. His anger was spent, and her little boy lay curled up in a ball whimpering like a frightened animal.

'Oh, my love...' She gathered him to her, and he clung like a limpet. She didn't care that he was covering her clothes in vomit.

'He's so mean.' Benny sounded much younger than his years as he buried his face in her chest. 'Why does he hate me, Mum? I don't want him to hate me.'

Janet rocked him as she had when he was a baby, aware his mind was still racing with the aftereffects of the seizure.

'Nettie's my friend.'

'Shh, it's all right.' She helped him wash and undress and put him to bed, where he fell into a fitful sleep. He didn't return downstairs that evening, which was probably for the best. Ola didn't come home from the Frog until late, and Janet guessed he had eaten at the pub. She sat with Emma as they shared their evening meal, trying to describe the events of the day.

'Benny's been hanging around with Nettie?' Emma looked as shocked as Janet had been. 'She didn't tell me.'

'You'll have to talk to her, Em. You need to tell her to keep away from him.'

'Mum, we don't know that Nettie's done anything wrong. I bet she was only being friendly. She hasn't got brothers or sisters. Maybe making a fuss of Benny felt nice.'

'You didn't see how angry your dad was, or how ill it made Benny,' Janet fretted, not stopping until Emma agreed to speak with Nettie.

Later that night, Emma knocked gingerly on her brother's bedroom door. Having received his muffled response, she entered to find him curled up on his bed still crying.

'Hey Pestie,' she soothed. 'Come on. Cheer up. Tomorrow's Christmas Eve, remember?'

'It's gonna be rubbish now cos Dad won't talk to me.'

'He doesn't talk to you much anyway, so what difference will it make?' She wanted to help him see reason. Nothing was working with Benny tonight.

'It's not fair, Emmie. He doesn't tell you who you can be friends with.'

'I'm older. You're still a kid.'

'He won't talk to me, so why does he care about who I talk to?'

'You know Dad.' It was the only answer she had. The truth was Benny didn't know their father, and Emma realised it the instant the words were spoken.

The Wellander family shared a quiet and strained Christmas as tensions ran high. Janet was hostile towards Ola for upsetting their son. He had announced that Benny would be grounded during the holiday, including a ban on him spending time with Damian, and Emma was stuck in the middle. She agreed their father had over-reacted, but she also found Benny's fascination with Nettie unfathomable. It just wasn't like him.

Emma hoped her gift for Benny would provide him one bright spot. It was a mobile phone, which she'd saved up her pay to buy.

'It'll mean Mum can keep tabs on you,' she explained. 'Hopefully she won't get so stressed about letting you go out by yourself or with Damo.'

Emma spent hours teaching Benny to use it, receiving a sharp reminder of how sluggishly her brother learned new skills. What came naturally to most kids his age was alien to Benny.

'It's pointless anyway. I can't go nowhere till Dad lets me out,' he sulked.

Emma bit down annoyance that he wasn't appreciating the gift she'd saved so hard for and tried to think of things from his point of view. 'He'll have to let you out when you go back to school, Pestie. So hang on in there and try not to keep annoying him.'

January was soon upon them and Ola was relieved the festivities were over. He had tried talking to Janet about buying the garage, but she'd merely said it was up to him. There had been no special gift, and the chasm between them seemed wider than ever.

The day before he returned to work, Ola went up to the attic to bring down the boxes for Janet to pack away the Christmas decorations. As he slid a crate out from its place, something caught his eye as it fluttered to the floor. He bent down and retrieved a tatty looking manilla envelope. Wondering what he had found, he took it down to his bedroom to study it in the light.

His first impulse was to return the item to the box out of which it had fallen. That box held the only things he had brought from Denmark that seemed to be worth keeping. Ola wondered why he held on to them. Somehow, he couldn't bring himself to throw them away.

Sitting on his bed, he couldn't resist opening the envelope, trying to recollect when he had last looked at its contents. His mind strayed back to a long-forgotten evening, with a curious three-year-old Emma asking him questions about his childhood. He had been alone with her in their poky rented flat. He recalled feeling unusually close to his daughter that night, and how he had entertained her questions.

'What did you look like when you was little like me, Daddy?'

'Well, not like you.' He smiled and pulled her down onto his lap. 'You look more like your mum.'

'Show me, please? I wanna see you when you was little. I seen Mummy.'

Janet had a couple of her childhood photographs, but Ola only had the one tucked away in an envelope with a few other keepsakes from Denmark. He hadn't even shown it to his wife. What harm would it do? If Emma wanted to see, then why shouldn't he indulge her?

Setting her down, he moved over to the drawer where he stored his private documents and retrieved the envelope. Pulling out the tattered old photograph of him standing with his mother on the steps of his childhood home, he held it out to Emma, and she beamed up at him.

'You was cute, Daddy.' That had made him laugh.

Now, as he opened the envelope and saw the photograph again, memories he tried not to recollect came flooding back. What was the use in thinking about his childhood? Why dwell on a mother who had walked out when he needed her most? She had been full of excuses: she didn't know where she was going, and she would struggle to support herself, let alone both of them. However, Ola had known the truth. She was involved with another man and didn't want to risk remnants of her old life clouding her future.

The boy in the photograph smiled innocently at Ola, and he saw something he had never noticed before. Those were Benny's eyes, and the smile was the same one he often saw on his son's face as he sped off on his bike with Damian.

Ola put the picture back in the envelope. It hurt to see it. His teenaged son might look like him, but that was where the similarities ended. Ola had always been strong and healthy. Benny was sickly, weak, and immature. At Benny's age, Ola had already known who he was and what he wanted. His parents' marriage was breaking down and his dad's drinking caused huge amounts of strain, so Ola had learned to take care of himself. That was something Benny would never be capable of doing. The boy would depend on them forever, but was that Benny's fault?

Ola shook off thoughts about whether he'd been fair on his son. Even if he hadn't, it was too late to change it now. Besides, he couldn't understand Benny. There was no point in even trying. Janet's fussing had put paid to any relationship they might have enjoyed. He would support the boy financially, which was more than his own father had done for him, but beyond that he had nothing to give.

Ola returned the worn envelope to the attic and took the boxes down to Janet. She worked in the living room with Benny beside her, obediently passing things her way. He knew Benny was still cross because he wasn't even acknowledging him anymore. They had spent Christmas avoiding one another. If Ola walked into the lounge, Benny went up to his room. If Benny entered the kitchen for a drink while Ola was making coffee, Ola left his task unfinished and returned later. They had shared the Christmas table in silence, and Benny had excused himself the minute the meal was over.

No doubt things would improve once school started. Ola would have to lift Benny's restrictions to enable him to spend time with Damian. He just hoped he had done enough to deter him from associating with the Thompson girl. If Benny hated him, so be it. They had never shared a meaningful relationship, so it would make little difference if things got worse.

Yet as Ola watched his wife and son working side by side, he felt a twinge of sadness over what might have been. He had wanted a boy so badly, and he'd been determined to give him everything his own father had withheld. Was he as bad as his father in his own way? Was detachment just as damaging as alcohol and fits of rage?

'I'm off down the Frog, Jan.'

His wife gave a curt nod of acknowledgement, and Ola left the house struggling with a new and surprising loneliness. He had always prided himself on not needing anyone. Was that really true? Hadn't he needed Janet? Wasn't that why he'd married her? Now they were poles apart, with the boy between them as he had been for nearly fourteen years. Yet could Ola blame Benny for everything?

14

It was the talk of the village. Sixteen-year-old Shanette Thompson was pregnant. Her family could no longer hide it, and Ola's suspicions had been justified. Now the truth was out and everyone understood why the girl's father had moved his family in such a rush. He was ashamed. Who could blame him?

'Surely now you understand why I didn't want you both associating with Nettie,' Ola said while delivering Emma another of his lectures.

'I feel sorry for her.' Emma had tried to explain her point of view. 'We all make mistakes.'

'Hopefully not you, Emma.' Her dad gave her a hard stare. 'I'd like to think I've brought you up to know better than that.'

'Come on, Dad. You were young once. Some people will always be led by their emotions.'

Ola studied his fingernails and for a moment, Emma thought he might reveal something about the past he held so tightly to his chest. But he didn't. 'There's no excuse for that kind of behaviour,' he said, then once again, he stormed down to the pub.

❧

'Is it true, Emmie?' Benny met her on the landing that night as she was getting ready for bed.

'Is what true?' She reached out to tousle his hair. 'Hey, I thought you were asleep.'

'I pretended I was so Mum would leave me alone.' He winked at her.

'You know you've got school in the morning.' Benny was still struggling, even with the extra help from Brian.

'I only wanna know if it's true about Nettie.'

'You mean the baby?'

Benny nodded.

'It's true.' Emma sighed. 'She's got the bump to prove it.'

'What's she gonna do?' Benny had told her he missed his friend. Despite being initially outspoken during the row with their dad, he hadn't been able to pluck up the courage to defy him and talk to Nettie again.

'Her parents want her to give the baby up for adoption. They say it'll be the best thing because of how young she is. I guess it makes sense, but...' Emma couldn't believe she was discussing this with her innocent little brother.

'That's really sad. Babies should be with their mums.'

'It's complicated, Pestie,' Emma replied. 'Go back to bed before Mum catches you and insists on spending the night in your room.' She exchanged a conspiratorial smile and a warm hug with her brother before saying goodnight.

❧

The following day, Benny saw Nettie in the street. Knowing his father wouldn't catch him because he was at work, he approached her cautiously, realising too late that he had no idea what to say.

'Hi.' Even though his greeting sounded pathetic, Nettie's smile was comfortingly familiar.

'Hi, Benny.'

There was a new sadness in her eyes despite her smile, and he had an unexpected urge to hug her.

'How're you doing? How's school?' Nettie asked.

'A bit better now Brian's helping me, but it's still hard.'

Mary Thompson brought a rapid end to their conversation by appearing in her doorway and calling her daughter in for tea. Benny had noticed that Mary never looked happy. Perhaps she was just worried about Nettie and her baby.

Later that evening, Benny sat at the kitchen table with Brian, working on his maths. They had already been at it for over half an hour, and Benny's brain hurt. Some days he found it harder to concentrate. Today was one of them, so he tried distraction tactics.

'Do you know Nettie Thompson's having a baby?'

Brian's head shot up and he stumbled over his response. 'Well yeah. Everyone knows. What's that got to do with you?'

'She was my friend before my dad found out and stopped me talking to her.'

'I guess he was worried. She's sixteen.'

'Do people like you, who go to church, think what she's done is really bad?' Benny asked.

'It's not ideal, is it?' Brian flicked his biro open and closed and shuffled his schoolbooks. 'I mean, it's pretty obvious she and the baby's father aren't still together, and she might have to give it up. That's going to be hard on her and the baby, but it won't stop God from loving her.'

'Does God love bad people?'

'Nettie's not bad,' Brian clarified.

'I know,' Benny agreed. 'But my dad thinks she is.' Brian probably hadn't expected to be discussing this with him. 'I don't think God would like the stuff my dad says. If he's real, he'd want us to be kind to one another, wouldn't he?'

'Yes, he does.' Brian paused, like he was thinking of saying something else, then he slid a book across the table and pointed at a column of numbers. 'Come on. We need to finish your maths.'

On Saturday afternoon, Benny was in the kitchen making a cup of tea when his mobile phone rang. The sudden sound accompanied by the vibration against the worktop made him jump and almost drop the milk. He wasn't used to receiving calls because hardly anyone phoned him.

Glancing down at the display, he saw Damian's name. 'Damo?' Benny put the phone to his ear as he carried his tea upstairs to his room. 'How come you're phoning me?'

Benny heard a gulp, followed by a sniff. Was Damo crying? He never cried. 'What's the matter?'

'I'm in the park. Some of the older boys from school...' Damian cleared his throat, clearly trying to control his emotions. 'They were waiting for me, and... and... They beat me up, Benny.'

'Why?' Damo was fit and sporty and he'd already been in a few fights. Why was this different?

'They told me I should go back where I came from.'

'Back to London?' Benny was struggling to understand.

Damian sighed with frustration. 'No, you idiot! To wherever my father came from. Or his father, or whoever it was who came over here from wherever it was.'

'You don't know your father.'

'It doesn't matter. They beat me up cos I'm black.'

Now Benny understood. 'Oh. Are you okay?' Benny regretted his stupid question as soon as he asked. It would serve him right if Damo cut him off.

'I've got a black eye and a split lip, and I'm pretty bruised from where they kicked me,' Damian paused, then continued. 'I don't want my gran to see me like this. She'll end up marching to the school to sort things out. That'll only make everything worse.'

'How come?' Benny asked. 'Those boys who beat you up should get into trouble. It was wrong, Damo.'

'We know that,' Damian explained, 'but it'll only cause more trouble for me in the long run. It'll be better if I make out what they've done hasn't bothered me. Maybe then they'll leave me alone.'

'How will you hide it from your gran if you're hurt?'

'Can I come back to your place?' Benny heard desperation in his friend's voice.

'Yeah, okay.'

'Will you ask your dad to fetch me? I don't wanna walk back in case they're waiting to jump me again or something.'

'I'm not talking to my dad. I can't ask him.'

'Benny!' Damo let his frustration show. 'Can you get over yourself for five minutes and try and think about someone else?'

His friend's words brought Benny up short. Damo needed him, and he was letting him down. His best mate was always supporting him. This was Benny's chance to give something back. 'Sorry. You're right. I am being stupid.'

'Don't start crying about it now,' Damian warned. 'Just ask your dad if he can come and pick me up.'

'Okay.' Benny ended the call and ventured back downstairs. It was one of the rare occasions when his mum had gone shopping with Emma, leaving him alone with Ola. He found his dad in the lounge and steeled himself for what would surely come. 'Dad?'

Ola looked up with surprise as Benny stood in the doorway. 'What? If you're ill, Benny, you can phone your mother and ask her to come home. I haven't got the patience for your nonsense today.'

'Damo just phoned me.' Benny couldn't afford to let his dad's coldness hurt him. Not today when he'd made a promise to his friend. 'Some boys beat him up down at the park. He doesn't want his gran knowing cos he thinks she'll make a fuss, and that'll make it worse for him with the boys who did it.' The words tumbled out in a nervous stream because Benny wasn't used to asking for help from his father.

Ola's body tensed with rage. This was a bad idea. Damo should have listened. His dad wouldn't help.

'Why did they go for him?' Ola barked.

'He said it's cos he's black.' Benny hung his head, preparing to return to his room and apologise to Damo.

'He's not going to let them get away with it, is he?' Was Ola mad at someone else for a change? Could Benny risk saying more?

'He wants to come here. He doesn't wanna upset his gran.'

'I'll fetch him.' Ola strode past Benny into the hallway and picked up his car keys. They were united in a common cause, and it felt strange but good.

'Can I come with you?' Benny hovered in the lounge doorway, not wanting to push his luck, but desiring to be there for his friend.

Ola nodded. Nothing more was said as Benny sat beside him while he drove the short distance to the park. Once there, Benny

117

sent Damo a text, and he appeared looking extremely bruised and dishevelled.

Back at home, Ola took charge, doctoring Damian's cuts and bruises. 'There's no way you'll hide this from your gran.'

'Could I stay here tonight? Please, Mr Wellander? I'll ring her and say I'm spending the night with Benny.'

Ola's eyebrows raised in admiration. 'Yes, if you want to.' He glanced at his watch. 'Jan and Emma will eat out. Should I order you both a pizza?'

Benny's jaw dropped at his dad's generosity, and he was even more startled at the way Ola talked to Damian as they ate. He was afraid to open his mouth in case he said something to spoil the moment. He listened as his friend talked about similar issues he had faced in the past.

'Did you ever have problems after you came over from Denmark?' Damian asked Ola.

'Not that I can remember.' Ola sighed. 'I had people poking fun at me for being a foreigner with a funny accent.'

Benny looked away so his father wouldn't see his smile.

'But I had one major thing in my favour.'

'You had the same colour skin as the rest of them.' Damian frowned down at his plate, and Ola put a hand on his shoulder.

'No one would blame you if you wanted to see these boys brought to justice, Damo.'

'What good would it do? It'd stress my gran, and they'll only do it again. Kids like that… They like getting a reaction out of you. If you don't give them what they want, sometimes they leave you alone.'

'You know best, Son.' Ola rose, patting Damian's back as he prepared to leave the room. 'Whatever you decide, you'll have our support.'

Watching his father interacting with his best mate in ways he never had with him gave Benny a pang of jealousy.

Ola paused in the doorway. 'I'll take another look at your face later. The bruising should've gone down enough for you to get away with saying you fell off your bike by the time you see your gran tomorrow.'

'Do we have to tell Mum and Emmie what happened? Can't we tell them he fell off his bike, too?' Benny feared his question would arouse Ola's anger, but they had to form a plan.

'It might be for the best.' Ola returned to the lounge, and the boys went upstairs.

When his mum and Emma returned home, Benny heard Ola telling them Damian was staying the night. Although his mum showed concern when she saw the state of Damo's face, she didn't pester them for details, and if Emma had her suspicions, she kept them to herself.

That night Benny broke with tradition by refusing to let his mum into his bedroom. He gave Damo his bed, intending to sleep on the floor. When Janet fussed, Benny remained insistent. It would be fun to share a room. He'd never had a sleepover before, and Emma had loads when she was growing up.

He even heard Ola warning Janet off when she made to follow them upstairs. 'Don't embarrass him in front of his friend, Jan.'

The two boys talked late into the night and snuck downstairs, once the house was quiet, for hot chocolate. They didn't mention the attack again. Damo seemed to want to put it behind him, and Benny respected his choice.

15

The following morning, Ola found the lads in the kitchen making breakfast. Damian was in command, with Benny successfully obeying orders.

'Want some scrambled eggs?' His son smiled from his position at the stove.

'Why not? You seem to have made enough.' Ola sat down at the table, enjoying the banter as they worked. Damian scolded Benny for his cluelessness, but Benny took it all in his stride.

'If you keep telling me off, I'm gonna throw this egg at you.'

Ola realised Benny hadn't spoken in his customary petulant tone signalling one of his temper tantrums. He was learning to stand up for himself.

With Janet still asleep, the three of them sat at the table eating in companionable silence, and Ola felt an unexpected surge of love for the two teenagers. 'What're you two planning for today?' He poured brown sauce over his egg, and Benny grimaced with disgust.

'Dunno.' Benny reached for the tomato ketchup, and it was Ola's turn to be appalled, yet he found he did it with a smile.

'There's a vintage car show on in town. I think I'm going to go.'

'Can we come with you?' Damian's eyes lit up, and although Benny seemed nonplussed, he didn't object.

'If you want to.' Ola usually went to such events by himself unless he persuaded Peter to accompany him. It might be interesting to have the boys tagging along. Damian was a bright and entertaining lad, and Benny wouldn't dare show himself up in front of his friend.

Janet expressed surprise when she heard of their plans. It was the first time Ola had ever considered taking Benny out alone, she argued. Would he know what to do if their son had one of his seizures? She was sure he would never be able to cope…

'We'll be fine, Jan.' Ola bit back his annoyance. 'I am his dad. Stop fussing.'

With Benny determined to go, Janet had no choice but to let him.

The morning passed without incident. The boys soon became bored and decided they wanted to do their own thing. Ola realised he didn't even have Benny's mobile number, so added it to his phone before he sent them off to amuse themselves.

It was about two pm when the call came, and he was alerted by the panic in Damian's voice.

'Mr Wellander! You've gotta come. Benny's had a seizure, and it's bad.'

'Where are you?'

Damian told him, and Ola found them in no time. Benny lay sprawled on the pavement with a crowd gathered around him, while Damian stood by looking helpless and scared.

'I thought he'd be okay.' He clutched Ola's arm. 'He normally just gets up after a while, but he hasn't, and he keeps being sick.'

'It's okay. I'm his father.' Ola pushed through the crowd that dispersed once they knew a responsible adult was on the scene. He knelt beside Benny, reaching for his hand as he had seen Janet do so many times. 'Can you hear me, Son? It's Dad.'

Benny's eyes flew open, and he mumbled something incoherent. Then he retched again, panic flooding his pale face as his tears fell.

Ola moved by instinct and pulled the boy into his arms, realising he hadn't allowed them to be this close in years. Benny was his son. He needed him. For now, nothing else mattered.

'Dad!' Benny clung as his body was seized by more violent shaking.

This was bad, and Ola knew they had to get help. He looked up and met Damian's gaze, mouthing for him to call an ambulance. 'It's all right, Benny,' he soothed. 'You're going to be okay.' By now, Janet would be crying too, but that only made their son worse. Ola had seen it, yet he'd never stepped in. If he

121

could calm Benny down, perhaps the shaking and sickness would stop.

Ola didn't care about the state he must be in as he encouraged Benny to take deep breaths. It shamed him to realise he knew so little about how to manage his seizures. Janet was the one who had been on all the courses and attended the doctor's appointments. Ola had buried his head in the sand, preferring to remain detached. Benny didn't need him. It was his mother he cried for and clung to. Except he wasn't crying for her now. He was looking to his dad, desperate for reassurance.

'We've got this, Benny.' Ola locked eyes with his son as he laid him gently down on the pavement, taking off his own vomit-stained jacket to place it under Benny's head. 'You're going to be fine.'

'I'm sorry, Dad.' Benny whispered.

Ola felt his throat constrict as love for his boy overwhelmed him. How had he let this happen? Benny was his son, and he desperately needed a father. He had achieved in minutes what Janet never had with her years of fussing and fretting. Benny held his gaze trustingly; all traces of fear having abated. He was drawing on his father's strength. His frightened little boy was growing up without him, and the realisation hit Ola like a kick in the gut.

'It's okay.' Ola squeezed his hand. 'It's not your fault. None of this is your fault. You can't help having seizures, but the sooner you can calm down, the more chance you've got of things getting back to normal.'

'It's scary, Dad. I can't stop it, and I can't stop being sick.'

'Yes, you can.' His tone was encouraging with none of its usual sternness. 'You're not being sick now.' Ola rose as he heard Damian conversing with a paramedic.

Benny was aware of it too and the terror was back in his eyes.

'Please, Dad? Please don't make me go to the hospital. I just want to go home.'

'Okay, Benny. Let's wait and see what happens. If you don't have another one, I think I can persuade them to let me take you home. You should let them check you over though, to make sure everything's all right.'

The paramedics stretchered Benny into the ambulance, but after a while they too were satisfied that although it had been a serious seizure, he was recovering well. Damian fetched him something to drink, and this revived him further, so they agreed to release him into his father's care.

They dropped Damian off at his gran's on the way, and Ola helped Benny into the house. Janet came running when she realised what had happened, but Ola insisted on helping Benny up to bed.

Janet stood wide-mouthed, too startled to object. By the time she joined them, Benny was already asleep. Ola stared down at their son, watching the rhythmic rise and fall of his chest as he used to do when Emma was little.

'He'll be okay, Jan.' Ola spoke softly before leading her out of Benny's room and into their own. He closed the door and sat on the bed, pulling his wife down beside him. She reached out, and he took her hand gladly.

'He must've been so scared.' Janet's lip trembled.

'I calmed him down.' He noticed there was pride in his voice.

'He needs you, Ola. He needs his dad. He always has.' She gave way to her tears as Ola drew her into his arms. 'I shouldn't have questioned you earlier. I just get so scared...'

'I know. I'm sorry, Jan.' He had nothing else to say. So many years of mistakes couldn't be undone overnight. 'That day when we had the row over Nettie Thompson... He thought I hated him.'

'He's such a sensitive little boy.'

'Oh, he's not a little boy anymore, despite how much you'd like to think he is.' Ola smiled as he relived the last twenty-four hours - how Benny had come asking for his help with Damian, the way he had stood by his friend, determined to give him somewhere to stay, the banter between the two boys earlier that morning in the kitchen, and finally how his son had clung to him on the pavement during his seizure. 'We've both got a lot to learn, Jan. Things will have to change around here, and that'll involve both of us.'

Janet rested her head on his shoulder. He'd forgotten how nice it felt to have her so physically and emotionally close. It took him back to their early years of marriage, when he held her at night and told her he loved her. It had been so long since they'd made love…

Ola embraced his wife, lowering her onto the bed. 'I still love you, Jan.' His voice was husky as he lay down beside her and pulled her towards him. And for once, she didn't pull away.

❧

Later that night, Ola cradled Janet in his arms and felt a sense of peace he had rarely enjoyed. He lay with his wife with both his children close by. They had a wonderful confident daughter, and a son he could learn to be proud of. This was everything he'd wanted. Why had he almost thrown it away?

He couldn't change what was past, but he could work on the future. He could help Janet release her stranglehold on Benny and help his son grow up to be a man – but not a man like himself. He realised Benny would always have his limitations and inhibitions. He needed to get to know him rather than focusing on the kind of person he could never be. It would take time and effort, and there would be many pitfalls along the way. His boy was intimidated by him, and Ola realised this was his fault. He couldn't pander to him as Janet did, but today had proved they could build on a foundation of trust. Ola felt overwhelmed by the enormity of the barriers he would have to break down, but he knew it would be worth it.

16

'Why d'you think my dad's acting all weird?' Benny expertly caught the drip that was about to fall from his ice cream cone as he sat on a park bench next to Damian.

'How d'you mean weird?' Damian's eyes were glued to a couple of loud and giggly girls circling the park arm in arm. Benny thought they were silly. He didn't get Damo's recent fascination with girls.

'He's talking to me more and stuff.'

'Isn't that good?'

'I dunno.' Benny's cone split and he deftly stuffed the rest into his mouth. Wasting ice cream was as daft as Damo chasing after girls.

'You're scared of him, aren't you?'

Benny looked away, hit by the force of his friend's insight. 'He's only ever shouted at me, except when he ignored me. Which was most of the time.' He shrugged, regretting his inability to find the right words.

'He wasn't shouting at you when I was at your house the other day.' Damian changed the CD in his diskman. His headphones were slung around his neck with the volume turned up to full, so he could still catch the music without putting them on his ears.

'I thought that was just cos you were around, and he likes you,' Benny admitted. 'But he was nice to me this morning too. He asked me to help him clean the car, and he didn't have a go when I said I didn't know how. He said he'd show me, and he did, and I got it. He even said *well done*, and he gave me money for ice cream.'

'You're lucky to have a dad, Benny.' Damian's tone was unusually melancholy. 'I wish I did.'

Benny didn't know how to respond. As he looked away, his gaze fell on Nettie Thompson walking towards them with Emma and Brian's sister, Kerry. Nettie's baby bump was obvious now. She'd given up trying to hide it.

'Hello, Benny.' She drew level with the bench, addressing him in her friendly way.

'Hi.' Her smile earned one from him in response

'You've got ice cream around your mouth, Pestie.' Emma handed him a tissue.

Benny blushed with embarrassment. He turned away to wipe his mouth, then screwed up the tissue into a ball in his hand. The girls moved on, but Nettie turned back with a wave.

'I wish I had brothers or sisters.'

Emma noticed Nettie's reflective tone as she walked between her and Kerry. 'Not sure you'd be saying that if you had mine,' she laughed merrily.

'I've always got on pretty well with my brother.' Kerry's voice was jaunty.

'Brian's different. He's a sensible kid.' Emma admired the whole Brooks family, even though she didn't share their religious convictions.

'How come your parents never had more children, Nettie?' Kerry had always been one to ask questions.

'I guess they reckoned I was trouble enough, and... Well... They've always been serious people. Their lives never revolved around me. Mum enjoys sports like tennis and badminton, and Dad's busy with his work.'

'How are they handling your pregnancy?'

Emma admired Kerry for enquiring about subjects she hesitated to broach.

'They're not.' Nettie sighed plaintively. 'They insisted on us moving, and buried their heads in the sand, pretending it wasn't happening for as long as they could. Then when they did face it, they started working on me about adoption.'

'They moved you all here, so they must've been thinking about it,' Kerry suggested.

'They didn't want me showing them up in front of their friends.' There was bitterness in Nettie's tone. 'Mum can't wait to get back to our *real* home. They've kept the old place. It's rented on a twelve month lease.'

'I always think it's a shame when families don't stick by one another.' Kerry's family were extremely close. No wonder she couldn't imagine living any other way.

'I dunno,' Emma said. 'Just look at mine. Though I guess we were close once, before Mum had Benny.'

'What changed?' Nettie could be as curious as Kerry.

'Everything after Benny was born. He took over Mum's life, and Dad struggled to relate to him from day one. Benny had separation anxiety when he was a toddler, and it was only Mum he wanted.'

'Your dad seems to be trying harder with him now,' Kerry interjected. 'I saw them walking back from the shop together the other day.'

'Yes, but didn't you notice how awkward they looked? It's true Dad's started spending more time with him. I'm not sure why, but it isn't coming naturally for either of them. Benny's still like a frightened animal around Dad. He sometimes does stupid things and Dad gets frustrated.'

'Your dad is pretty imposing.' Nettie grinned. 'Has he still got it in for my family?'

'I was hoping you hadn't noticed.' Emma sighed.

'It's pretty hard not to with the looks he gives us. That man can scowl!'

Nettie was right. It was impossible for Ola to hide his feelings.

'What do you think it is he doesn't like?' Nettie asked.

'The fact that he thinks you're so different, I guess.'

'Am I, Em? Am I really?' Nettie accompanied her question with a penetrating stare.

'Now I've got to know you, I don't think you are.' Emma gave a nervous laugh. 'Dad's trouble is that he won't allow his mind to be changed.'

'It's a pity. Your brother… He's a sweet kid. He and I used to chat sometimes. Now it's like he's scared to.'

'I'm afraid Dad laid the law down with him about that.'

'Shame. I got the feeling Benny needed more friends.'

127

'He does. He only has the one, and they only started hanging around together a couple of months ago. Before that, Benny was always with me or Mum.'

❧

'Dad?'

'What?' Ola dragged his attention away from the television to focus on his son. He'd learned that eye-contact was important when communicating with Benny. When he was scared or vague, the boy looked away. They could have whole conversations with none of it registering unless he made Benny focus by looking him squarely in the eye. Ola still had much to learn, and there were days when he wondered if it was worth the effort. Yet there were other increasingly frequent times when he felt a bond forming between them. Today Benny had sought him out, and that was a first.

'I wanna earn some money.'

'Why? What do you want to buy?' Ola kept his voice neutral.

'Dunno, but lots of kids my age do stuff like that so I think I should too.' Benny wriggled but kept eye-contact.

Understanding dawned. Benny was trying to fit in. 'They're usually older. Perhaps you should wait awhile.'

'Okay.' Benny turned to walk away.

Finding himself wanting to extend their time together, Ola patted the sofa beside him and offered a half-eaten bag of crisps. 'Want to share?'

Benny hesitated, nodded, and sat stiffly beside him. They crunched in silence.

Janet bustled in and out of the room more often than necessary. She didn't say a word, simply cast nervous glances at her husband and son. Ola sighed. It seemed Janet still worried that any time he and Benny spent together would end in disaster. However, tonight Benny seemed happy to sit beside his father as he watched the news and Ola was content to have him there.

The words on the television caught Ola's attention. He reached for the remote to switch it off.

'Why did you do that?' Benny asked, then winced, as if expecting Ola to be cross with him.

Ola smiled and explained, 'They said there was going to be flash photography.'

Benny looked at him blankly.

'People like you can't watch news reports where there are lots of cameras flashing. It can bring on a seizure.'

'You could've just told me to go away.'

Ola's smile drooped. Was he still such a monster to his son? 'I could've.' He scrunched up the crisp packet and hurled it into a nearby wastepaper basket then took a breath. 'But I didn't want to.'

Benny laughed as the packet hit its mark. 'I can't do that. I always miss.'

'Like most things, it takes practice.'

Again they sat in silence. Ola sensed Benny had something on his mind. He wanted to ask but didn't want to appear to be prying, so he waited.

'You know Nettie Thompson?' Benny blurted the question, glancing sideways at him.

Ola nodded, silently wondering what Nettie Thompson had to do with anything.

The nod was enough for Benny to carry on. 'I know you don't like her cos she's pregnant and stuff.'

'It's not because she's pregnant, Benny. It's because...' Ola frantically searched for the right words as the memory of a vivacious red-head so much like the Thompson girl fought to invade his thoughts. He was unwilling to explore his aversion to the Thompsons himself, let alone with his son. 'Well, she's different. The whole family is.'

'Damo's different too. You like him.' Benny looked away. 'Sometimes I think you like him more than me.'

Ola put a hand on his son's shoulder, urging him not to withdraw. He couldn't let this moment slip by without somehow reassuring Benny that he loved him. Actually saying it would be too much. While Benny and Janet exchanged endearments freely, Ola wasn't ready for that yet. It would be harder with a boy

129

than it ever had been with Emma. 'Benny, Damo's a nice kid and I'm glad he's your friend, but you're my son.' He hoped he had put enough feeling into those words so Benny would understand.

'You wanted a son like Damo.' Benny's words were matter-of-fact.

Ola winced. 'I won't deny that. We all have ideas of how things should be, and when you were little, you only wanted your mum.' He paused, carefully weighing up his words. 'I've never been around illness before. When I was your age, I had to be tough. I didn't have people to look after me like you do. I guess that gave me ideas of how a boy should be.'

'You think I'm a silly wimp, like the kids at school.'

'No I don't.' Ola knew the time had come to say it outright, and it was only as the words came out of his mouth that he realised for sure how much he meant them. 'I love you just as much as your mother and Emma do, Benny.'

Benny looked away, but not before Ola spotted sudden tears in his eyes. His heart ached when Benny brushed them away, as if crying would prove he wasn't the tough son his father had wanted.

'I'm sorry I haven't been much of a father to you.' Now Ola had begun sharing his heart it was getting easier. 'I just hope that from here on in we can start working on things.' He grimaced. 'I'm not a patient man. I'm still going to get cross, and you'll have to learn to deal with it.' He twisted to face Benny, who turned back so they were eye to eye. Ola patted his son's shoulder. 'But I know you can. You don't need to run away when I get angry. You just need to give me space.'

Benny blinked. 'Like Damo.'

'What? What about Damo?'

'I bug him sometimes, and he tells me he needs space, so I give it to him.'

Ola realised afresh that Benny was growing up. His understanding of other people's needs was deepening. 'Yes, like Damo.' A long pause ensued as they stared at one another. Only one thing remained. Benny was an affectionate boy, always hugging those he loved. This was yet another thing Ola would have to become accustomed to if he truly wanted to break through. He reached out an arm to encircle Benny, surprised and gratified at how willingly his son leaned into him. The moment was brief as Ola hugged him then gently pulled away, but the look of pleasure on Benny's face was worth the unease.

Ola leaned back on the sofa, Benny still sitting close beside him. 'So we were talking about the Thompson girl.'

'It doesn't matter.'

Ola wasn't sure about that. While all these truths were coming out, this one might be important too. 'Tell me what you were going to say.' It was a request rather than a demand.

'I was…' Benny looked briefly away before turning back. 'I was gonna say…'

'Spit it out.' Ola's tone was teasing. He was surprised to be enjoying Benny's company.

'If you like Damo even though he's different, why can't you like Nettie? Why can't you let her be my friend the same as Damo?'

Ola grasped the first plausible excuse. 'She's a good bit older than you, Benny.'

'It doesn't matter. She'll probably make lots of other friends soon, and then she won't wanna talk to me no more. But she's lonely, Dad.'

'How do you know that?'

'Cos sometimes I am too. I used to be, before Damo.' The words came slowly, and Ola suspected that learning to express his feelings was as new to Benny as listening was to him. 'I only ever had Mum, and Damo says you can't make your mum your best friend. It's not cool.'

'What if Nettie doesn't want to hang out with you?'

Benny shrugged. 'It's up to her, but I wanna be her friend if she wants me. She's nice, Dad. She's just like Emmie, only she dresses different.'

'And she's having a baby.' Ola narrowed his eyes, unsure what he felt about that despite his earlier insistence that it wasn't the problem.

'I reckon that must be really hard.'

Again, Ola was impressed by Benny's maturity. 'I'm sure it must be.' He sighed, realising his boy had well and truly shown him up. 'All right, Benny. I won't say anything if you want to chat to her. Just remember how old she is. Don't annoy her like you sometimes do with your sister.'

'I won't. Thanks, Dad.' That earned Ola another hug, before Benny rose.

Ola stared after him, thankful they were learning to communicate. He was determined to put to rest the memory of the Shanette Thompson lookalike whose wild ways and unfaithfulness had made him swear he would never trust another woman. Only Janet's simplicity and predictability had broken down his defences and made him dare to believe in love again.

Benny lay on his bed, remembering the conversation he'd had with his father. It had taken courage to open up about Nettie. He had learned it was okay to ask questions as long as he tried to do it sensibly. Although his dad still had no patience with his childishness, they were finding their own way of communicating. Still, it was hard to admit he wanted to be friends with Nettie when Ola didn't approve. Why did he dislike the Thompsons so much? He hadn't given a decent explanation and there were still many things Benny didn't understand.

However, Benny was glad he'd asked, because they'd ended up talking about themselves, about how Benny knew his dad wanted a son like Damo, and then when Ola said he loved him just like his mum and sister... Benny grinned at the thought, before shivering. He'd nearly ruined everything by crying. That was a stupid thing to do when he was happy. At least his dad hadn't got angry this time.

He'd worried about messing it up again when they'd gone back to talking about Nettie. Benny hadn't wanted to ruin the moment they'd shared. He was finally learning what it felt like to have a father, and it gave him a sense of pride like nothing he'd ever known. His strong, capable dad had admitted he loved him. This time he let his grin spread wide as he stared up at the ceiling.

If only Nettie would talk to him again, his life would be pretty good.

17

Over the next couple of weeks, life moved into an easier rhythm for the Wellanders. Ola completed his purchase of the garage and celebrated by treating his family to a slap-up meal at a restaurant in a nearby town. Benny didn't want to go. It sounded boring, and the promise of food held little appeal. However, Emma persuaded him it would mean a lot to their father and showed him how happy it made their mum.

It was one of the first times they'd shared a meal in public. For Emma, it almost felt like they were a normal family again. Her mum swelled with pride and Ola was relaxed and happy as they chatted around the table. Though Benny picked at his food and hid in a corner, their dad didn't react. In fact, Emma reckoned it was their dad's confidence that gave Benny the strength he needed to get through the evening. He stuck to Ola rather than Janet, even though it likely grieved their mum.

One Saturday afternoon while he was out on his bike, Benny saw Nettie struggling down the road carrying several heavy-looking shopping bags. She was tired and breathless a lot these days. Now Ola had consented to them spending time together, Benny liked to help her as much as he could. He had been eager to renew their friendship following his conversation with his father and though Nettie's friendships with Emma and the other girls had flourished, she still made time for him.

'My mum says you're not supposed to carry heavy stuff when you're pregnant.'

'What made your mum tell you that?' she grinned at him as she relinquished her shopping and offered to push his bike.

'She's been helping Karen a lot.'

Karen's baby was due just weeks before Nettie's. Being a much older mother, the pregnancy had taken its toll, and Janet was often at the Moss house assisting her friend.

'Have you heard about Kerry?'

'No. What's going on?' Nettie had told him she enjoyed their chats despite the difference in their ages, so Benny didn't mind admitting when there was something he didn't know.

'I'm surprised Emma hasn't told you.'

'Emmie don't tell me nothing much.' He sighed.

'Kerry's getting married. It's happening over the Easter weekend.'

'She can't be! She's the same age as my sister.' His outrage made Nettie laugh out loud.

'She's been with the same guy for a while, hasn't she?'

'I dunno.' He'd never taken much interest in his sister's friends.

'I think it has something to do with the fact that they're Christians, and Christians don't approve of sex before marriage.'

Nettie's use of *that word* made Benny blush because he still didn't altogether understand what went on between men and women when they were married. He had heard rumours, but it all sounded disgusting and confusing, and he didn't need to know.

'I guess they didn't see the point in waiting,' Nettie concluded.

Benny asked Emma about it later and learned that Nettie had been right. Nineteen-year-old Kerry Brooks was getting married. It worried him, with his sister being the same age. 'You're not gonna get married too, are you, Emmie?' Benny depended on the security of his family. He feared change and losing her would be one of the scariest changes of all.

She chuckled and hugged him tenderly. 'I don't even have a boyfriend yet, Pestie.'

She cheered him up by making hot chocolate and sitting with him in the garden to drink it.

❦

A few days later, Janet was in the kitchen when Benny slammed his way into the house, threw down his schoolbag, and

135

announced through tears, 'I hate him, and I'm not gonna be his friend no more!' before charging upstairs. Janet followed, and finding him on his bed crying, she drew him to her, muttering the soothing endearments she'd used all his life.

'It's okay, sweetheart. I'm here. I love you, Benny. Please, darling, tell me what's wrong.'

She got no sense out of him. All he did was cling to her as his body shook with sobs, and Janet waited fearfully for the seizure that was sure to follow. When it didn't, she tucked her little boy into bed and told him to sleep until teatime.

She wasn't sure what to say to Ola and Emma when they arrived home from work. All too aware of how easily they became frustrated with Benny, Janet was once again fearful of rocking the boat. Things had been so much better for their family since Ola started making more of an effort to get to know their son. When tea was on the table, she prepared a tray, intending to carry Benny's meal up to his room.

'What's the matter with him?' Emma asked.

'I'm not sure. Something upset him at school. He wouldn't tell me what.' Janet chewed on her bottom lip, waiting for a negative reaction from Ola.

'I'll talk to him.' Her husband rose and made for the door.

'Ola?' There was pleading in her eyes. 'Please don't shout at him. He was in a terrible state.'

'You told me the boy needs a father, Jan. So let me be a father to him.'

'There's still so much he can't understand. When he's upset like this... well you know how he is.'

Emma chipped in. 'No matter how frustrated you get, Dad, if you yell, you'll only make him worse.'

Ola acknowledged Emma's advice with a nod and left Janet to keep their meals warm in the oven while he talked to Benny.

Ola found his son still lying in bed staring hopelessly up at the ceiling. His eyes were red-rimmed, and his nose was running. Ola sat on the bed and Benny turned away. 'It's no good, son. It won't go away unless you talk about it.'

'I don't wanna.'

Benny's petulance almost earned him an irritable response. Ola forced it down, walked into the bathroom, and fetched a tissue. 'Blow your nose.' He felt like he was dealing with a five-year-old.

Benny blew his nose and made to hand back the used tissue as he was accustomed to doing with Janet.

Ola shook his head. 'I don't want it! Put it in the bin, and then we'll talk.'

Benny disposed of the tissue, then returned to his bed. Ola was pleased to see that this time he had the decency to sit up and face him.

'Want to tell me what happened? Was someone mean to you at school?'

'Damo's got a girlfriend.' The tears were falling again, and Benny's hand balled into a fist as he rubbed at his streaming eyes.

'And?' Ola probed.

'And I hate him! I said I don't wanna be his friend no more!'

'Benny.' Ola struggled to understand such an extreme reaction, but as he gazed at his boy, several things seemed to occur to him all at once. Damian was his son's first friend, and Benny saw this newfound relationship as a betrayal and a threat. It was yet another complication the boy didn't understand. Lack of understanding made Benny default to his childhood patterns of sulking and temper tantrums.

Yet something was changing, because now Benny was looking to him for help. Ola could sense he wanted to process things, but it was too overwhelming. If he handled this tactfully, he could help his son. If he didn't, he would push Benny away and the lesson would never be learned. 'Damo can still be friends with you and have a girlfriend.'

'No he can't.'

'Why do you think that?' Ola wanted to make inroads into Benny's unusual thought patterns.

'He won't wanna hang round with me no more. He'll only wanna be with her, and she doesn't like me. None of the kids do,

137

Dad. Only Damo, and he won't now he's got her cos she'll make him make fun of me too.'

Understanding brought empathy to the surface. 'Lots of boys your age have girlfriends, Benny. It's a big part of growing up. It'll happen to you one day.'

'No it won't, cos no one will ever wanna go out with me, and girls are silly.'

Ola looked away to hide a smile. 'You might think that now, but one day you'll change your mind.'

'No I won't.'

Benny seemed adamant, so Ola decided not to push. 'Well even if you don't, you'll still have to learn to accept that what's happening to Damian is natural. It doesn't mean he won't carry on being your friend. Take Kerry Brooks across the road.'

'She's getting married,' Benny stated.

'But she's still friends with Emma and Erin.'

'And Nettie.' Benny was so literal. He wouldn't let his friend be left out of the list.

'It'll be the same for Damo. Although he'll want to spend time with his girlfriend, he'll still choose to do things with you too. Even though you'll have to accept the fact that you might see less of him for a while, he'll always need his best mate.'

'No he won't.' Benny looked downcast with shame written all over his face. 'He won't now cos I messed everything up by being stupid.'

'Did you get stressed in front of him?'

Benny nodded soberly.

Ola noted with pleasure that the tears and tantrums were gone. They were having a sensible conversation, and Benny was facing up to his mistakes. 'You could always say sorry.'

'I'm so stupid sometimes, Dad!'

His despair was touching, and Ola drew him into his arms. This was getting easier. 'We're all allowed to be silly when we're growing up. The important thing is to learn from this and try not to make the same mistakes again.'

'I wanna learn.' Benny rested his head on Ola's shoulder.

'I know you do.' Ola pulled away and climbed off the bed. 'So will you show us how grown-up you can be by coming down for tea instead of expecting your mum to bring your food up here?'

Benny nodded, rose, and walked past him into the bathroom to wash his face and comb his dishevelled hair.

Janet fussed over their son as they ate. Benny dismissed her with a shrug, then surprised his dad by offering to help with the washing up. Ola said they would do it together, and he sent Janet for a sit down. Nothing was said about the row with Damian until the last item was put away.

Then Benny announced, 'I sent Damo a text and said sorry.'

'Have you heard back from him yet?' Ola asked.

'Yeah. He said it's cool.'

'Good. I'm glad.' Ola gave his best fatherly smile. 'I'm proud of you, Benny.'

Benny bounced out of the room in delight.

❧

Later, Ola and Emma sat around their dining room table indulging in an intense chess match. It had thrilled Ola when his daughter warmed to the game he had loved since childhood. She was as serious a contestant as him. They both played to win. Janet usually left them alone and retired with her knitting, and Benny either accompanied her or hid away in his room. Tonight, he stayed and chatted with them while they played. Emma chided him for asking too many questions, and Ola frequently told him to shut up when he was concentrating on a strategic move. However, Benny was strangely unperturbed.

'It looks really hard.' Benny gazed in bewilderment at the board. 'How d'you know what to do?'

'You learn,' Emma explained. 'There are different rules for each chess piece.'

'I couldn't do that.'

'There are other games we could play.' Ola thought about it as he took his next move. 'Your mum and I used to play cards when we were first married, and we couldn't afford to do much else. Maybe we could teach you some of the games we enjoyed.'

Benny shook his head. 'I'll be rubbish and you'll get cross.'

'Bet you won't. I can start you with something simple.'

Ola was true to his word. Friday evenings became card playing nights in the Wellander house, as the four of them sat around the dining room table with pizza, French fries and a generous amount of junk food. Benny often lost track of the games and he never won, but even that grew to be a source of loving family banter because Benny was finally learning to laugh at himself. When he became confused, he threw down his cards with a smile, telling them to carry on without him while he munched on a packet of crisps or another slice of pizza.

Sometimes Benny and Janet played together, giving him half a chance of beating Ola or his sister. Emma brought home a set of Uno cards, and Benny understood that better. When he won his first game, he was so excited he almost knocked over his father's glass of beer. He gloated over it for days until Ola brought him back down with a bump the following Friday.

The Wellanders were interacting like a normal family, and as Benny felt more secure, his confidence grew. Although Damian's first relationship fizzled out in a fortnight, it was soon followed by another, and Benny learned to tease his friend about his fascination with girls.

18

With spring fast approaching, plans for Kerry's upcoming wedding were the talk of the street, and both Nettie and Karen grew rounder by the day as they waited for their babies.

Nettie wasn't sure what lay ahead. Her parents still saw adoption as the only way out of the mess she'd created. Yet as her child grew inside her, Nettie's feelings became more conflicted, and she wondered if she would find the strength to allow her baby to be brought up by strangers.

'You'll have your life back,' her mother encouraged. 'Everything will be normal.'

'No it won't. We're living in a different place for a start.' Nettie was growing accustomed to village life, and much to her surprise, she liked it. However, she suspected Mary was planning to work on her dad about moving again as soon as possible. They hadn't considered making new friends. They were living in limbo, watching her stomach grow and waiting for the day when they could return to the city, putting her unfortunate mistake behind them.

Nettie was pondering all these things as she sat in a recliner on the front lawn with a cup of tea, enjoying a rare chance to lift her swelling feet.

'Your garden's a mess, Nettie.'

She loved the way Benny didn't waste time on pleasantries. His bluntness was refreshing.

'I know.' A closed gate was between them. Benny had been to the post office to collect his father's Saturday newspaper, and Nettie noted the healthy glow on his cheeks. He'd told her he liked running errands for his dad. It made him feel grown-up. 'We never had a garden at our old house,' Nettie said. 'None of us know what to do with it.'

'You didn't have a garden?' Benny screwed up his face, like he couldn't imagine houses other than his own.

'We lived in a flat. We had neighbours above and below and to the left and the right.'

'Your house didn't have an upstairs?'

'No. It was all on one floor. Haven't you ever known anyone who lived in a flat?'

Benny shook his head. 'Damo's gran's house is smaller than ours, but it still has an upstairs. Where did you sleep?'

'We had bedrooms, silly!'

Benny glanced around self-consciously, then back at her. 'D'you want me to help with your garden?'

'What do you know about gardening?'

'Lots. I helped my mum all the time when I was little. I still do when I'm not out with Damo, cos Emmie and Dad hate gardening.'

Nettie looked across the street, admiring the neatness and symmetry of Janet Wellander's garden which was showing signs of early blooming. 'We'd have to pay you.'

'You don't have to do that.' His smile lit up his face. 'I wanna help cos you're my friend.'

'You shouldn't let people walk all over you, Benny. If someone does a job well, they should get paid.'

'Damo doesn't pay me when I help him wash his bike, and my dad doesn't give me no money when I take the bin out or help him clean the car. Why should you?'

Not knowing how to respond, she suggested, 'You should check with your dad first.'

'I told you; He's okay with you now.'

Perhaps he was right. Ola had even exchanged brief pleasantries with Nettie, and she hoped the frost between them was thawing. 'I still think he'd prefer it if you asked.'

So Benny did, and surprised Nettie by returning the following Saturday with gloves and secateurs.

'Dad was fine. He even seemed a bit happy I was thinking of others. I said you'd never had a garden before. That you lived

142

somewhere weird with no upstairs and people living all around you.'

Nettie laughed at his confused description.

'Dad showed me some photos of one of the places he and mum rented when Emmie was little. They had a flat too!'

Nettie smiled as her mum brought them glasses of lemonade and she flopped onto a lounger to rest. It was a bit cold to have the loungers out, but her back needed a break from the digging. 'Are you and your parents going to Kerry's wedding?'

'No.' Benny tossed a pile of earth into a wheelbarrow. 'My mum and dad never go to stuff like that.'

'I'd noticed they keep themselves to themselves.'

'They do stuff with Karen and Peter sometimes, cos Karen is mum's friend and Dad works with Peter at the garage. Only Emmie's going to the wedding. She's one of Kerry's bridesmaids.'

'I'm dreading it.' Nettie scowled down at her protruding stomach. 'I'll never find anything to wear.'

'Girls think too much about clothes.'

'I can see you don't give it much thought.' Nettie grinned teasingly as she sipped on her drink. 'The only time I ever see you in anything other than jeans and the same couple of t-shirts is when you're wearing your school uniform.'

He laughed along with her as he sat down in the opposite chair. 'Clothes are boring.'

'Kids your age reckon everything's boring.' Nettie sighed, wondering if she had ever been as innocent as Benny. She hadn't grown up in the country, and her parents didn't stifle her. She supposed she had always been mature for her age.

'I don't think you having a baby is boring.'

His intense gaze surprised her, and Nettie felt the need to look away. 'My parents still want me to give it up for adoption as soon as it's born.'

'What do you want?'

Nettie couldn't believe she was having this conversation with Emma's little brother. 'I don't know. That's the problem.' She rested her chin on her hand as she allowed her guard to slip. 'In

143

the beginning before the baby started moving around inside me, it was easy to pretend it wasn't happening.' She could see he was endeavouring to understand. Of course he couldn't. He was too young. 'It's probably the right thing to give it up and give my child the chance to have two parents who love it, rather than land it with a mum who doesn't know what she's doing.'

'You could learn.'

In Benny's mind it was so simple, and Nettie envied him that.

'I've had to learn loads of stuff, especially lately,' he continued. 'I bet people would help you, like your mum. Maybe even mine and Karen. Karen's having a baby too. She'd tell you what to do.'

'My mum will be disappointed if I keep it. She might not want to help.'

'I bet she would. Mums and dads get cross sometimes when we don't do stuff how they want, but they usually work it out with us in the end...' Nettie guessed Benny was thinking of his own relationship with Ola. 'If you decide to keep it, I reckon lots of us would help.'

'Are you including yourself in that?'

He nodded seriously.

'So tell me, Benny Wellander. What would a boy like you know about handling a small child?'

'Not a lot.' He blushed. 'I guess I wouldn't be able to do nothing much.' His face brightened into an eager smile. 'I could give you a break by cuddling it when it cries. I know babies do that a lot, but they're pretty cute.'

His offer was incredibly touching. No one else had shown any interest in the baby's needs. 'Just how old are you?' She had never asked but assumed he was around twelve.

'Not as young as everyone thinks I am.' He laughed. 'I'm fourteen next week.'

That was a surprise. He didn't look like most fourteen year olds. 'Are you doing anything for your birthday?' Nettie loved birthdays.

'I don't care about them much. I'll come here again if you like.'

'Why would you want to help me on your birthday?'

His smile was broad as he reached out and touched her hand. 'Cos I like you, Nettie. You don't treat me like everyone else does. Well everyone except Damo.'

'How do you mean?'

'You didn't have to be my friend. You could've ignored me after that day I dropped the ice cream.'

She smiled as she remembered. 'You didn't have to spend time with me either.'

He rose and went back to his work as Nettie watched him, pondering the reasons why she persisted with this unconventional friendship.

'I knew a girl who was adopted once.' Benny didn't look up as he focused on the task at hand.

'What was she like?'

'She was always angry. She was in my class till they had to move her to another school cos the teachers couldn't handle her.'

'Did she know she was adopted?' Nettie leaned forward in her seat.

'Yeah, and her mum and dad seemed nice. I dunno why she did what she did.'

'Not all adoption stories turn out like that, Benny. I've heard some great ones about kids being brought up in loving families.' Was she trying to convince him or herself?

'You won't know how it will be for your baby though, will you? I mean, you won't know who it's going to, or if they'll be kind or mean.'

There was a lull in their conversation as Nettie pondered what he'd said, until Benny asked, 'What would you call it if you keep the baby?'

'I haven't thought about that. Any suggestions?' She expected him to shake his head and reply with his customary *Dunno*, so his rapid response surprised her.

'Beth if it's a girl. Dunno about if it's a boy.'

'Beth?' Nettie was baffled by his choice. 'Isn't that a bit old-fashioned?'

'It's little. Babies are small so they need little names.'

'They don't stay small.' She was enjoying their conversation.

'It's sweet, and it suits a baby.'

'Babies grow up. Would it suit an older child, or would she end up hating me?'

'Kids shouldn't hate their mums.'

When Benny left shortly afterwards, Nettie joined her mum in the kitchen.

'I've arranged for the lady from the adoption agency to visit on Monday evening,' Mary announced.

Nettie baulked under her mum's pressure. 'You know I haven't made my final decision yet.' She wouldn't tell Mary about her conversation with Benny.

'This way you'll have more information to help you decide. There's no harm in that, is there?'

Nettie had nothing to say.

'It was kind of the Wellander boy to help with our garden. He's a sweet kid.'

'Yes, he is.' Nettie smiled wryly, wondering how Mary would feel about him if she knew Benny had been trying to persuade her to keep her baby.

❧

Nettie stood in front of the Wellander house under a clear blue Easter Saturday sky, shuffling nervously as she reached up to ring the doorbell. She'd never been inside their home before. Despite Benny's reassurances, she remained convinced his dad still disliked her.

The door opened wide. 'Have you come for the flowers?' Janet greeted her with a smile.

Nettie nodded. 'Kerry's mum asked me if I'd mind fetching them.'

'Come on in. They're ready.' Janet guided her into the kitchen where a lavish bouquet stood in a bucket of water in a corner of the room, prepared for Kerry's wedding later that day.

'They look lovely, Mrs Wellander.' Encouraged by Benny's friendly face, Nettie scanned the kitchen's other occupants, acknowledging each with a nod.

'Anything else we can do to help?' Janet lifted the flowers out of the bucket, allowing the excess water to drip off before handing them over.

'Are you heading over there now?' Emma rose and put her plate and mug in the sink.

'Yeah. The earlier we start with your hair and makeup, the better.'

'None of us has a clue what to do. We're hoping you know – coming from a city.'

'I feel pretty out of touch now.' Nettie shrugged.

'Would you like something to eat or drink before you go?' Janet was being surprisingly hospitable.

'I'd better not.' Nettie rested a hand on her middle. 'There's not much room for food or drink anymore.'

'How long do you have left?'

'Two weeks.' Nettie sighed plaintively. 'My midwife warned me it could happen any time now.'

'Well, Karen and her little one are coming along nicely.' Janet leaned over to kiss Benny's cheek. 'Seeing baby Marcus takes me right back. It only seems like yesterday when I had a baby in my arms.' She hugged her son, who squirmed and attempted to pull away.

'I don't think he wants reminding of his babyhood, Jan.' Ola laced his comment with amusement.

'Especially some of the stories we could tell.' Emma's teasing earned her a glare from her brother.

'I think I'd better head off with the flowers,' Nettie said, sensing a need to rescue poor Benny from his embarrassment and relieved that her time with the Wellanders had gone smoothly.

Later that afternoon, the Brooks family hosted a small gathering in their garden following the marriage ceremony. Nettie had never attended a Christian wedding. It differed from anything she had previously experienced. Kerry and Neal had written their own vows, and Nettie wiped away tears over their sincerity and unmasked devotion. She wondered if anyone would ever make those kinds of promises to her. Would any guy

147

in his right mind choose a girl who'd allowed herself to get pregnant at sixteen? Of course, if she gave the baby up, he need never know, but could she live the rest of her life denying the fact that she had carried this child?

The afternoon was unseasonably warm, the baby kicked incessantly under the maxi-dress Nettie had squeezed into, and Emma and Erin giggled with Kerry. Nettie felt like an outsider in their midst. She walked around the side of the Brooks house, spotting Damian, Dale, Brian, and Benny in the road. Dale handed something to Damian, and as she moved closer, Nettie realised it was a cigarette.

'Don't be stupid, Damo.' Brian's face paled with worry. No doubt he would receive a telling off from his parents if they got wind of what was happening.

'I smoked when I was his age,' Dale gloated.

Dale had developed a swagger when he walked, and Nettie felt the urge to wipe the satisfied smirk off his horrible face.

'It's no big deal, Brian,' Damian insisted. 'I've smoked before.'

'You have?' Brian stared at him open-mouthed.

'Yeah.' Damian lit the cigarette from Dale's match and inhaled deeply.

'You're gonna get into trouble, Damo!' Nettie could see the panic in Benny's eyes. 'If my dad catches you, he'll take you home to your gran and make you tell her what you've done.'

'How's your dad gonna find out unless someone tells him, little snitch?' Dale sneered at Benny, and Nettie's young friend visibly shrank. She could sense he was on the verge of tears. Poor Benny.

'I won't tell him, but my dad always finds stuff out.' Benny looked helpless as Damian handed the cigarette back to Dale.

'It's okay, mate. I only had one drag to prove my point. I don't wanna start smoking. It's a filthy habit.'

Dale smarted at Damian's criticism.

'Let's go, Damo.' Benny grabbed hold of his friend's arm.

'Well, there's a surprise! Weedy Wellander's running away again,' Dale taunted.

'Leave him alone.' Brian seemed torn between staying to make sure Dale didn't hurt Benny further and escaping to the safety of his sister's wedding reception.

Dale laughed eagerly. 'If he had a puff of this, it would probably give him one of his fits. Then he'd go crying to his mummy about what nasty Dale made him do.'

Nettie clenched her fists as she saw the tears in Benny's eyes. He couldn't hide it now. He was crying openly.

'No it wouldn't. You're mean, Dale Moss!' He always reverted to childish speech when he was upset, and that played into Dale's hands. He had Benny right where he wanted him.

'So, prove it then.' Dale held out the cigarette, revelling in his power.

Nettie's heart pounded as she wondered what Benny would do.

'Don't do it, Benny,' Damian urged, as the same words echoed around Nettie's head. 'You don't have to prove anything to him.'

Brian moved forward to reach for the cigarette as Benny snatched it from Dale and stepped away. A challenging look crossed Benny's tear-filled eyes as he fixed them on Dale. Before anyone could say or do anything else, he inhaled deeply, then promptly gagged as the cigarette fell from his hand.

Dale ran away laughing, while Brian and Damian rushed to Benny's side. Benny bent double and heaved over the pavement as shaking racked his body.

'You idiot,' Damian cried, while Brian hovered, looking equally clueless.

Nettie had to step in. She moved forward, reached for Benny and gently rubbed his back. 'Hey. You'll be okay. Just take deep breaths.'

'Did you see what happened?' Brian's eyes rounded like saucers.

'I saw it all. It's all right, Brian. Leave him to me. Damo, you keep an eye out for either of his parents. Let us know if they're coming.'

149

Nettie dragged Benny gagging and sobbing down the street and into her parents' garden and fetched a glass of water. He still looked pretty green, and she wondered how she would handle it if the shock brought on one of his seizures.

'Why did you do it?' She gazed at him sternly.

'Dale was winding me up.' He cried. 'He's so mean.'

'You should've walked away like Damo and Brian said. What were you thinking, Benny?'

'I dunno.' He gazed sorrowfully down at his feet.

'Don't give me that.' Nettie was becoming familiar with his avoidance tactics.

'What d'you want me to say?'

'I want you to tell me the truth.' She reached out and took hold of his hand. 'You must've known what would happen.'

'Damo did it. I thought it'd be okay.'

'And you think it's always cool to do things just because your best mate does?'

He shook his head, still unwilling to look her in the eye. 'They're always picking on me, Nettie.'

'Who?'

'All of them!'

'Damian doesn't, and Brian wasn't either from what I could see. Dale's not everyone.'

'It's not just him. All the kids at school do it too. They bully me cos of my seizures and cos I'm thick.'

'So you thought you'd prove how mature you are by smoking?'

Benny shrank further into himself. 'I wanna be like everyone else.'

'Hey.' Compassion rose in Nettie's chest. 'You don't need to. You just need to be Benny.'

'But who's he?' Benny sighed.

His petulance was gone, replaced by a sadness so intense that Nettie wanted to hug him. 'He's sweet and funny and kind, and he's one of my best friends.'

'You don't mean that.'

'Why not?'

'Cos you're sixteen, you're beautiful, and you're cool. I'm just...'

'Just Benny.' She patted his hand as she spoke. 'And I'm knocked-up Nettie Thompson – who half the people in this place don't like either. We can only be who we are, and we shouldn't want to be anything else.' She hoped she was explaining things clearly. She knew his brain didn't function normally, yet she had wondered lately how much of that was medical and how much was a consequence of Janet's overprotectiveness. She felt sure there was more to Benny than anyone realised.

'Made a fool of myself, didn't I?' He had finally stopped crying and looked straight at her.

'You did a bit.' She smiled, earning herself one of his wide grins in return. 'That's part of being a teenager.'

'Bet you never looked as stupid as me.'

'I got pregnant, didn't I?' Nettie surprised herself by making a joke of it.

'And your baby will be here soon,' Benny stated.

'Yeah.' It was her turn to look away. The closer her delivery date loomed, the harder she tried to push it out of her mind.

19

'What did she have?' Emma placed a glass of coke on the table beside her and luxuriated in her deckchair, making the most of the late April sunshine.

'It's a little girl.' Kerry's voice replied through the loud speaker of her phone.

'What will happen now?' Emma wasn't sure how to react.

'Nettie said the people from the adoption agency are coming for the baby tomorrow,' Kerry said.

'Is she sure?'

'I don't know, Em.' Kerry sighed. 'She keeps saying it's what her mum and dad want.'

'It's Nettie's child.'

'She hasn't even held her. She was afraid that if she did, she'd feel something.'

'Sounds like she's not sure.' Emma's eyebrows narrowed in concern, coupled with frustration over Nettie's parents and their dismissal of the baby.

'What do you think you'd do if it was happening to you?' Kerry's question caught Emma off guard.

'I can't imagine. Especially as I'm not even in a relationship.'

'Nettie said she should be home tomorrow.'

'And her parents will expect her to carry on like the baby never existed?'

'I doubt whether she'll be able to.'

'Me too.' Emma's voice dropped.

The conversation ended moments later, leaving Emma overwhelmed by sadness for her friend. Should she visit her at the hospital? She doubted whether the staff or Mary Thompson would let her in.

'It's not fair.'

Emma had been unaware of Benny loitering nearby.

'What isn't?' She wasn't in the mood for his nonsense today. No doubt someone had said something to shatter his fragile little world.

'The way Nettie's mum and dad are making her give up her baby.' Benny shuffled from foot to foot.

'They can't make her, Benny. No one can. It's Nettie's choice.'

'But Kerry said the adoption people are coming tomorrow.'

'Nettie can still change her mind.'

'You should go and talk to her. I bet she'd like to see you.'

Emma's attitude warmed. Her brother was genuinely concerned for their mutual friend. He was growing up, becoming less self-absorbed. 'I doubt they'd let me in. We've just gotta be here for her when she comes home.'

Leaving his sister to sunbathe, Benny wandered into the house, thinking about his friend, Nettie. She had a little girl she hadn't even held. Babies were meant to be cuddled by their mums. He still indulged in his mum's hugs, and he was fourteen. It wasn't right.

An idea formed in his head, but he doubted he had the courage to act upon it. There was a bus that went to the hospital. He and his mum had travelled on it for some of his doctor's appointments. What number was it? And what time did it leave? Benny had no idea. How could he find out? Brian would know. He travelled by bus all the time. Benny rushed up to his room and rang Brian.

'You know about buses and stuff, don't you?' His mind was racing so much that he launched straight into his questions.

Brian sounded amused at the unusual beginning to their conversation 'Yeah. Why? What do you want to know?'

'Which one goes to the hospital?'

'Are you ill?' Brian sounded concerned.

'No. I wanna see someone.' Benny hoped he wouldn't have to say who, because Brian wouldn't understand.

Thankfully Brian didn't question him further and told him what he had to do.

Benny scribbled himself a note and stuffed it in his jeans pocket. He was rubbish at remembering numbers and times.

Half an hour later, he sat on the bus next to an elderly lady who made funny noises when she breathed.

'Sorry, love. Too many years on the ciggies according to my doctor. I keep telling him I'm too old to give it up now.'

Was this why Benny's parents said it was wrong to smoke? It made him even more grateful he'd only tried it once. That had put him off for life.

Benny closed his eyes as they travelled, valiantly battling the motion-sickness that always threatened to overwhelm him. He was more successful at controlling it since he'd started taking the bus to school. His dad's changed attitude had also helped. On long car journeys, Ola let him sit in the front with the window open, distracting him with conversation if Benny said he felt ill. The nausea sometimes passed if he didn't give in to it.

Today was harder though, because he was anxious. His parents would be mad if they knew what he was doing. He'd told his mum he was going for a walk. If she knew he was on the bus by himself she'd panic, especially if she had an inkling about where he was going and why.

Benny was so focused on trying not to be sick that he almost missed his stop, but the woman beside him was also alighting at the hospital, so he followed her off the bus.

Once inside the large and confusing building, he wondered how he would find out where he needed to go. It would involve asking questions, and Benny hated talking to strangers. He found a map that made no sense. Then he spotted some shops near the entrance, and that gave him another idea. You couldn't visit a baby without taking a present.

Benny thought about Chloe as he walked through the shop that sold children's toys. He remembered bringing her here once during their time together on the children's ward. She had fallen in love with a rabbit with huge floppy ears, and he'd asked his mum to buy it for her. Chloe had loved that bunny, naming it Benny after him. He still missed his friend and thought it was a shame she had to die. He remembered how her mum held her when she was ill and thought again about Nettie's baby. Who would play with her, or hold her when she cried?

Benny's resolve strengthened as he paid for a small white teddy out of the pocket money he'd been saving for ice cream. Maybe he should have bought something pink, but he hated pink. It was so girlie. Emma would be quick to remind him the baby was a girl. Well, this was his gift. It didn't have to be something his mum or sister would choose. The lady at the cash register seemed nice, so he thought it was safe to ask her where he would find Nettie.

'Where's the place where people have babies?' Benny shifted from foot to foot, aware of how stupid his question sounded. No doubt there was a posh name for the ward. They all had names.

'The maternity ward?' She handed over his change.

Benny nodded, hoping he would remember the strange-sounding word in case he needed it again.

'It's up the stairs and first right.'

Those instructions sounded simple enough, so Benny thanked her and climbed the stairs.

Finding maternity was easier than he had hoped. Benny was heaving a mental sigh of relief when another hurdle presented itself. He'd found the ward. How was he going to find Nettie? There was a reception desk like the ones he and his mum had waited at when he had appointments. He strolled over to it, drawing on every ounce of confidence he could muster to speak to yet another stranger.

'Hello.' The receptionist was friendly.

Benny supposed this would be a happy ward if people came there to have babies. 'I'm looking for Nettie...' He cleared his throat and started again. 'I'm looking for Shanette Thompson. She's just had a baby.'

'It's close family only here. So you are?' She raised an eyebrow.

Benny replied without thinking. 'Her brother.' There would be no going back now.

A nurse came over with a file and the two women disappeared into a side room.

Benny's heart threatened to pound out of his chest. What had he done? Were they checking if he'd told a lie? Because he had. Even his over-indulgent mum would be cross with him about that.

'Benny!'

He spun to see Mary Thompson standing next to a glass sliding door. She looked more than a little shocked to see him.

'I'm sorry.' Benny jumped. He hung his head, certain she was going to send him away. 'I just wanted to see Nettie.'

'How did you get here?'

Benny glanced behind him. The two ladies hadn't come back. 'On the bus.' He couldn't look at Mary, fearing the condemnation in her eyes.

'You'd better follow me.'

He stood stock still, unable to believe his ears.

'Come on then!' An exasperated Mary motioned to a side room. 'You might as well since you've come all this way.'

Benny found himself in a room not unlike the ones he had stayed in during his frequent and prolonged hospital visits. Nettie lay in the bed looking tired and pale, but her eyes twinkled mischievously as she greeted him.

'Hello, little brother.' His gaze met hers and they both laughed. 'You gave my poor mum quite a scare. She didn't realise she had a son.'

'Sorry.' Benny looked bashfully at Mary. Even she had a trace of a smile.

'What made you come here, Benny?' Nettie gazed at him intently.

Benny was so proud that this beautiful girl was his friend. That was why he had come. Nettie needed him. She just didn't realise it yet. 'I wanted to give you this for Beth.'

He held out the white teddy, chiding himself for letting his pet-name for the baby slip out. He hadn't told Nettie he'd thought of her child as Beth since their conversation about suitable names. It wasn't right to call her *the baby*. Everyone deserved a name, even if he wished his was different.

'Beth?' Mary gave him a questioning glance.

'It's what Benny thinks I should name the baby.'

So Nettie remembered. He had only told her once, and she was so disgusted, Benny presumed she would forget.

Nettie reached for the gift, stroking the teddy's soft fur with a weak smile. 'He's lovely.'

'I know it should be pink for a girl, but... I hate pink.' Benny blushed, and Nettie laughed again.

'It's not my favourite colour either.'

'Will they let her have it?'

'I suppose so.' Nettie's eyes were downcast. 'She's in the nursery. I haven't seen her yet.'

'I could take you to see her, Benny, if you want me to,' Mary said, then looked surprised by her own offer.

'I'm touched you came all this way on the bus.' Nettie reached for his hand, and Benny let her take it. 'I didn't think you were used to going places by yourself.'

'I'm not. Only to school, and Damo's always with me.'

'Where do your parents think you are?' Nettie had suspected the truth before he admitted it.

Benny wrinkled his nose. 'I told my mum I was going for a walk.'

'You are a little rebel,' Mary chuckled. 'Perhaps I misjudged you.'

'Do you think I'm silly?' He addressed the question to his friend.

'No way.' Nettie squeezed his hand. 'It's sweet, the way you care about my baby. You're the first person to buy her a present.'

'I wanted her to know someone loves her.' Benny had spoken without thinking. He immediately pulled his hand away, convinced his hasty words would make them cross. Surely now he had blown his chances. They would send him home.

But Nettie wasn't angry. He saw sad tears pooling in her eyes as she gripped his hand again. 'I love her too, Benny.'

'If you love her, why isn't she in here with you? She might be lonely or scared.' His courage was bolstered by her reaction. Wasn't this why he had come?

'It wouldn't be fair if Nettie had the baby in here, since she's intending to give her up. It would be cruel.' Mary's tone was firm.

Uncharacteristically, Benny wasn't deterred. All he cared about was Nettie, and she still held his hand. She wasn't angry.

'I thought it was best for the nurses to take her.' Nettie looked from Benny to her mother as her tears fell. 'But I do want to see her. This is the hardest thing I've ever had to do.'

'I bet it's hard on Beth too, being by herself with a load of other crying babies and wondering where her mum is.' Now Benny had started, he couldn't stop.

'She won't be thinking anything of the sort at such a young age.' Mary sniffed her disgust.

'How d'you know?' Benny fought the urge to cry. 'No one knows what babies think. People reckon I don't think nothing when I'm having my seizures, but I do. Sometimes there's loads of stuff going round in my head. I just can't talk about it.'

'Don't you realise Nettie feels bad enough as it is?' Mary was angry even if her daughter wasn't.

'Mum,' Nettie gazed imploringly. 'I know how you and Dad feel, and I've been listening to everything you've said, but... Now she's here...'

'I was only just born when I had my first seizure.' Benny had to make Nettie understand. 'What if something like that happened to Beth? The nurses are looking after lots of babies. They might not know until it was too late. Even if she doesn't have seizures, she'll still get ill. All kids do, Nettie, and they need their mums. I still do, and I'm meant to be growing up.'

'If I don't keep her, she'll have an adoptive mother. I'm sure she'll love her very much and take great care of her when she's ill...'

'She might not.' Benny heard the note of desperation in his voice. 'She might be cruel to Beth, and you'll never know!'

'You're a pretty determined kid, aren't you, Benny Wellander?' Nettie's tone was wistful.

'Most people reckon I'm a wimp.' Benny lowered his head, the courage having drained out of him.

'A wimp wouldn't have come here today to fight for a little girl who has nothing to do with him.'

'She does.' He spoke in barely more than a whisper. 'You're my friend, and she's your baby, so I love her.'

'You're right. She is my baby.' There was a new resolve in Nettie's eyes. 'She's mine, and she should be in here with me.'

'Nettie?' Mary's lips had narrowed into a firm line, and she shifted on her feet.

'I'm not going to know what I feel until I hold her, Mum. The nurses said I could.'

Mary released a deep sigh. She glanced from Benny to Nettie then shrugged and left the room, calling for a nurse.

Benny and Nettie made small talk as they waited. Benny sensed he needed to distract Nettie as she prepared for what would surely be one of the biggest moments in her life. She still clutched his hand, like he used to hold his mum's when he was nervous.

A nurse entered with a wrapped bundle and Mary shuffled in behind. Nettie caught her breath as her baby was placed in her arms. She seemed awkward at first, as she struggled to position the infant. She looked to her mum for advice, and Mary moved forward to show her how to support the baby's head. Once she was more comfortable, Nettie gazed down in awe at the bundle she held.

'I can't believe she's the baby I've carried for the past nine months. Even so, I feel like I know her.'

'She looks exactly like you did as a newborn.' Mary stroked her granddaughter's downy red hair, visibly softening. Benny wondered what she was thinking. Would she love Beth too, and let Nettie keep her?

'She's beautiful.' Nettie's voice came out as a reverent whisper, as she pulled her daughter close. The baby whimpered, and she hushed her with a kiss and tender words. 'It's okay, Beth. Mummy's here.'

'You're really going to call her Beth?' Mary asked. 'It's such an old-fashioned name. You usually like everything new and modern.'

'It feels like this little girl's always had a name.' Nettie's eyes met Benny's, and they exchanged a smile. 'Do you want to hold her?'

'Dunno.' He did, but he was too frightened. 'She's so small. She might get scared.'

'She could never be scared of someone who loves her so much.'

Nettie was right. He did love this baby, even though he couldn't understand why. Benny nodded, and Nettie placed Beth in his arms. She was tiny. She barely weighed anything. Yet the weight of her life in his hands was heavy. Mary hovered, but Benny didn't need her help. Beth snuggled into him as though she belonged.

He held her more confidently than Nettie had, whispering as he looked down at her sleeping form. 'Hi, Bethy.'

Benny was barely aware of Mary and Nettie's watchful eyes as his heart burst for the little bundle in his arms. They couldn't say goodbye to her now, could they? Not if they loved her like he did.

Eventually, he realised it was time to leave. 'I'd better go.' He handed Beth back to Nettie and leaned down to hug them both. 'I'm gonna be in loads of trouble when I get home.'

'I'm sorry for causing that.' Nettie lifted her baby to her shoulder. 'But I'm glad you came.'

'You're not gonna change your mind again now, are you?'

Nettie shook her head firmly, and Benny was satisfied.

Once he was back outside, Benny switched his phone on and saw several messages from his dad. His heart raced as he rang his parents' number and steeled himself for Ola's response.

'Benny, where are you?' His mum sounded frantic. 'Are you okay, sweetheart? I've been worried sick.'

'Let me talk to him, Jan.' Ola's loud voice echoed over the line, and Benny waited for his angry explosion.

'I'm sorry, Dad,' he croaked. He had used up all his courage for the day. Probably for the year!

'Tell me where you are.' Ola sounded like he was stifling the urge to shout.

'I'm outside the hospital.'

'The hospital. What're you doing there?'

'Has he had an accident?' His mum's fear was palpable over the line.

'No. Tell Mum I'm fine. I came… I came on the bus, to see Nettie and her baby.'

'Stay there and I'll fetch you.' Ola hung up.

Twenty minutes later, Ola pulled up in the drop-off bay, waiting surprisingly patiently while Benny clambered into the passenger seat. Instead of heading home as Benny expected, he drove to the park in town and bought them both ice cream.

Could this day get any weirder? Benny had never eaten ice cream with his dad, only with his mum or Emma.

'So, tell me what happened.'

Ola listened with interest as Benny explained. He didn't get mad. He even seemed impressed by the stuff flowing effortlessly from Benny's lips. Benny was surprising himself. Had holding Beth given him extra words?

'I even got to cuddle her. She's cute, Dad; and Nettie's gonna keep her now.'

'Sounds as though that's partly thanks to you. You were very brave, son.' Having finished their ice creams, they stood to head back to the car. Benny was amazed when his dad reached out to give him a hug. It filled him with so much warmth that when Ola said the next words, they didn't scare Benny into trembling. 'Even so, you should've told me and your mum where you were going.'

Benny nodded. 'I know, but you would've said no.'

A smile crept onto his dad's face, then he laughed. 'Probably. Still, now I know you're more than capable of catching buses, there'll be no excuse for you not to run errands when I ask.'

'Mum won't let me.' Benny studied his toes.

'Your mother will have to learn.'

Back at home, Ola immediately put paid to Janet's fussing. 'He's okay, Jan. He only caught a bus. Most kids his age do.'

'How did you know where to go?' Janet gaped at Benny.

He was almost annoyed with the question but swallowed it down and answered her calmly. 'I rang Brian and asked, and I wrote it all down. I had my phone. I could've called if something was wrong.'

It looked like a swordfight was going on behind Janet's eyes. She didn't want to see him grow up. Accepting it would mean letting him go. Still, he loved his mum and when she drew him towards her, he let her hold him, happy to be her little boy again if only for a few moments.

It had been a momentous day. Benny was exhausted and overwhelmed by everything he had achieved. Was this what growing up felt like? And was that what he wanted?

20

'She's beautiful, Nettie.' Kerry leaned over Beth's pram with wonder in her eyes, stroking her tiny cheek with her little finger. 'A wonderful gift from God.'

Although Nettie didn't share Kerry's beliefs, she appreciated the sentiment. 'It'll be your turn next,' she teased as they stood together on her parents' driveway.

Kerry shook her head emphatically. 'Oh no. Neal and I aren't planning on having children for a while. We've got plenty of time.'

Nettie's mood sobered as she reflected on Kerry's words. 'I don't blame you. Babies are hard work.'

Kerry peered at her, probably noticing the dark circles around her eyes. 'Keeping you up, is she?'

A sigh escaped Nettie's lips. 'Sometimes she cries and cries. No matter what I do, nothing seems to work. It's weird. I love her so much. I'm sure I was right to keep her, but it's still so hard. She's taken over my whole life.'

Nettie wouldn't be going back to work for a while, and when the time came, she wondered how she would cope. What would she do with Beth? She hadn't dared broach the subject with her mum. Mary was still struggling to come to terms with her choices.

As if on cue, Beth let out a wail. Nettie lifted her out of the pram and stood rocking her daughter, feeling helpless to calm the crying.

A door opened further down the street, and Karen Moss stepped out, cradling her own infant. 'Giving you a hard time, is she, Nettie?' Karen smiled.

'I'm sure you must have all heard her, the amount of noise she makes when she gets going.'

Karen shot Nettie a look of sympathy, then beckoned. 'Want a cuppa?'

Nettie wasn't sure if she should leave Kerry, but her friend soon settled it. 'You go. I've got to visit my mum.' Kerry excused herself, crossing the road to her parents' house.

Karen's warmth drew Nettie in as she accepted the older woman's suggestion. She pushed the pram with one hand while holding Beth in the crook of her arm and approached Karen's door.

'You can park it in here.' Karen pointed into her hallway.

Nettie gingerly manoeuvred the large and cumbersome object into the house. She'd had nothing when Beth was born because she hadn't been expecting to keep her. Mary had reluctantly helped her get the necessities, finding this pram at a local charity shop. Nettie had been shocked. She didn't think her mum had ever stepped foot in a charity shop before.

'I hope she doesn't disturb Marcus.' Nettie followed Karen into the kitchen, where the more experienced mother placed her baby in a Moses basket and prepared the tea.

'He's just been fed. He should stay quiet for a while if we're lucky.'

'I've fed Beth too, but that doesn't seem to shut her up.' Nettie jostled her squirming baby, noticing that Beth felt heavy and aware her observation was fuelled by exhaustion.

'Seeing how far she can push you, is she?' Karen reached out, and Beth quietened in her arms.

'How did you do that?' Nettie leaned against a worktop.

'Years of practice.'

Karen's motherliness made her want to cry. A lump rose in her throat as she looked away. 'Will I ever get better at this?' she asked.

Having expertly made a cuppa one-handed, Karen passed it over. 'Of course you will. It's only been two weeks. Beth still needs to settle into a routine, and you have to get used to being her mummy.'

'Did I do the right thing, Karen?' The tears were falling. Nettie could do nothing to stem the flow.

'I don't think you need me to answer that.'

Nettie nodded, aware of how much she loved her daughter even though they were still getting used to one another. 'Every time she cries, and I get stressed, I see my mum looking at me. I know what she's thinking.'

'It's difficult for mothers when we see our daughters going through hard things. We instinctively want to do everything we can to protect them. You'll discover that for yourself one day with Beth.'

Nettie laughed through her tears. Imagining Beth as a teenager was more than she could handle.

Time with Karen replenished her, and she left a few hours later feeling refreshed. Beth was calmer having been fed and changed yet again, and Nettie had observed the differences in the way Karen handled her. She had also seen Karen breastfeeding Marcus and was astonished by the ease with which she did it. Karen could do most things with Marcus at her breast. She carried him around in a sling much of the time, letting him feed whenever he wanted to. When Nettie had decided to keep Beth, she had convinced herself breastfeeding would be too painful, taking her mum's advice and putting her daughter on the bottle. Now she found making up bottles and keeping them at the right temperature yet another stress to add into the mix.

'Are you still sulking?' Ola turned to Benny as he swung his red Ford onto their driveway.

Benny shook his head, then regretted the action when his brain swam.

'You know why I had to do it,' his dad continued.

'You didn't. I'm okay.'

'You weren't when I had to carry you out to the car a few hours ago.' Ola switched off the engine. 'You ought to be glad I talked your mother out of calling an ambulance.'

'I guess,' Benny sighed.

He had just started his third year of secondary school. His dad kept telling him it was going to be important, with big choices to make. Benny just wanted to ignore that and hope it passed quickly.

Ola climbed out of the car and Benny made to follow. However, an unexpected attack of dizziness had him clutching onto the door

'You see?' His father rushed to his side to steady him. 'Not quite as okay as you pretend to be, are you?'

Benny shrugged, fighting the annoying urge to cry that always plagued him most after a seizure. This morning he had suffered two in succession, and it was after they struggled to rouse him following the second that his dad had insisted on driving him to the hospital.

'Still feeling sick?'

They'd had to pull over half-way home for him to vomit into the grass verge. He still felt embarrassed that Ola had been forced to hold him up while he was sick. It hadn't worried him so much when he was younger. Now his bouts of sickness annoyed him. Yet he was grateful his father handled it all better these days. So much so that Benny preferred turning to him because he remained calm, whereas his mum's panic made things worse.

'Let's get you inside before you fall down.'

Benny allowed himself a moment of weakness as he leaned into the safety of his dad's embrace.

'You're all right, Benny. I've got you.'

As they neared the house, the all-too familiar sounds of Beth's wailing reached their ears. Ola sighed. 'Sounds like that friend of yours is still having problems with her baby.'

Benny looked across to where a frazzled-looking Nettie paced her parents' garden with five-month-old Beth screaming in her arms. 'I bet she brought her out cos her mum and dad were giving her funny looks.'

Nettie had confided her parents' impatience with Beth's crying when they went out for an ice cream on her seventeenth birthday. He was so proud that she wanted to spend time with him, and they'd chatted in the park for a couple of hours while he held Beth to give his friend a break. Nettie made him relax and talk more than anyone else ever had. She asked for his opinions, and he was discovering he had them. They discussed things he'd never considered before. Nettie challenged him, making him feel more mature. Benny realised he was accustomed to having all his decisions made by his parents, but Nettie was encouraging him to take control of his own life.

'You're your own person, Benny,' she urged. 'You've got a right to express what you feel.'

He had never seen it like that, always considering himself to be clueless and incapable of feeling anything worthy of expression. Nettie gave his self-confidence an unexpected boost.

'Should I invite her over for a coffee?' Ola's question startled him. 'Having Beth in the house will give your mum someone else to fuss over and take the pressure off you while you recover.'

Ola smiled, and Benny nodded, thrilled at the prospect of seeing his friend and her baby. He had made plans to spend his Saturday with Damian, but it would be unsafe to go out on his bike after the seizures. He'd sent Damo a text while they were in the car. Benny suspected he would be forced to spend the afternoon resting. It would be more fun with Nettie to talk to and Beth to cuddle.

Nettie's eyes widened at Ola's offer. However, she gladly accepted, passing Beth into Janet's eager arms as soon as she stepped through the door.

Benny headed into the garden and grabbed a seat, then dusted the leaves off another for Nettie, who sank into it with a grateful smile. His parents soon joined them with Beth. Ola carried two drinks, one of which he passed to Nettie. Wary of him at first, Nettie gradually relaxed as they sipped and talked. Her eyebrows went up when Ola unexpectedly took her daughter from Janet.

Benny was amazed too as Beth babbled up at his dad. Ola spoke back to her, not in the sing-song way Janet used with small children, but in a more adult tone, as if he expected the baby to understand.

'She's going to be a bright one, Nettie.' He spoke confidently whilst disentangling Beth's fingers from his glasses.

'Right now I just wish she'd sleep.' Nettie groaned as she dipped another biscuit in her tea.

Benny slid the plate away from her with a boyish wink.

'What did you do that for?' She scowled.

'You said you didn't wanna get fat.'

'Yes, but I didn't say you could steal my biscuits.'

'They're not yours. They're my mum's.' He poked his tongue out, and Nettie jabbed him with her elbow. His dad laughed, and Benny realised he was enjoying being teased, something he'd never appreciated when he was younger.

A text alert sounded on Nettie's phone. She glanced down to see who it was from.

'What's wrong?' Benny noticed her subtle change of expression.

'That was Kerry.' Nettie cast her phone aside. 'She's in town with Erin and Emma. They wanted to know if I'd go shopping, but I can't.'

'How come?' Benny asked.

'What would I do with Beth?' Nettie sighed wistfully. 'She gets stroppy if I take her shopping. I guess this is what my mum tried to warn me about. I've got to learn to put up with it and accept that my life will be different from now on.'

'You can still have fun sometimes, can't you?' He didn't think shopping sounded fun, but Nettie clearly did.

'Not according to Mum.' She leaned back in her chair looking defeated.

A spark of an idea formed in Benny's mind. 'You could go if someone else looked after Beth.'

'Yes, but who? Mum's not going to do it. She's out to prove a point.'

'I will.' He was sure she wouldn't like the idea, so added, 'Me and my mum.' Nettie knew about his seizures, and with today having already started badly there was no way he would offer to care for Beth alone. Besides, he had never looked after a baby. Even so, he was good at soothing Beth when she cried. Hadn't he proved that already? Although he didn't know about changing nappies or making up bottles, his mum could show him. None of it could be as complicated as Maths, English or Science.

'You'd really want to look after my baby?' Nettie drew her brows together.

How could he make her see? Benny reached out to take Beth from his dad, holding her protectively. 'I said I would. She likes me, don't you, Bethy?'

Beth smiled up at him. Surely that was her way of saying she liked him a lot?

From the next chair, he heard his mum's fretting voice. 'You should be resting.'

Benny braced himself for the moan that would put paid to Nettie's plans. However, his dad surprised him again by stepping in. 'Holding babies means a lot of sitting down, so he should be fine.' Ola rose as he spoke, preparing to leave for his game of golf with Peter. 'Like he said, you'll be here to keep an eye on them both.' He turned his attention to Nettie. 'Enjoy yourself, young lady. You won't get too many offers like this, so make the most of them when you do.'

'She'll have lots from me.' Benny smiled. 'Me and Beth get each other, don't we, Bethy?' he tickled her under the chin and the baby laughed.

Nettie dashed off a response to Kerry, then rose to hug Benny with her daughter between them. 'Thank you. I'll just pop home to put my face on, then I'll catch the bus into town. I'll be back before four, alright?'

Benny glanced at the time on his phone. Nearly three hours to cuddle Beth. Yeah, he'd like that a lot.

❧

When Nettie returned, she showed her gratitude by taking Benny to the park and buying him an ice cream from the shop. Nettie felt guilty for always resorting to the same treat, but it was the only thing he ever wanted.

'It'll be easy for your future girlfriend to find the way to your heart,' she teased. They sat together on a bench with their Cornettos, Beth sleeping beside them in her pram. Nettie hadn't been an ice cream fan before she met Benny, but his passion for it was converting her.

'No one's never gonna wanna go out with me.' He spoke absent-mindedly while watching a group of children jostling over whose turn it was to go down the slide.

'What makes you so sure?' Nettie was always questioning him, never letting him get away with his negative self-assessment.

'Cos I say stupid stuff, I'm rubbish at school, I have seizures and I throw up all the time.'

Nettie tried not to laugh at his comical answer, but she also felt an urge to encourage him. 'Someone will see past all that one day.' She wanted to put an arm around his narrow shoulders but thought better of it. 'You've got to let people get to know the real you.'

'I get scared of people.'

'You're never scared around me or Damo.' She had seen the two boys cavorting on their bikes, and she knew Damian brought out another side of Benny.

'That's different. You're my friends.'

'You could have more friends.'

'I don't need loads.' He reached for her hand and Nettie had no qualms about letting him take it. 'Only you and Damo.'

Nettie felt honoured to be included as one of the special people in his life. She hoped she would never let him down. She sensed Benny would be easily hurt. Although Emma had warned her he could become difficult, she hadn't yet seen that side of him. 'Thanks for what you did for me today. I needed a break from Beth.'

'I like looking after her.' Benny grinned, still holding her hand. 'Even when I've gotta change her smelly nappies.'

'You were looking rough earlier. I felt bad leaving you.'

'I'm okay now.' He lapsed into thoughtfulness. 'I reckon having Beth helped. You can't think about your problems when someone else needs you. I know I can't never look after her by myself. But Mum doesn't go far, and I reckon she likes making a fuss of Beth as much as she likes babying me.' They both laughed and Benny reluctantly released Nettie's hand.

From then on, Nettie found herself with a regular babysitter, and Benny's bond with Beth grew. He even discovered he could focus more on his studies with her in his arms. Beth's warmth and need for comfort settled his brain and stopped him panicking over the things he struggled to understand. Even Brian noticed it when he came to tutor him when Beth was at the house.

Damian, on the other hand, teased him mercilessly. 'I wouldn't want to look after someone's kid! I don't get you sometimes.'

'I don't get you wanting to kiss girls,' Benny responded. 'Girls are stupid.' He thought better of his rash statement as he gazed down at Beth eagerly sucking from her bottle. 'Except for Nettie. She's different.'

'She's still a girl.' Damo laughed.

'She's not a silly giggly one.'

'Even Beth's a girl.' Damian pointed at the baby with disdain.

'She's not gonna be a stupid one, are you, Bethy?' Benny put the bottle down and lifted Beth to his shoulder to bring up her wind, causing Damian to look away in disgust.

'I guess you won't want to catch the bus into town with me this afternoon then.'

'I will when Nettie gets back.'

Travelling on buses had become more familiar since the incident at the hospital, and Ola had given him a grilling on which ones went where.

'I'll meet you outside Tesco.'

Damian left placated, and Benny enjoyed what he considered to be an ideal Saturday. He spent the morning taking care of Beth, followed by an afternoon watching Damo waste his pocket money on CD's and computer games. He was no longer the little boy who gazed wistfully up and down the street watching everyone come and go and wishing he had a friend. Janet had lost her primary place in his world, yet he still loved her as much as ever. He earned his dad's favour by mowing the lawn and emptying the bins, and even Emma criticised him less frequently.

The only blot on the horizon was his schoolwork. Benny figured that was a lost cause, so why worry about it?

21

Nettie went back to work when Beth was six months old and was pleasantly surprised when her mum offered to care for Beth in her absence. Karen had been right. They were settling into a routine, although Beth was still a more demanding baby than Marcus.

One evening in November, Nettie, Emma, Erin, and Kerry met for a girls' night at Kerry and Neal's house. Neal was attending the men's fellowship group at their church, leaving Kerry free to invite her closest friends for pizza and a film.

Nettie was grateful for an opportunity to go out alone. Beth slept through most nights now, so leaving after putting her to bed caused few problems for Mary and John.

Emma arrived late. She stormed into the room, throwing off her coat in disgust.

'What's eating at you?' Kerry asked. Emma always wore her heart on her sleeve.

'My brother,' Emma spat.

'What's he done now?'

'Just when I thought he was growing up, he went and showed me how much of a child he still is!'

'Tears and temper tantrums?' Clearly, Erin knew the drill.

'And then some. I had to get away before I did or said something I'd end up regretting. Mum was babying him like she always does.'

'He was okay when I saw him yesterday,' Nettie felt someone needed to stick up for Benny.

'I told you. He only shows you his better side. You ought to try living with him!'

'What upset him?' There had to be a reason for Benny's odd behaviour.

'I bet I can guess.' Erin patted the sofa for Emma to sit next to her. 'I warned you there'd be fireworks when he found out we're searching for a flat to share. Benny hates change. Losing you was always going to come as a massive blow. I can't believe you didn't expect it.'

'He doesn't understand anything.' Emma tossed her head. 'It's impossible to even try talking to him about serious things. He'll always be a child.'

Emma calmed down as the evening wore on, seeming to forget about her row with Benny, but Nettie resolved to do all she could to help.

Her opportunity came the following morning when she spotted Benny heading down the street on his bike.

'Benny, wait!' Nettie stood in her parents' front garden flagging him down. She could immediately see something was wrong. He got off his bike, wheeled it to where she stood, and stared at her forlornly. 'What's got you in a grumpy strop?'

She hoped her use of one of his favourite phrases would make him smile. This time it didn't have the desired effect.

'Emmie's moving out.' Benny's expression was downcast, as though he was announcing the end of the world.

Nettie's heart went out to him. Benny's life was so limited that every change struck him as monumental. 'Yes. I heard she and Erin are looking for a flat.'

'It's not fair,' he sulked.

'Not fair on whom?'

He shrugged, and his attention turned to the pavement.

'On you?' Nettie pressed.

Benny nodded, and she saw the glint of tears in his eyes.

'She's my sister.' Even Benny seemed to realise he sounded pathetic as he screwed up his nose in a gesture of self-disgust.

'She's an adult now, and she wants more independence. You'll understand when you get to her age.'

'Mum reckons I'll always live at home with her and Dad.'

'I'm sure that's what she wants.' Was Nettie saying too much? 'I bet you'll want to move out one day.'

'I won't wanna go nowhere.' Benny sounded convinced. 'I only like being here.'

Nettie could sense he was backing down, ashamed of his outburst. 'If you love Emma as much as you say you do, you'll be happy for her. It's not as if she and Erin are planning on going far.' Both girls had local jobs. It made sense for them to stay in the area.

'Emmie hates me now.'

'No she doesn't.' Nettie bridged the space between them with an outstretched hand. 'She's pretty cross. I saw that last night, but she'll never hate you. Brothers and sisters squabble all the time. Even when they're grown up.' Explaining things to Benny came naturally. Nettie found she could do so without resorting to a patronising tone.

'I wasn't being grown-up, Nettie. I was being a baby.' He looked straight at her this time.

Maintaining eye-contact was a rare thing for Benny. Nettie felt honoured that he trusted her enough to let her into his world so completely, making himself vulnerable enough to admit his failings.

'Well you're not now.' A warm look passed between them that Nettie couldn't read. It had been happening a lot lately. She kept dismissing it by telling herself Benny was just an affectionate boy who was always open about his feelings.

'I'm gonna say sorry.'

'Good for you.' She smiled to show her approval and squeezed his hand. 'When you're done, come back here and we'll go somewhere together.' She was about to turn away, but added, 'Not just to the park this time. I need to broaden your horizons.'

'You what?' He looked confused.

'Trust me.'

Benny returned a short while later, his change of expression telling Nettie everything she needed to know. 'I said sorry, and Emmie is ok now. She said she was proud of me for owning up to my mistake.'

'There you go.' Nettie flashed him a smile. 'I knew she'd be fine.'

'I had to say sorry to Dad too. He hates it when I go off in a grumpy strop. I don't want him to stop liking me again.'

'How did that go?' Nettie asked.

'He gave me a hug and thanked me for trying.'

Feeling proud of him, Nettie took Benny to town in her car. She had passed her driving test quickly and had been thrilled when Ola helped her parents find her a reliable used vehicle.

With Beth in her car-seat, Nettie drove to her favourite café, where they sat outside sharing cake and drinking hot chocolate, whilst chatting and watching the world go by.

~⚘~

'What's going on, Nettie?' Kerry stared at her with probing eyes as Nettie showed her some recent photographs of Beth.

'How do you mean?' Nettie sounded distracted.

Kerry responded by pointing at one of the images. Nettie held Beth, while Benny stood with his arm looped through hers, his head resting against her shoulder. They were both grinning, and Beth chuckled at the camera. At nine months, Nettie thought her baby had one of the best belly laughs she had ever heard.

'You and Benny,' Kerry said pointedly.

'What about us? He's a good friend, and he's great with Beth.'

'You sure that's all it is?' Kerry folded her arms. 'Seems like a weird friendship with a fourteen-year-old boy. You're spending a lot of time together.'

'I suppose.' Nettie had nothing further to say.

'Doesn't that seem odd? I mean, shouldn't you prefer hanging around with someone your own age?'

'What difference does age make?' Nettie couldn't hide the hurt in her voice. Kerry's Christian values usually made her more understanding.

'I guess it depends on how you see him.'

'Well he's… He's just Benny.' Nettie laughed self-consciously.

'And his sister is one of your best friends.' Kerry took a sip of her tea. 'He's young for his age, Nettie. We all know that.'

'Not so much anymore. He's changed.' Why did she feel the urge to rush to Benny's defence?

'And most of that has been down to you. Even Emma's seen it. It was you who got him to back down when he was in a state about her leaving home.'

'He sometimes needs someone to explain things, that's all. He's lived a sheltered life.'

'That's what I mean.' Kerry pointed at the picture. 'If I didn't know better, by looking at this I'd presume the two of you were a couple.'

'That's ridiculous!'

'Then how come you don't seem to want a boyfriend?' Kerry fixed Nettie with a challenging stare. 'You push away all the guys who act like they're interested. I know there have been a few.'

'Most of them back off when they find out about Beth.' Nettie gathered up her photographs, wishing she hadn't shared them with Kerry after all.

'But Benny's never minded...'

'He's like a little brother to me,' Nettie stammered. She couldn't believe what Kerry was hinting at.

'The girl in that photo didn't look like she saw him that way.'

Nettie found the photograph again and studied it more closely. Realisation dawned. Why hadn't she seen it before? She hadn't been looking at the camera when a stranger in the park offered to take their picture. She had eyes only for Benny, her smile revealing her affection. Kerry was right. How long had she been in denial?

Kerry reached for her hand and squeezed it tightly. 'When did it happen, Nettie?'

'I don't know.' Nettie gulped. 'I'm not even sure what *it* is. I just know...' She rose to pace the room, musing over how many times she had seen Benny do the same thing during an intense conversation. He said pacing helped him concentrate. 'I enjoy being with him, Kerry. He makes me laugh like no one ever has before, and he's great with Beth.'

'Of course he is, but you must know it can never go anywhere. Not with him being so young. Plus, there are his other problems.'

'What do you think I should do?' Nettie asked.

'Pull away, for both your sakes.'

'Don't worry about Benny. Any feelings are only on my side. He just sees me as a friend, and he loves any excuse to be around Beth. I know there can never be anything between us other than friendship, and I can handle it.'

Kerry looked unconvinced.

22

'So, tell me all about it!' Nettie sat in the Wellanders' lounge with Emma one late February afternoon. It was pelting it down with rain outside but fortunately, Beth had stayed asleep in her buggy when Nettie had manoeuvred her into the hall. Emma and Erin had found a flat, and Nettie wanted to know everything.

'It's small but exactly what we need, and it's affordable.' Emma looked pleased with herself.

'Have you broken the news to your family yet?' Nettie hesitated to ask.

'Yes, and they were fine.'

'Even Benny?'

'Even Benny.' Emma ran her fingers through her hair. 'He barely reacted. I think his mind is on choosing his GCSE subjects, though I doubt his choices will make much difference.'

'What do you mean?' A protective instinct rose in Nettie's belly.

'He'll most likely fail them all. I've been trying to help him.' Emma sighed. 'It's a pretty fruitless exercise.'

As if to counteract his sister's negative thoughts, Benny chose that moment to bound into the room, a proud grin lighting up his pale face. 'Emmie, I did it!' He threw his hands into the air in a show of pure glee, then blushed as his eyes caught Nettie's.

Beth stirred and whimpered, so Benny rushed to pick her up. 'Sorry, Bethy. I didn't know you were sleeping,' he said from the hall and emerged moments later with Beth in his arms.

'Don't worry. She was due to wake up soon. If she sleeps too long in the afternoons, she's awake all night.' Nettie longed to see the joy return to his face. He had looked young and alive in his moment of euphoria. 'So tell us. What did you do?'

'I passed my science test.' Benny tickled Beth under the chin and her cries turned to giggles. 'I'm not so thick after all, Bethy.'

He sobered and met his sister's gaze. 'It's okay, Emmie. I know it was cos of Brian. Science is his best subject, and he's good at explaining stuff.'

'I'm sure he helped, but you had to do your bit too.' Emma rose to hug him. 'Well done, Pestie. I'm proud of you.'

'Me too.' Nettie took her turn at giving him a hug. He felt so comfortable in her arms, his skinny frame moulding into her body. She pushed the thought swiftly from her mind and pulled away.

As Emma watched her brother enjoying Nettie's hug, alarm bells rang in her head. She had already observed how Benny acted differently around Nettie. He did things for her without being asked. Every word of praise or affirmation from her lips seemed to make him swell with pride. He stood taller, spoke more carefully, and showed genuine concern for hers and Beth's wellbeing. Was her baby brother experiencing his first crush?

She cornered Damian the following day when he came to meet Benny for a bike ride. 'Benny's never had a girlfriend, has he?'

'No. He doesn't seem interested,' Damian answered.

'You sure about that, Damo?' Emma probed. 'That's not what I saw yesterday when he was with Nettie.'

'Benny and Nettie?' Damian scoffed. 'As if he'd get that lucky!'

Not convinced by Damian's quick dismissal, Emma felt she had to confront her brother. She was due to move out that weekend. This might be her last chance. She made hot chocolate when Benny returned home and asked him to sit with her.

'I'm still gonna miss you, Emmie.' Benny was handling it more maturely now.

Emma smiled and reached for his hand. Her brother was still a compulsive hand holder. 'I'll miss you too.'

'No you won't.'

'I will, Pestie.' She looked lovingly into his eyes, seeing glimpses of the man he might become if their mum ever allowed it. Although his voice was on the verge of breaking, he still had the looks and many of the mannerisms of a child. His skinniness didn't help, and most of his clothes were shabby and hung off him. He had no interest in his appearance, but gone were the days when he walked around in stained t-shirts with his hair sticking up, and he no longer needed Janet to remind him to wash his face or clean his teeth. Emma realised he made more of an effort when Nettie was around.

'So can I come and see you?' Benny was asking.

'As long as it's not all the time.' She smiled and sipped her hot chocolate, still holding his hand. 'You'll have a lot more going on during the next couple of years.'

'You mean with my GCSE's and stuff?' He paused. 'I still dunno what to do, Emmie. Whatever subjects I pick, I'll be rubbish.'

'Go into it with that attitude and you will.'

'You sound like Dad.' He grinned, and they both laughed.

'I didn't just mean your exams,' she pressed. 'Lots of things will change. You're bound to find a girlfriend one day.'

'No I won't.' He spoke with such confidence that Emma was taken aback. 'I told Nettie. No one's never gonna wanna go out with me.'

'You might be surprised; but about Nettie...' she wasn't sure where to begin, desperate to keep him engaged so he would understand. 'I can see the two of you are close, and... Well, you know that's bound to change, don't you?'

'How d'you mean?' Benny's face looked almost ghostly in the dimming light.

'You've been a big help to her during this first year with Beth, but she's more settled now, and... She's bound to want more out of life than just being our friend and Beth's mum. She's had boyfriends before. There was at least one because she got pregnant.'

Benny shook his head. 'Nettie's not interested in boys.'

'She hasn't had time for a relationship lately. She'll have more of it once Beth grows up.'

'Doesn't matter. She doesn't want a boyfriend. She told me.'

'What if that changes?' Emma pressed on. 'How would you feel if one day you found out Nettie had a boyfriend?'

'Dunno.' He shrugged.

'Don't give me your standard "I don't wanna talk about this" answer, Benny Wellander.' Emma tried not to let her exasperation show. 'You know it's likely that one day you'll have to face seeing Nettie with another man.'

'It wouldn't be *another man*, cos I'm not a man. I'm a stupid little kid.'

Emma saw the tears threatening and feared they were in for one of his tantrums. However, Benny pulled himself together and took another swig of his hot chocolate.

'You really like her, don't you?' This was more serious than Emma had feared.

'There's no point talking about all this stuff.' He rose to pace. 'It's stupid.'

'No, it's not.' Emma stood and pulled him into her arms. 'There's nothing stupid about thinking you've fallen for a girl, and it must be very confusing because it's your first time.'

'I hate thinking about her with someone else, Emmie.'

He was crying on her shoulder, and Emma was glad Janet was out grocery shopping. These weren't childish tears of temper or rage. Benny was simply struggling to understand the complex emotions that went along with growing up. She held him and let him cry it out. 'This habit you have of pushing away the things that hurt or challenge you... You've been doing it all your life. It's not good, Benny.'

He nodded, telling her he understood.

'I've gotta push this away. Nettie's seventeen and she'll never be interested in me. It doesn't matter if I can't stand thinking about her and Beth with no one else, cos it's gonna happen one day, isn't it? If I want her to still be my friend, I'm gonna have to make out I'm not bothered and pretend I'm happy and stuff.'

'Do you think you can?' Emma asked.

'I'll have to.' Benny pulled away and wiped his eyes with the back of a hand. 'I'm still not gonna think about it now. I can't. I wanna enjoy being with her while I can.'

What could Emma say to that? She hugged him again, even tighter than before, loving him more than ever.

'Emma said some stuff tonight about me and Nettie.' Benny lay on his bed talking to Damian on his mobile phone. He needed to be honest with his friend. Damo knew more about girls than he did.

'Like what?' Silence stretched between them. What was Damo expecting him to say? Had he guessed Benny's feelings for Nettie were growing?

'She wants me to get ready for when Nettie finds a boyfriend. Someone her own age.' The image of Nettie with another boy made Benny's head hurt.

'I guess that will happen.'

'Nettie told me she's not interested in none of that stuff. She's too busy with Beth.'

'Benny, what's really going on?' Damian probed. 'I reckon there's more than you're saying.'

'Emma said I don't face hard stuff.' Benny looked towards the window, unaware of his surroundings. His mind was consumed by his problem.

'She's right; you don't. The way you're handling your GCSE choices proves it. You're hoping burying your head in the sand will make it all go away. Well, it won't. You're gonna have to face it.'

'I just figure there's stuff I can't do nothing about, so why worry?'

'Only you do worry.' Damo knew him too well. 'There's stuff you're not facing about Nettie, isn't there?'

Benny nodded, although he knew Damian couldn't see him.

'Fallen for her, haven't you?'

'I dunno!' Benny's voice sounded panicked. 'How can I know when I've never felt none of this stuff before? I never thought I would.'

'Just because you're a slow learner doesn't mean you're not gonna have normal feelings, mate. Falling for a girl... That's about as normal as it gets.' Damian waited for a reply that never came. Benny had no answer. 'Benny? This is gonna be really awkward, but someone's gotta help you understand. So, what kind of stuff are you feeling for Nettie?'

'Stuff I don't wanna talk about, not even with my best mate.'

Damian chuckled. 'It's normal, Benny.'

'It's not!' The pitch of Benny's voice rose with his growing agitation. 'I don't understand none of it, and I can't tell no one. Not even you.'

'You don't need to. I know. And I'm not gonna blab if that's what you're worried about.'

'I get made fun of enough as it is.' Benny's tone contained an edge of bitterness. 'Dale Moss would love telling everyone Weedy Wellander fancies Nettie Thompson.'

'He's had girlfriends,' Damo encouraged. 'Lots of them.'

'He doesn't think I will. No one does.'

'Are you…' Damian faltered. 'Are you having thoughts about Nettie you wouldn't want to talk about?'

'Yeah.'

Benny buried his head in his pillow. Argh. He couldn't hide forever. Stupid! When he spoke again, his voice was muffled. 'Some things never meant nothing to me before, but now they kind of do. I mean, I never saw the point. You know?' Benny heard a snort of laughter from his friend. 'Don't laugh at me!' Was Damo going to start acting like Dale?

'Sorry, mate.' Damian sounded genuine. 'But you're acting like you're the first bloke to find a gorgeous girl like Nettie hot, and you're not. I get it.'

'This is getting too weird.' Benny searched for a way to lighten the mood and came up with the only thing he could think of. 'You're bugging me, Damo.'

Damian roared with laughter, but Benny soon realised his mate wasn't ready to back down in his efforts to help him face the truth. 'So what're you gonna do about it?'

'I said you're bugging me.'

'Grow up, Benny.'

'Yeah, okay.' Benny sighed. 'There's nothing I can do, is there? She'll never wanna be my girlfriend. I've gotta forget about it. I'm just her mate who sometimes helps with Beth.'

'I wonder if she feels more for you than that?'

Benny scoffed.

'Nah, hear me out. Some things don't add up. You two act like a weird couple sometimes. It's like… Maybe there is more going on than either of you wants to admit.'

'I'd be too scared to tell her. She'd say stuff about what a nice kid I am, and she'd stop hanging around with me cos it'd be weird.'

'Then you'll have to keep your feelings to yourself and hope they go away.' Damian's gran was calling, and he said he'd be there in a minute.

'I don't think they will.' Benny rose and paced from his bed to the window, to the door and back again. 'I wish she was my age, or I was older. Yeah, that'd be better, if I was older.'

'You can't do anything about how old you are.' Damian's response was practical, even if it wasn't what Benny wanted to hear.

'I'm sick of being a kid, Damo. It feels like I always will be.'

'I know what you mean.' Except he couldn't. Damian's family had treated him as an adult at a much earlier age. He didn't have a mum determined to keep him as her baby.

'Come on, mate.' Damian's tone brightened. 'You've changed loads since I've known you.'

'Nettie says that too, and Emmie. But it's not enough though, is it?'

❦

On the day Erin and Emma moved into their new flat, Ola and Peter borrowed a van, while Janet and Karen handled the breakables with care. Karen asked Nettie to look after Marcus, so Nettie took the babies along to watch what was happening. She didn't want to miss out on sharing in her two friends' big adventure. She was excited for them, yet wondered if she would ever have their courage to go it alone.

Erin was fuming because Dale had found an excuse not to help. However, Benny surprised them by offering to lend a hand in his place. It seemed that now he'd adjusted to the idea of his sister moving out, he was determined to help.

'What if the exertion makes him ill?' Janet fretted. 'He might drop something and get upset?'

Fortunately, Ola appeared confident in his son's newfound ability to obey instructions. Nettie was pleased when he stood up for Benny and allowed him to help. 'Do what I ask, and it'll be okay. Don't presume you know what needs doing. Wait to be told.' He laid the law down from the outset, and Benny kept quiet and busy for the next few hours.

'You're a great help. Don't know what we would've done without you.' Peter patted Benny's back as he passed by carrying yet more boxes. 'How can two girls have so much stuff?'

That made Nettie giggle. They didn't have nearly so much as her and Beth.

'You're stronger than I realised.' Ola smiled as his son helped him carry a wardrobe up the awkward metal staircase.

Nettie also watched him work with a sense of pride. The little boy who had dropped his ice cream on the day they met had come a long way. He might look like a gust of wind would blow him over, but he could hold his own with the older men.

By the end of the day, Benny was exhausted. Although he had never worked so hard, he wasn't about to confess his tiredness to his dad. His mum sensed it though and insisted on taking him home. They sat together in the garden sharing a pot of tea while Ola took the van back, and Erin and Emma settled into their new flat.

'I'm going to miss her so much,' Janet admitted.

'Me too.' Benny snuggled closer to his mum as they watched the sun set, jumping awake several minutes later. He had dozed off with his head on her shoulder.

'Go to bed, sweetheart.' Janet hugged him tenderly, and Benny made his way up the stairs.

'Thanks for your help today.' Ola stood in his bedroom doorway half an hour later, and Benny pretended he hadn't already been asleep.

'It's okay.' He yawned, stretched, and reached to pick up his phone. He had vaguely heard a text alert but had been too tired to bother finding out what it was. It was from Nettie.

'You did a good job today. You're pretty strong under all that skinniness.'

He dashed off a reply, turned over, and went straight back to sleep, too tired to think about the fact that his sister might never sleep in their parents' house again.

23

One Saturday morning in March, Nettie was strolling down the street pushing the buggy when Beth let out a loud squeal. Nettie instantly guessed why. They were passing the Wellander house. Beth knew where Benny lived, and she wanted to see him. She just didn't have the vocabulary to say so.

'Not today, Bethy.' Nettie felt especially lonely and fragile. If she saw Benny, it would be harder than ever to resist saying or doing something that might damage their relationship beyond repair. She was constantly reminding herself of his age, but he hadn't seemed so young when he was lifting Emma and Erin's heavy furniture.

Beth refused to be pacified, even when Nettie tried distracting her with a favourite toy. 'Anyone would think you're trying to match-make!' She smiled down at her daughter, and Beth babbled as though she was ready to start a conversation. 'So, you want to see your friend Benny, do you?'

Beth waved her arms gleefully, happy because she was about to have her way.

'All right, Bethy. You win. Mummy will be brave. You've got to help me though. You can't let me make a fool of myself over a fourteen-year-old boy.'

Nettie parked the buggy on the driveway, lifted Beth out and knocked on the front door, which was opened by a smiling Janet.

'Morning, Nettie.' When Janet reached for the baby, Beth ignored her cuddles and looked past her into the house.

'Sorry, Jan. I don't think it's you she's come to see.' They laughed together as Nettie followed her inside, and Janet encouraged Beth to call Benny's name.

Benny was in the kitchen with Ola, opening birthday cards. Beth tried to wrestle herself free of Janet's grasp as soon as she saw him, and Janet struggled not to drop her as she handed her over. Abandoning his cards, Benny gave Beth a loving squeeze. She chattered away at him in her own language.

Nettie watched Benny closely. His love for Beth was obvious, but what about his feelings for her? He hadn't caught her eye like he usually did.

'We were going for a walk,' Nettie explained. 'And it looks like she won't be satisfied unless you come with us. Hey. Is it your birthday?' She pointed at the cards.

Benny nodded, still not looking her way.

'We're having a birthday breakfast,' Janet put in.

Nettie looked at the array of food Janet had prepared, aware Benny probably wouldn't eat any of it. 'Are you doing anything nice afterwards?'

'I told you. I don't do birthdays.' Benny murmured.

'We can't have that,' Nettie grinned at Janet, whose face had resumed a look of despair as Benny fed his toast to Beth.

'How about I buy you ice cream after breakfast? Nettie said.'

Benny finally glanced her way, rewarding her with one of the smiles she was growing to love.

'If that's alright with you, Jan?'

'He'd eat it for breakfast, dinner and tea if we let him.' Ola looked up from his newspaper and waved at Beth in Benny's arms.

'Of course,' Janet said as Benny jumped up and practically ran out of the door.

Once outside, Nettie tried putting her daughter back in the buggy, but Beth cried and clung to Benny.

He carried her all the way to the park, telling her about the people and places they passed. Many of his observances amused Nettie, such as his description of a neighbour's untidy garden.

'Auntie Jan would wanna tidy that up, Bethy. She says he's lazy.'

Nettie had never heard him talk so freely. His chatter didn't stop when they reached the park, and she handed him the Cornish ice cream she'd nipped inside the inn to buy.

189

'Posh stuff today?' Benny studied the chocolate-covered cone.

'Of course. It's your birthday.'

He grinned, sharing the ice-cream with Beth.

'You're honoured, Bethy,' Nettie reached out to stroke her daughter's hand. 'He wouldn't share that with just anyone.'

'I'd share it with you if you wanted.' The look he gave her caught her off-guard.

Benny blushed with embarrassment and looked away, distracting himself by alerting Beth to someone who hadn't picked up their dog's mess.

Beth eventually dropped off to sleep, but Benny was still happy to hold her as they sat companionably on a bench watching a group of children at play.

'Have you chosen your GCSE subjects yet?' Nettie asked.

'Yeah, but it's not gonna make no difference. I'll still fail cos I'm rubbish at school.' He rolled his eyes. 'They say I've gotta have extra help.'

'I thought you had that from Brian.'

'I'll need more, from a teacher in the special unit place. If I do it, they've promised they'll try and keep me in the normal classes.'

Aware of his fears, Nettie was glad. He inched closer to her, and Nettie battled an urge to reciprocate. Although she had hugged him before, it was different now because of her growing feelings.

'Nettie, can I talk to you?'

His direct question broke into her musings. 'Course you can.' She imagined it would be more about school, or perhaps he would confess how much he was missing Emma.

'It's hard.' He looked away.

Despite her misgivings, Nettie had to reach for his hand to draw him back. 'You've never struggled to talk to me before.' She tightened her grasp, enjoying the feel of their fingers intertwined. 'Known each other a while, haven't we?'

He nodded.

'So come on then. Maybe if you tell me what's wrong, I can help.'

'I'm scared I'm gonna mess stuff up. Damo said… He said I should talk to you, but I think I'm bottling out.'

Nettie waited for him to continue. When he seemed uncertain, she knew it would be up to her to push the conversation further. 'You said Damo thought you should talk to me about something?'

'We were talking the other day about what would happen if you and Beth moved away, and how much I'd miss you both.'

'I'd miss you too, and Beth would turn into Little Miss Strop-A-Lot. Look at how she's been with you today.'

'Emmie said something too.' Benny adjusted his back against the wooden slats. 'She said one day you'll want a boyfriend. Now you've got used to looking after Beth, I expect that's what you'll want.'

How could she tell him the only boyfriend she wanted was sitting beside her? Nettie chided herself. She needed to take her feelings in hand for both their sakes.

'It was bugging me when me and Emmie talked, cos I can't think about you and Beth not being a part of my life.'

His deepening voice and growing ability to put his thoughts into words was only making things worse for Nettie. She desperately wanted to reassure him, so draped an arm around his shoulders. 'It's all right, Benny. Me and Beth aren't going anywhere.'

'When you find a boyfriend… He won't want you hanging around with a kid like me. He might want you to live somewhere else.'

'Trust me, that won't happen.' Her words sounded feeble even to her own ears.

'Emmie says it will.'

'You can tell your sister she doesn't know everything about me.'

Silence settled between them as they watched the comings and goings of other people. Was that the end of the conversation?

'Have you ever talked to anyone about me?' Benny suddenly asked.

Nettie chewed her lip. Did she dare say more? 'I've been chatting to Kerry.'

'Really?' His jaw hung open.

'She got me to face up to things I didn't realise I've been hiding from for quite a while. I guess it was easier to do that, because admitting them was downright scary. I don't know how we'd handle it.' Why had she said all that? Her mouth had run away with her, just as she'd feared it would on a day when she felt lonely and in need of love.

'Who's *we*?' Benny sounded confused.

Nettie had been hoping he wouldn't pick up on that. Perhaps his learning difficulties would benefit her, but no. Today he was taking it all in and he had questions. 'Me and you.'

Shame washed over her as the familiar look of confusion crossed Benny's face. He was panicking, and Nettie feared she was going to make him cry. Giving him a brief hug, she added, 'All you need to know is that I've got no intention of looking for a boyfriend or of leaving the village. You can relax, okay?' She longed for his smile to return.

'How come you're so sure?'

'Not now. Please? Let it go.' Nettie pleaded as she fought to remain in control. 'I don't want to answer that, Benny. Not yet.' She tried a chiding tone she had heard Emma using, then felt ashamed for talking down to him.

'Why not?' he challenged, and Nettie looked away.

'Because you're only fifteen.' She was glad she could add a year to his age today, but he still seemed too young.

'I don't get it.' Benny rose and placed Beth gently into the buggy. His hands trembled and tension lined every feature of his face. He lifted up and down on his toes, like he wanted to run away, and familiar tears pricked at his eyes. Would he run back to the safety of Janet's embrace, or would Benny show himself mature enough to handle the conversation?

Nettie waited on tenterhooks, wondering if the stress was going to bring on a seizure.

'Please, Nettie?' His eyes darted to and fro as his words came out in a strangled sob. 'I'm so muddled up about lots of stuff.'

'It's all right. I'm sorry, Benny.' She rose, grateful he was turning to her instead of his mum. 'I wanted to put your mind at rest, not scare you. Things won't change, okay? You and I will carry on being good friends like we always have, and you'll still be a huge part of Beth's life. I promise.'

'What if...' He leaned closer, as if drawing strength from her nearness. 'What if I want them to change?'

'In what way?'

He didn't answer for a while. Nettie waited until Benny pulled away and rubbed his eyes. 'You know I've never had a girlfriend, don't you?'

She nodded soberly. 'You're still young. There's plenty of time.'

'Damo's had loads.' Benny was calmer now. The shaking had stopped. He stood facing her, his attention fixed on her eyes. 'I didn't get it. I thought it was all stupid. I never wanted to be with no one like that. Not until...'

Was he trying to say what she thought he was? Would he go on? 'Do you like someone?' she asked.

'It's complicated.' He carefully enunciated the uncharacteristically long word.

'Oh, believe me, I understand complicated.'

'Nettie, it feels like we're... talking but not talking; like we're going round in circles. I'm getting more muddled up.'

'Do you think that's because we both have secrets we don't want the other one to know?' The air hung still and heavy between them.

'I'm scared if I tell you, you'll say I'm stupid.'

'And I'm afraid that if I tell you, you'll run away like you almost did just now.'

She could see the thoughts congregating behind his eyes. 'I wouldn't. I won't run away.'

'And I'd never call you stupid. You're very special to me, Benny. A lot more special than you realise.' The spell seemed to break with her unplanned revelation. Was it time? 'That's the problem.' Nettie sighed and sat back down. 'Okay, I'll be as honest as I can. I'm struggling because I'm feeling things I shouldn't be feeling for someone as young as you.'

Benny stared at her open-mouthed.

'Is this the point where you run away scared?' she asked.

'No,' he whispered, 'Cos your secret's a lot like mine. I didn't wanna say nothing cos I'm only fifteen. I thought you'd be angry if you knew I...' He paused, reaching for words. 'The kids at school talk about fancying someone. That sounds childish with you being older and having a baby.'

'Benny?' Nettie needed to be sure she fully grasped his meaning. 'Let's imagine things were different.' Ignoring his baffled look, she pressed on. 'If you weren't only fifteen... If you were sixteen, seventeen or even older... What do you think you'd want then?'

'I'd wanna ask you to be my girlfriend. I'd wanna help you look after Beth.' He had rarely spoken with such assurance. He even looked surprised at himself. 'If I was older, I know I'd have stuff to give you.'

'And you don't feel you have anything to give me now?'

'Just a stupid little kid who's gonna mess up in school and fail his GCSE's.'

'No, Benny. You were a little kid when I moved to the village. You aren't anymore.'

'Most people reckon I still am.'

They had laid their cards out on the table. Where did they go from here? Though she thought she probably should, Nettie wasn't ready to give up. Not now she knew he had feelings too, even if he didn't understand the full weight of them. 'Shall we take things slowly and see how it goes?'

'Dunno.'

He clearly wasn't sure what that meant, so she explained further. 'We've both admitted we like each other.'

'I dunno how to handle relationships and stuff. I'm pretty thick, Nettie.'

She dismissed his second sentence and focused on the first. 'You won't until you actually have one. Maybe if we take things slowly, you can learn gradually, and if you decide it isn't what you want, we can still be good friends.'

'Damo says you can't go back to being just friends after you've gone out with a girl.'

'That's more if the relationship gets physical. That wouldn't be happening to us - not yet anyway.'

'It wouldn't be a proper relationship for someone your age without all that stuff.' Benny's brow creased.

Nettie wondered how much information Damian had shared. 'Benny,' She smiled at him, reaching for his hand again. 'If we go for this, nothing will be normal for either of us. We'll both have a lot to learn, and if we're meant to, we'll get through it.'

'I know I like you a lot, but Mum, Dad and Emmie... They say you're like another big sister, but I don't think of you like I think of Emma. I never have.'

'Okay. Embarrassing question time.' His face reddened before she could ask, enhancing her tenderness towards him. 'I've got to do this, to help you sort out your feelings.'

He nodded.

'Have you ever imagined kissing me?'

Benny's blush transformed into a bashful grin. 'Yeah, like all the time! Sometimes I have to stop myself hugging you and stuff, and it's not like the way I hug Emmie. I know we've hugged each other, but I reckon it'd be different if we were going out, wouldn't it?'

'I think it already kind of is. Shall we give it a go - being together, I mean?' Nettie feared he would still say no.

'Our parents will go mad.'

That was the truth. Should they tell them? Nettie wasn't sure, but she knew that if her mum found out, she'd put a stop to it right away. And she wasn't sure she could handle that. 'Maybe we don't tell them for now? Not until we're sure where this is going.'

'How long will that take?' Benny had so many questions. Nettie guessed that was inevitable.

'Probably longer for us than for most couples.'

'So… What do we do now?' He looked at her apologetically. 'I've never had a girlfriend. I dunno what to do.'

'Nothing has to change between us. You can still hang out with me and Beth like always. We'll come here, go to town, that sort of thing.'

'That'll still be like we're just friends.'

'No, because now we've faced up to our feelings. We'll let things happen as they're meant to. I don't want you doing anything you feel uncomfortable with or trying to change just to impress me. You don't need to act more mature than you can be. Remember, I like you for who you are.'

'So, are we…' Nettie could tell he was paddling in mental waters that threatened to sweep him away. 'Asking if we're going out sounds as childish as saying I fancy you. It doesn't feel right cos you're so grown-up.'

'For someone your age, those words are natural. I need to handle this like I would have when I was fifteen.'

'That sounds weird, Nettie.'

Her laughter broke the nervous tension between them. 'What I mean is that we have to go at your pace. So yeah, we're going out, in a casual kind of way with no pressure.'

'I dunno what people my age do when they're going out. I never took no notice of Damo and his girlfriends. I think he's kissed some of them.'

Nettie wondered how many girlfriends fourteen-year-old Damian had actually had. 'You can kiss me one day if you want, but don't worry about that yet. It doesn't matter when that happens, or if it ever does. Like I said, no pressure. Plus, we'll have to be careful if we're going to keep this from our families. I don't think much in our relationship should change until you're older. You need time to figure out what you want, but you need to know I'll always be here to answer anything you want to know.'

'Okay.' He re-took his seat on the bench, shuffling even closer to her now Beth wasn't between them. His eyes remained fixed at a point in the distance while his lip twitched, like he wanted to smile but wasn't sure if he should. They sat in silence as Nettie gave him space to process everything that had passed between them. Then he turned to her with a smile, holding out his arms, and Nettie leaned gratefully into them.

They hugged for a long time, enjoying being close. Earlier they had hugged as friends. Now she was his girlfriend. Although Nettie wasn't quite sure how it had happened, or what the future held, her heart warmed.

24

Nettie slammed the bedroom door and flopped down on her bed. Her mother's timing was impeccable! Mary had been full of excitement when Nettie arrived home from work, eager to share her plans for John's week of annual leave. He'd timed it to coincide with Nettie's, so they could visit Gran and Gramps.

Mary had raved about their eagerness to meet Beth, suggesting it would also be the ideal opportunity for Nettie to re-connect with her old friends. 'I know we had to delay our return because of Beth,' her mum said, 'but we can't stay here forever, and you don't want to lose your real friends.'

Under normal circumstances, Nettie would have looked forward to seeing her grandparents. They had always been close, and they were devastated when her family moved away. They couldn't understand why because they hadn't known their cherished only granddaughter was pregnant. Mary had kept it from them, believing there would be no need for them to know if Nettie gave up her baby. Subsequently, it had come as a shock to her elderly grandparents when Nettie phoned them to break the news about Beth.

'Why didn't your mother tell us?' Gran was unable to conceal her hurt.

'I guess she was just trying to protect me,' Nettie had tried making excuses. 'Hardly anyone knew. I didn't even tell my friends.' It had all been carefully hidden until Nettie's decision to keep her baby threw a spanner into the works.

Now she faced the prospect of leaving Benny just days after starting their relationship. There was still so much he didn't understand. Would he view this as a rejection? Would he think she was having regrets and running away? Yet, if she refused to go, what plausible excuse would she give? She would have to explain it to Benny, keep in touch as much as possible, and deal with the fallout when she got back.

Benny had become more bashful around her since the day they admitted their feelings. Nettie found this endearing. She was still able to put him at his ease by finding something to make him laugh. They held hands constantly when they were away from prying eyes, taking every opportunity to be close. Nettie had always known he was physically demonstrative, and he was making her aware of how much affection she had missed out on during her formative years. Yet despite the hugs and hand holding, there was still an innocence about their relationship that Nettie found strangely refreshing.

She took Beth to visit Kerry that evening to have some space from her mum. Mary was asking awkward questions about her attitude, and Nettie couldn't come up with a satisfactory explanation. However, when she complained to Kerry about the trip, her friend was also confused.

'Why don't you want to go?'

How could Nettie explain without sharing something she wasn't ready to divulge?

'Are you worried you might have to face Beth's father?'

Nettie hadn't even thought about Simon. Now she wondered if her friend had inadvertently given her the perfect excuse. If she told her parents she was worried about seeing him, they might understand why she couldn't go.

However, Mary put paid to her argument when she explained, 'According to your gran, he doesn't live there anymore.'

Nettie didn't know whether to be pleased or disappointed by the results of her mother's enquiries.

'He went off to study or something.' Mary looked impressed. She'd always fallen for Simon's swagger. Even when Simon had gotten Nettie pregnant, it hadn't stopped her mum liking him. Her dad, by contrast, had been furious. 'There's nothing for you to worry about. We'll have a brilliant time. And maybe your dad and I will even start setting the wheels in motion towards moving back home.'

Nettie had suspected that was coming, but she'd been trying not to think about it.

She broke the news to Benny the following day when they took Beth to the park to feed the ducks. They stood together on the bridge over the pond with Beth in her buggy, Beth and Benny already having used up half of the dry bread.

'I guess it'll be nice to see your grandparents,' Benny had taken it better than she had expected.

Nettie squeezed his hand more tightly.

'I've never seen much of mine.' He tossed more bread to the ducks.

Nettie had never asked him about other relatives. Now she wanted to know more. 'So you do have them?'

He nodded. 'I only know about Mum's parents. Dad never talks about his. I guess they're in Denmark somewhere, so we can't see them.'

'You could if you flew.'

Benny shook his head and smiled. 'Dad never says nothing about them. Maybe they're dead.'

'Don't you ever want to ask?' Nettie probed.

'Dad doesn't like a lot of questions.'

'What about your mum's parents?' she took her own turn at throwing bread to the ducks.

'Emma stayed with them when we were little. We've all visited them sometimes, but my dad doesn't like them much.'

'How come it was only Emma they had to stay?'

'Maybe they were scared of my seizures. I don't wanna go nowhere, anyway. I like being here.'

More like Janet wouldn't let him go, Nettie suspected. She told him about her own grandparents, sharing happy memories of the times they'd spent together, and he loved hearing her stories. She also said she would probably meet up with some of her old friends. Having created an opening, Nettie wondered if he would ask about Beth's father, but the thought didn't seem to enter his head. Benny had never asked about who had fathered her baby.

On the morning they left, Benny stood on his parents' driveway waving to their retreating car. Beth waved back from her car-seat, and Nettie helped her blow him a kiss. Moments later, he texted to inform her he was going out on his bike with Damian.

A steady stream of texts passed between them during the time she was away. Nettie had quickly learned to unscramble Benny's bad spelling and lazy shorthand. He told her everything, and she did likewise. She wrote about how her grandparents were spoiling Beth, and about the friends she had seen.

While Mary was in her element, fitting back into city life like a duck to water, Nettie missed the quiet of their sleepy village. She no longer fitted in amongst her old friends. Some of them were awkward in her presence because she had a baby, and even those who had kept in touch and knew about Beth seemed shallow and fickle compared to Emma, Erin, and Kerry.

They stayed for a week, and as the time wore on, Nettie became increasingly eager to get back home. At first, her text exchanges with Benny were casual, until finally one lonely evening she wrote, 'I miss you. x'

His response came back quickly. 'Miss you too. xx' A new precedent had been set. From then on, they always peppered their messages with kisses.

Needing to hear his voice, she phoned him once while she was out walking with Beth in her buggy. The minute he answered, calm swept over her.

'What're you doing?' She guessed he was either at home or at the park with Damo. Benny's daily activities were as predictable as Beth's.

'Trying to learn for a maths test.' He sounded glum.

She knew how much he struggled with his studies. 'Wish I could help.'

'You could take it for me.' He laughed, and Nettie joined in. 'Bet you'd pass too.'

'I suppose I wasn't bad at maths.' Nettie decided to offer him more support with his schoolwork when she got back home. She wondered if she could find ways of explaining things more clearly, since she seemed to understand his thought patterns.

'Karen's having a birthday party for Marcus on Saturday.' His typically random change of subject made her smile. 'She wants you to bring Beth.'

'Are you going?'

Benny replied in the affirmative.

'Good. Then we'll see each other. We should be back late Friday night.' Their conversation left Nettie feeling warm and reassured.

As the Thompsons travelled home on Friday, Nettie was relieved. A few good things had come out of their trip. Her grandparents had enjoyed meeting Beth, and John had told Mary that despite her longings, they couldn't afford another house move yet. Moving was expensive, even when renting, and they'd given their tenants another 12-month lease. As a result, Nettie had time to work on her relationship with Benny without the prospect of another upheaval in their lives.

The following afternoon, she stood in front of her bedroom mirror, marvelling over the fact that she was making more of an effort over her appearance to attend a one-year-old's birthday party than she had during her entire week away. She recalled her dates with Simon, when he had taken her out in his flashy car, snuck her bottles of wine, and spoiled her with expensive chocolates. Now here she was getting dressed up to meet her fifteen-year-old boyfriend. 'If Simon could see me now...' Nettie giggled while applying eye liner, then dashed downstairs when she heard Beth's cries.

On entering the lounge, she found her dad rocking Beth and singing one of her daughter's favourite nursery rhymes. Nettie paused in the doorway, overcome by love for her quiet, dependable dad. He had said little during her pregnancy, always deferring to Mary, but when she brought Beth home, he had been the first to offer his support. Nettie wondered if he had been going along with his wife while secretly longing for her to keep her child.

'You look lovely, Nettie.' John gave her a gentle smile. 'Bit dolled up for a baby's birthday party though, aren't you?'

'I haven't bothered much about how I look since Beth.' She wanted to put him off the scent as quickly as possible.

'I guess you don't have much time to think about hair and makeup. It's been strange though, because those things were always so important to you.'

'They need to be again. I'm sick of looking in the mirror and seeing black circles under my eyes.'

'There's been a new spark in your eyes lately.' John winked. 'Makes me wonder if you might have a secret.'

Nettie looked away to hide her reddening face.

'You'd tell your old dad if you had a boyfriend, wouldn't you, Nettie love?'

'I haven't got time for a man.' Nettie tossed her hair as if to dismiss the suggestion.

'I hope you will make time one of these days, love.' John's smile faded into a frown. 'You deserve to be happy. What happened with Simon shouldn't change that.'

'I am happy.' Relief washed over Nettie as the doorbell sounded and she took Beth from her father. Benny had unwittingly saved the day. Her heart beat faster as she opened the door.

'Hello, you.' Nettie couldn't conceal her joy. Benny stood on her doorstep wearing his usual ripped jeans and faded t-shirt. She ached to throw herself into his arms, but there were too many prying eyes. She needed to keep reminding herself that they were moving slowly.

'Hi.' Benny's awkwardness had returned, He was trying not to look at her.

Nettie closed the front door and moved to his side. 'Why do you always do that?'

'Do what?'

'You act all weird when you see me. You never used to,' she teased.

'Dunno. Sorry. Just dunno how to be and stuff.' He took a deep breath then blurted out, 'Nettie, I'm sorry. I told Damo about us.'

She wondered what reaction he was expecting. All she gave was a warm smile. 'I'm glad.'

'You said…'

'I said we weren't going to tell our parents. I didn't say anything about close friends we can trust.'

'Bet you didn't tell none of yours.'

'Not while I was away, no. Besides, my close friends are Emma, Kerry, and Erin, and I haven't been around them much lately.'

'I don't think you should tell Emma.' He looked worried.

Nettie couldn't help laughing. 'No, that would definitely be a bad idea.' Her merriment lightened the atmosphere between them.

Beth reached out her arms and Benny took her, squeezing her tightly and spinning around until she let out a gleeful squeal. 'I missed you, Bethy.' He planted a kiss on her cheek, and Beth wrapped her little arms around his neck.

Nettie's throat constricted with love for them both. 'Only her?' She feigned disappointment, and Benny surprised her by pulling her round to the side of her parents' house with an uncharacteristic twinkle in his eyes.

Having established that they were alone, he drew her into a hug with Beth nestled between them. 'You look really nice.' He stepped back to admire her, and Nettie was glad he had noticed.

'Dad asked if I've got a boyfriend.'

'What did you say?' He looked concerned.

'I tried to put him off, but it's good to feel like I've got a reason to make more of an effort.' She winked playfully. 'And your reaction just now made it all worthwhile.' He was trying to learn, and she wanted to teach him. She suspected he had also sought guidance from Damian.

'I still don't get why you wanna be with me.' Benny shrugged. 'I thought you'd change your mind while you were away.'

'You've got it all wrong, Benny. The truth is - I'm having to work hard at not showing you how strong my feelings are. Now we've finally been open with one another, they all want to gush out. But I've got to think about your age.'

'And I'm trying not to be stupid like I always am.' He looped an arm through hers as he held Beth snugly with the other. When Nettie reminded him, for what felt like the umpteenth time, that he wasn't stupid, he rapidly changed the subject. 'We'd better go.'

'Will your mum be at Karen's?'

He nodded, and Nettie reluctantly withdrew her arm from his as they walked around her parents' house and across the road.

'There you both are.' Janet pounced on them the moment they arrived at the Moss' house. 'I was wondering where you'd got to.' No doubt she presumed the worst when Benny was out of her sight.

Nettie covered for him by reminding Janet that nothing was ever straight-forward when you had to dress and change a baby.

Janet led them into the garden where the whole Moss family waited with Emma and Ola.

Dale's eyes feasted on Nettie, looking her up and down. He even released a quiet whistle before his attention turned to Benny, and a sneer settled on his features.

Nettie ignored him and smiled as Marcus came toddling towards her. She commented on how he had learned to walk before his first birthday, while Beth showed little interest in standing on her own two feet.

'Babies do things at their own pace, Nettie,' Karen reassured.

'Benny held on to the furniture until he was eighteen months old. Even after that he still preferred to be carried,' Janet reminisced.

Benny's cheeks turned a shade of pink. Still carrying Beth, he moved to a quieter part of the garden, while Nettie continued chatting with everyone else.

When Karen said she needed to fetch the food, Nettie offered to give her a hand. Once they were alone in Karen's cosy kitchen, the older woman complimented her on her appearance.

'You've got a sparkle in your eyes. See? I told you everything would be fine once you got used to being a mum.'

'You were right. Thanks for being there for me, Karen.' Nettie removed cling film from a plate of sandwiches.

'Any time.' Karen poured crisps into a bowl, then turned back to Nettie with a wink. 'So, can I ask who he is?'

'Who?' Nettie couldn't hide her confusion.

'Whoever it is that's responsible for putting the sparkle back in your eyes.' Karen paused. 'I am right in thinking there is someone, aren't I?'

Nettie could have denied it. Yet she had an overwhelming urge to confide. Despite their age difference, Karen had become a close friend.

'If I tell you, will you give me your word that you'll keep it to yourself?'

'It's okay, Nettie.' Karen placed a hand on her shoulder. 'I was a teenager once, remember? I even had a baby at your age, so I know what that's like.'

Nettie leaned forward. 'I do feel like I need to talk to someone, but my secret… It's not what you might expect. I need to say it to reassure myself I'm not going crazy.'

'I'm listening.'

She had Karen's full attention, and there was no going back. 'This might surprise you.' Nettie inhaled deeply before taking the plunge. 'The guy… It's Benny.' She waited for Karen's expression to change to one of horror or disgust, but a gentle smile settled on her face.

'I'm not as surprised as you might think. I've been watching you lately, and I could see there was an attraction. You've spent so much time together. Does he know how you feel?'

'He says he has feelings for me too. We started a relationship a few days before I went to visit my grandparents, but no one knows yet. Don't worry though. I'm letting things move along at his pace. I don't want to put him under any pressure.'

'Do you think he's able to understand his own feelings?' Karen's eyebrows lifted.

'I know he's young for his age in a lot of ways. I understand his problems, but I saw a different side of him that day he came to the hospital and persuaded me to keep Beth.'

'Are you sure he doesn't see you in the same way he sees Emma?' Karen put a hand to her head, clearly unconvinced. 'Maybe he's confused.'

'I spent a lot of time watching him with his sister before I told him how I felt. It's definitely not the same.'

'Well in that case…' Karen was choosing her words carefully. 'The only thing I can say is what I'm sure you're already aware of. You're going to have to take things very slowly if you and Benny are going to make a relationship work. There's no doubt he's matured a lot during the past eighteen months, but he's still young. And very dependent on his mother. A lot of that is Janet's own doing, but Benny clings to her too when it suits him. There's also his epilepsy to think about.'

Nettie nodded, affirming her understanding of everything Karen had said. 'He hasn't had a seizure around me yet. It's bound to happen, and I'd rather get it over with.'

'He's usually very ill afterwards.'

'I just want to be there for him.'

'Not to mother him, I hope?' Karen cautioned. 'That's no basis for a relationship. He already has more than his fair share of mothering from Janet.'

'No. But in some ways, he still needs looking after. For now anyway.'

Karen smiled again while loading plates onto trays. 'When will you tell your families?'

'I don't know. I'm dreading how they'll react. Especially Janet.'

'It will hit her hard. You'll have problems with Ola too. He's still very old-fashioned.' They each picked up a tray. 'Janet will only ever see Benny as her baby. He didn't have a problem with that until recently, but he's changing. That's what makes me think he might be ready for this relationship. As long as you don't push.'

'So you won't tell anyone?' Nettie had risked confiding in Karen, having an inkling her hunch would pay off.

'No, of course not.'

25

Nettie gazed down at her sleeping daughter on the morning of Beth's first birthday, marvelling over how far they'd come.

This time last year, she had been labouring to bring Beth into the world, holding on to the misguided assumption that her only option was to relinquish her baby into the hands of a more responsible mother. Now she was thankful every day that she'd chosen to keep her.

Beth stirred and held up her arms, and Nettie covered her little face with kisses. 'Happy birthday, sweet girl.' She held her tightly, overwhelmed by tender maternal emotions. 'Mummy loves you so much, Bethy.'

Beth chuckled and Nettie wondered what she found so funny. Carrying her downstairs, she began the tasks of feeding and changing that had become a regular part of her daily routine.

She hadn't organised a party, but Karen had said she would bring Marcus round to play.

As the morning wore on, friends and neighbours dropped by with gifts and well-wishes, confirming that Nettie and her daughter were truly part of this close-knit community. They had welcomed them into their hearts and lives, and Nettie loved them for it.

Benny had started delivering papers on a Saturday morning, fulfilling his long-held desire to supplement his pocket money with his own earnings. Ola had helped him get the job, and Benny was fairly organised once he'd worked with his dad to establish a strategy. Janet worried over the risks to his health, but after seeing how it improved Benny's self-esteem, even she eventually backed down.

'Did you get chased by dogs today?' Nettie asked as they sat in her parents' garden sharing some of Beth's birthday cake while her daughter enjoyed her late morning nap. Benny loved telling her crazy stories from his paper round.

He shook his head, feeling the awkwardness between them under the scrutiny of Nettie's parents. There could be no subtle hand holding or hugs if they wanted to keep their secret.

Beth stirred in the house and Nettie rose to attend to her. 'Come with me. She'll be excited to see you.'

Benny followed her inside, clutching the doorframe for support as a wave of dizziness hit him.

'Sorry Nettie. I've gotta go.' He'd had warnings of an impending seizure all morning. Some days it was obvious, while other times they caught him off-guard. Nettie hadn't witnessed one yet, and he didn't want today to be the first. Not on Beth's birthday.

'Why?' Nettie looked hurt as she picked Beth up.

Benny wanted to explain, but it was too late. His final coherent thought before he hit the floor and started fitting was that he should never have come. He had recognised the signals. Why had he been so stupid? Yet he knew, even as his brain whirled with a million disjointed thoughts and his body jolted. He had wanted to see Nettie; longed to be with her and Beth.

Nettie looked down in sheer panic as Benny lay fitting on her parents' kitchen floor. They had talked about this. He had told her what to do, but could she remember his instructions? What if she did something wrong? She ran into the lounge to put Beth down before returning to Benny and easing him into the recovery position. She had been reading up on epilepsy. She'd thought she had a handle on it. However, watching someone she cared about in the throes of a seizure was another matter. He mumbled incoherently, and she stroked his hand. 'I'm here. You'll be okay.' Then, without thinking, 'I love you, Benny.' It didn't matter that the words had slipped out. He wouldn't be able to hear her.

Nettie glanced at her watch, aware that if this went on too long, she would have to call for help, but Benny gradually calmed. The seizure was over as quickly as it had started. His eyes flew open, seeming to look right through her, and he vomited over the kitchen floor.

Why hadn't she thought to grab a bowl? He had warned her about the sickness. He said it always happened, and the doctors had never figured out why. They supposed he just had a weak stomach because lots of things made him sick.

Benny looked up at her with tear-filled eyes. 'I'm sorry, Nettie.' He attempted to stand, stumbling in his dizziness.

Nettie reached out an arm to steady him. 'It's okay.'

They stood together, with Benny leaning heavily against her. She was relieved he weighed so little. 'What can I do?' She held on tighter as the tears rolled unchecked down his cheeks.

'Get my dad.'

Nettie eased him into a kitchen chair and picked up her phone to call Ola. He was there within minutes to take Benny home, leaving Nettie to mop the kitchen floor. Ola had offered to do it, but she said it was fine. She was used to cleaning up after Beth.

Benny didn't speak to her again before he left with his dad. Nettie sensed his shame. He couldn't even look her in the eye. She would put his mind at ease later, after he'd rested. Right now he was confused and scared, and there was little she could say with Ola in earshot.

'I'm sorry you had to cope with this, and on Beth's birthday of all days.' Ola offered his apology as he guided his son out of the house.

Nettie had to bite back an angry retort. He didn't need to apologise for his son. His words felt like a subtle way of putting Benny down and implying he was a burden. She knew that was how his dad had seen him for the first thirteen years of his life, and she suspected it was easy for him to still fall into that trap when Benny's illness caused embarrassment. It was no wonder Ola and Janet always kept him close.

Kerry arrived with her gift for Beth shortly after Nettie finished tidying up, and they chatted in the kitchen over more tea and cake.

'I saw Benny leaving. Did he have a seizure?' There was compassion in her friend's eyes. 'That must've been a nightmare.'

Nettie scowled. 'It's hardest on him. He's the one who's got to live with it. Just imagine how awkward he must feel about having a fit and throwing up in someone else's house.'

'I guess those of us who've known him all his life don't often think about it.'

'That's the trouble,' Nettie fumed. 'No one bothers to look at it from Benny's point of view.' She clamped her lips tightly shut. There was so much more she wanted to say. When others looked at Benny, they saw the inconvenience, whereas Nettie saw the person. She understood his sensitivities and his longing to be what he called *normal*.

'I'm sorry, Nettie. I know you're close to him.' Kerry shuffled nervously in her seat.

'We're close to each other.' It was time to confide. Nettie needed another of her friends on-side to help her face what lay ahead.

'Well yes. You've helped him a lot.'

Kerry clearly hadn't grasped her meaning. 'We're more than just friends, Kerry.' She steeled herself for a negative reaction. 'Those feelings you got me to admit... It turned out he was having them too.'

'But Nettie!' Kerry was wide-eyed. 'He's only fifteen, and... Let's face it; in some ways he's still much younger.'

'And in others much older.' Nettie was the first person who had appreciated that despite his limitations, Benny's feelings ran deep. It was why he cried so easily, why he allowed his parents to shield him from hard things and from change. 'I told you it was him who persuaded me to keep Beth.'

'That doesn't mean you're meant to be more than friends.'

'It's not the only reason.' Nettie looked her friend in the eye. 'I want this because I love him.'

Kerry's jaw dropped.

'Don't panic,' Nettie reassured. 'I know nothing major can happen between us for a long time, but I'm willing to wait. I wanted him to know someone other than his family sees him as worth loving.'

'There are lots of different kinds of love, Nettie.' Kerry spoke falteringly. 'Are you sure what you're feeling isn't just protectiveness? I'll admit Benny's a big help with Beth, and your life's been more limited since she was born, but to date a fifteen-year-old!'

'You were the one who got me to admit my feelings.' Nettie gathered up their plates and stacked them near the sink.

'For you to face them and move on, not so you'd start dating him.' Kerry looked away. 'Don't tell me he knows how to handle a relationship, because I won't believe you. We all know how he struggles to understand things.'

'He's got a lot to learn,' Nettie conceded, 'but I'd prefer to wait for him to mature than to end up with someone like Beth's father again. He was so shallow. With Benny, what you see is what you get. If he says he wants to be with me, he means it.'

'Are you sure you aren't going for the safe option because of how badly you were hurt last time?' Kerry asked.

Nettie laughed sardonically. 'Once his parents find out, this will be anything but safe, but I'll stick with it for as long as he wants. I could do with your support.' She re-took her seat opposite Kerry at the table. 'I need my friends now more than ever.'

'Your mind's made up, isn't it?' Kerry reached across to cover her hand as Nettie nodded. 'Who else knows?'

'Only his friend Damian and Karen Moss.'

'Karen? You told his mother's best friend!' Kerry rolled her eyes.

'Don't ask me to explain why. It just felt right.' Nettie gazed at Kerry with sincerity. 'I know what you stand for, and I promise I won't do anything you'd be ashamed of. I learned my lesson the hard way with Beth's father.'

'I'm sorry, Nettie.' Kerry walked around the table to hug her. 'I'll be here to support you, and you may not want to hear this, but I'll be praying.'

'I reckon we can use all the help we'll get, so thanks.' Nettie knew an offer of prayer from Kerry was a compliment of sorts. She had never thought much about God, but if Kerry felt he could help them, then wasn't that a good thing?

❧

Benny spent the afternoon of Beth's birthday lying on his bed alternating between tears and rage. He had told his mum he still felt sick, and thankfully she'd taken the hint and left him alone. In reality, the sickness had passed quickly. It was his embarrassment that lingered. Things had been going so well. Nettie had wanted to be his girlfriend. She wouldn't anymore. Not after what had happened in her parents' kitchen. He ignored several texts and just lay there feeling sorry for himself.

Later, he heard the doorbell and presumed it was Karen. His eyes were red rimmed from crying, and he felt dehydrated. He should have been eating and drinking, but he didn't think he deserved it after what had happened. Refusing food was often his way of punishing himself for his insecurities and lack of understanding. He would force something down later. For now he would stay where he was, especially if his mum had a visitor. He didn't want anyone to see him like this.

'Nettie's here, Benny.' Ola's voice boomed up the stairs.

Why had she come? Should he tell his dad to send her away? He could say he still felt sick. His mum would stick up for him even if his dad was cross. Still, if Nettie was going to end things between them, he would have to face it eventually. Considering he already felt rubbish, perhaps now would be the best time.

Benny rose and ambled down the stairs, not bothering to concern himself with his appearance. There wouldn't be any point if she broke up with him. Nettie stood in the hallway, smiling as he drew near.

'He's been cooped up in his bedroom all afternoon. Take him out for some fresh air will you, Nettie?' Ola nudged Benny towards the door.

'But Ola!' Janet appeared behind her husband. 'He hasn't eaten all day! And he was ill, so he'll be weak.'

'I haven't eaten much either except for loads of Beth's cake.' Nettie turned and headed out of the door. 'I'll buy us both a burger in town.'

Benny followed her without a word, stopping in his tracks once the door was closed and his parents could no longer hear them. 'Can we just go for a walk?'

'Why?' When Nettie tried to touch him, Benny shrank away.

His eyes darted to the road in front of his home where the ice-cream van had idled eighteen months earlier on the day he'd met the girl who'd changed his life. Everyone said his confidence had grown and he'd come a long way. They were wrong. Today he was the old Benny, scared and pathetic. 'If we go somewhere in your car, I won't be able to get back home.'

'You'll come back with me, silly. I'm not going to take you somewhere and leave you.'

'I won't handle it once you've said what you're gonna say. I'll do something stupid, Nettie. Just say it, and I'll go back to my room.' He already felt like he was about to cry again or pass out. Maybe going all day without food or drink had been a bad idea.

'What do you think I'm going to say?' She took a firm grip of his arm, drawing him further down the street and behind a copse of trees, away from the risk of prying eyes.

'That you know what a stupid, messed up idiot you're going out with.' Benny hung his head.

'So this is all about your seizure?'

He nodded, looking at his trainers. They were worn and shabby. He needed new ones. He'd been planning on asking Nettie to help him choose. That wouldn't be happening now.

'Did you honestly think we'd be able to have a relationship without me learning to handle your seizures?' Nettie was speaking quietly, and she leaned back to check no-one had seen them.

Benny raised his eyes and looked past her, withdrawing further into his shell.

'Benny?' Nettie reached for his hand. He wouldn't let her take it. 'Please, don't do that.'

'Do what?' Holding her hand would be wrong because he knew it would be the last time.

'You're shutting me out. You're doing that thing where you pull away when things get hard.'

'I've got to.' He forced a certainty into his voice that he didn't feel.

'I knew you were epileptic. What happened today wasn't a surprise.'

'Seeing it is always worse, and you even had to clean up after me.' He swallowed the lump in his throat. 'It's gross, Nettie. No one should have to put up with that. My parents only do cos they have to.'

'Do you realise I sat with you the whole time you were fitting?'

He nodded. He had been aware but couldn't communicate. 'I do sometimes know what's going on. It depends how bad the seizure is.'

'I'm glad you knew I was there.' After stepping further behind the trees, she drew him close.

Benny stiffened but couldn't resist her hug. She felt so amazing, and she even smelt good.

'I want you to always know I'll be here when you need me.'

'I don't want that, Nettie.' His tone was sorrowful. 'I don't want you acting like my mum or my big sister.'

'I'm not.' He tried to disentangle himself, but she refused to let him go. 'I'm acting like a girlfriend who's going to be there to support her guy when he needs it, and who knows he'll do the same for her.' Nettie sounded as choked as he was. 'You already did when I had Beth. You were so brave that day. You stopped me making a huge mistake, and to think we weren't even together then.'

'I dunno what made me go to the hospital that day.' Could he dare to hope that Nettie's feelings hadn't changed? 'I just knew I had to. I thought you might need me.'

215

'I did, even though I didn't realise how much until later.'

He was still in her arms. She hadn't let go, and he was starting to think she wouldn't. He pulled away enough to see her face and spoke the words that were uppermost in his mind. 'Nettie, when I was out of it, I think… I think I heard you say you loved me?'

'I did.' Her gaze was unflinching. 'I didn't plan on saying anything like that so soon. It just felt right.'

Benny finally relaxed enough to allow his lips to stretch into a smile. Had they reached another milestone in their relationship? 'D'you think I'm the first guy ever to have thrown up after his girlfriend said she loved him?'

'Oh, Benny!' She laughed, hugging him tighter. 'I can't help it. I love you to bits.'

Benny's heart swelled with pride. Nettie loved him? This amazing, wonderful girl loved stupid Benny Wellander? His disbelief turned into laughter that joined hers, until Nettie sobered.

'I'm glad we talked things through. We couldn't talk in front of your dad, and you were feeling rubbish. That's why I had to leave things. I know you thought I was backing out on you, and I'm sorry if I let that happen.'

'I'm sorry I nearly ran away again.'

It was his turn to draw her into his arms, and he brushed aside the strand of her fiery hair that had blown forward in the breeze. As he looked into her eyes and realised afresh how beautiful she was, Benny's emotions skyrocketed. Nettie had seen him at his worst, and she loved him. He knew he loved her too, even though so many things about their fledgeling relationship still baffled him. She had said they would take things at his pace. Well, maybe the pace needed to speed up. Benny was consumed by an urgent desire to kiss her. Except he didn't know how. Surely Nettie would know? She must have kissed at least one boy because she had Beth. His lips found hers and instinct took over.

Nettie was afraid to breathe, terrified to break the moment she had been dreaming about for longer than she cared to admit.

Benny's kisses were tentative at first then charged with ever-growing certainty. His confidence grew as each second passed until the moment ended, and they stood facing one another holding hands.

'You okay?' Had she rushed things when she'd promised she wouldn't? No; Benny had instigated the kiss.

'Yeah!' he beamed, looking boyish but pleased with himself.

'Good, because now I've kissed you once, I don't want to stop.'

'Or me.' He laughed self-consciously and leaned in for another, before withdrawing with a cheeky grin. 'D'you still wanna go for that burger, Nettie? I reckon kissing makes you hungry, cos I'm starving.'

'Benny Wellander!' She gave him a playful swipe. 'Did those words really come out of your mouth?' Nettie was constantly baffled by his lack of appetite. 'All right, and I suppose it'll have to be me who pays because you've never got any money.'

Her parents had Beth, so Nettie was free to enjoy their time alone. After nipping back for the car and picking Benny up by the side of the road, she drove to the closest McDonalds drive through, then once they'd grabbed their food, parked in her favourite quiet spot beside a lake. Nettie often found solace there when she needed time to walk and think. She sometimes brought Beth in her buggy, but she had never been there with Benny before. Now she wanted to share everything with him, and it was strangely rewarding to introduce him to a new spot near where he'd grown up.

They walked hand-in-hand until well past sunset, their chatter occasionally fading into silence. Even that felt effortless. The boy who had kissed her moments before was a child again, swinging her hand as they walked. Yet his complete transparency and inability to be anything other than what he was drew her like a magnet.

As they drew near their street, Nettie stopped the car. 'We'll have to tell our parents soon. Hiding it will be even harder now,' she said as she stroked his pale cheek.

Benny looked frightened, but he nodded before she started the car up and drove round the corner to her parents' driveway.

'Whatever happens, we'll face it together. Okay?' she said, squeezing his hand.

He nodded, waved, and blew her a subtle kiss as he climbed out of the car and turned to walk the short distance home.

26

Something was different about Benny. As Janet gazed out of the kitchen window with her hands in the dishwater, aimlessly feeling around for a plate that wasn't there, she felt it with every fibre of her being. But she couldn't place the cause.

When she had broached the subject with Ola, he had dismissed her concerns by saying Benny was probably worried about returning to school in September to start his GCSE's. 'He's going to struggle, Jan. He's bound to be dreading it.'

Unconvinced, Janet mentioned her worries to Emma, who dismissed them without a thought. 'You're always fretting about Benny. Give it a rest.'

That was another thing. Emma was considering changing jobs. The factory-work she'd taken after leaving school no longer satisfied her. She wanted to do something more challenging and was chatting to her dad about fulfilling his long-held desire for her to go to college and further her education. At twenty, she wouldn't be that much older than her fellow-students.

Janet could hear Ola from the other room, asking their daughter about her long-term plans. Benny sat behind her at the kitchen table.

Emma mentioned social work. 'There are a lot of needy kids out there. I think I could help them, Dad.'

Benny must have been listening too, because he suddenly stood up and wandered into the lounge. 'I reckon you'd be good at it, Emmie.'

Janet followed and held her breath, waiting for Emma or Ola to reprimand Benny for eavesdropping. Instead, Emma offered him a smile. 'Thanks, Pestie.'

'Your sister can do anything she puts her mind to,' Ola stated, with pride visible in the lift of his shoulders and the gleam of his eyes.

Benny's face fell as he picked up their dirty mugs and carried them back into the kitchen.

'What's the matter, my love?' Janet trailed him and stroked his back as he plunged the mugs into the soapy water.

'Dad's never gonna say stuff like that about me.'

It couldn't be denied. Emma was Ola's pride and joy. She was intelligent and confident; all the things Benny would never be.

❦

'You'll gloat about this for days, won't you?' Ola forced a smile onto his face as he and Janet stood on the Moss's driveway with Karen and Peter. The men had just returned from a game of golf which Peter had won. It irked Ola because he was usually the better golfer, and his competitive spirit hated coming second. Today, his friend and employee had outsmarted him, and he was struggling to be gracious.

'I'll try not to. Well, not too much anyway.' Peter waved the Wellanders off with a satisfied smile.

'I'm sure you'll beat him next time,' Janet soothed as Ola strode purposefully ahead of her towards their house.

Ola grunted. It was ridiculous for a grown man to be sulking over a trivial game of golf. Shameful even. Heck - he was acting like Benny.

Ola shook his head. He wondered if Benny had inherited some bad habits from his side of the family. Ola prided himself on setting a good example, but he wasn't doing that today.

'It doesn't matter, Jan,' he said to his wife who stood beside him, waiting for him to unlock their front door. 'It was only a game.'

Ola turned the key in the lock and ushered Janet inside, only to stand frozen in place as they entered their lounge. Benny was there, sharing a lingering embrace with Shanette Thompson. 'What on earth?' Ola couldn't believe his eyes.

'Dad!' Benny and Nettie sprang apart.

'Ola, please...' Nettie darted helpless glances from Ola, to Janet, to Benny, whose face had turned ashen.

'Don't you dare tell me this isn't what I think!' Ola's voice was eerily quiet while he shook with rage. 'I know what I just saw.'

Nettie bent to pick up her crying daughter who had abandoned her toys. 'Please, Ola, if you calm down, we can explain.' Her tone was even as she patted Beth's back.

How dare she? Ola's pent-up rage could not be restrained, and his next tirade came out in a bellow that seemed to shake the house. 'Explain what? How you've taken advantage of my fifteen-year-old son?'

Benny resembled a rabbit caught in a trap. Nettie moved closer to him, then swiftly changed her mind and backed away.

'Get out of my house!' Ola might have marched her to the door if it weren't for the baby she was trying to calm. 'I knew when you first came here that you were trouble. I should have listened to my instincts. I was fooled into thinking I was wrong.'

'You weren't wrong.' Nettie's eyes pleaded for understanding. 'I'm the same person I was when we sat in your garden chatting yesterday evening.'

'Oh, I know you haven't changed.' Ola glared at her viciously. 'Once a cheap tart always a cheap tart!'

'Dad!' The single word exploded from Benny in a strangled sob.

Nettie was touched that Benny was defending her, despite his tears and the way his body quivered. She considered staying and having this out with Ola but realised it would do no good. She had to abide by his wishes, even though the insult stung, and Benny might not understand.

'I'm so sorry, Benny.' Holding Beth snugly against her chest, Nettie headed for the door. 'This wasn't how it was supposed to be. We should have told them sooner. I'm older. I should have known better.'

'Don't go, Nettie!' As Benny made to follow her, Janet pulled him back holding him firmly in the circle of her arms.

'I'm so sorry, Benny. I never wanted it to happen like this.' They had left it too late. For the past week she'd had the urge to talk to their parents, but she'd done nothing about it. How much of this could have been avoided? But even if they had come clean, would Ola have handled it any differently?

'What are you saying?' Benny struggled to free himself from Janet's grip, but she held him even tighter.

'It's okay. Nothing's changed. We'll talk later.' Nettie was desperate to reassure him. She needed him to understand she was still committed to their relationship.

'Oh no, you will not!' Ola barked.

Nettie decided to leave. If she stayed, things would only get worse. Beth's cries had turned into a wail, and she knew her daughter had to be her priority. Whatever she said to Benny now would be undermined by his father.

Janet's grasp on her son loosened as the front door closed and Benny pulled free. He turned angry eyes on Ola, his rage mingling with his tears. 'You can't tell me who I can go out with!' He slumped heavily against the wall. In turmoil, Janet witnessed his dizziness and despair, but he turned away from her, as if unwilling to let her see his weakness.

'Oh yes I can young man, because you're a child and I'm your father!'

Janet reached for Benny again, longing to soothe him as she always had. She had to make this better before he made himself ill. He had always clung to her in the past. Why was he pushing her away now? Had Nettie poisoned him against his own mother?

'Oh, my love...' Her baby was out of his depth and suffering for it, and she yearned to draw him back into the shield of her protection. 'What on earth has she got you into?'

'It's not her,' Benny wailed pitifully, turning stone cold eyes her way. 'Why won't you believe me? You've always taken my side before. I want Nettie too!'

'You're a child, Benny.' Ola towered imposingly over his son, his eyes flashing and his body rigid with rage. 'You don't know what you want. You're not capable of it. You never have been.'

Benny clenched his side, as if Ola had stabbed him. All the progress they'd made, all the steps Ola had taken to understand their son. It had all been pointless.

'I can't talk to you right now, or I'll do something I'll regret.' Ola was heading out into the hallway. He turned to inflict one final verbal blow. 'But I'm telling you now, whatever you think you were doing with Shanette Thompson... It's over.' He pointed a finger at Benny for emphasis. 'No more, Benny!'

Benny crumpled to the floor as the front door slammed behind his father, and Janet knelt beside him, sure he would have a seizure. 'You've got to calm down, love,' she urged. 'You know what will happen if you don't.' Now they were alone, she was sure she could break down the barrier that had formed between them.

However, her son refused to meet her gaze.

Benny wanted to pound the carpet and scream his heart out, but that would give his parents the satisfaction of knowing they were right. He wasn't a child anymore, and he couldn't let them rule his life. He had to show them he was sure of what he wanted. He rose unsteadily, still struggling to quench his choking sobs.

For the first time he could remember, Benny was furious with his mum. She had let him down when he needed her most. All she wanted was to keep him as her baby. She wasn't interested in who he was becoming or what made him happy. 'I don't care, Mum,' he spat. 'I don't care about nothing if he stops me seeing Nettie!'

Now it was Benny's turn to stride into the hallway. He flung open the front door and was in the back garden unlatching the shed by the time his mum caught up with him.

'Benny! Please, love? You'll only make things worse with your dad if you go out now. Stay here and calm down.' This was the first time she hadn't been able to persuade him, and she looked terrified.

'I don't care what he wants.' Benny dragged his bike out of the shed and climbed onto it, not bothering to shut the door. He had to get away. He couldn't stand being around his parents any longer.

He heard Janet calling after him, but he didn't look back as he pedalled down the road in a frenzy. At first he rode aimlessly, blinded by his tears. Then common sense kicked in and he knew he needed to calm down. It was dangerous riding his bike without focusing on what he was doing. He could hurt himself or someone else. He got off and walked for a while, taking deep breaths, and slowly bringing his emotions under control. He briefly wondered where he was going. Then he knew, and he climbed back onto the bike and carefully pedalled his way to Emma and Erin's flat.

Emma was in the lounge on her phone, having just received a call from a frantic Nettie, when she heard the pounding on the door. Erin went to see who it was and didn't question Benny as she led the shaking and red-eyed boy inside.

'I'm worried about him, Em,' Nettie fretted. 'I saw him tearing past our house on his bike, but there was nothing I could do because I was still trying to calm Beth down.'

'It's okay, Nettie. He's just turned up here.' Emma glanced over at her brother and could only guess at the state he had got himself into. She switched her phone onto loud-speaker.

Nettie's voice gushed. 'Thank goodness!' Her relief was palpable. 'Can I talk to him?'

'I don't think my parents would like that.' Emma didn't feel it was her place to interfere.

'Please, Emma? Despite how this looks, you need to know that I do genuinely care about your brother.'

That brother had visibly relaxed as he heard Nettie's voice. He perched on the edge of a chair, and his eyelids drooped.

'How long has this been going on, Nettie?' The first Emma had known about it was in a frantic call from Janet moments after Benny left the house, but her mum had been too hysterical to make much sense.

'About three months,' Nettie admitted.

Emma struggled to comprehend how they had kept it a secret for so long. Her brother was normally an open book. 'All right, Nettie. You can talk to him.' She held out the phone to Benny, who gave an emphatic shake of his head as his face reddened with embarrassment. 'Oh no you don't, Benny Wellander!' Emma thrust the phone into his hand. 'You're half responsible for this mess, so you can do the adult thing and face up to it.'

Benny felt a glimmer of hope at Emma's words. If she was urging him to behave like an adult, then maybe she would start treating him like one. Now all he had to do was find some courage. He took the phone and squeaked out the only word he could form, 'Nettie?'

Her response was full of tenderness, and the moment he heard it his world fell back into place. 'Are you okay?'

If Emma or Janet had said those words, they would have sounded patronising, yet they were different coming from Nettie. 'Yeah…' Benny had to pull himself together. The time for crying and childishness was past. 'Yeah, I'll be okay.'

'I wish I could be there with you.' Each word she spoke calmed his pulse a little. 'I'm sorry, Benny. Things shouldn't have happened this way. I should've had more sense.'

'It wasn't your fault.'

'This will work out, okay?' Nettie sounded more convinced than he was. 'I want you to know nothing has changed between us. Your parents are gonna be pretty mad for a while. Especially your dad. We'll have to keep a low profile, but I'm not ready to give up on us unless it's what you want.'

'What are we gonna do if Dad won't let me see you?' It was hard for him not to sound like a child.

'We'll hang on and prove to him that our feelings are genuine, but I'm gonna need you to show him how mature you can be. Now's your chance to prove that what you're feeling for me is more than a childish crush.'

'You know it is.' Benny spoke with conviction.

'We both know that, but they don't. They still see you as the little boy they need to protect. Right now, your dad's thinking all those assumptions he made about me in the beginning were true. He can't see how much I love you, and he can't believe you can love me back.'

'I do, Nettie. I do love you.' It was the first time Benny had summoned up the courage to admit it. Quite how he loved her he still wasn't sure. Even he knew his age was still a barrier. 'I wish we could just be together, and we didn't have to do what they say all the time.'

'Well we do, so we're gonna have to try to win them over.'

'What d'you want me to do, Nettie?' He would do his utmost to follow her advice. He needed to prove his growing maturity to her as well as his parents, and even to himself.

'Be calm when you see your dad. I'm not asking you to back down. You can stick to your guns about our relationship, but be respectful. We'll still see one another, I promise.'

'Dad will ground me.'

'If he does, stick to his rules. If you break them, he'll see you as immature and rebellious. If we have to put up with chatting on the phone for a while, then that's how it's got to be. I promise we will see each other when we can. I'm not going anywhere, okay?' The more Nettie said it, the more he believed her. 'Remember, you've got to show him what you're made of.'

'What's that, Nettie?' Benny's gaze fell to the carpet, noticing the indents where Emma and Erin had recently moved some furniture. 'I don't think I'm made of nothing.'

'I don't know whether I want to shake or hug you.' Nettie sounded exasperated. Then her tone gentled. 'I wish you saw yourself the way I see you.'

'You're the only one who believes in me,' Benny muttered.

'Maybe I'm the only one who has to. But talk to Emma. Try to get her on-side. We're going to need her support, because she can usually get through to your dad. Oh, and calm down. The last thing we need is for you to make yourself ill.' Nettie hung up, and Benny held the phone out.

Emma stared at her brother open-mouthed, unable to believe what she had heard. 'Are you serious, Benny?'

'Will you talk to me without getting all cross?' Benny sounded pathetic, but Emma supposed she was being a little intimidating. 'I came here cos I need your help.'

She looked at Benny with a fresh perspective. This wasn't her baby brother coming to cry on her shoulder and tell her everyone was being mean. He was seeking practical help, not coddling. He was growing up, and she could either push him away or support him.

Still, no matter how hard he was trying, Emma knew what Benny needed most. She suspected this much about her brother would never change. She crossed the room and knelt in front of him, pulling him tenderly into her arms. Although he nestled into her embrace, he didn't start crying again, and this too surprised Emma.

'Okay, Pestie.' She drew him over to the sofa and wrapped her arm around his shoulders. 'Talk to me. What have you gone and got yourself into?'

'Me and Nettie...'

Emma suppressed the urge to correct his speech. Although she had been encouraging him to talk more carefully for years, he never seemed to care.

'We've been together for a while.'

'When you say together...' She had to make sure she was understanding him correctly. With Benny, she never dared presume.

'I mean boyfriend and girlfriend. Going out and stuff. It was what we both wanted.'

'But Benny, she's nearly eighteen, and she's got a baby.'

'I know that. I've always helped her look after Beth.'

Emma couldn't deny the truth in his words.

'You, Mum and Dad... It's like you won't let me grow up. I reckon you don't think I can.'

Emma rubbed at her nose, ashamed to admit he was right. In their defence, he'd never seemed like he wanted to before. 'Okay, but did you have to do it quite so dramatically?'

'Nettie and me...'

227

'Nettie and I.' If Benny wanted to be treated like an adult, he would have to learn to talk like one.

Benny smiled at her correction as he pondered his next words. 'We didn't make this happen. I reckon we both knew we wanted it to for a long time, but we didn't think it could.'

'I'm still not sure it can. I can't see Dad ever agreeing to you going out with her.' The spark of determination in Benny's eyes almost made Emma proud of him.

'He'll have to,' Benny confirmed. 'Cos I'm not gonna change my mind. And Nettie isn't neither.'

Their conversation was interrupted by the ringing of Emma's phone again. Realising it was their dad, she allowed Benny to see the caller ID before answering.

'Do you know what's happened, Emma?' Ola was cutting straight to the chase, sure he would find an ally in his level-headed daughter.

'Yes, Dad.' Emma sighed. 'Benny's here with me. He came over on his bike.'

'At least that's one less thing for your mother to worry about. She just rang me in a state because he'd run off. Typical Benny!'

Emma wondered if all the bridge-building between her father and brother had been for nothing.

'I'll come round and pick him up.' Ola's words earned Emma a pleading glance from Benny.

'Don't you think it might be better to let him stay here tonight?'

Her brother gave her a thumbs up and a smile, but Ola breathed heavily. His next words sounded like they were through gritted teeth. 'You hiding him away won't make a scrap of difference to how I feel. He must face the music some time.'

'He knows that, but it wouldn't hurt for him to stay here tonight, so you both have some cooling off time.'

'I still can't believe it. The gall of that girl! And to think I let it happen.'

Emma didn't bother arguing that he hadn't even known.

'If I'd stuck to my guns in the beginning and hadn't let her into my home, she wouldn't have taken advantage of your brother.'

228

'Dad,' Emma figured he wasn't going to listen to anything she had to say while he was still in such a temper, but maybe he would think about her words later, so she had to try. 'You might have to come to terms with the fact that Nettie didn't take advantage of him. Benny and I have been talking, and it sounds as though he went into this with his eyes open.'

'Don't be ridiculous!' Ola barked. 'He's a child having his first silly crush. I would've thought I could count on you for some common sense.'

'Kids Benny's age can sometimes know what they want, Dad. I remember being pretty sure of some things when I was fifteen.'

'You were different. You were a sensible girl. Benny's young for his age because of his limitations and the way we've protected him.'

'He used to be, but I think he's done some pretty fast growing up.'

'I don't want to hear any more of this nonsense!' Ola sounded about ready to explode.

'Fair enough. Tell Mum Benny will be fine here with us for tonight. I'll be round later to pick up his medication.'

When Ola hung up with a grunt, Emma turned back to her brother.

'Thanks, Emmie.' Benny leaned against her, and she couldn't help but place an arm about his shoulders.

'This will only be for tonight, Benny. You're going to have to go home tomorrow.' She was using her best stern older sister tone.

Benny tried not to laugh. 'I know that, and I'm gonna do what Nettie said and show him I can handle stuff right. If I want him and Mum to take me serious, then I know I've gotta act it.'

Emma's heart swelled with love, and she smiled at him encouragingly.

In response, his nose twitched. 'But you're gonna have to help me, cos I dunno if I know how.'

'You're learning, Little Pest. And you know you'll always have my help.' Emma made Benny a drink and left the flat to calm her mother down and pick up what he needed for the night.

Nettie glanced at the buzzing phone and her heart jumped when Benny's name flashed up.

'Are you still at Emma's?' she asked.

'Yeah. She convinced Dad to let me stay.' Benny sounded much calmer. Now they could work out a plan. Things suddenly didn't seem so bleak.

Nettie could hear Benny laughing when Beth wrestled the phone out of her hand and began babbling away in his ear. When she got the phone back, he told Nettie he knew exactly what Beth had said, which made her laugh with him. 'You're crazy!'

It was just one of the many things Nettie loved about him. He was as devoted to her daughter as he was to her. That had never changed. Ola Wellander would have to see sense, because despite her best efforts, Nettie was falling hook line and sinker for his son.

27

'I don't understand you, Nettie!' Mary Thompson gazed across the dining table in horror as Nettie broke the news about her relationship with Benny. 'He's a child.'

'I know it's hard for you to understand.' It was even more difficult for Nettie to explain because she still sometimes wondered how she had ended up here. She certainly hadn't planned it.

'It would explain the look of thunder I saw on his father's face when he passed me in the street yesterday.' John sprinkled pepper onto his meal. 'It'll never work, love. Even if the pair of you stood half a chance, Ola Wellander will never allow it.'

'How could you go from Simon to this?' Mary threw up her hands in horror.

Nettie couldn't deny her relationships had gone from one extreme to the other, but she'd never understood why her mum liked Simon.

'I know you were hurt, Nettie.' John tried another tactic. 'Simon treated you shamefully, but there are lots of other men out there who would act differently, even though you have Beth.'

'I'm not interested in anyone else, Dad. I love Benny.'

Nettie's words were met with stony silence.

Though there was little they could do, her parents took every opportunity to make their disapproval known, and she overheard them confessing that they were glad Ola was doing everything within his power to keep her and Benny apart.

During the weeks that followed the explosive revelation of her son's relationship with Nettie, Janet felt like she was living in a pressure cooker of tension. Ola was more distant than ever, and

Benny only answered when spoken to. As time passed and the outside temperature soared, Janet suffered from continual headaches and took to her bed. She had never felt so lonely. In the past, her difficulties with Ola were overridden by her closeness to her son. Now her clingy little boy had turned into a silent and sullen teenager overnight. It was all the fault of that Thompson girl.

'I don't know what to do, Karen.' Janet once again found herself weeping in her friend's kitchen as Karen sat opposite her feeding a loudly appreciative Marcus.

'Are you sure you can't get Ola to back down?' Karen pressed.

Janet couldn't believe she was daring to suggest such a thing. 'Why should he? It's wrong. Benny's still a child, and she's a young woman with a baby. He's too young to know what he wants.'

'But she cares about him, Jan. Isn't that what matters most?'

'She's ruined him!' Janet wailed. 'I've lost my lovely little boy, and it's all her fault.'

To Janet's slight annoyance, Karen didn't back her up. She remained silent and made her another cup of tea.

❧

Ola was sure Benny was still in regular contact with Nettie. He even suspected him of sneaking out to meet her when he was at work and Janet was resting. Despite his anger, part of him admired his boy's determination. Ola hadn't realised Benny was capable of such fortitude. He noticed with interest that his son was going out of his way not to cause arguments. If Ola asked him to carry out a task, Benny silently obeyed.

Ola wished he could find something to chastise him for, but Benny wasn't giving him the opportunity. Through it all, the thing hitting Ola hardest was how much he missed their times together. He hadn't realised how close they'd become until Benny withdrew, and with Emma no longer living at home and Janet in a state of constant tension, Ola felt lonelier than he had in years.

On the eve of Nettie's eighteenth birthday, Benny came downstairs to find his mother in the kitchen with tears pouring down her face. Although two months had passed, he was still smarting over the way she hadn't stood by him the day his father threw Nettie and Beth out of the house.

Yet Benny's tender heart hurt when he saw the state she was in. He'd been so absorbed in his own problems that he'd paid little attention to his mum, but tonight he saw her struggles. She was pale and tired, and her flimsy summer dress practically hung off her because she had lost weight. He had heard Ola snapping at her earlier in the evening, and he guessed that was what had brought on her tears.

'Mum?' He placed a hand on her back, and she looked up at him, her eyes still streaming. 'D'you want a tissue?' It had always been her offering one to him, and it felt strange for their roles to be reversed.

'I'll be okay.' Janet's lip trembled and although she leant gently on his shoulder, she didn't pull him closer or hold him tight. He wondered if she missed the feel of his arms entwined around her neck. He'd always needed her. Did she now need him?

Benny made two cups of hot chocolate and passed one to his mum before carrying the second up to his room. He was spending most of his time up there now, either chatting to Nettie on his phone, texting Damian or watching television. What else was there to do? Damian had taken advantage of their school holidays to visit his mother in London, and even Benny's tuition with Brian was on hold for the summer.

The only person Benny went anywhere with was Emma. She had drawn closer to him than ever, taking him out for ice cream and sending him encouraging messages every time she sensed he was struggling. He still couldn't believe he'd got her to see things from his point of view.

'Don't give up now, Pestie,' she kept encouraging. 'It'll be worth it in the end.'

'But what if Dad never changes his mind?' This was his constant fear.

'He will.'

❧

After chatting to both Benny and Nettie separately, Emma could see there was a strong bond between them, even if her brother was still in the early stages of understanding it. All her fears about Nettie's intentions towards him were also evaporating. She didn't show any signs of wanting to push Benny into something he wasn't ready for, and she was being careful to stay away and respect Ola's wishes.

Emma had tried explaining this to their father, but he wasn't willing to listen and had shut her out too. It felt alien for Emma to be taking Benny's side against their dad. Yet the more time passed, the more she thought Ola was overreacting.

Emma had just got in from work and collapsed on the sofa when Benny rang her. She could hear him slurping what was likely hot chocolate before he spoke.

'Mum was crying in the kitchen tonight,' he said, leaving out the usual pleasantries.

'Yeah. She's been doing that a lot lately, and you know she's been having loads of headaches.'

'Is it my fault, Emmie?' Benny asked.

'I guess it is,' she sighed, 'but I don't know what you can do about it.' There was no sense in shielding him from the truth now. He was up to his neck in an adult-sized problem, so he had to face the consequences like an adult. 'The only way she and Dad will go back to normal is if you give up on you and Nettie.'

'I don't wanna do that, but I don't wanna see Mum crying either. Even though I was mad with her the day Dad chucked Nettie out, she's still our mum. She's always looked after me and stuff.'

'That's part of the problem,' Emma explained. 'She can't accept that you don't need as much mothering anymore.' Emma wanted to be honest with him. He was trying so hard to understand, and she was proud of the way he was learning to read other people's feelings. Had they all been under-estimating his abilities for the past fifteen years?

'I do still need her, but it's not like how it used to be.'

'I think right now she needs you more.'

'I was wondering that...' Benny's voice trailed off and Emma heard another slurp.

'Her whole life has revolved around caring for you since you were born,' she clarified. 'Once we found out you were ill, she became obsessed. It was hard on me and Dad because it felt like you were all that mattered.'

'Is that why you sometimes got in a grumpy strop with me?'

'Sometimes I was jealous, yeah,' she admitted.

'What should I do, Emmie?'

She had been answering that question all his life. Tonight was going to be different. 'I think you already know.'

After ending the conversation with his sister, Benny knocked on his parents' closed bedroom door. He knew he would find his mum lying in bed alone. She always retreated to her room early these days. He could hear the television on downstairs and suspected his dad was watching the news.

'Mum?' He stood looking down at her pitiful form. Janet lay curled up in a ball cuddling her pillow. Benny realised this was the same way she had so often found him when he was struggling. Unable to find the right words, he lay down on the bed beside her and wrapped his arms around her back.

'Oh, Benny... I've missed you so much! I'm so lonely.' She cried as she clung to him.

Benny felt ashamed of his anger towards her. His mum was just as needy as him. He'd been wrong to push her away. 'I'm sorry, Mum.' He couldn't apologise for the way he felt about Nettie, but he could show remorse for hurting her and for making her ill.

At first Janet snuggled into his nearness. Then she slowly let him go, and he sat up beside her, resting his back against the headboard as he held her hand. They had always talked easily, but now they were hesitant, both afraid to bring up the one subject that hung heavy in the air between them.

His mum asked if he was looking forward to the weekend, and he said no. Although he didn't want to hurt her again, he couldn't help but blurt the truth.

'It's Nettie's birthday tomorrow. You know how sad you were feeling cos I wasn't talking to you? Well that's how I feel about not seeing Nettie on her birthday,' he said. 'Birthdays are really important to her.'

Janet looked into his eyes and her brow furrowed. 'How did it happen, Benny? You and Nettie?' She paused, giving him time to explain.

'I dunno.' He shrugged. 'It just did.'

When his mum smiled at his unsatisfactory explanation, Benny heard Ola switching off the hall light and ascending the stairs. Making up with his mother was one thing, but he wasn't ready to tackle his dad yet. He gave her a half smile then slipped back to his room.

❧

Nettie woke him up on the morning of her birthday with a phone call. When Benny answered, he could hear Beth in the background yelling, 'Enny! Enny!'

Benny laughed at her attempts to say his name.

'I'm in the middle of getting her dressed, and she's refusing to cooperate. She wants to put her leggings on her head.'

'Let me talk to her,' Benny said, then gave Beth a mini lecture about letting her mum get her ready. 'It's Mummy's birthday, Bethy. You have to be good today.'

'I wish I could see you,' Nettie bemoaned. 'Spending the day without you doesn't feel right. Do you think your Dad would let you come over, just for a few minutes?'

'I doubt it.' And it was Saturday, so Ola wouldn't be at work.

When Benny arrived downstairs, his mum had made pancakes, which they enjoyed together in the kitchen while Ola read his newspaper. Her eyes were brighter, and the smile was back on her face.

'What would you like to do today, sweetheart?' She seemed desperate to make him happy.

'See Nettie and Beth.' It was the only answer he could give because he refused to lie.

Janet sighed and filled the sink to wash the dishes.

Benny stayed to dry up, then retreated to his room. Emma had promised to take him out for a pizza to distract him, but he still had several hours to kill, and it was safer to be upstairs when his dad was close by.

'Did you realise it's Nettie's birthday today?' Janet had brought Ola a cup of coffee, and they sat together in the lounge.

'So?' Ola was being defensive, and Janet feared yet another conversation would end in disaster. He had already had a run-in with Emma over Benny that morning. She was still trying to talk him into letting her brother see Nettie.

'I don't want to go against you, Ola, but we can't go on as we are. It's not healthy for any of us.' Although being so outspoken with her husband was alien to Janet, she had spent a lot of time mulling over her conversation with Benny the previous night. She had also been chatting to Emma, and she was realising that somehow, they had to make Ola listen. 'This is probably the last thing you want to hear, but you might have to back down over Benny and Nettie.' There. She had said it. Now she waited for his admonishment.

'And allow my son to be taken in by her? Never!'

'He came and cuddled me last night, Ola. He hasn't done that for such a long time.'

'I know you miss the closeness you used to share.' Ola's anger was deflating. He studied her, perhaps wondering if she was willing to talk sensibly without dissolving into floods of tears. She didn't blame him. The tension of the last two months had affected her so much it had made her ill, and Ola always withdrew when she became emotional.

'It hasn't felt like he's needed me lately. That's been hard to take,' Janet admitted.

'You have to let him grow up.'

'Yes.' She reached for his hand, wondering if he would pull away, but he held it between both of his. 'Maybe we both do.'

'You're not the only one who's been missing him.'

Janet felt honoured that her tight-lipped husband was opening up. It wasn't easy for Ola to make himself vulnerable, even to her.

'I worked so hard to build up a relationship with him, and it was all gone overnight.'

'You could have it back, Ola.' She leaned over to kiss him, then worried he would think she was manipulating him to get what she wanted. He smiled and drew her closer.

'Only if I give him what he wants.' Ola's tone was reflective. Even if he was desperate to restore the harmony in their home, giving in was against her husband's principles. He'd feel like Benny had him over a barrel.

'Ola,' Janet didn't want to spoil the moment by saying the wrong thing, but she had to express her son's point of view. 'I think Benny does feel something for Nettie. I mean, we both know he's too young to understand the full weight of his feelings, but they seem genuine enough. I know she's made mistakes, but from what I've seen, Nettie's basically a good girl, and you know our Emma's convinced she's not out to take advantage of him.'

'We can't let him have a relationship with an eighteen-year-old with a baby, Jan. Not when he's so vulnerable. We're his parents. It's our job to protect him.'

'They already are in relationship. He won't give up on that, no matter how hard we push against him. You can attempt to keep them apart for as long as you like, but he'll still spend hours on the phone and sneak out to meet her if he can.'

'So you know he's been doing that?' Ola gave her a wry smile. 'I've been waiting for you to challenge him.'

'I've been admiring his determination.' Ola grinned. 'I'm discovering our son can be as pig-headed as his dad when he finds something he wants. Has Nettie encouraged him?'

'Emma maintains she hasn't. I wonder if, instead of forbidding them and encouraging his defiance, we could work together with them? Supervising them and showing them how to be responsible?'

'It goes against my better judgement to allow them to see each other at all.'

'Mine too,' she confessed. 'I want nothing more than to keep Benny safe here with me, but perhaps if we treat them more like adults, he and Nettie will act like it. I think...' She took a deep breath. 'I think that whether I like it or not, I'm going to have to start taking my little boy more seriously. The tide is shifting, Ola, and if I want to get close to him again, I'll have to learn to move with it.'

Ola said no more, and Janet left him to return to the kitchen. She had done all she could. It was up to him now.

❧

When Benny came down for lunch, his parents were waiting at the table, ready to share another strained and silent meal.

'Not having the best of Saturdays, are you, son?'

Benny couldn't believe he was hearing those words from his dad's mouth, and he didn't know how he should respond. 'Doesn't matter.' He tried to brush it off as he pretended to focus on yet another meal he didn't want. 'Damo will be back soon, then I'll have something to do.'

'How are you feeling about going back to school in a couple of weeks?'

Why was his dad asking about school? Did he want to make his day worse? 'Dunno. S'pose it's just part of getting older, doing GCSEs.'

'You feel you've done a lot of growing up during this past year, don't you?'

Benny wished Ola would just eat and not talk. He nodded, hoping that was the end of it.

'And in your eyes, you feel that makes you mature enough to handle a relationship, even if you have chosen a much older girl.'

Benny glanced up. His dad wanted to talk about Nettie? 'She's not even three years older than me. No one will care when I'm an adult.' If his dad wanted to talk, he would say what he had to,

239

even if it made Ola angry. The worst he could do was send Benny back up to his room, and that would be a relief. 'You wouldn't be saying nothing if I was eighteen.'

'Have you given much thought to the fact that when you're eighteen, Nettie will have a four-year-old?'

'Course I have. I think about Beth all the time. We don't pretend like she's not there, Dad.'

Ola raised his eyebrows, looking more impressed than angry.

Benny wondered if he was being respectful enough or if his dad would accuse him of insolence. 'I've been helping Nettie look after her since she was born,' he added.

'And you've done it well.'

Now Benny was thoroughly confused. What was his dad trying to get at?

'I've got to admit you've surprised me.' Ola looked straight into his eyes, and his next question nearly made Benny fall off his chair in shock. 'Tell me, when did you realise you were having feelings for Shanette?'

'Dunno.' Benny couldn't sit still anymore. He abandoned his lunch and gave in to his itchy feet. 'It just happened. We were always together, and I realised I wanna be with her all the time.' Benny thought Ola would chastise him for pacing, but he only nodded thoughtfully.

'That serious, huh?'

'I give her space to do stuff with her mates, but when they're not around, I just wanna hang out with her and Beth.' He waited for a negative retort, but it still didn't come. 'She... she gets me, Dad. And she makes me happy.'

'Don't you think all this happened too quickly?' That was the closest Ola had come to a rebuke, although his tone was still patient.

'Feels like we've been together a long time, so no.' Benny stopped pacing and leant against the kitchen sink.

Ola rose and approached. 'I'm not going to talk you out of this, am I, Benny?'

'No.' Benny dropped his gaze to the ground and was shocked to feel his father's arm around his shoulders. He had missed him so much, but he couldn't say that now, and he couldn't let himself cry.

'All right, Son. Your mother and I will support you in this.'

'What d'you mean?'

'I mean that Shanette and Beth are welcome to visit as often as they want to, but there is one thing I want to make very clear. You are not an adult yet, whereas as of today, Nettie is. That changes things. It means you must abide by our rules, which we're not making to hurt you, but to protect you. Do you understand?'

Benny thought that depended on what the rules were, but for now, he just nodded. He wasn't going to mess up his one chance to be back with Nettie.

'If you want to be given freedom, you've got to earn it. I expect you to behave responsibly. Nettie too. You and Emma keep assuring me she's a sensible girl, so I'm going to give her the chance to prove it. But she got pregnant before, remember? Some things are worth waiting for, son.' His dad was looking deep into his eyes, like he was assessing whether he got it. Benny did. He knew how Nettie made him feel, and he was starting to figure out how that sometimes led to babies.

'We won't do nothing stupid, Dad. We've gotta look after Beth.'

'Hoping you won't isn't good enough. Things happen by accident when you least expect them. So, I'm going to set some strict ground rules. When we found out about you and Nettie, you were alone together in the house. That isn't allowed. From now on, you're only allowed to be alone of it's in a public place, like the park. As I said, Nettie is welcome to come here, but only when we are here. And you must stay where we can see you.'

The idea of always being in front of his parents was almost enough to make Benny object, but he chewed his lip and kept his thoughts to himself.

Ola continued. 'I'm going to ask Nettie's parents over for a drink and make sure they enforce this too, okay? And you must always remember, Benny. Beth isn't your daughter.'

'It'd be a bit weird if she was.'

Ola let out a laugh and Benny was shocked to find himself pulled into a full-blown hug. As relief and warmth flooded through him, Benny wrapped his arms around his dad's waist and leaned in.

'So I imagine that now we've cleared things up, you'll be wanting to spend the rest of the day with your...' Ola's lip twitched. 'With your girlfriend. It's going to take a while for me to adjust to the idea that my son has a girlfriend.'

'Well, I do.' Benny grinned, even though he knew there was still work to be done.

Not finishing his lunch, Benny headed straight to the Thompson house. Ola followed shortly afterwards and shocked them both by apologising for the things he'd said to Nettie. She graciously accepted, and when Beth grabbed Ola's legs and squeezed them, asking for a cuddle, the tension broke.

'So that's it. It's all out in the open.' Nettie walked hand-in-hand with Benny later that evening. Beth rode on his shoulders as they headed for the park. It felt almost unreal, coming out of hiding and no longer having to constantly check if they were being watched. 'I can't believe your dad apologised for the things he said to me. That must've taken a lot of guts.'

'He's okay I guess.' Benny pulled her close as they stood on a bridge and Beth babbled down at the ducks.

'I'm sorry for the way I had to handle things with him.' Nettie had been placed in an awkward position when Ola came over. Knowing there were things he needed reassurance about, they'd inadvertently ended up talking about Benny as though he wasn't in the room. She sensed this was a common occurrence, and didn't want to become yet another person who fell into that trap.

Benny looked at her blankly. Was he so accustomed to it that he didn't realise it wasn't normal? Nettie would hate for people to talk about her like she wasn't there.

Nettie snuggled into his shoulder. Benny was on a steep learning curve with a lot of maturing still ahead, but she vowed to wait patiently and help him all she could. She was sure the end result would be worth it.

'Happy birthday.' Benny leaned in for a kiss and she closed her eyes as their lips met. There was still much to work out, but for now, she just wanted to enjoy being with him, celebrating what remained of the day.

28

Ola hated the fact that his family was under scrutiny. This was the very thing he had always striven to avoid and one of the aspects he despised about small village life, but there was no helping it now. Benny and Nettie had gone public, and it was the talk of the village. Not least because they were virtually inseparable when they weren't at work or school.

Ola often felt as though Shanette and her child had taken up permanent residence in his house. However, the changes in Benny were mostly for the good. Gone were the days of him hiding away in his room. Nettie even helped with his schoolwork, although it was still a major source of struggle.

Nettie was under pressure at home, which was the main reason she frequented the Wellanders. Her mother was trying to persuade her to visit her grandparents again, presuming some time with her old friends would help her see sense, but Nettie barely kept in touch with her city friends these days, and had no desire to.

Near the end of October, Nettie gave in and agreed to spend a week with her grandparents. Her granddad's health was shaky, and she knew time with Beth would lift his spirits. At eighteen months, her daughter was full of fun and mischief. Nettie's own energy reserves were running low, and like Ola, she struggled with knowing her relationship was the primary source of village gossip. With Christmas fast approaching, she would have to work extra hours at the shop. She worried how she would juggle her longer working days, taking care of Beth, and spending quality time with Benny.

They had their first serious row the day before she left. Beth was having one of her difficult toddler moments. She was going through the 'I want' stage, and had figured out that if Nettie said *no* to her demands, all she had to do was cry and Benny would give in. This was happening frequently, sometimes over seemingly inconsequential things, and it had started grating on Nettie.

'We can't always give her everything she wants,' she fumed.

'But she's crying, Nettie.' Benny hated seeing Beth cry.

'She's got to learn that turning on the tears won't always work.' Nettie's harsh tone resulted in both Benny and Beth remaining sulky for the rest of the evening. By the time she arrived home, she felt physically and mentally exhausted. Benny had picked up on her tension, causing his insecurities to resurface. It made Nettie wonder if her unwelcome holiday wasn't coming at the right time after all.

Later that night, once Beth was asleep and Nettie had indulged in a long bath, she realised Benny was only treating her daughter the way Janet treated him. He had so much to learn, and she wondered if it would take more patience than she possessed. Could she sustain their unusual relationship?

Dropping her head in her hands, she thought of the day they'd first kissed. She loved him. She couldn't deny it. That love must keep her pressing on. If she left tomorrow with things as they were, he would fret all week, and their hard work would be undone.

'Want to go for a walk?' She guessed he was in his room stewing when he answered her call.

'It's dark, Nettie.' He sounded tired and peeved.

'So?' She put teasing into her tone as she pictured him sprawled out on his bed, mindlessly flicking through the TV channels without actually watching anything. 'Not scared of the dark, are you?'

That worked. Benny slipped out without Janet knowing, and they met at the bottom of the street. Nettie's heart instantly softened at the sight of him walking towards her. Their eyes met, and she melted into his arms.

'I'm sorry.' Benny likely wasn't sure what he was apologising for. He just knew something had upset her and was desperate to put it right.

They walked for a while in silence as Nettie carefully formulated her words. Then she explained the reasons why they both needed to be on the same page with Beth. 'She'll play us off against one another,' she explained. 'She might not be able to talk properly yet, but Beth's clever, and she knows you hate seeing her cry. I know it's easier to give in, but I don't want her being spoiled. I know you shouldn't have to be thinking about things like this at your age, but it's part of the price you've gotta pay if you want to be my boyfriend.'

Benny didn't answer right away, yet one glance at his expression assured Nettie he was no longer sulking. He was taking time to process her words before giving his reply. She waited, squeezing his hand in a tender gesture of reassurance.

'I don't want her thinking I don't love her, cos I do, Nettie.' Benny was also choosing his words carefully. 'I love her loads.'

This was just the opening Nettie needed. Now he had explained his reasoning, she could help him understand. 'What about your dad? Do you think he loves you?'

Benny nodded, and they spent the next half hour talking about how discipline could be a way of showing love. She assured him that boundaries would help Beth feel more secure, and even suggested that some of his own inhibitions might have stemmed from his mother's pampering.

Benny listened with interest. 'Mum did spoil me, didn't she?' he finally said. 'And though I loved it when I was little, I was scared of everything that wasn't her. Now I'm older, I feel safer with Emmie and Dad because I know where I stand with them. That makes me brave.'

A smile spread over Nettie's face as he spoke. He could understand. By the time they shared a lingering goodnight kiss, Nettie was sure their honest talk was a huge step forward in their relationship. She left with Beth the following morning, feeling more hopeful than she had in recent weeks. The next few months would be tiring, but it would all be worth it. She would work the extra hours needed to make Christmas special for Beth, and she would continue working through things with Benny.

'Should I confiscate your phone?' This was the fourth text Benny had received during their study session, and Brian's frustration was growing. Sometimes he wondered why he bothered because since commencing his relationship with Nettie, Benny was showing less interest in his schoolwork than ever.

'How come you're in a grumpy strop?' Benny asked.

Brian couldn't deny he was in a bad mood, and it wasn't all because Benny was unwilling to focus. 'Let's give up on this for tonight.'

While Nettie distracted Benny's thoughts, Brian had his own issues. He was battling with an ongoing and unnerving feeling that God wanted him to talk to Benny about his Christian faith. He hadn't forgotten that day in the park when they had briefly discussed prayer after Benny had suffered one of his seizures.

Often since, Brian had felt this inner nudge around Benny, but he'd come up with every excuse he could muster not to obey it. He was being paid to help Benny study. Even if he tried talking to him about God or Jesus, Benny wouldn't understand. Explaining even the simplest mathematical or scientific concepts to him could often be frustrating.

'D'you want a hot chocolate?' Benny asked as he gathered up his schoolbooks, tossing them onto the floor in an untidy pile.

Brian was about to decline and head for home. He never stayed beyond the time allotted, and the only conversations they usually had were about Benny's schoolwork.

'Yeah, okay. Thanks.' The words were out before he had time to retract them, as if someone else had spoken on his behalf. Sighing, he followed Benny out to the kitchen.

'I bet doing A-levels must be pretty stressful.' Benny set the kettle to boil.

Brian was surprised Benny was thinking about him. He didn't usually invite him to stay either, as they had nothing in common. Not even Dale. Brian had stopped hanging out with Benny's tormentor when Dale left school after GCSEs.

'A-levels are the least of my worries right now.' He flopped down into a kitchen chair while Benny worked. 'Schoolwork I can handle. It's logical. I like it when I only have to rely on myself to make things happen. When I need to depend on other people for help and they let me down, it drives me crazy.' He was rambling, but there was no one else to listen, so Benny would have to do. Not that he expected anything in return. Benny probably wasn't capable of understanding what he was saying, let alone making helpful suggestions.

'Who's let you down?'

Brian sighed and took his drink with a nod of thanks. 'We've got a big youth event happening at church on Sunday for the teens and twenties group. Our pastor – that's the church leader – put me in charge of setting everything up. It's going to take all day Saturday if I can't find anyone to help me. Trouble is, whenever I ask people, they make excuses.'

'What've you gotta do?'

'Organise chairs, tables and that sort of thing. It's not complicated, but it's a two-man job.'

'I'll help if you want.'

'You?' Brian's jaw hung open.

'You've been helping me with my schoolwork. It'd be nice if I help you with something.'

Benny's generosity caused Brian to feel a pang of shame. Ola paid him for the tuition, but Benny was offering his help for free.

'I won't do nothing stupid if you tell me what you want,' Benny reassured, 'and if someone else wants to do it, then that's cool. Text me and I won't come.'

Brian smiled, well aware of Benny's fear of strangers.

When Saturday came with no one else having volunteered, Brian was amazed at how quickly they got the task done. He saw a new side to Benny as they seamlessly worked together, lifting tables and chairs into place. When Brian's pastor called in to see how things were progressing, Benny backed into a corner and pulled out his phone, obviously hoping he wouldn't be noticed. Brian chuckled. He knew that Pastor Tim was a warm, easy-going man, but Benny didn't know that.

When Tim stayed to help, he caught on quickly. Rather than asking Benny direct questions that made him freeze, he chatted to Brian, subtly drawing Benny into the conversation whenever he could.

When Benny left, Tim asked Brian about his young friend, and Brian had to admit they weren't exactly friends. He explained about their weekly study sessions. 'Benny's got a lot of problems. He has severe epileptic seizures, and I think they've affected his brain. His mother's sort of spoiled him all his life, and it's left him with a lot of hang-ups.'

'I could see that.' Pastor Tim absent-mindedly clicked the biro on his desk. 'Have you ever thought about sharing your faith with him?'

Brian said he had, but he didn't know how. He told Tim about Benny's seizure in the park and recalled the questions the younger boy had asked. 'I know I should've done something about it by now, but I wouldn't know how to get through to someone like Benny. You should see him with his schoolwork.' Brian knew he was making excuses to explain away his inaction. 'He hates anything that involves reading. He'd never cope with the Bible.'

'Don't be so sure about that. If God wants to speak to Benny, he'll do it despite his limitations.'

Tim left Brian with much to consider, and he resolved to spend more time praying about his dilemma, concluding that if God wanted him to reach Benny, then he would have to show him the way.

∽✒

'How did the youth thing at church go?' They were having another study session, and this time Benny was in one of his more cooperative moods, probably sparked by the return of Nettie and Beth.

'It was interesting.' Brian felt an all-too familiar pounding in his heart alerting him to the fact that God was at work. He prayed silently. If God wanted him to speak, he would need the right words.

'What goes on at your church?' Benny asked.

'Why don't you come and find out?' That wasn't the answer Brian had expected to give, but it was the one that popped into his head.

'I hate lots of people.'

'There are only about twenty of us at our Friday night youth group,' Brian explained, knowing that was still a lot for Benny. 'It's for people in their teens and early twenties. Pastor Tim gives us a talk from the Bible, and we have the chance to ask him questions.' Foreseeing Benny's next objection, he added, 'You don't have to ask anything. Some people don't. Then afterwards, some of us hang around to chat, play pool or whatever, but some people go straight home. It's all very relaxed.'

Benny thought about it, then shook his head. 'I couldn't come.'

'Why?' Brian sensed he had to push.

'They'd make fun of me. I'd say something stupid, or I'd have a seizure. You know what happens then.' He sighed. 'It's weird when I throw up everywhere.'

'The people at my youth group… They're not like Dale.' Brian was all too aware of his former friend's attitude to Benny.

'How come you don't hang round with him no more?' Benny asked.

'He doesn't want to grow up. He still acts the way he did when we were your age. It gets old. Plus, the way he treats people like you who are different from him… Well, it's wrong.'

'I get why people bully me and why no one wants to be my friend.'

'What about Nettie and Damo?' Brian smiled. 'You've got something I haven't.'

Benny looked confused, so Brian clarified, 'A girlfriend.'

'Bet you could get whatever girl you want to go out with you.'

'I don't think so.' Brian sighed. 'There is someone I like, but I don't have the guts to tell her.' It felt strange to be confiding in Benny, because he had only ever seen him as a slow kid who needed help. Yet, here they were having a normal conversation, and Brian found he was enjoying it. 'How did you find the courage to tell Nettie you fancied her?'

'I messed it up,' Benny confessed, and they both chuckled. 'I still reckon it's weird she wants to be with me. She could have whoever she wanted.'

'I've seen the way other guys look at her. Does it bother you?' Brian was still more than a little baffled by Nettie's choices.

'No.' Benny scribbled absent-mindedly on a piece of paper, then scowled when he realised he had defaced his maths homework. 'I'll have to do it again now!'

Brian laughed again. That was typical Benny. 'So will you come?'

'Where?' Benny had already lost the gist of the conversation as he glared down at his homework.

'To youth group.'

'You don't really want me to.'

'Wouldn't ask if I didn't. I don't mind sitting with you at the back.'

'No one else will wanna know you if you do that.'

Brian assured him he was wrong, but he also sensed it was time to let the subject drop.

Later that evening, Nettie met Benny after work for a walk. She wasn't getting home as early these days because of the late-night shopping and, as expected, the extended hours were taking their toll.

As he often did, Benny blurted out the last thing he'd been thinking about as soon as he saw her. 'Brian wants me to go to his youth group at church.'

Nettie laughed as she took his hand, and they began to walk. 'Don't I even get a proper hello before you start offloading onto me?'

He kissed her distractedly. Nettie sensed his growing agitation and mused that it was a good thing this was one of her better days. If this had happened after a long day of struggling with difficult and demanding customers, she might have accused him of being self-absorbed. He could still be that way sometimes when worries consumed him.

'I can't do it, Nettie.' He stopped walking and turned. She saw panic in his eyes as a streetlight eerily illuminated his pale face.

'So don't. No one's forcing you. I bet Brian only asked to be nice.' Benny got himself worked up over the strangest things.

'But he wants me to. No one's ever asked me to do nothing like that before. Not even you or Damo.'

'That's because me and Damo know you don't do groups.'

'I'm so stupid.' Benny let go of her hand and charged full steam ahead, causing Nettie to totter after him on her high heels. When she caught up with him, he was leaning against a wall looking like he was trying not to cry. 'And now you're gonna be mad with me too.' He hung his head and fought the tears, unwilling to meet her gaze.

Any anger Nettie had harboured over being forced to run after him evaporated as her heart was overwhelmed with love. The strength of her feelings for Benny still sometimes caught her off-guard. How had this happened? How had he stolen her heart without even trying? 'I'm not mad.' She took both his hands, forcing him to look at her. 'No one will make you do what Brian's asked, but I think your biggest problem is that you want to.'

He nodded. 'I do,' he whispered, 'and I dunno why.'

'What've you got to lose? If you hate it, you never have to go back, and if you like it... Well, you never know. You might make some more friends.'

'I've got you and Damo. I don't need no more friends.'

Nettie looked away, hiding a smile over the way he put her and Damian in the same bracket. 'Maybe now your confidence is growing you need more.'

'I don't reckon it is.'

'I know it is.' She leaned towards him for a kiss, and this time he gratified her with a proper one.

'Wanna come with me?' he asked hopefully as they hugged.

'No. Church isn't my scene. You should go with Brian like he's asked.'

They pulled apart and began walking again. Benny was calmer now and able to be more attentive.

'I think it's good for us to do things separately sometimes,' she said. 'It gives us more to talk about when we're alone like this.'

'I dunno...' He clearly wasn't convinced.

'We don't have to be together all the time, and it's good if we're interested in different things.' Nettie searched for an example and reached for the first thing that popped into her head. 'Imagine how you'd feel if I made you come shopping for clothes and makeup with me.'

'Bored.' He grinned.

'Yeah. So I wouldn't ask. I enjoy those things, and you like hearing about them when I get back because they make me happy.' She rewarded him with a beaming smile. 'I might not want to go to church, but you can bet I'll want to know all about it.'

❧

Benny's first night at the youth group was terrifying. He would have changed his mind if he hadn't been worried about letting Brian down. He wondered if Brian would cancel if Dale found out, but thankfully Dale was nowhere to be seen. They slipped into the building five minutes before the start of the meeting and sat at the back. Pastor Tim smiled at Benny but said nothing beyond hello.

The discussion was interesting, although much of it went over Benny's head. He knew little about the Bible beyond the basics they had all been taught at school and the stories he'd heard Chloe's mother reading at the hospital. She'd had a book of Children's Bible stories, and Benny had found listening to them calming, even if they were written for six-year-olds.

Pastor Tim talked about a guy called Paul who had something wrong with him. No one knew for sure what it was. It had obviously got on Paul's nerves, because he asked God three times to take it away. Benny could relate to that, although he had never thought to pray about his epilepsy. The doctors said the untreatable kind he had was rare, and they had given up trying to find a cure. All they did was help him manage it.

He wondered if Paul had something like epilepsy. Pastor Tim said he might have had a problem with his eyes because of something that happened on a road somewhere. Benny lost that part, but he became interested again when the pastor read something out of his Bible.

'So to keep me from becoming proud, I was given a thorn in my flesh, a messenger from Satan to torment me and keep me from becoming proud. Three different times I begged the Lord to take it away. Each time he said, 'My grace is all you need. My power works best in weakness.' So now I am glad to boast about my weaknesses, so that the power of Christ can work through me.'

Pastor Tim explained that God didn't take the problem away even though Paul begged him to. Instead, he taught Paul to use his weakness to lean more on his heavenly Father. Benny thought about the number of times his dad had to carry him after a seizure, and how safe he felt in Ola's arms. Did some people feel like that with God?

Benny was sure he would never feel that way, because God wouldn't want someone like him. He considered Paul boasting about his weaknesses, and decided Paul couldn't have had epilepsy. Epilepsy could never be boasted about. It had messed with his brain and ruined his chances of ever being normal.

The discussion ended soon after and Brian rose, signalling for Benny to follow him out of the church.

'I thought you said they all hang around afterwards.'

'Well yeah they do, but I guessed you wouldn't want to.'

'I'll walk home by myself. I've gotta meet Nettie, and you need to talk to that blonde girl in the front row.' Benny grinned, and Brian blushed.

'How did you know it was her?'

'Cos you were looking at her the way I look at Nettie.'

They exchanged a smile, then Benny left without a backward glance, relieved to be returning to his safe space, his family, and the girl he loved. It hadn't been as scary as he'd feared, though.

No one had bothered him, Pastor Tim was nice, and he'd enjoyed listening. If Brian didn't mind, Benny thought he might go to the Friday night youth group again.

29

'So who's the girl?' Tim asked as a wind-swept Benny battled his way into the church one Friday evening.

Benny had become a regular at the youth group for the past four months, even surprising Tim by attending the Christmas services. Although one or two of the others were subtly including him in their conversations, it was still Tim who spoke to him most.

'What?' Benny held what Tim privately christened his *deer caught in the headlights look* as he tried to stop the heavy door slamming behind him. It was so easy to get this lad into a panic.

'I saw you outside with a girl and a toddler.' Tim smiled. 'She kissed you goodbye, so I'm presuming she's your girlfriend.'

'That was Nettie.'

Tim noted the pride with which Benny said her name. Although he had learned about Benny's relationship from Brian, his goal from the start had been to encourage Benny to talk. Lately that was happening more, but Tim knew he still had to tread carefully. 'And the little girl's hers?'

When Benny just nodded, Tim sensed that was enough for tonight. He moved to the front of the gathering and began his evening's teaching. He often wondered how much Benny understood. Sometimes he looked vacant, but on other occasions, Tim saw a spark of something that gave him hope. He longed to offer the boy some private Bible study at a level he could understand, but sensed it wasn't time for that yet.

Benny was still skirting on the edge of the group, not speaking to anyone beyond basic pleasantries. However he had kept coming, even after the inevitable happened and he suffered a seizure in the middle of a meeting. Tim had handled it calmly, and Brian had rushed to help. No one mocked and, after it was over, a few of them had asked if Benny was okay. He was embarrassed and wanted to go home, so Brian had taken him.

Tim had feared that would mark the end of his time at the youth group, yet Benny came back the following week, more nervous than ever, but at least he was there.

'It's okay, Benny,' Tim had reassured. 'You can't help being epileptic. We're all fine with it.' During their prayer time, some of the other youths had prayed for Benny's seizures and the lad had looked surprised but pleased.

He stayed back for a while occasionally, just watching while the others milled around and played pool and other table games. Tim always took time to chat to him, but also gave him space to observe. Like Brian, he felt compelled to share with Benny how Jesus could change his life. Benny was clearly suffering from a significant case of low self-esteem, and Tim knew just what that felt like. That had been him once.

That night, Tim was teaching from Matthew chapter seventeen, about the healing of a boy possessed by a demon. Despite the subject matter, which might seem strange to many, the youngsters were eagerly engaging in the story.

'I think it would've been pretty scary to be around that boy,' Heather put in. 'The way it says he had seizures and fell into fire and water and stuff... That would've been terrifying for his parents.'

'But what about the boy?' Tim was always trying to encourage the youths to consider all angles of the Bible stories. 'How do you think he felt?'

'More scared than everyone else I reckon.'

Tim had to hide his shock that Benny had spoken up, and as he looked over at him, he sensed Benny's distress. He must have been so caught up in the story that he'd temporarily forgotten the others were present. Now about twenty pairs of eyes were on him, and Benny looked like he wanted to dart home.

'I imagine you'd understand more about this boy's plight than most of us.' Tim had spent long hours deliberating whether to teach from this passage. Having read studies drawing parallels between the boy's condition and epilepsy, he had wondered how Benny would react to the story.

'When you had a seizure here the other week, we weren't scared.' One of the more talkative boys stepped in, and Tim was glad the onus had been temporarily taken from Benny. 'I mean, okay it was a bit weird. I'd never seen anything like that before, but it isn't as if you can help it. I guess this boy in the Bible couldn't either.'

'People always get scared of things they don't understand,' Brian muttered thoughtfully.

The conversation moved on and Tim saw Benny relax, but when the meeting was over and the socialising had begun, Benny made a beeline for him. 'That boy in the story you read…' He paused, staring down at his feet. 'What happened to him was a bit like what happens to me.'

'Yes, I know.' Tim didn't want to put ideas into his head.

'Jesus said it was a demon.' Benny shrugged. 'That sounds scary.'

Tim was horrified as he realised what Benny was thinking, and he reached out to put a hand on his shoulder, surprised and gratified that Benny didn't flinch.

'That's where this boy's problem was different from yours. You see, some issues are physical, and some are spiritual. This boy's problem looked like epilepsy, but Jesus knew there was something more serious going on.'

'Epilepsy's pretty serious, especially when they can't give you nothing to stop it.'

'I'm not trying to deny that. Of course it's serious, particularly for someone like you who must live with its unpredictability every day. What I want is for you to understand the differences between this Bible story and your own.'

'So you don't reckon I'm like him?'

Tim was thrilled with the breakthrough they were having.

'You don't think I've got a demon inside me?' Benny asked.

'Absolutely not,' Tim reassured. 'You have a medical condition.'

'But some of that other stuff you've read about Jesus healing people… Some of those were blind, or deaf, or they couldn't walk… That's physical too, right?'

Tim nodded.

'So if Jesus healed them... D'you reckon he could take my epilepsy away and make me normal?'

'You are normal, Benny.'

'No, I'm not,' Benny stated. 'It's done stuff to my brain. I'm rubbish at school, and I don't remember stuff. Sometimes my dad gets mad with me cos he has to explain stuff loads cos I don't get it the first time. Or sometimes the second, or the third.' Benny gave a half smile and Tim allowed himself a chuckle. It seemed to set Benny at ease.

'That doesn't mean you're not normal.' Tim noted Benny was finally maintaining eye-contact, and he uttered a silent prayer of thanks. 'I believe the first step on your road to healing is to accept that you are who God made you to be, and to realise he loves you just the way you are.'

'But then I might be stuck with having epilepsy forever.'

'You might, or Jesus might take it away one day. It's up to him. We can all pray for you, but you need to understand that whether he heals you or not, Jesus loves you and wants to be your friend.'

'D'you think my epilepsy could be like that thing you talked about the first time I came here?'

Tim couldn't recall what he'd said on Benny's first visit to the group, and he was amazed the boy did.

'You went on about a guy called Paul,' Benny clarified, 'and how he asked God to take something away, but God didn't. D'you think my epilepsy could be like that?'

'A thorn in the flesh?'

Benny nodded.

'If it is, he'll give you the strength to bear it, like he did with Paul.'

Benny nodded and headed for the door, whilst Tim prayed his words had made an impact.

259

'You don't believe all that rubbish, do you?' Damian sat on a chair in Ola and Janet's back garden on a warm spring Saturday morning while Benny played with Beth on the lawn.

'I dunno.' Benny still wasn't sure where he stood with God and Jesus, and he still didn't get how they could be the same but different, like Pastor Tim said.

'So why do you keep going?' his friend probed.

'I like it, and no one makes fun of me.' Benny pulled Beth back as she attempted to approach Ola who was painting the fence. 'No, Bethy. You'll get yucky paint all over you.'

'But church is boring,' Damian persisted.

'I reckon the stuff that happens on Sundays is, but youth group isn't. They talk about good stuff, and I like Pastor Tim.'

When Beth squealed and made another dart towards Ola, Benny scooped her up and sat in the chair next to Damian, pinning Beth firmly in his lap. Beth released all her pent-up frustrations in a wail, but he remained unmoved. 'You can yell if you want to, Bethy, but I'm still not gonna let you get covered in paint.'

She struggled and kicked, but Benny held his ground until she gave up the fight and leaned into him for a cuddle.

'Are you gonna be good now?' He rubbed circles around her back, and Beth cooed contentedly, then smiled up at him with a toothy grin. 'Love you, Bethy.' Benny kissed her cheek, amazed by the strength of his affection for his girlfriend's feisty little daughter.

'Are you coming for a bike ride or what?' Damian asked.

'I can't cos I've got Beth. I'll meet you when Nettie gets back.'

They arranged a time, and Damian headed down to the park.

Ola indulged in a contented smile as he continued with his painting, thankful for his son's offer of a cup of coffee. He snuck a glance at Benny over his shoulder and saw him talking quietly to Beth, who now gazed adoringly up at him, hanging on his every word. Had it not been for Benny's age, they could be mistaken for father and daughter. Ola couldn't help being pleased with how things were working out in his boy's life.

Benny's growing maturity had shone moments before in the way he had disciplined Beth, and she seemed to love him more because of it.

Despite his initial misgivings, Ola was forced to conclude that the relationship with Nettie had been the making of his son. Benny's confidence was growing in other areas too. Though Ola held no religious convictions, he was pleased Benny was socialising at the youth group, and especially that he'd stuck it out after the seizure. Ola wouldn't have thought that possible a year ago.

❦

'I've had it up to here with you today!' Nettie was tired and cross because Beth had pushed her patience beyond its limits. They were at the park with Benny, and no matter what she tried, her daughter wouldn't stop her incessant grizzling.

'Want me to have her?' Benny had grown more accustomed to her temper flareups, and they didn't seem to unsettle him as they had in the beginning. They had been together for over a year now.

'She'll only want some of your ice cream, and she doesn't deserve it after the way she's behaved.' Nettie sat on a bench, pulled a biro and a tatty piece of paper out of her handbag, and handed them to Beth. 'There. You like drawing, so maybe this will keep you quiet for a while.'

'You can't let her have a pen, Nettie,' Benny said.

'Why?' Her anger was rising.

'Cos you don't give pens to little kids. Even I know that. She might put it in her mouth or something. Little kids have gotta have crayons and stuff that's safe.'

'Well if I had crayons, I'd give them to her,' Nettie snapped. 'Since when did you become the parenting expert?'

'Can't get nothing right with you, can I?' His eyes flashed with anger that matched hers. 'You said you wanted me to help with teaching Beth stuff, so I've been learning. I'm trying not to be childish and give in to her, even though it's easier cos it shuts her up, but now you don't like it cos I'm telling you something and you know I'm right.'

'Okay, fine.' Nettie rose, Beth in her arms. 'Is this the point where I should head for home before this turns into a full-scale row?'

'You're doing what I do.'

Nettie looked at him questioningly.

'Running away when stuff gets hard.' He approached her, having consumed the last of his ice cream, and Nettie was taken aback by his confidence. 'I'm sorry, okay?' He rested his hand on the small of her back. 'She's your kid, and I won't say nothing no more.'

'I'm surprised you ever know where you are with me. I can be so moody.' Nettie allowed herself to relax into Benny's embrace, all her anger and frustration evaporating as his arms encircled her.

'It's okay.' He kissed her tenderly.

'No it's not. You shouldn't let me treat you like that. You've got a right to be angry because I was being a brat.'

'You know a lot more stuff than me, Nettie.'

'Not always. You acted like the responsible parent just now, and I behaved like a child. You were right – it is dangerous to let Beth play with pens. I knew that, but I'd had enough, and I wasn't thinking straight. Then when I realised I was wrong, I jumped down your throat. I'm sorry, Benny.' She silenced him with a penetrating stare as he seemed about to respond. 'And you need to learn to accept it when I apologise and not pretend I haven't hurt you, when I know I have.'

'Okay.'

Nettie still wasn't sure he understood, so she pressed, 'I need you to tell me what you're thinking.'

'I'm thinking I love you loads.' He smiled, but she shook her head.

'Don't back down. I know you love me, but I also know I hurt you.'

'I'm muddled up, I guess.' He released his hold on her and took a few paces away before returning to her side. 'I dunno what you want. D'you want me to help you teach Beth stuff, or to let you do it?'

'That's a fair question.' She sighed heavily. 'We're both learning this parenting thing together, aren't we?'

'Kind of,' he admitted, 'but I know I'm not Beth's dad.'

'Let's face it; you're the only one she's ever known.'

'Yeah, but I'm too young.' It was his turn to release a plaintive sigh. 'I just wanna be what you want, Nettie.'

'Well, I just want you to be Benny - the quirky, funny, caring, and sometimes very silly guy I fell in love with.'

'I hate how stupid I am. Even my name is stupid. I told Mum and Dad I wish they'd called me Ben, cos that's normal. Benny was okay when I was little, but it sounds silly now.'

'Well you'll always be Benny to me, and I'll never let you change it.' She leaned in for the affection he was always more than eager to give. 'You are what you are, and you must learn to accept and enjoy it.'

'That's like what Pastor Tim said.'

'What did he say?'

'That I've gotta like who God made me to be. Trouble is, I don't even know if I believe in God yet, Nettie.'

'I'm afraid I can't help you with things like that because I've never given God much thought, but I think going to that youth group is good for you, so you should keep it up.'

'You were right about us needing to do stuff with other people as well as together,' he conceded.

'And you were right about Beth. I do need your help with her. It's so hard doing all this by myself. Mum puts me under a lot of pressure by constantly telling me how she thinks I should do things, or how Karen does such a good job with Marcus. It stresses me out.'

'Karen's older and she's had more kids and stuff. Is that why you were in a grumpy strop? Cos your mum was going on?'

She nodded. 'Every time Beth plays up, Mum acts as though it's my fault.'

'It's not, Nettie. Little kids are naughty all the time. Even my dad says you're a good mum.'

Nettie knew that coming from Ola, such words were high praise indeed. 'And Beth's lucky to have you in her life. We both are.'

They lapsed into companionable silence as they joined hands and gazed out over the duck pond, and Nettie felt her peace return. She was grateful for Benny, for his constant encouragement, love, and companionship.

30

Shortly after Benny's sixteenth birthday, Nettie's life changed with a letter.

She rarely received mail, so she wondered who her correspondent could be when her mum called up the stairs. Nettie was intrigued, maybe even a little excited, until she glanced at the handwriting on the envelope. That was enough to produce a strong urge to throw it straight in the bin. Having retreated upstairs and read its contents, she gave herself the satisfaction of tearing the paper into tiny pieces and disposing of it.

Though her mum noticed her change of mood, Nettie was unwilling to divulge her secret, forcibly convincing herself that this was a one-off. Surely nothing more would come of it? Desperate for distraction, she left Beth with her parents to spend some much-needed time with Benny. She felt more grateful than ever that he asked few questions and always accepted her just as she was.

'I've gotta do work experience before the summer holidays.' His words mercifully interrupted her thoughts, which had meandered to a dark place.

'Where have you got to go?'

'Dunno.' They sat outside a cafe sharing a large mug of hot chocolate, their hands touching under the table. 'Whatever I do I'll be rubbish.'

'Don't say that.' She gave his hand an encouraging squeeze. 'You've got to learn to stop putting yourself down. I bet there's something you'd like to do.'

'I'm no good at nothing, Nettie.'

She stole a kiss and grinned playfully. 'You sure about that?'

He laughed, and after swigging the last contents of the cup, she pulled him to his feet and dragged him into a nearby shop, earning herself a scowl and a stream of grumbling.

'If you wanna go shopping, you should do it with Kerry or Emma.'

'I'm coming to that beach trip with your church group,' she reminded him, 'so this is your payback.'

'I reckon you'll like the beach a lot more than I like shopping.'

She knew he was right, but Nettie was desperate for some retail therapy to take her mind off the discarded letter.

❧

A few weeks later, Nettie was playing with Beth in her parents' front garden when a strange vehicle pulled up on the driveway. An immediate sense of foreboding told her who it was before he even opened the door. She wanted to pick her daughter up and run, but Mary had seen him and was already inviting him inside.

'Simon!' Her mother beckoned, delivering a flirtatious smile that made Nettie feel sick. It forced her to glance at her former partner and try not to notice how handsome he looked.

Four years older than her, Simon had always maintained an air of confidence. They had made a striking couple, until she fell pregnant with Beth, leaving Simon horrified at the thought of becoming a father.

Before Nettie could stop her, Mary was ushering Simon into the house and offering him a cup of coffee. Nettie felt trapped. She knew she could take Beth over to Benny's house, but she sensed that even if she avoided Simon today, he would inevitably come back. Ignoring his letter hadn't been enough.

'Hello, Nettie.' Simon's eyes caressed her as she entered her parents' lounge with their daughter in her arms, and she felt ashamed of the blush that came to her cheeks. Why could he still play with her emotions?

'What are you doing here, Simon?' Nettie's tone was harsh, and she registered the shock on her mother's face.

'I told you in my letter. I want to see my daughter, and I needed to check that you're okay.'

266

'How did you know I'd kept Beth?' she asked.

'Beth?' Simon was startled. 'That's not the type of name I would have imagined you choosing.'

'A friend named her.' She didn't need to explain further. She owed him nothing.

'I bumped into one of your old friends a while back and she told me all about you.' Simon sank into a chair, while Nettie perched on the edge of the sofa.

Nettie guessed which of her former friends had been talking, and she wished she had never taken those trips to visit her grandparents. She didn't want Simon knowing anything about her or Beth. He didn't deserve to.

Perhaps sensing her coolness, he spoke in a more placating tone. 'I know I hurt you. What I did was inexcusable, but you have to understand, I was scared.'

'And you think I wasn't?' Nettie's temper bubbled to the surface.

'Of course you were, and what you did… Keeping our baby… It was very brave.'

'I nearly didn't.' Nettie tightened her hold on a squirming Beth who was eager to be down on the floor playing with her toys. 'I nearly gave her up for adoption.'

'Well I'm glad you didn't.'

He seemed sincere, with a gentler side Nettie had never seen before. Or was it an act? Everyone had been worried about her taking advantage of Benny, but the truth was, Simon had taken advantage of her first. She'd never do that to the boy she loved. 'You can't just come here and expect to be Beth's dad, Simon. It doesn't work like that.'

'I know she'll need time to get used to me,' he admitted.

'What if I don't want her to?' Her eyes challenged him, but his gaze was unflinching.

'I'm her father,' he countered. Nettie couldn't deny it, even though he hadn't taken responsibility for his child. 'I'd say we're both older and wiser now.'

'Having a baby makes you grow up pretty fast.' She sighed. 'It's been hard doing this by myself.' She regretted her words the moment they were out. She hadn't been alone. She'd had her parents, and more than that, she'd had Benny.

'No woman should have to bring up a baby alone. I'm so sorry, Nettie. Please, will you forgive me?'

She couldn't look at him anymore. Long-buried feelings were fighting their way back to the surface. Simon's presence had always made her go weak at the knees. All her friends had been jealous that it was Nettie he wanted. He'd had the pick of almost every girl, but he'd chosen her. He'd paraded her around like a trophy and treated her like a queen until the awful day when she burst his bubble with the news of her unwanted pregnancy.

'I need time to think. You should at least have the decency to give me that.'

'Yes of course.'

The speed with which Simon backed down surprised Nettie, but before he left, he pointed at Beth with a smile. 'She's beautiful; the spitting image of her mum.'

❧

Later that evening, Nettie rang Kerry and cried her heart out.

'What am I going to do?' she wailed.

'Can you refuse him access to Beth? I don't know a lot about these things, Nettie.' Kerry sounded concerned.

'Me neither. I never thought I'd have to.'

'What do your parents say?'

'Mum's adamant I should give in to him, but she always fell for his charm.' She also suspected Mary had an ulterior motive. She still hadn't accepted her daughter's relationship with Benny, although she tolerated his presence for Nettie's sake.

'And Benny? What does he say?'

Kerry's question brought her up short. 'I haven't told him yet.'

'Don't you think you should? He is your boyfriend.'

'I don't know if he's up to coping with all this.'

'Well if you're gonna stay together, he'll have to be.'

Nettie knew her friend was right, so she sent Benny a text after they hung up and asked him to meet her in their usual place at the end of their road.

As he walked towards her, she compared him to Simon, then felt a sense of betrayal. They were total opposites. That wasn't surprising with Benny being only sixteen compared to Simon's twenty-three.

'What's wrong, Nettie?' He reached out his arms to encircle her.

Nettie thought, not for the first time, that no one could hug like her Benny, and she rested her cheek against his. 'Oh, Benny...' As her tears came unbidden, he held her more tightly.

With difficulty, she told him about the letter and Simon's unexpected visit, and he listened calmly, still unwilling to relinquish his hold on her as her words tumbled out. 'I'm sorry. I know I should've told you about the letter straight away. I don't know why I didn't.'

'Did you think I'd be mad?'

'No, but I wasn't sure how you'd take it or whether you'd be able to cope.' She was loath to admit it, but the time had come for her to be honest.

'Is he gonna come back?'

'He says so. He seems to want to be a part of Beth's life. He feels he has rights as her father.'

'Maybe he does.' Benny rested his chin on her shoulder. His silence spoke volumes, but Nettie appreciated every moment he didn't crumble. He was trying to be strong for her, and she loved him for it.

'Simon will come back. I'd love to pretend it's not happening, like it'll all go away, but I know Simon. Once he's got an idea into his head, there's no stopping him.'

'Nettie...' Benny was grasping for words. 'I think... If my mum and dad split up... I think I'd still wanna see both of them. Maybe you should let Beth do that too.'

He was only voicing what she knew to be true. She pulled away from his hug, gave him a kiss and held his hand as they strolled down the street.

They walked for a while before Nettie bade him goodnight and returned to her parents' home. She lay awake all night with her fears. The one thing she could never admit to Benny was the affect Simon had on her, and in his innocence Benny hadn't even asked. His concerns had only been for Beth. Had it not occurred to him that spending time with Simon would put Nettie's own heart at risk?

As she rose the following morning and sent a brief message to Simon arranging his first visit with their daughter, Nettie vowed not to let him spoil things between her and Benny. She couldn't allow herself to be carried away by him again. The relationship she and Benny shared was much more sincere than anything that had ever existed between her and Simon. Despite his age and his limitations, Benny had given her everything. He trusted her wholeheartedly, and she couldn't let him down.

When Simon visited on Wednesday evening, Beth refused to make eye-contact with him. Instead, she horrified Nettie by sidling up to her with doleful eyes and asking for Benny.

'Who's Benny?' Simon was instantly on the alert.

'My friend from down the road. He's been helping me look after Beth.' Nettie excused her lie with the thought that Simon would never understand what she and Benny shared, but guilt soon had her rushing out to the kitchen to send Benny a text telling him how much she loved him.

His answer came back instantly. 'Love you too. How's Beth?'

Nettie's heart warmed at his concern. 'She won't even look at him,' she typed back.

'Well she doesn't know him yet, I guess.'

'She's been asking for you.' Nettie felt good about adding that part.

His reply was a little slower in coming. 'Tell her I'll come and see her after he's gone.'

Nettie put her phone down and spun to see Beth standing at her side holding up her little arms imploringly. She picked her up and kissed her cheek. 'Benny will come and see you later, Bethy,' she soothed.

'Want Benny!' Beth wailed, and Nettie felt totally out of her depth as she cuddled her and returned to Simon.

'I suppose I should have expected her to be hesitant with me.' Simon looked disappointed as Nettie saw him out an hour later. In all that time, Beth had clung to her and failed to respond to him.

'You're going to have to be prepared for this if you want to get to know her,' Nettie stated.

'I know,' he replied, 'and I am.'

As soon as Simon's car drove off, Benny appeared walking down the street towards them. Nettie realised he must have been watching Simon's departure. She was saved the stress of explanations by Beth launching herself straight into Benny's arms. He caught her, and Nettie was relieved that all his attention was consumed by her child. Where Beth had been silent with Simon, she now began a stream of constant babbling. Benny understood virtually every word.

As Nettie watched them that evening, she was hit by the realisation that Beth already thought she had a father. There was nothing Benny wouldn't do for her daughter. He fed and changed her and even consented to read haltingly when a tired and cranky Beth brought over one of her favourite bedtime books. He rocked her to sleep with tender whispers of love and comfort, before carrying her up to bed. She monopolised him all evening, as though she needed him closer now Simon was on the scene.

'That won't help her bond with her father.' Mary pulled Nettie aside while Benny was upstairs with Beth. Although he rarely spent much time at the Thompson house, tonight he'd done it for Beth and Nettie was touched. 'She's going to get more confused, Nettie.'

'What can I do about it?' Nettie threw up her hands in a gesture of despair.

'You can think about what's best for Beth.'

Mary's words cut her to the core, but she was saved the agony of replying by Benny returning to the kitchen and telling her Beth was asleep.

'You were amazing with her tonight.' They stood holding hands in her parents' garden under a moonlit sky. 'She was so grizzly while Simon was here. I didn't know how to handle her.'

'Maybe she'll be better next time.' Once again, there was no malice in his tone, and he left her with a kiss.

Nettie retreated upstairs to stand over her sleeping child, her thoughts awhirl. Why had Simon come and turned their lives upside down? And perhaps more importantly, why did she feel so conflicted?

31

'We need to think about your work experience.' Ola reached out to pat his son on the back as he realised his words were falling on deaf ears. 'Benny?'

'What?' Benny looked up from the slice of toast he was covering with lavish amounts of strawberry jam.

'You're getting more of that on the worktop than on your toast,' Ola reprimanded. 'Use a plate.' He tossed him a cloth, and Benny made a feeble attempt at cleaning up, earning him another scowl.

Janet bustled into the room with an armful of washing. 'I would have done that for you, my love.' It was her standard comment whenever she found Benny in the kitchen. She still resisted letting Benny do anything for himself.

'It's okay.' Benny bit into his toast, scattering a shower of crumbs.

Ola handed him a plate. 'Do you know what this is?'

'Sorry, Dad.' Noticing the mess he had made, Benny focused on cleaning it up. 'I wasn't thinking.'

'I can see that.' Ola's anger subsided as quickly as it had flared up. He pointed at the clean work-surface and smiled. 'Thank you. Now about what I was saying.'

'What were you saying?' Benny stood leaning against the worktop eating his toast.

'Can't you at least sit down with us to eat?' Janet asked.

His wife had always enjoyed family meals around their kitchen table, but with Emma having moved out and Benny being such an irregular eater, those times were now rare. In the past Benny had always sat with them even if he wasn't eating, but these days he was out more than he was at home. Their only guaranteed family time was when Emma came round for their weekly card games, but even they were often gate-crashed by Nettie or Damian.

'Sorry, Mum. I've gotta go out.'

His wife pouted. 'Why the hurry?'

'Simon's taking Beth out by himself today, and I wanna be there for Nettie. She's gonna be upset, and I reckon Beth won't like it neither.'

'That's very thoughtful of you.' Ola knew this would be the first time Benny met Beth's father, and he was surprised he was even considering it. His son normally avoided strangers at all costs, but he'd amazed him several times during the past six months, first with the church youth group, and now with this.

'I expect we'll go somewhere while Beth's out, so Nettie doesn't have to sit around worrying.'

'We still have to discuss your work experience,' Ola reminded him. 'These decisions don't make themselves.'

'Can we talk about it later?' Benny's expression was pleading, and Ola had the sense to let it go.

'This evening then?'

'Yeah, Dad. I promise.'

Simon had already arrived, and Nettie was anxious as Beth clung to her arm, wailing about not wanting to leave. Suddenly Beth stopped, reached out her arms and yelled, 'Benny!'

Benny approached, still munching the last of his toast. He was going to meet Simon. What would they make of each other? Nettie's knees weakened as the anxiety compounded and she struggled to control her wriggling daughter.

'She'll be fine with me, Nettie. She's getting used to me now.' Simon had seen Beth about a dozen times during the past few weeks. She was beginning to interact with him, but she still asked for Benny more often than not, proved by her present screeching.

Realising his daughter was looking beyond him, Simon turned his head. His eyebrows drew together. 'Who's that?'

'Hi, Bethy.' Benny blew Nettie's daughter a kiss as he stood at a distance, obviously unsure whether he should come closer.

Beth automatically reached out for him, but Nettie held her back. 'You'll see Benny later, sweetheart. You're going out with Simon in his car today, remember?' She felt even more flustered as Simon's expression changed. She could read him like a book. He was assessing Benny, his ripped jeans, faded t-shirt and slightly vacant expression. Nettie hadn't counted on Benny turning up early. She knew this was his way of offering support, but she wished he'd waited.

'That's Benny?' Simon muttered.

'Oh dear.' Nettie held Beth out to Simon. 'I've just realised I haven't given you her changing bag.'

'She won't need changing in the next two hours, will she?' Simon's nose twitched at the prospect of handling Beth's personal care.

'You never know with kids her age.' Nettie hurried into the house, leaving Beth looking uncertain in Simon's arms and Benny still hovering, gazing at his feet.

'Beth talks about you a lot.'

Benny hadn't expected Simon to speak to him.

'It sounds as though you've been a good friend to her and Nettie.' As Simon's gaze penetrated, Benny felt like he was under the scrutiny of an older, better-looking Dale Moss. 'Thank you.'

Then Benny realised what Simon had said. Had he heard him correctly? Simon had called him Nettie's *friend*. His head swam and his brain went into panic mode. He could feel himself shaking and he didn't know how to respond.

Nettie reappeared carrying Beth's bag and handed it to Simon. 'You be good.' She planted a loving kiss on her daughter's cheek, and Beth cried when she realised she was being placed in a strange car. 'You'll be okay, Bethy.' Nettie smiled at Beth through the back window as she sat wailing in her car-seat. 'You'll have fun!'

'I'm sure she'll settle down once we're on the move.' Simon climbed confidently into his vehicle, rolled down his window and revved the engine. 'We'll see you later.'

'Call if you need me. Don't let her make herself sick with crying.'

'I won't.'

As Simon drove away, Nettie's tears streamed. Despite his confusion over Simon's words, Benny instinctively reached out his arms, and she fell gratefully into them. 'What have I done, Benny?'

'She'll probably be okay once she gets used to him.' Benny was just as worried about Beth as her mother. He felt hugely protective of the toddler, but was all that about to change? He forced himself to pull away from the girl he loved and stared penetratingly into her eyes. 'Nettie, Simon said you told him I was your friend.'

Nettie looked horrified. 'Some things are so difficult to explain.' She was fumbling for the right words.

'Like how you've been going out with a guy who's loads younger than you?' He tried not to sound bitter, but he couldn't help it.

'Benny,' she squeaked. 'I don't know what to say to you. I'm so confused about everything.'

'Are you confused about if you wanna be with me or Simon?' He had known they were spending more time together. He'd presumed that was all because of Beth. Now he wondered whether he'd been naïve.

'I never thought I'd see him again.' She was wringing her hands in despair. 'Mum says… She says Beth needs a father. She says I'll only confuse her if…' She stumbled over her words again. 'I do… I do love you, Benny.'

'Yeah, I know you do.' He could no longer maintain eye-contact with her. 'But maybe you love him too, and you think you and Beth should be with him cos he's her dad.' He made to walk away, but Nettie pulled him back.

'Please don't go!'

'I've got to.' He shrugged out of her grasp. 'I don't wanna lose it and act stupid.' He swallowed hard to get rid of the lump forming in his throat. 'Maybe we need to split up so you can decide what you want.'

'Benny, no!'

'You didn't wanna tell him I'm your boyfriend.' He was crying now, tears of sadness not of rage. 'It's okay, Nettie. I get it.'

'Do you?' She hung her head in defeat. 'Because I'm not sure if I do. I'm so confused. I thought I knew what I wanted. I was so sure, but you have to believe me when I tell you I've never lied about my feelings for you.'

'I do,' he replied. 'I've gotta go now.' Benny longed for the safety of his bedroom where he could release his tears without shame.

'So this is it?' She darted him a nervous glance. 'You're breaking up with me?'

'I've got to, Nettie. Don't you get it?' He was shaking. Would the stress bring on a seizure? 'I love you and Beth, and if I'm gonna have to let you go, then I've gotta do it now.'

'Will I hear from you at all?' She called after him as he walked away.

'Text me if you like. We said we'd always be friends.'

As soon as he was a few strides away, Benny's feet quickened.

Ola was in the hallway preparing to clean his car when his son came barrelling through the front door with tears streaming down his cheeks.

'Hey, what's going on?' He put out a steadying hand, then watched as Benny crumpled into a heap on the bottom step of the staircase. At first Ola thought it was a seizure, but he soon realised Benny was extremely upset.

Sorrowful blue eyes lifted as Benny mumbled, 'Me and Nettie split up.' Then he rose and mounted the stairs alone. Ola followed him into his bedroom and closed the door behind them.

'Please, Dad?' Benny begged. 'I wanna be by myself. I don't want you to be mad with me. I know you hate it when I cry like a baby.' He stood with his back to Ola, gazing forlornly out of the window.

'Splitting up with your girlfriend is a good reason to be down, son. You don't have to hide it from me.'

277

Benny turned and Ola held out his arms. They embraced for several long moments, and Ola could tell Benny was still fighting to compose himself. How should he handle this unexpected turn of events?

'She told Simon I was her friend.' Benny sat down on his bed and rubbed at his streaming eyes with a tissue. 'She doesn't know what she wants. I had to break up with her, cos things are getting pretty serious for me, and if I've gotta let go of her and Beth, I need to do it now before…' He lowered his gaze and Ola finished his sentence for him.

'Before you let yourself fall in love with her.'

Benny's eyes glimmered in surprise before he nodded. 'Bit late for that.'

Ola had never expected Benny to be capable of the emotions he was expressing, but as he witnessed his grief, he knew they were real. Ola wasn't accustomed to discussing emotions, least of all with his son. Even so, he sat down beside Benny and put an arm around his shoulders. 'I'm proud of you, Benny. You're having to show maturity that's far beyond your years.' He smiled ruefully. 'I have to admit that until today, I wasn't sure whether you had it in you.'

'Yeah, well I don't feel very grown-up now. I feel like the stupid kid I've always been.'

'Not buying into that rubbish that real men don't cry, are you?'

'You don't.'

'You'd be surprised.' He handed Benny another tissue and waited for him to blow his nose. 'I won't have you putting yourself down over this.' When Benny shrugged, Ola took a firmer grip of his shoulders, forcing his son to turn and face him. 'Listen to me, Benny. I've never been prouder of you than I am today. It took a lot of guts to do what you just did.'

'You said it wouldn't work.' Benny looked so young and helpless. It was hard to believe he was dealing with his first relationship breakup.

'There's no pleasure in being right when my boy's been hurt. I wanted it to work out because I can see how much you care for Nettie and Beth.' He paused for thought, then continued. 'Letting her go and giving her this opportunity to make her own decision is proof of how deep your feelings run.'

'I dunno, Dad. Maybe it's best for Nettie, Simon and Beth to be together as a family cos he can give them what I can't. He can drive, he's grown-up, and he doesn't have stupid seizures.'

'None of that is essential. The main thing is, you wouldn't want Nettie being with you only out of a sense of duty, would you?'

Benny shook his head. 'I just want her and Beth to be happy.'

'And what about you?' There was tenderness in Ola's voice as he realised this was the closest he had ever felt to his son.

'I've just gotta get on with stuff I guess.'

Although it wasn't a satisfactory answer, it would have to do. 'Well, you know your mum and I will do what we can to help. We're here for you, Benny, and I'm sure your sister and Damo will be too.'

'Will you tell Mum?' he pleaded. 'I don't want her making a fuss. It'll wind me up.'

In the past, Benny would have run straight to Janet for pampering and sympathy. Now he wanted to handle his greatest challenge alone. Ola's chest swelled again.

'I will, but I'm not gonna let you hide up here by yourself all the time. You need to keep your mind occupied so you're not constantly dwelling on what's happened. It will be bad enough at night. You need to keep yourself busy during the day, so you'll sleep.' Ola could give practical support and was learning to supplement it with the emotional too. He realised that in some ways he and Benny were learning together.

'Thanks for not saying I'm stupid, Dad.' The crying had stopped for now, and Benny rose to throw away the tissues he had screwed up into an untidy ball.

'Well since I'm here, shall we have that talk about your work experience?' Ola pressed.

Benny groaned. 'I don't wanna think about that now.'

'Well you've got to,' Ola insisted. 'You're running out of time, and I can't continue letting you avoid the hard things the way your mother does.'

'There's nothing I wanna do. I'm rubbish at everything. No one's gonna want me working for them.'

'I do.' Ola's words brought Benny up short. 'I've been giving this a lot of thought, and I think you should do your work experience with me at the garage.' He had no idea whether he would find suitable work for Benny. His son's capabilities were still something of a mystery, but he wanted to protect him from the fears he would inevitably face if he was sent to a strange workplace. That seemed more vital than ever after his breakup with Nettie.

'You'll get mad with me. I'll be rubbish, like I am at everything.'

'No you will not.' Ola put a little of the familiar sternness back into his voice for emphasis. 'I'm a good teacher, and I'm sure I'll be able to find something for you to do.'

'I don't learn stuff quick. It doesn't go in.'

'I think you'll surprise yourself if you bother to try, but it would help if you wanted to do it. I'm afraid that's a lot of your problem, Benny. You've never taken a genuine interest in anything. Especially your schoolwork.'

'I'm… kind of afraid to want to do stuff, cos I'm scared I'll mess it up before I start.'

'Then you need to change your attitude and come at things with the belief that you're going to succeed. This week at the garage with me could be your starting point.'

'Mum won't let me do it,' he argued. 'She'll say it's too dangerous.'

'She'll know you're with me. Any signs of a seizure and you stop what you're doing straight away. That's something you'll have to learn to do no matter what job you decide on.'

Ola left Benny alone with his thoughts while he went to discuss things with Janet. When she heard about Benny's breakup with Nettie, she wanted to comfort him, but Ola persuaded her to give their son some space. He knew Benny would spend the rest of the day crying up in his room, and he was willing to grant him that concession. Janet's objections to Benny doing work experience at the garage were also quickly quashed, and on an impulse, Ola took his wife out for a walk to make sure she left Benny alone.

Benny lay on his bed for hours staring up at the ceiling. He had cried himself empty as he wondered what his life would be like without Nettie and Beth. A text message from Nettie arrived at about seven-thirty, after he'd excused himself from going downstairs for tea. He couldn't have eaten even if he'd wanted to.

She told him again that she was sorry, admitting that Beth had come home from her time with Simon in a worse state than when she'd left. Benny said he was sorry and offered to look after the toddler any time Nettie felt she needed a break. Perhaps that was a mistake, but he figured Beth shouldn't have to suffer because of their breakup, and he knew how wearing she could be. He still instinctively wanted to make Nettie's life easier.

He rang Damian and told him what had happened, and his friend offered to come straight over, just as Benny had known he would. Damo spent the night on his bedroom floor and held the bowl for him when he vomited after a seizure.

The following morning, Damian cajoled Benny into joining him on a bike ride. 'You can't sit in here and mope forever over a girl.' Damo was the expert in relationship breakups, although he'd never maintained anything as serious as Benny had with Nettie. 'You've gotta eat something. I'll buy you an ice cream.'

At that, Benny gave in. He was glad he still had Damo.

32

'You're gonna buy what?'

Benny grinned at Damian's disbelief as he propped his bike against a tree in the park. 'I told you; a skateboard,' he stated, with the same voice he'd use to suggest buying a second ice cream cone.

'But why?' Damo asked.

'Why not? You've got one.'

'And when you had a go, you fell off and twisted your ankle, and your mum went mad,' his friend reminded him.

'I fell off when I was learning to ride a bike too, but I don't no more.' Benny shrugged.

'You haven't got any money.'

'I've got enough to get the one I saw in the charity shop. Wanna come with me, or not?'

'I suppose. I mean, if you're gonna do something stupid, I guess I'd better be there to teach you how to do it properly.'

When Emma arrived to join the family for tea, Benny's purchase was the talk of the table. Predictably, their mum was worried about her *precious boy,* who'd already fallen off several times, but Emma was pleased to see Ola taking it in his stride. She even spotted her dad winking at her.

After they'd eaten, Emma decided to surprise her brother with her own prowess on the skateboard. She felt the years slip away as she went hurtling down the street, her hair flying out behind her in the breeze.

'How's Nettie?' Benny asked as they sat side by side on a wall.

Emma was breathless and smiling as she swung her legs back and forth whilst munching on a chocolate bar. 'I thought you'd know. She's told me she's still texting you.'

'She doesn't say nothing much. It's just normal stuff. She never says nothing about her and Simon, or if Beth's got used to him.' Benny leaned over to take a bite of her chocolate, and Emma playfully pulled it out of his reach.

'She doesn't say much about those things around me either.' Emma stuffed the chocolate into her mouth and grinned at him with bulging cheeks.

'Piggy!' Her brother laughed at the spectacle.

'You've always brought out the kid in me, Pestie.' She put an arm around him and drew him close, wondering how he was coping with Nettie's sudden withdrawal of physical affection.

Benny inched closer, looping his arm through hers. 'I miss her, Emmie.'

The simple statement contained far more meaning than he was able to express, and Emma didn't need to respond. She offered quiet support and a hand to hold, until Benny pulled away, climbed down from the wall, and took his turn with the skateboard. Amazingly, this time he didn't fall off.

❧

'Hey, Benny! We've missed you at youth group the past couple of Fridays.' Brian had walked over when Benny was practicing on his skateboard and started chatting.

'I don't think I'll come no more.' Benny hoped Brian wouldn't ask him why.

'They've all been asking after you.'

'They'll forget about me pretty quick.' Benny saw Nettie's car pulling into the street out of the corner of his eye and began backing up his parents' driveway. He was doing everything he could to avoid seeing her. Texts from her were one thing, but being near her without the right to hug her or hold her hand was more than he could bear.

Brian's shoulders dropped. He nodded then walked away.

Less than an hour later, Benny's mobile rang. When he realised who was the calling, he wasn't sure if he should answer. His heart-rate increased with both fear and excitement at the prospect of hearing her voice, and before he realised it, he was holding his phone up to his ear.

'Hi, Nettie.' He tried to sound casual.

'I saw you earlier when I was coming home, but before I could park up, you were gone.'

'Yeah.' His one-word utterance felt pathetic, but what more could he say? She must know why he hadn't been able to face her.

'Beth saw you too. She was with me in the car, and I had a terrible time calming her down when she realised we weren't gonna see you.'

'Hasn't she forgotten me yet?' Although he tried to put amusement into his tone, even he knew it wasn't working.

'No, of course she hasn't. She loves you.' Did Nettie still love him too?

'She's gotta get used to her dad now.'

'Yes, I know.' Nettie let out a sigh, and Benny could picture her creased forehead and worried frown. He wanted to run over the road and kiss her until her worry-lines faded into a smile, but that wouldn't happen anymore because she wouldn't want to be kissed by him now she had Simon.

When Nettie hung up, she felt worse than she had before. Their conversation had been awkward and stilted without the endearments and intimacies that had been an everyday part of their former relationship.

When she went back downstairs, she found Beth throwing a tantrum, and her mum not knowing what to do. So Nettie put Beth in her buggy and walked over to visit Kerry. Eventually Beth cried herself out and settled down for a nap, and Nettie inhaled the scent of roses carried on the balmy summer air.

'You're looking awful, Nettie.'

She couldn't help smiling at Kerry's greeting. 'I've had a difficult few days with Beth. She wakes up crying and doesn't seem to stop until she falls asleep again.'

'What's started all that?' Kerry asked, raising an eyebrow. She obviously had her own theories.

'It's got worse since I started insisting on her going out with Simon.' Nettie flopped into an armchair, having left Beth in the hallway to sleep. 'No matter how hard I try, she doesn't seem to be taking to him.'

'How hard is he trying?' Kerry probed.

'As hard as he can, I guess. I suppose parenthood doesn't come naturally to all men. I mean, he buys her things, and he tries to interact with her, but he doesn't know how to play with her like Benny did.' The comparison had slipped out before she had time to stop it.

'Do you think that's partly because of how young Benny is?' Kerry asked.

'No!' Nettie jumped eagerly to his defence. 'He's always been responsible around Beth. Sometimes more so than me.' She recalled incidences when Benny had anticipated danger before she did and had calmly diverted Beth's attention without incurring one of her tantrums.

'What do you want, Nettie?'

Kerry's intense stare was penetrating, and Nettie averted her eyes. 'I don't know.' She felt the tears coming. They seemed to fall unbidden these days. 'It's so complicated, Kerry. The more we see one another, the more convinced I am that Simon wants to get back with me. He keeps dropping hints. He's even suggesting I go out with him and Beth, and maybe he's right. Perhaps seeing us together as a family would make her feel more secure.'

'I hear a *but* in there somewhere,' Kerry persisted.

'Why isn't it Simon's face I think about last thing at night? Why do I do everything I can to avoid him getting physically close to me? And why isn't it him I text at least five times a day, just because I know I'll get a reply?'

'I can't answer that question.' Kerry spoke quietly. 'I wish I could.'

'I don't love Simon, Kerry.' Nettie was finally brave enough to meet her friend's gaze. 'I'm not sure I ever did. Our relationship was always based on the physical rather than on feelings.'

'And Benny?'

'That was all about feelings.' Nettie smiled reflectively. 'Well I guess there was more than that too. There was an incredible friendship, and more trust and honesty than I've ever known. He's also a lot of fun. I let myself laugh and be silly when I'm with Benny. When we were together, I could just be me, and he took me as I was. On my grumpy days, he either teased me out of it or let me have my strop, and he was so good with Beth.' She sighed. 'Why do I feel as though I've thrown away the best thing I ever had?'

'You haven't; not if you're still in contact with him.'

'Even by doing that I'm not being fair. Mum keeps telling me I have to think of what's best for Beth.'

'You're a person as well as a mum,' Kerry reminded her, 'and Beth won't be happy unless you are. Maybe you're already seeing that with her now?'

Nettie thought long and hard about what Kerry had said as she pushed Beth's buggy back home. However, when she arrived Simon had come for an unexpected visit, and this turn of events threw her into an even deeper state of confusion.

Benny stood at his bedroom window watching Nettie walking down the street with Simon and Beth. Simon had Beth riding on his shoulders, and Benny fought the jealousy trying to consume him. How many times had he carried her that way? How many times had he and Beth run to the park ahead of Nettie as she tottered after them on her ridiculously high heels? He had kept telling her to get rid of them and buy a pair of trainers, but Nettie always said she wouldn't be seen dead in flat shoes. It had become yet another of their shared jokes.

They didn't have any of that anymore, and he felt empty without it. He was trying to move on, to learn new things like skateboarding, but nothing was filling the void.

Turning away from the window, he saw the Bible he had used at youth group. He hadn't read it much; only when he had to. Even then, half the time he had only pretended to look up the verses Pastor Tim told them to read. Benny was too slow at finding chapters and verses, and when he did, the words often turned into a jumbled mess in his head. Well, he wouldn't be needing it anymore.

He stuffed the Bible into a drawer and switched on his TV. There was nothing he wanted to watch, but scrolling aimlessly through the channels temporarily numbed the bitter pain of rejection.

33

'Mrs Wellander?'

Janet peered cautiously at the clean-shaven young man standing on her doorstep. She wondered if he was a salesman and was about to send him away, but the fact that he knew her name had disarmed her. 'Yes?' She chewed on her bottom lip whilst acknowledging that Benny had most definitely inherited his wariness of strangers from her.

'I'm Pastor Tim Gordon from the local Baptist church.' He smiled to prove he meant her no harm. 'Your son's been attending my youth group.'

'Oh yes.' Janet found herself returning his smile. The young pastor had an uncanny way of putting even the most nervous person at ease, causing Janet to wonder if this was why Benny had taken to him? 'Would you like to come in?'

'Thank you.' Tim followed Janet into the lounge, where Ola sat in front of the television.

'Ola, this is Pastor Tim from Benny's youth group,' Janet explained.

Ola switched off the television, rose, and shook Tim's hand. 'Nice to meet you.'

'I was wondering…' Tim looked like he didn't know where to begin, even though he was the one who'd called on them. 'Is Benny okay?'

'Well yes…' Janet wasn't sure how much she should divulge.

'Only we haven't seen him at our meetings for a while.'

'He's been having a rough time of it.' Ola said, clearly less worried than she. 'He split up with his girlfriend.'

'I heard about that from Brian.'

'It's hit him hard,' Janet admitted. The pastor had been kind to Benny. 'He's been putting a brave face on things, but… Well, he's so young. I was always worried the relationship was getting too serious, and now it looks like I was right.'

'Do you think Benny would talk to me?' Tim asked.

'I'm not sure...' Janet twisted her wedding ring around on her finger. 'He hasn't been seeing many people since it happened except for his sister and his friend Damian.'

'But if you think you could get through to him...?' Without a backward glance, Ola walked purposefully out of the room and ascended the stairs.

Ola returned moments later with his son. One glance told Tim that the boy had lost even more weight, and his eyes were full of sadness. 'Hi, Benny.'

'Hi.' Benny stood in the doorway ready to bolt at the slightest provocation, and Tim felt grieved that all his hard work in forming a relationship with this youngster had been undone so rapidly.

'Do you fancy coming for a walk with me?' Something told Tim that Benny would feel more comfortable if they were moving.

Benny shifted on his heels before replying, 'Yeah okay.'

Tim began by making small-talk as they walked, and thanks to Brian he had the perfect opening. 'Brian told me you did your work experience with your dad at his garage before school broke up for the summer.'

Benny's eyes widened. Had he thought they wouldn't care?

'How did it go?' Tim asked.

'Better than I thought it would.' Benny paused for reflection. 'Better than Dad did too, I reckon. I liked it, and Dad wants me to carry on working there sometimes in the holidays.'

'That's great. So you think you might go into the family business when you leave school?' Tim smiled encouragingly.

'I don't think a lot about what I wanna do after school. Well, I didn't till I realised there might be something I could be a bit good at.'

'We're all good at something, Benny.'

'Not me.' His confession broke Tim's heart. 'I'm pretty stupid. You probably know... There's something wrong with my brain.

It's cos of the seizures and stuff, and if I keep on having them, it might get worse.'

'Lots of people have limitations. It doesn't make them useless or mean they can't contribute to society. It sounds to me like you might have found your niche.'

'I've gotta do something, I guess. I can't just live with my mum and dad forever and make them look after me. Mum would probably like to, but...'

'Fusses over you, does she?' Tim smiled, already knowing the answer.

'A lot.' Benny's face relaxed, and Tim saw glimpses of the boy whose confidence had grown at the youth group. 'I liked it when I was little. I guess I sometimes still do, but a lot of stuff's changed for me.' Benny became reflective and stopped walking. 'In the beginning it changed in a good way. Now it's all gone wrong again.'

'Your girlfriend?' Tim placed a hand on his shoulder, and Benny didn't shrug it off. 'I remember you telling me about Nettie and her little girl. Beth, isn't it?'

Benny teared up and glanced away. 'Me and Nettie split up.'

Tim gave him a few moments to elaborate, but when Benny didn't, he spoke again. 'Can I ask why?" He pointed at a bench, and they sat down.

'Beth's dad turned up. He wanted Nettie to get rid of Beth when she told him she was pregnant, but then he came here, and he wanted to know Beth. Only I think he wants Nettie too. I thought Nettie wanted me, but she told Simon I was only her friend.'

His words poured out as the dam burst, and Tim said a silent prayer of thanks.

'When I found out what Nettie said, I told her we should split up. I've seen her a lot with him since, so I guess they're gonna be a family now.'

'Simon, Nettie and Beth?' Tim clarified.

Benny nodded.

'And how does that make you feel?' He could tell without asking, but he felt Benny needed to admit it.

290

'Rubbish, cos I love her.' Tears filled Benny's eyes again, and he rose, turning his back.

Tim waited until his young friend had composed himself and sat back down. 'So you've been shutting yourself away from everyone again, like you used to before you got together with Nettie?' Tim had filled in the blanks with help from Brian.

'I still hang round with Damo.' Benny's eyes narrowed.

It was likely a good sign that the lad had become defensive. 'And do you think Damo is your only friend?'

Benny nodded assertively.

'What about all of us at the youth group, Benny?' Tim probed. 'I thought we were your friends too.'

'I reckon most of them think I'm stupid.'

'Why do you always presume people think you're stupid?'

'Cos I am. The kids at school make fun of me when I have a seizure because I throw up afterwards. No one knows why that happens. Mum and Dad have asked loads of doctors, and most of them don't reckon it's cos of the epilepsy. Mum thinks it's cos I get so scared of everything, and Dad... Well, it took him ages to like me, cos I wasn't the son he wanted.'

'From what I just saw, your dad loves you very much. I think that's why he wanted me to talk to you.'

'I guess he's hoping you can help, cos you're a pastor and stuff.'

'What would you like me to do, Benny?'

'Nothing. There's nothing no one can do.' Benny rose again, but this time he didn't turn away.

Tim took a deep breath. 'There's plenty Jesus can do.'

'What? Like get rid of my epilepsy, make my brain normal and stop me throwing up all the time?' Benny's agitation increased with every word.

'He could do all of those things, but I was thinking more about what's going on inside you rather than the physical. I was thinking about how he could help you deal with all your hurt over Nettie and Beth.'

'Yeah, cos he doesn't always heal people, does he? I remember that from what you said at youth group. There's all that thorn in the flesh stuff that Paul guy went on about.'

'For someone who claims to be stupid, you have a good memory.'

'I remember stuff when it means something.' Benny shrugged. 'That's why Dad thinks I can learn at the garage. I enjoyed what he was teaching me, and by the end of the week I guess I did remember some stuff.'

Tim stood, and they continued their walk. 'I think the reason why you remember what I said about Paul and his thorn in the flesh is because Jesus wants to use that bit of the Bible to speak to you,' he suggested.

'Jesus wouldn't wanna talk to me.'

'Why not?' Tim knew he had to keep pushing, no matter how uncomfortable Benny might be feeling. They had come too far now, and the quickening in his own chest compelled him to continue.

'Cos he's got better people to talk to. I thought Nettie wanted to be with me, but she didn't want me when someone better turned up.'

'And you think Jesus would do that too?' Tim asked.

'Well yeah. I don't even know if Jesus and God are real. How can you know when you can't see them?'

'Those are good questions. Shall I tell you how I know Jesus is real?'

Benny nodded.

'I know because I've seen him working in my life, time and time again. Like you working at the garage on a car - moving things around, fixing bits and topping the engine up with oil - Jesus works on my heart. He has to fix bits there too and keep me topped up with what I need to get through each day. Sometimes I find it really hard to be around people too, but Jesus has helped me overcome those fears.'

Benny raised an eyebrow. 'But you're so confident.'

'Now I am. I wasn't always this way, and sometimes, what you see on the outside isn't what's happening within. I'll admit Jesus doesn't always do what I want him to, but when I look back, I can usually see that what he's done has been for the best.'

'I'll never be able to say stuff like that about losing Nettie.' Benny shook his head in bewilderment.

'Right now you don't have to. I think Jesus would just like it if you tried talking to him, like you're talking to me now.'

As Tim caught Benny's gaze, the lad's eyes weren't vacant or shallow but were deep pools. Tim realised he wasn't seeing the brain-damaged, fearful young man most people saw when they looked at Benny Wellander. He was perceiving the character beneath. How much of Benny's reticence was caused by his fears and inhibitions? Tim felt convinced the boy could learn, and he wanted to help him. 'Can I ask you something?'

'If you want.'

'Will you let me teach you about Jesus?'

'Thought you were already doing that.'

'You've stopped coming to youth.' A grin passed between them, reassuring Tim that they were still friends.

'I don't wanna be with loads of people no more. I can't handle it. Maybe one day I'll come back.'

'I bet you could handle it if we spent some time together like this. Say once a week? We could go for a walk, talk, and read the Bible together.'

'I'm a slow reader, and I can never find none of those chapters and verses and stuff you go on about.' Benny was looking for excuses, but Tim wasn't about to let him indulge.

'You'd learn. You'd get quicker in time. Everyone finds the Bible overwhelming at first because it's so big.'

'Why do you wanna teach me?' Benny asked in barely more than a whisper.

'Because you're my friend, and when you have a friend, you want what's best for them. I believe the best thing for you is being introduced to the greatest friend of all. You know, if you'd been the only person alive in this world, Jesus would still have thought it was worth coming here to save you.'

He continued. 'I want you to read John 3:16, where it says that God loved the world so much that he sent his only son to die in your place and be confident enough to put your own name into that verse. Like this: "For this is how God loved Benny Wellander…" I hope you'll accept Jesus' friendship so he can give you strength to face things you never thought you'd be able to handle before. Even a future without Nettie.'

'I can't believe that will happen.' Benny was shaking his head.

'That's fair enough. Just agree to let me help you. I won't put you under pressure or expect more than you're able to give. You don't have to feel ashamed or nervous about what you can't understand, and I hope you'll become confident enough to ask me questions.'

'Yeah, okay.'

Benny's agreement to Tim's request surprised even himself, but as he reflected on it while walking back, he realised he had nothing left to lose. If there was someone who could help him, then maybe he should dare to reach out and take hold of what was offered.

When he snuck through the front door, he was relieved that Ola and Janet didn't question him. He guessed his dad must have had words with his mum.

Benny made himself a mug of warm milk and took it up to bed. He pulled his discarded Bible out of the drawer and put it back on his bedside cabinet. What was that verse Pastor Tim had talked about? He tried to remember, then it came back to him. It was John 3:16. Benny opened the Bible, pouring over the contents several times until he found the right page for John.

'Stupid,' he chided himself, but something compelled him not to cast the book aside. Finally he found it. Benny's eyes rested on the words. They jumbled and danced on the page and then became clear. 'For this is how God loved the world; He gave His One and Only Son, so that everyone who believes in Him will not perish but have eternal life.'

They danced again, but something kept pushing him to read them. So he read, and read, and read them again. It took him awhile, pausing between phrases. *His Only Son.* Who was that?

That was Jesus, wasn't it? He was sure Tim had said something at youth group about Jesus being God's son.

Ok. So God gave Jesus. For what? What else had Pastor Tim said? He'd said that Benny should put his own name into that verse. 'For this is how God loved Benny Wellander…' He stopped there, unable to go on. 'For this is how God loved stupid, thick, rubbish, Benny Wellander…'

He felt a nudge, telling him he shouldn't be thinking of himself like that. That was weird. It was like Dale had poked his ribs, except it didn't hurt. And it made him feel better, like when Nettie told him off for putting himself down. Did the nudge come from God? Benny tried again. "For this is how God loved Benny Wellander: He gave Jesus." Had God really given Jesus to him? Could God love him that much?

Benny placed a scrap of paper in the page and shut the Bible. That was enough for now. The second bit would have to wait. He was still unsure of what to believe, but he knew he would go back to it again. Was it possible that one day he would understand? He turned out his bedside lamp and fell asleep, and his dreams were undisturbed by images of Nettie.

34

'Is that Simon over there with Beth?' Damian pointed them out to Benny as they rode into the park on their bikes one sultry August afternoon.

'Yeah. I don't want her to see me.' Benny considered going back home, but he knew if he did, Damo would accuse him of wimping out. Seeing Beth with her real dad was about to make a rubbish day even worse. He'd already had to put up with teasing from Dale, who revelled in taunting him about his failed relationship with Nettie.

'You don't have to let on you've seen them,' Damian encouraged. 'We can eat our ice creams at the other end of the park.' He pointed to where the ice-cream van idled with only a short queue.

Although Benny agreed, as he waited and put his order in, his eyes kept straying to Beth, and he felt a magnetic pull towards her as she started crying.

'Looks like she's giving him a hard time, doesn't it?' Damian's cone split, and he swore under his breath as ice cream dripped down his arm.

Benny had never been perturbed by Damo's cursing, so why was it irking him now? 'It's cos he's putting her in the baby swing. She hates them.'

Almost against his will, Benny found himself walking towards Simon and Beth. The little girl's face lit up as she saw him, and he blew her a kiss. 'Hi, Bethy.' It wasn't her fault he and Nettie had split up. She was only a child, and she needed his love now as much as ever. Besides, he couldn't withhold it from her even if he tried.

'Benny!' Beth's crying instantly stopped as she smiled and held up her arms, but Benny knew he couldn't pick her up without Simon's permission. She was with her father now.

'D'you mind if I give her a hug?' He summoned up all his courage to ask, but Beth was worth it.

'Go ahead.' Simon looked as though he was coming to the end of his patience. 'I can't seem to do anything right today.'

'Are you being a naughty girl, Bethy?' Benny passed his ice-cream to Damian and Beth clung to him as he lifted her. Her weight in his arms brought immediate relief. She covered his cheek in wet kisses, and he laughed. 'Yuck!' Benny blew a raspberry on the little girl's neck, causing her whole body to shake with giggles, and he momentarily forgot himself as he played their familiar games. Beth remembered them all, as she held up her fingers for him to count, first on the left hand, then the right.

'Haven't you learned to do that yet?' Benny was so focused on amusing Beth that he forgot Simon was there, until he looked up, and their eyes met. The strain on Simon's face made him nervous, and Benny averted his gaze, knowing he should put the toddler down.

'Thank you for stopping her crying.' Simon muttered awkwardly.

'It was cos she doesn't like the baby swings. She'll only go on the swings if you have her on your lap. If you do that, she loves it.' Benny relinquished Beth to her father, but she immediately resumed her crying, whimpering Benny's name.

'No, Bethy. Be good.' Why was he still talking as though he was her dad?

'I should let you get on with whatever you were doing,' Simon said as he turned away, signalling the end of their conversation.

Forcing himself not to witness Beth's continued crying, Benny returned to Damian with a heavy heart. Then, making his excuses, he left the park.

❧

'Simon said he saw you at the park today.'

Benny had answered the phone to Nettie again despite his internal warning signals. She had rung just after his first Bible study with Tim, and he was exhausted. His brain hurt from the effort of wanting to learn, because that was a whole new experience. They'd discussed the John 3:16 verse Benny had been reading every morning and every night before he went to sleep. Especially the end part about not perishing and having eternal life. He'd wanted to know what that meant.

'Sorry, Nettie. She was crying, and I knew it was cos he was putting her in one of the baby swings.'

'He said she was excited to see you.'

'Yeah, but I don't reckon he liked it. I shouldn't have done it.'

'Yes, you should.'

What was that meant to mean? It sounded like she wanted to say more but she didn't, so Benny just massaged his head and collapsed into bed.

An hour after Nettie hung up, Benny found himself on the bathroom floor vomiting violently after a seizure. He reached for his phone, thankful he always kept it in his pocket, and dashed off a nonsensical text to his dad.

Moments later, he heard Ola mounting the stairs two at a time. His dad only paused a moment before sweeping Benny up, as though he weighed nothing, and carrying him to his room.

Benny's body was soon battered by another seizure, followed by a third. They continued throughout the night until he saw the flash of ambulance lights through the curtains. He was incoherent and dehydrated but he knew what that meant.

They pumped him with fluids at the hospital and gave him something for the sickness, until finally, after a sleepless night, he was released to go home. He slumped down in the back of the car as Ola drove, refusing his mother's offer to sit beside him.

'I'm not a baby no more, Mum.' Benny struggled to even get the simplest of words out. His body and mind were beyond his control, and it was scary.

'Are you there, Jesus? Do you really love me?' The cry came from his heart as Benny fought not to be sick again. What would happen if he kept on throwing up? Would he die? He supposed he might. Right now, he wasn't even sure he cared. If Jesus loved him as much as Pastor Tim claimed, then Benny would be better off in heaven. At least then he wouldn't cause so much trouble for his parents.

When they reached the house, his dad helped him inside, lowering him onto the sofa as his mum hovered over him. Benny felt weak and pathetic, knowing he wouldn't even get to the bathroom by himself.

He must have slept for a while, because when he woke, his dad was standing beside him, asking if he wanted help to get upstairs. He accepted gratefully, but found he was more able to stand. Perhaps the worst was over.

'He hasn't been this ill for a long time, Ola,' Janet fretted as they shared a meal while Benny slept.

'I know.' Her husband didn't tell her not to worry. He surprised her by reaching for her hand.

'He's been trying to be so brave lately, so grown-up.' Tears filled Janet's eyes, and Ola's hand squeezed tighter. They were united in a common cause, as they both worried over their boy.

'But he's still only sixteen.' Ola sighed.

'It was so much easier when he was little,' Janet mused. 'I could sit him on my lap, cuddle him, and tell him everything was going to be okay. These days he pushes me away.'

'That's because of his age, Jan.'

'It's more than that. He's gone from needing help with everything to never wanting help at all. It's like he believes he has to cope with everything by himself.'

'Do you think so? I know I pushed him to be more independent, but that's not what I wanted.'

'I know that more than anything, he wants to make you proud. He's so thrilled to have finally got closer to you.'

'I am proud of him. I hoped he'd know that by now.'

'He hasn't eaten since yesterday.' Worry filled Janet's heart. Benny couldn't afford to get any thinner.

'Then it's no wonder he's so weak.' Ola paused. 'He's struggling without Nettie and Beth, isn't he, Jan?'

'Yes.' She wondered how much she could say without arousing his anger. 'I think he does love her. It might not be the kind of love a mature adult feels, but it's very real to Benny. It's breaking his heart to see Nettie and Beth with Simon.'

'You should go to him. Perhaps you can give him some of the comfort he used to enjoy when he was a child.'

'If he'll let me near him.' She stood and prepared to leave.

'Whatever happens, tell him it'll be just between the two of you. He doesn't need the pressure of thinking you'll tell me if he gets upset.'

Janet climbed the stairs and knocked on Benny's bedroom door. Receiving a feeble response, she entered the room, finding her son curled up on his bed in the foetal position. All Janet could see as she gazed down upon his pitiful form was the little boy who had clung to her during his formative years.

'Benny love ...' She ignored his grunt of protest as she sat down beside him. 'I wish you'd talk to me.'

'Nothing to say.'

'Oh, but I think there is. Between everything that's happened with Nettie and how ill you've been, I'd say you've just about had all you can take.'

Benny turned away, burying his face in the pillow. Janet knew he was trying to hide his tears.

'Darling...' She stroked his back in a gesture that had always brought him so much comfort. 'I'm still your mum, and you're still my boy, no matter how old you get. I know you don't want to hear it, but there's nothing shameful about letting go when everything is too much.'

Benny's chest heaved. Then he turned, propelled himself into Janet's waiting arms and sobbed his heart out. Janet held him, muttering soothing endearments as her own tears mingled with his.

'I'm sorry!' Her son sniffed as he pulled away, his eyes and nose running.

Janet stifled the urge to hold the tissue for him as he blew his nose, knowing such an act would undo all her good work and make him angry.

'I'm always gonna be a stupid little kid, Mum!' Benny wailed. 'I get why Nettie doesn't want me.'

'You are not stupid.' Janet steadied him with an arm around his back. 'And you aren't little anymore either, despite how much I sometimes wish you were.'

He gave her a weak smile.

'I didn't come up here to embarrass you, Benny. I came to help. I've been watching you struggle, and although I've been trying to respect your desire to be treated like a grown-up, today I wondered whether you might need your mum.'

'I do.' He reached for her hand.

'I'm here for you, love. Like I've always been. Your dad is too. I know our relationship had to change, and I'm sorry for trying to hold on to things the way they were. I realise I haven't supported you like I could have. I was too preoccupied with missing the little boy you were, instead of enjoying the young man you're becoming.'

'Everything's changed, Mum.'

'But most of those changes are for the good. It's been nice watching you getting closer to your dad, and Damo is the friend you've always wanted. Then there's Pastor Tim. I know he's become a big help to you, and I can see he genuinely cares about you just as we do.'

'Damo and Pastor Tim get me,' was his blunt response.

'I hope we do too.'

'Yeah, sometimes, when you're not wishing I was still a baby.'

A chuckle escaped her lips as Janet leaned over to kiss his cheek.

'I guess it was hard for you though, cos I wanted you all the time, and then I started pushing you away. I'm sorry, Mum. It's really hard growing up.'

'Yes. I remember. Benny, you need to know how proud your father and I are of you. Especially lately, with everything you've had to handle.'

'You never took me and Nettie seriously, did you? You thought it was a silly crush.' There was no accusation in his tone. He was stating the facts, and Janet couldn't deny them.

'I didn't want to see what it was, because it felt like another part of letting you go, but since you and Nettie broke up, I've hated watching you suffer. You've been trying so hard to hold it all together.'

'I love her, Mum.' Benny rested his head on her shoulder. 'I know it's weird, but I can't help it.'

'You've always felt things intensely. Like when you were little, and you had that awful separation anxiety every time I left the room. You wouldn't let anyone else hold you. I think that's part of why your dad struggled to get close to you.'

'I wish I was normal.' Benny sighed.

'Oh, you are.' Janet hugged him tightly. 'You're working it all out, mostly by yourself from what I can see.'

'A lot of it was cos of Nettie. She made me feel good about myself, like I could do stuff.'

'You can.' Janet stared deeply into his eyes, wanting him to know with all her heart that she believed in him. 'You can do anything you want to.'

'I feel weird without her, Mum, like there's nothing left, but Pastor Tim keeps telling me there is. He keeps trying to get me to ask Jesus for help.'

'I don't pretend to know a lot about faith, my love,' Janet ventured, 'but I can tell you, I believe Jesus is real and that I'm sure he wants to help you.'

'So you don't think he's a made-up guy, like some people do?'

'No, Benny. I don't.' She paused for reflection, then went on. 'Have I ever told you I went to Sunday School as a child?'

He said she hadn't.

'I loved it. All the beautiful stories and songs…'

'How come you stopped going?'

'I guess that as I grew up, other things in life took over. Then I met your dad, and… Well, we never talked about what we believed.'

'I think Dad's okay with Tim.'

'Yes. He seems to like him.'

'I think I wanna go back to youth group, Mum. I guess... I guess I need to carry on doing stuff, even if I've gotta get used to being without Nettie.'

'That sounds like a great idea.'

Janet sat talking to him for another half hour, after which Benny agreed to go downstairs for something to eat. They sat in the kitchen with Ola, enjoying time together as a family.

When Emma came round later for their customary card games, Benny was still thinking about Nettie. Still, his sister cheered him up somewhat and he went to bed grateful for his family. As he read John 3:16 again, he wondered if those words might really be true. Perhaps God and Jesus did really love Benny Wellander.

35

'So what've I gotta do?' Benny asked, unable to wait much longer for his opportunity to speak.

Pastor Tim spun away from his conversation with Brian and smiled. 'What've you gotta do about what, Benny?'

It was Benny's first week back at youth group. He had slipped in five minutes late hoping no one would notice him, but the heavy church door creaked, ruining his plans. His face warmed when everyone turned round, but Tim had waved him in then gone on with his lesson, giving Benny the chance to sit at the back and resist running back home.

'You said tonight that we've gotta be sure about what we believe; that we need to make a commitment,' Benny stated. 'So how do I do it? How can I show God I'm serious?' He no longer spoke of God and Jesus as two separate people. He was learning to use the two names interchangeably during his study sessions with the pastor.

'Are you saying you're ready to become a Christian?' Tim enquired.

Benny nodded emphatically.

'Should I go?' Brian asked.

'No. It was you who got me to come here, so I guess you can be here now.' Benny was no longer scared of looking stupid in front of him like he used to be.

'Can you give me a moment to see everyone out?' Tim asked.

Benny said he could wait, but rather than returning to his seat at the back, he stood with Brian while the others left. He didn't back away when a few of them stopped to chat before leaving, although he only responded when spoken to.

'I'm glad you came back.' One of the quieter girls addressed him hesitantly. 'We prayed for you when you weren't here. We thought it might be because of your seizures, but Brian told us you'd split up with your girlfriend. Sorry about that. I had a breakup a while ago too, and it sucks.'

'Yeah.' Benny didn't know what else to say. Part of him wanted to add that she seemed to have got over her break-up pretty fast, judging by the hand-holding with the boy next to her every time Tim's back was turned. He controlled himself but couldn't resist sharing his observation with Brian the moment she left.

When the three of them were alone, Tim led Brian and Benny into his office and made them both a cup of tea. They made small-talk for a while about the meeting and some of the other youths, until finally Tim looked straight at Benny and asked, 'Can you tell me what's made you so sure that you're ready to commit your life to Jesus?'

Benny held out his Bible open at John 3:16, pointed to the verse, and stated, 'This.'

Tim and Brian waited for him to elaborate further, but rather than feeling pressure, a new sense of peace washed over Benny. For the first time in his life, he felt confident enough to express his thoughts without agitation or pacing. He could feel Jesus' calming presence as surely as he could see his two companions. When Benny had first started reading his Bible, he'd wondered if the nudges he felt were from God. As he'd kept reading, he'd begun to recognise the different the indications that God was talking. When he felt strongly he must do or say something, and the sensation during or after he did. It wasn't just about feelings, either. His brain was getting stuff. He was understanding things he never thought he could or would. He was understanding Jesus.

Turning first to Brian, he began. 'I've always known you were different, since I was a kid, but I didn't know why. You never picked on me like Dale did, even though he was one of your best mates. Then that day in the park, when you prayed while I was having a seizure...'

Brian's brows drew together, and he leaned forward.

'People think I don't remember stuff cos I'm thick, but I do when it matters.' Benny paused then continued, 'You've helped me with my schoolwork when no one else wanted to, and no matter how many times you have to go through stuff, you just keep trying until I get it. Mum reckons that's cos you wanna be a teacher, but it's more than that. Then you talked about setting up for the youth meeting...'

'I'd felt God nudging me to talk to you about my faith for a long time,' Brian admitted, 'but I kept resisting. I made all kinds of excuses. The worst one was that you wouldn't understand.'

Benny nodded. 'I don't a lot of the time. Just ask Tim. He has to tell me stuff about the Bible over and over, like you do with schoolwork. I'm hard work. I know that, but...' He turned from Brian to the pastor. 'I dunno what made me come to your youth group.'

'Well, I think I do, and it's not a what, Benny. It's a who,' Tim said.

'Yeah, I guess. When I started coming, the stuff you said made sense, and everyone seemed to want me to be here. I've never had that before, except...' He looked away, 'except with Nettie.' He shrugged as if to dismiss thoughts of her before continuing, 'When we split up, I reckon I was in a grumpy strop with God, but to be in a grumpy strop with someone means you believe they're real, doesn't it?'

A smile crept onto Tim's face as he sipped his tea.

'I reckon I get in grumpy strops a lot when I don't get what I want.'

'I think we all sometimes do that,' Tim confirmed.

Benny grinned at the pastor who had become his friend. 'I don't reckon you ever get in a grumpy strop with no one.'

'Then you haven't known me long enough.' They exchanged a conspiratorial grin. 'You never know; one day I might even get in one with you.'

'That's okay. My dad does all the time. I reckon getting like that with someone you hang out with a lot must mean you care about them. Sometimes I had to yell at Beth, but it was only to stop her doing something stupid. She didn't know stuff was bad until we told her.' He felt a yearning for the little girl he loved so dearly as he spoke, but he went on bravely. 'When you came to see me at home, I realised you cared. I started wondering if God

306

cared too. I read that verse you told me about every morning and every night. I don't even need to read it no more, cos I can remember what it says without looking at it. I've never done that with nothing before.'

Benny fiddled with the pages of his Bible. 'You told me to put myself in that verse where it talks about the world. It felt stupid doing that in the beginning, but then I started believing it. Maybe this is how God loved Benny Wellander: He gave His One and Only Son - that's Jesus, right? - so that if Benny Wellander believes in Him, he will not perish - which means die - but will have eternal life. Will live forever.'

Benny checked the smiles on his friend's faces to make sure he'd got it right, then continued. 'I didn't reckon living forever would be all that great. I've always hated everything about myself, 'especially the stupid name my mum gave me when I was a baby. But when I put my name in the verse like that, I don't hate it so much. It's who God made me. Even though there's something weird wrong with my brain, I have seizures, and I'm always throwing up, God still loved me enough to give me Jesus. Not cos I'm nothing special, but just cos I'm me. I mess up all the time, but when I do, I can ask Jesus to forgive me, and he will. I might not never have many friends, and I know I've lost Nettie, but I'll never lose Jesus. He's with me all the time, and I can talk to him about everything. He doesn't care how messed up my words come out, cos he just loves me, and he gets me.'

Benny's words had run dry, and he shuffled restlessly, wondering if he had said too much.

Fortunately, Tim was quick to put him at ease. 'I think you're already a Christian, Benny, but I can lead you in a prayer if you'd like me to?'

Benny nodded. 'Don't have to say nothing out loud, do I? I talk to God all the time now, but I can't do the out loud stuff like the rest of you.'

'You don't need to, because He hears what we say in our hearts.'

Benny nodded, relaxing again as the pressure eased. Then Pastor Tim prayed, and the words wrapped around Benny like one of his mum's comforting hugs. When Tim left space for silence, Benny thought he and Brian would be shocked if they could hear the conversation he was having with the person he now considered his God and Friend:

'Thank You, Jesus. Thank You for Tim and Brian. Thank You for getting me to come to this church, and thank You for loving me just cos of who I am. I'm not gonna get stuff right all the time, but You know that anyway, cos Tim says You know about everything we're gonna do and it doesn't change how much You love us. Thank you for my mum and dad, and for Emmie and Damo. I don't reckon I'll never be able to help them the way Brian and Tim have helped me, but maybe I could if You wanted me to, cos I know they need You too.'

He took a breath, knowing this part would be the most difficult of all. 'And thank You for bringing Nettie and Beth into my life, cos Nettie showed me I was worth loving. I probably wouldn't have believed You loved me if she didn't. I dunno what's gonna happen to them now. Maybe they'll go away with Simon, and I'll have to get on with stuff. Pastor Tim read that bit tonight from that book with a weird long name about how there's a time for everything. I didn't like some of what it said, cos I wish I was still laughing with Nettie and Beth, and not crying without them, and I still wanna hug her, not turn away from her, but maybe I've just gotta get that it's over. I've gotta thank You for what we had instead of letting it wind me up.'

A tear rolled unbidden down Benny's cheek. He brushed it away, relieved that both Brian and Tim had their eyes closed. 'You know what I want, but Tim's trying to get me to understand that it's what You want that matters most. He says that sometimes the things we want aren't what's best, but it's hard when you love someone as much as I love Nettie. I guess all I can do is ask You to help me. If it's time to let go, then please help me, cos I can't do it by myself. But I'm not by myself no more, am I?'

He sat in silence, allowing his new Friend to give him strength and peace. Then he heard shuffling, and he opened his eyes.

Brian rose and smiled at him. 'Guess we'd better be heading home.'

They bade Tim goodnight and walked together back to their street. Brian spoke of his enthusiasm over leaving for university, and about his sister's pregnancy and how excited his family were. 'They're disappointed because I'm not acting like becoming an uncle is the most brilliant thing in the world. I guess I'm not as thrilled by babies as some people.'

'I wasn't neither until Beth.' As he spoke her name, Benny spotted Nettie standing on the Thompson's driveway with her daughter in her arms. They were waving to Simon as he drove away, and Benny knew he had to break the ice and talk to them. He had delayed it for long enough. He and Nettie lived in the same street. It was childish to run away every time he saw her.

Brian had spotted them too, and he gave Benny a questioning glance.

'I've gotta talk to Nettie.'

'Hope it goes all right.' Brian patted him on the back as they prepared to part. 'I'll be praying for you.'

'Thanks, cos I need it.'

Benny steeled himself as he crossed to Nettie's side. Then he remembered his newfound friend, and he silently prayed, 'Please give me the right stuff to say.'

'Benny!' Beth spotted him first and strained to be free. Nettie handed her over without hesitation, and Benny held her lovingly.

'Hi, Bethy. What've you been up to?'

She babbled a stream of nonsensical words, then looked up at him, waiting for a response.

'Hey, I reckon you should be in bed.'

'We only just got back.' Benny glanced up at Nettie, even though it was hard to look her in the face rather than focusing on Beth. She looked weird, like her eyes were seeing him for the first time. Was that even a thing? 'Can we talk?' she said.

'Yeah, if you want.' Was she going to tell him about her future with Simon? If so, he hoped Jesus would help him handle it, and that he could honestly tell her he wanted her to be happy, because Nettie's happiness meant everything to him.

Nettie hesitated, looking like she might head back inside, but she didn't. 'Simon asked me tonight if we could get back together; if we could be a family, for Beth's sake.'

'It'll be nice for her to have a mum and dad. Every kid needs that, I reckon.'

'Would it? Would it really, Benny? Would it be fair if she knew her mum had settled for second best?'

'What d'you mean?' Their conversation was taking an unexpected turn, and he shuffled restlessly, unable to maintain eye-contact.

'I can't be with Simon, because I don't love him. He'll always be Beth's dad, and I can never take that away from him. He's going to have to do a lot more work if he wants to develop a relationship with her though, because she's still very wary of him.'

'So, you and Simon...?'

'There is no me and Simon, and there never could be. There never should have been. Except that now I've got her, I could never wish I hadn't had Beth.'

'She's great, Nettie.' Beth was becoming heavier in his arms, and Benny knew she was ready for sleep.

'Yes she is, and it was you who helped me see that. You've taught me so much.'

'Me?' He couldn't help being surprised. 'I can't teach no one nothing.'

'Yes you can.' She beamed at him. 'And d'you know the most amazing thing of all?'

He shook his head, more confused than ever.

'You've taught me what it means to love and be loved.' Nettie's fingers reached forward, like she wanted to touch him.

Benny saw tears in her eyes. He longed to hug her and tell her how much he still loved her, but he was holding Beth, and he still wasn't fully convinced of where their conversation was going. 'What're you saying, Nettie?' He had to know for sure before he risked his heart again.

'What d'you think I'm saying?'

'I don't wanna think what I'm thinking.' He laughed self-consciously. 'I say some stupid stuff.'

'No you don't. I know you like straight talk, so I'll give it to you plainly.' Her eyes locked with his and Benny held his breath. 'I love you, Benny Wellander. You're the only guy I've ever loved, and I reckon you're the only guy I ever will.'

Could it be true? 'I'm only sixteen. You might change your mind. Even if you don't love Simon, there might be someone else one day.'

'Oh, there is, and his name's Benny Wellander, and I've treated him like dirt.'

'No you haven't, Nettie,' he whispered.

'Yes I have, and before we can move on from this, I need to ask you to forgive me.'

'Yeah okay, if it'll make you feel better.' At that moment he thought he could forgive her anything.

'I shouldn't be asking you this because we shouldn't have ended up where we did, but can we get back to where we were?' It was Nettie's turn to laugh at her fumbling words.

Benny nodded with a satisfied smile, before indulging in the thing he'd been dreaming about ever since their breakup. He leaned towards her, their lips meeting in a mutually satisfying kiss. 'I love you, Nettie.' He didn't doubt it; despite his age, despite everything. He meant every word.

'I love you too, and I've missed you so much.'

They hugged with Beth between them. She was asleep now, nestled between the two people she trusted most.

'I think Beth will be more settled now things are back as they should be.' Nettie sighed contentedly.

'What about Simon?' Before he allowed his world to slide back into place, Benny needed to know.

'That's up to him. I can't stop him being Beth's Dad, but he'll need to accept that there's always been another guy in her life who's loved her since the day she was born.'

Benny carried Beth into the house and waited while Nettie put her to bed. Then they walked back outside hand-in-hand, revelling in the comfort and familiarity of being together. Their time apart melted away as they laughed, kissed, and chatted.

Yet despite his joy, Benny knew there were no longer just two of them in this relationship. His heart was overwhelmed with gratitude as they strolled through the moonlit park. God had given Nettie and Beth back to him. This had to be the most amazing day of his life. He knew there were still things he and Nettie needed to talk about – his newfound faith being right at the top of the list. It was a part of him now, just as she and Beth were, and Benny wondered how she would feel about it. They would have plenty to work through. Yet Benny's confidence no longer just came from the girl at his side, but from the friend he communicated with in his heart.

'Thank You, Jesus.' He breathed the silent prayer as he and Nettie sat together on a park bench in the darkness, their arms entwined, her head resting on his shoulder where it belonged.

THE END

Coming Soon...

Janet's identity is drawn from her role as Benny's mother. Her epileptic son has needed her all his life, to the detriment of Janet's own needs. Yet, she lives in the shadow of a childhood secret that her family never speak about. Not her distant parents, nor her rarely seen older brothers. Her husband and children? They don't even know she holds it.

When Benny's blossoming independence creates a chasm in Janet's heart, it's time for the secret to come out. Will she find the reasons for her parents' rejection so many years ago? Is there hope for healing - for her to be more than Benny's mother?

Pre-order from broadplacepublishing.co.uk
More than Benny's Mother, by Alex Banwell.
ISBN: 9781915034632

About the Author

Alex Banwell lives in the beautiful Forest of Dean with her husband, Jonathan.

As a child, she made up stories on the swings at the park. Later, she began writing them down, firstly on a Perkins Brailler, then later on a typewriter, and finally a laptop computer.

In 2021, she felt led to take the plunge, adapting some of her earlier writings into a full-length novel. It began as an experiment, a secret project between her and her Saviour. She had no idea it would lead to where she is now, a published author of Contemporary Christian fiction.

To sign up to Alex's newsletter head to
https://subscribepage.io/alexbanwell

About Broad Place Publishing

Broad Place Publishing is a new Christian imprint whose aim is to bring Jesus-centred books to the market. We want to see good-quality books, inspired by the Holy Spirit, brought to life and made available across the world.

We work in partnership with the Holy Spirit at every step, encouraging our writers to listen to Him in their creativity, asking our editors to trust Him as they strive for excellence, and seeking Him for finances and marketing strategy.

We also strive to be an accessible publisher, using dyslexic friendly fonts and making the book available in multiple formats. Please contact us if you see any ways we can improve in this.

If you wish to support us in this missional work, either in prayer or financially, please see the website, or email us directly on: support@broadplacepublishing.co.uk.

You can find out more about our work at: broadplacepublishing.co.uk

Also from the Publisher

Encouraging families in their walk with Jesus
by Joy Vee

The Kai Series (5-8s):
Kai: Born to be Super
Kai: Making it Count
Kai: Playing his Part

The Sienna Series (8-12s):
Love from Sienna
Left Out, Sienna?

The Petrov Series:
The Letters She Never Sent (8-12s)
They Whisper About Us (12+)

Available at broadplacepublishing.co.uk/shop

Bible-based Fiction
by Natasha Woodcraft

The Wanderer Series - *Cain & Abel Reimagined*

1. The Wanderer Scorned
2. The Wanderer Reborn

Non-Fiction

The Wardrobe by Alan Hoare

Encountering the Kingdom of Heaven through the Bible

Historical Fiction

The Stranger by Joy Margetts

Will a wandering soul find his heart a home?

Available at broadplacepublishing.co.uk/shop